TWISTED PICCOLO

BASED ON A TRUE STORY

STEVEN LANE SMITH

outskirts
press

Outskirts Press, Inc.
http://www.outskirtspress.com

ISBN: 978-1-9772-4778-0

Outskirts Press and the "OP" logo are trademarks belonging to Outskirts Press, Inc.

PRINTED IN THE UNITED STATES OF AMERICA

Books by Steven Lane Smith

Reaper's Lament

A Dolphin and a Pilot

Fair Share

Salvation at Rio Feo

Caledonia Switch

Alibi for a Vigilante

Twisted Piccolo

stevenlanesmith.com

for Austin and Travis

Chapter 1

Treasure:
a death certificate and an expired
CIA non-disclosure agreement

IT USUALLY TAKES years to wreck a life. I ruined mine in fewer than thirty seconds. It all started when my engine quit. The silence was creepy. I had simulated engine failures many times in the past but always with the engine at idle. A bitter taste of fear and adrenaline fouled my mouth. I mashed the engine starter button hard enough to bond it there forever. Treetops rushed up toward the cockpit. I threw down full flaps and pulled the yoke back deep into stall buffet. Surely Elizabeth knew we were going down but she didn't utter a sound.

At the last second before impact, I shouted, "Brace." The airplane slapped onto barren branches like a pancake tossed onto a tumbleweed before slashing through a labyrinth of limbs, slamming onto the forest floor, and bursting into flames. Fire from the engine compartment turned the cockpit into a kiln. I visualized layers of flesh curling off my face like overbaked potato skins. I ruined my hands in failed attempts to claw open the jammed cabin door. By the time I frantically broke the left side window out with my fists, the entire forward half of the airplane was an inferno.

Elizabeth clambered over me. I saw her squeeze through the left window frame before my eyes scrunched shut against the blistering heat. The blaze licked at my legs as I scrambled blindly in the same direction she had gone. I fell onto the left wing, rolled onto the ground, then staggered away from the flames. I regained sight and found Elizabeth lying in a clearing to the left of the burning wreckage. Heat had melted the artificial fabric of her dress, so I covered her against the cold with my sweater and shirt.

She asked, "Are we dead?"

Leaving my new bride alone on a California mountainside to hike in the direction of an approaching siren was the hardest decision I had ever made in my 23 years. I waved down an all-terrain search-and-rescue ambulance groaning over uneven ground toward the column of black smoke. The ambulance reached me, and a husky emergency medical technician leaped out. He ran to me and grasped a dog tag on my neck chain.

"Lieutenant Cromwell, we're taking you to Reno."

The technician's jugular veins were as thick as licorice sticks, which oddly reassured me. I told him where Elizabeth was lying. He loaded me onto an ambulance gurney and gave me an injection that turned off the lights. I was told, but didn't remember, that the Air Force airlifted Elizabeth and me by Air Force C-9 hospital plane from Reno to the burn center at Brooke Army Medical Center at Fort Sam

Houston in San Antonio, Texas. It was Thanksgiving Day. What a cruel way to return to my hometown.

I had no inkling of the prejudice, cynical manipulation, blackmail, and kidnapping I was destined to face. If I had known about nothing more than the physical pain I would suffer, I would have willed my heart still. At the time, I didn't believe that Elizabeth or I would survive to see 1970.

———=((◉))=———

On a Sunday morning nine years before the crash, I was slumped on a wooden pew way in the back of the chapel trying to elude parental oversight. Fidgeting in woolen pants as itchy as poison ivy, I was a scatterbrained fourteen-year-old chaplain's son — yes, the son of a preacher man – whose attention was divided between the bosoms of a cute alto in the choir and my father's voice booming from the pulpit.

"For where your treasure is, there your heart will be also. Dearly beloved, where is *your* treasure?"

Tough question. I thought a lot about my treasure from that moment on, although it took a long time to identify it. The armada of plastic fighter planes hanging from my bedroom ceiling at home was a hint that my treasure was located somewhere overhead. Any run-of-the-mill psychic could have predicted that I was going to be a fighter pilot if I ever grew up. I peppered my adolescent speech with aviation terms: "Roger" this and "affirmative" that. I obsessed for a time on the Geneva Convention. It required a prisoner of war to reveal only his name, rank, and serial number. I didn't have a rank or serial number so, if interrogated or, God forbid, tortured, I planned to divulge only my name — Daniel Cromwell.

I abided by most rules and regulations like the Geneva Convention and the Ten Commandments. Number Ten: "Thou shalt not covet thy neighbor's ass," was problematic. I envied my handicapped next-door neighbor because his van was the only private vehicle in Abilene, Texas equipped with an elevator. He toiled not, neither did he spin, yet neighbors laughed at his sorry jokes and did chores for him at no charge. My juvenile mind reasoned erroneously that my life would be peaches and cream if only I also was physically handicapped.

My father was a stern West Point graduate who upended orthodoxy by attending a post-graduate seminary to become an Air Force chaplain. "Give me sixty," he'd say every night as if the number "sixty" had randomly popped into his head. Cue the pushups. "One-legged deep knee bends," he'd announce. Bam, like a trained seal, forty on each leg. I developed the legs of a gazelle, which paid off in high school and college when I put on spikes and became a blur for a quarter of a mile on a cinder track.

Dad insisted I establish goals like acing Latin and trigonometry. I graduated from college *sine laude*. I married Elizabeth Van Drake, daughter of the Sacramento Van Drakes, noteworthy because Elizabeth was a society thoroughbred and I was a social plow horse. I observed that people treasured beauty above all else, which put Elizabeth in life's pole position. She was gorgeous.

Shortly after our wedding, one month before I started

Air Force pilot training, a cereal manufacturer hired us to appear in a loopy thirty-second television commercial that must have sold a boat load of puffed rice because the company kept airing it. Elizabeth and I had eaten the product exactly once before the shoot, but technicians made it look like we were addicted to the stuff. A stream of royalty checks paid for our favorite hobbies, skiing and flying. It could be said that, indirectly, my life was ruined by puffed rice.

Chapter 2

Treasure:
a hotel key fob — "Hilton Palacio del Rio 606"

THIS WASN'T MY first lap on the burn ward circuit. I was living in Edinburgh, Scotland at the age of eight when a pot full of boiling water scalded my head and chest. I spent six months in the Royal Hospital for Sick Children recovering from burns. Three vivid memories survived the fifteen-year span between burnings: an Indian doctor, a nurse named McCloddy, and a pair of twins.

"This is our young American, Master Cromwell," Dr. Patel told his peers during morning rounds. He touched my arm, and I imagined pulses of healing flowing from his fingertips. "Master Cromwell never complains."

Nurse McCloddy, the patron saint of derision, never smiled. "You should be in your own country across the sea," she scolded me. It seemed she had a grudge against Americans. Perhaps a Yank had wronged her. After I became ambulatory, a jollier nurse named Ramsay encouraged me to read stories every afternoon to a five-year-old set of twins who had survived a house fire. A week's worth of stories later, she intercepted me on my way to the twins' room.

"The wee bairns have been taken elsewhere," she said. "You may go back to your bed."

When I figured out where the twins really had gone, my heart disintegrated. For the first time, I felt an awful ache in my chest that I diagnosed as a heart attack. I reported the symptoms to Nurse McCloddy. She frowned and said, "You'll live." As I understood things, adults were always right, so Nurse McCloddy's reproach made me profoundly sad. I stopped speaking until I was spoken to. Heartbreak left a scar, so the next time I felt the ache it was less traumatic.

Fifteen years later, I lay helplessly on a burn ward again. My brain was no more than a metronome for my heart. Morphine calmed the pain at brief intervals, but it opened a door to disoriented meandering among foggy pathways of denial and guilt. Everyone in my paranoid delusions condemned me for the accident. How could the plane have gone down unless I had done something wrong?

A nurse appropriately named Lieutenant Wheeler pushed me in a wheelchair from my bed on the main burn ward into the Burn Intensive Care Unit so I could see Elizabeth. A Doughnut Dolly who was brushing Elizabeth's long, naturally blonde hair left so Elizabeth and I could have privacy. I concentrated on every exquisite detail of Elizabeth's face. Her mind resided a long way from reality. She was fascinated with a Barbie doll the Doughnut Dolly had given her.

"Darling, your head is gigantic." My head had swollen bigger than a pumpkin ripe for bursting. "We're going to do big things when we leave here." She inclined her head toward Barbie. "Aren't we?"

Those were the last words I ever heard her speak. She didn't glance my way again. Perhaps my appearance was too revolting. I imagined that God had turned His countenance away, too. Elizabeth continued humming and stroking Barbie's hair as though I didn't exist. Even squeezing my eyes shut couldn't stop the flow of hot tears.

The next morning, an Army nurse major closed privacy curtains around my bed. She whispered, "Lieutenant Cromwell, Elizabeth died during the night." With a heart of pure kindness wrapped in a starched white uniform, she stayed with me for a long time. I lay there remembering how Elizabeth had changed me. Before falling in love with her, my life had been a solitary passage. I had grown up accompanying my parents from one air base to another, never knowing whether kids at the new school would find me adequate, but almost certain that my austere father never would. Elizabeth tore away my veil of inadequacy and showed me how brilliant a shared life could be. When Elizabeth died, my world went dark again. To compensate, I swore that I would return to flying, my only remaining treasure.

<hr />

I didn't know what pain was until I checked into the Cut House. I remained flat on my back in one of sixty burn ward beds comprising a repository of misery that was blizzard-white: white floors, sheets, curtains, uniforms. Everything was the color of snow except American blood. None of us knew how long we were going to be in the Cut House. An inmate on Death Row at least had a target date for firing up Ol' Sparky. I couldn't kill myself because my charred hands hung uselessly from hospital floor stands like *piñatas*. Every four hours, a nurse jabbed a hundred milligrams of fake tranquility into my thigh through skin tightened like a snare drum by scores of previous shots. Temporary relief descended on me in the flush of an opioid hot flash. Beads of sweat and heart palpitations were the price of admission to levitation and blessed sleep. Suspended in an expectant lull, I gazed at Corporal Angelo Costello as he dawdled around the ward.

Surely, no other medic in the Army could appear as busy while accomplishing so little. He wouldn't have recognized the Hippocratic Oath if it had sashayed right up to him and kicked him in the nuts. Costello's first words to me were, "Welcome to the Cut House, Flyboy." I learned that the self-centered egomaniac could make almost anything happen. Costello was a fixer. He looked like James Dean in scrubs. He showed me proof of his conquest of a nurse in the Hilton Palacio del Rio. For no reason that I could fathom, he gave me the plastic key fob to Room 606 as if it were his to give. The gesture loosened my tongue; among other things, I told him that I used to resemble Robert Conrad.

"Not any more you don't," he said. "In fact, you don't look like nobody." Costello was no comforter and not much of a grammarian either. He used my mirror to comb his hair. Tears filled me eyes involuntarily. "Not to overstate the obvious," Costello said, "you've got to toughen up. You can't start bawling every time your feelings get hurt." I retreated to a safe place inside my head. I ruminated on Elizabeth all the time. I was humiliated without the benefit of humility. Resentment festered in my victim's heart. I alternated between self-loathing and a stubborn longing to prove that I wasn't to blame for the accident.

I had other problems, too. My formerly clear speaking voice had degenerated to a jumble of mumbles. I sounded like a drunk when I tried to pronounce "subliminally," "minimalism," or "abominable." A speech therapist made a list of ten problematic sentences for me to recite twenty times every day: like "tell Tom to tread tentatively on tangled tree twigs" and "today's high is eighty-two degrees."

Every other Crispy Critter on the ward had sacrificed his future for his country. A helicopter pilot named Tom Speer who clung to life in the bed next to mine had been shot down for the third time near Tuy Hua. Twisted metal had trapped him in the flaming cockpit. He couldn't remember how he got out. He held the New Jersey high school hundred-yard dash record, but he wasn't going to race ever again on stumps where his legs used to be.

Ken Lacey, in the next bed, lost half his face to a white phosphorous grenade. The left side of his face was fine, but the burned right side could have been the surface of the moon. He said he was going back to Montana to raise sheep because sheep didn't care about appearances. Tom, Ken, and the other Crispy Critters received Purple Hearts for being wounded in combat. No Purple Heart for me. I was a military student pilot who had punched his ticket to Fort Sam Houston by crashing a civilian airplane in the States. I was ashamed that I hadn't been wounded in combat. I avoided discussing the accident. I didn't want anyone to know that I hadn't been in the plane alone. Remembering Elizabeth's agony was so excruciating that I tried to think of nothing at all, which was the same as not being alive.

I imagined Tom Speer praying himself dead during the dark hours after midnight. I didn't actually hear him die, but I did hear him stop living. His ventilator-assisted breathing stopped. I didn't detect a sob or see a choir of angels. The main hint of his passing was the faint hiss of pressurized oxygen leaking between his mask and his scarred face. A corpsman arrived to check Tom's pulse. When he draped a sheet over Tom's face, it felt like he was covering my face too. I felt suffocated by a powerful dark force bigger than my mind, bigger than the burn ward, bigger even than the universe. It was a bleak expanse, a place uninhabited by God. It absorbed light into its blackness, this punishment for what I had done. Inside the Cut House, I was an exception because I was less mutilated than the other guys. Outside the Cut House, I was a disfigured freak. I didn't belong in either place. I had never known an enemy, but I had one now: Boundless Gloom. I had felt loneliness before, but I was convinced that I would spend the rest of my life alone — high octane, 200 proof alone.

Chapter 3

Treasure: a 27th Tactical Fighter Squadron patch,
an eagle silhouetted against a brilliant yellow sun

DOCTORS PERFORMED TWO dozen surgeries on my face and hands so I wouldn't end up on a street corner pounding on a tom-tom and hustling loose change. Surgeons routinely operated on one hand at a time, but, when they scheduled a double-header, I had to cope post-operatively for a while without hands. I learned to put a sock onto my left foot with my right toes monkey style, a modest achievement compared to a double-arm amputee on the fourth floor who painted landscapes with his toes. Following six months at Fort Sam Houston, I logged another twenty months of hospitalization at the Air Force's Wilford Hall Medical Center at Lackland Air Force Base on the west side of San Antonio. I gritted my teeth and pressed on toward eternity, in the way taught by my father. "Don't ever quit," he used to say. "Your forefathers never quit, else they never would've tamed Texas."

Even though I was descended from a long line of Texas-taming non-quitters, I found the legacy hard to sustain for

777 consecutive days in hospital. During year two, my parents moved from Tokyo to Sacramento. I received convalescent leave to fly to California to spend Christmas with them. I felt obligated to speak in person for the first time with Elizabeth's parents, the Van Drakes, in Rancho Cordova but I didn't have the fortitude to add their sorrows to my own, so I didn't make the telephone call. I was a coward. Dad coerced me to sit in on his Sunday School class of ninth graders. What a gaggle: a dozen fifteen-year-olds with more pimples than brains sitting on beige metal folding chairs arranged in a circle. The kids looked everywhere except at me, refraining from staring until they believed I wouldn't notice.

Dad ambushed me, proclaiming, "God makes use of broken vessels. God can use even *these*," he thrust my hands into the air, "no matter how deformed, how repulsive. He can use *these* to accomplish great things for His glory." I was an involuntary prop. The kids were as embarrassed as I was. I radiated humiliation and shivered in the cold blast of disgrace because I hadn't achieved even *mediocre* things for the glory of God. It was a relief to return to my kind in hospital where I could reside inside my head. Some people told me I was brave, but I knew better. Bravery was throwing your body on a hand grenade to protect your friends when you had the option of running to safety. All I had done was refuse to quit. I didn't want to be known as "the burned guy" for the rest of my life. I was afraid that sympathy, not merit, might be credited for any achievement.

Despite my gloomy outlook, however, I kept one hope alive: I wanted to fly fighters more than I wanted to breathe. The smart money was against me because I was missing finger joints required by regulations that seemed intended to block my return. On the other hand, Vietnamese missiles and triple A were shooting down hundreds of American pilots during the late 1960s, so I hoped that the Air Force brass would view my previous pilot training as a sunk cost and would want to salvage their investment. A Flight Evaluation Board loomed, and even though doctors and nurses were humans, not robots, my chances of returning to flying actually were slim.

A nurse called Marla telephoned me in my hospital room on the third floor on Day 753: "Daniel, you know Doctor Jones, Bones, the flight surgeon? He's doing flight physicals today down on the first floor. He told me to put you on the standby list and have you wait down here in case something opens up." I was surprised that anyone was looking out for my interests. I quickly reported downstairs in Air Force standard issue pajamas and dressing gown. Marla told me I was third on the standby list. The first "no-show" occurred at 1145. A Captain Kilgore didn't respond to Marla's call. She called the first name on the standby list, "Lieutenant Colonel Wilson," and he trotted off down the hallway to whiz and burp and cough and bend over for his annual spelunker's probe.

San Antonio was protected from Russian invasion by four Air Force bases: Lackland, Kelly, Randolph, and Brooks. Pilots from all four bases showed up punctually for appointments all afternoon. By 4:28 my future was looking grim. The pilot ahead of me on the standby list, Major Knight from the Texas Air National Guard unit at Kelly AFB, left the waiting room in search of a restroom. Marla announced, "Lieutenant Bush. Lieutenant George Bush." A captain from

Randolph AFB whispered an explanation why Lieutenant Bush couldn't report for his flight physical. I overheard scattered words: "B School ... Harvard."

Marla didn't miss a beat. She struck through Lieutenant Bush's name and called, "Major Knight."

I cunningly offered a narrow version of the truth: "Major Knight had to leave."

"Well, Lieutenant Cromwell," Marla said brightly, "you're next."

My heart was racing and I felt dizzy as I followed Marla down the hallway to the examining room. Bones entered the room and said, "You made it." He looked me over in my sad sack military pajamas and gown and said, "Snappy dresser." When he had discharged his medical duties, he directed me to one of two chairs and he sat on the other. "Dan, I don't want you to meet a Flight Evaluation Board. There are too many reasons to reject you. I'm going to issue this flight physical, and, if anything comes up, I'll play dumb. America has plenty of fighter pilots with perfect fingers and handsome faces." He inspected my reconstructed hands and face, then he thumped a fist against my chest. "America needs fighter plots with savage hearts, and that's what you've got." He signed his name on the medical certificate and said, "Congratulations, Lieutenant Cromwell." A nurse's empathy, a doctor's compassion, a major's distended bladder, and a future President's decision to give up flying F-102s to attend Harvard Business School made my dream come true.

I received orders to pilot training at Laughlin AFB near Del Rio, Texas. Eighty new college graduates started training in my pilot training class. Forty washed out along the way. I was one of the forty survivors who earned pilot's wings. Top-ranked graduates always chose fighters. My class received four fighters, and I graduated high enough in the class to get one. I learned to fly the F-4 Phantom, the greatest all-around fighter in the world at the time, in the 27th TFS, one of four squadrons that made up the 1st Tactical Fighter Wing (TFW), stationed at MacDill AFB in Tampa. I had doubts and insecurities but I told no one, not even my best friend Dinger.

First Lieutenant Tyler "Dinger" Countryman, a native of Tampa, was a real asset to the squadron because he knew every watering hole worth knowing in the Tampa Bay area. He clipped his blond hair as short as his list of worries. His pulse idled at about forty. I never saw him get excited during seven months of F-4 replacement training, which was significant because the Phantom presented plenty of opportunities for excitation. Maintaining silence was a fundamental competence in the military, but Dinger never got the hang of it. He butchered metaphors and analogies left and right as deftly as Yogi Berra in his prime. At a squadron soirée, for example, with no sense that his words could be taken as anything but a loving compliment of his wife, Dinger said, "Shelley's tits could sink a thousand ships." I asked him if his gaffes were for real. He said, "When you're as close to perfection as I am, people will resent you unless you have a flaw." I acted as though I believed him.

The war ended before Dinger and I graduated from F-4 replacement training, so, instead of heading to Southeast Asia, we received orders to join the 612th TFS "Eagles" based at Torrejón Air Base near Madrid, Spain. What luck:

my best friend, Spain, the Phantom. If the burn ward was my Hell, I had every expectation that the Six-Twelfth would be my Heaven. I contrasted my life before and after the accident. Before the crash, plenty of guys wished they could be me. After I was burned on the mountain, no one wanted to be me ever again.

Chapter 4

Treasure: a 612th Tactical Fighter Squadron patch,
an irate black eagle silhouetted against a blue sky

THE SIX-TWELFTH PILOT who gave me my F-4 local area checkout was D Flight Commander Captain Bobby Joe "Hacksaw" Ballantine from Austin, Texas. (My device for remembering names was to link them to their hometowns.) Hacksaw was a graduate of Texas A&M. His credo was simple: "I make noise, therefore I am." His voice was a replica of Roger Whitaker's, minus the British-Kenyan embellishments. Hacksaw volunteered his wife to drive me around the countryside outside Madrid in search of a rental cottage, a *casa de campo*. She was pleasant company and she offered me tips galore. I retained three nuggets of advice. One: avoid the appearance of black-market transactions by giving Spaniards gifts bought only in Spain, not bought at the American base exchange. Two: don't bother trying to have a home phone installed in Spain because the installation would take months and then the phone would work only intermittently. Three: stay away from Gunner Gunnerson.

Gunner was the notorious Six-Twelfth B Flight Commander and squadron bully. He was a past collegiate football player and present self-anointed aviation idol. He maintained his blond hair clipped short and his facial features in a permanent scowl. He admired his own muscular body more overtly than etiquette allowed. I knew from the start that I didn't want to cross him when he left me at attention instead of parade rest on the day I reported to him for duty. In less than a week, he had added me to his shit list.

I shadowed a junior captain named Zacrzhewscii for my orientation at the Bardenas gunnery range near Zaragoza, two hundred miles from Torrejón. Zacrzhewscii's cumbersome name showed up in grease pencil on the flying schedule as "Z+11." The carefree grandson of Russian immigrants to Oregon, he earned the call sign of Zip. During a two-hour break between bombing missions on Thursday, he bagged a combat nap while I roamed around the inactive bombing range collecting trinkets. On the run-in to the closest strafe panel, I found loads of 20 millimeter brass casings piled up like snow drifts on the ground. An operating F-4 Gatling gun fired bullets and ejected empty cases at a rate of 100 rounds a second, so brass was everywhere. I collected scores of unblemished four-inch-long empty shells. I hoarded my spoils of peacetime in a parachute bag to take home. I didn't have anything in mind; I wasn't planning a war or intending to sell the brass. When Zip and I returned to the squadron late Friday afternoon, Gunner demanded to see inside my bag. Oblivious to any wrongdoing, I willingly showed off my haul of several pounds of brass. Gunner said, "We've got a problem." Zip shrugged and looked damn glad that he had taken a nap while I was prospecting. I didn't press to find out Gunner's intent because I hoped he'd forget about it.

A month later, I flew a ground attack sortie on Gunner's wing on a Friday afternoon. My bombs were decent and my strafing was red-hot. We armed up for rocket passes. My first rocket had a faulty fin and it went haywire, corkscrewing crazily toward the range tower. The range officer sprinted toward the exit. The rocket missed the tower. Regaining composure on the radio, he deflected blame from me to the malfunctioning rocket. I considered this chapter closed until Gunner brought it up at a squadron party at the Torrejón Officers Club pool the following evening in front of the Ballantines and Countrymans. Gunner camouflaged disdain as banter: "Cromwell almost shot the range officer in the lips yesterday."

"Not really," I said.

"Don't contradict your flight leader, Rookie," Gunner growled. He glared scornfully at my scarred hands and face and shook his head. "You're a mess, Cromwell. This isn't a damn rehab center."

My psychological callouses from the Cut House couldn't protect me from Gunner's derision, so, preferring numbness to wounded feelings, I selected booze as my anesthetic of choice. Half in my cups, I couldn't come up with a retort witty enough to meet my needs, so I remained spinelessly silent.

"You don't belong here," Gunner said, moving away without looking back at me even once.

Dinger tried to cheer me up: "Loose lips are the devil's workshop. Ignore him."

Gunner's barb was still stinging as Dinger and I

mercilessly raided an appetizer tray. Gunner's dazzling wife Jennifer, who bore a startling resemblance to Elizabeth, joined us. My knees went wobbly.

"I apologize for Gunner's bad manners," she said. Gunner was still nearby, thronged by a clutch of admiring women as noisy as a flock of sea gulls. Jennifer asked, "Is your wife here?"

"I'm not married." I sensed that she already knew that.

"Divorced?"

"My wife died," I said. I sensed that she knew that, too.

Jennifer put her arm around my back and lowered her voice. "I'm so sorry. Where did you meet?"

I had to guard against my *S*'s getting mushy when I was inebriated: "Columbia, Missouri. She went to Stephens College while I was at Mizzou."

"My best friend in Boston went to Stephens for two years before she transferred to B. C."

I asked her friend's name but, before she could answer, a squadron mate shouted, "Dead Bug."

Every pilot within earshot collapsed onto the patio on his back with arms and feet jutted into the air. The last man to hit the deck would buy the next round of drinks. Dead Bug might have seemed an adolescent ritual to thoughtful people, but the game had solid roots in military aviation. Dinger and I popped back up to our feet beside Jennifer.

"Aren't you a spunky pair?" She assessed the chaos with intense, sparkling eyes. "It's amazing what you guys will do in public, things you'd never do if you were alone."

I sensed that Jennifer Gunnersson could be trouble. I saw her leave with Gunner as the crowd thinned out. Dinger and

I sat astraddle the low diving board at the deep end of the pool drinking cognac and recapping the evening.

"Gunner wasn't thrilled about you bundling with his *frau*," Dinger mumbled drunkenly. "In the words of Red Robin Hood, *my, my, what big balls you have.*"

———— ⊗ ————

I was 25 when I was discharged from the Cut House. The rest of the world had forged ahead during my absence. A black jailbird described the abandoned feeling on a summer night in the back of a Greyhound bus bound for Montgomery, Alabama. Recently released from a four-year stretch, he got his kicks telling me hair-raising prison stories. "You the first cracker ever paid me no mind, know what I'm saying?" I chipped in five dollars to listen to his blood-chilling tales and share his cache of warm Jax beers. We did the math together and figured out that he was older than I was by four years. "Woo-ee," he said, "next thing you know, I be an old man, know what I'm saying?" I couldn't make out his facial features in the dark bus interior except when refracted headlights of passing cars revealed a lot of wrinkles for his years. He asked, "What's that shit on your face?"

"I got burned."

"That's some bad shit, know what I'm saying? Don't go getting burned. Don't do the Big House, neither. It puts you *behind.*"

There I was, three years after that night in Alabama, feeling left out, *behind.* Thanks to plastic surgery, I no longer scared the wits out of people, but the only times I forgot that I was a Crispy Critter was when I was flying. In my efforts to counter Boundless Gloom, I corrupted the virtue of fighter pilot assertiveness into a sin. The back seaters who tolerated my stunts probably deserved medals for bravery. I snubbed speed and altitude rules. The rulebook prohibited flying the Phantom slower than 200 knots except for landing, but I cheated by throwing down flaps at disapproved slow speeds to win dogfights. Flying above 50,000 feet was forbidden because we didn't wear pressure suits. If you lost cockpit pressurization without a pressure suit above 50,000 feet, your blood would boil and your mother would collect your government life insurance benefit. Making up my own rules, I climbed in full afterburners up to 59,000 feet and, weightless, watched the airspeed fall to zero. The sky turned black in the middle of the day, stars became visible, and the curvature of the earth was obvious. Like a bullet fired straight up and running out of energy, the Phantom tumbled backwards tail-first. The nose flipped toward earth, usually to the left, as I retarded the throttles to idle. The Phantom dove straight down, blowing through the sound barrier with ease. It was exhilarating.

I also was a nuisance flying single-ship down on the deck. In Turkey, where radar technology was frozen-in-time at 2,000 B.C., I went hunting down in the weeds at 600 knots just a few feet above the desert. During tactical turns, my lower wingtip and its shadow almost merged. While flying that low and fast, a twitch of the stick would have turned me and my back seater into briquettes. I intercepted Turkish Air Force fighters flying low-level navigation routes and I thumped them by passing a few feet above them so my supersonic shock wave slammed into them. I'm sure it scared the living *kebap* out of them, but maybe it taught my NATO brothers to keep a sharp lookout. The adrenaline rush was addictive. Behind my back, detractors may have regarded me as a nut job, but, except for Gunner, they were kinder than saints to my face. They even gave me that most treasured of gifts, a cool call sign.

A fighter pilot without a call sign was like a rock star without a guitar: not illegal, but peculiar. My assigned back seater was First Lieutenant John "Rim Shot" Remington. A native of Fort Worth, Texas, big Rim Shot would accept any dare at a party. He could eat a light bulb without shredding his guts by not swallowing the filament or the metal parts. One night he split his scalp on a coffee table corner while attempting a limbo pass. I told our hostess that he'd bleed out if I didn't stitch him up. Nonsense. She produced her sewing kit. My first operation of this kind was a challenge because Rim Shot's hair was thicker than a raccoon pelt. Skinning a wolverine would have been easier than shaving the margins around his wound. He had drunk as much as I had, so anesthesia was unnecessary. I sewed the edges of the gash together with burnt orange thread in honor of his beloved University of Texas Longhorns. As a reward for my lightning quick reflexes and rock-steady hand, I received my own *nom de l'air*. "Stitch." I believed that audacious flying and a madcap social life would defend against Boundless Gloom and prove that I wasn't to blame for Elizabeth's death. Perhaps I could persuade even myself.

The Saturday after my return from altitude chamber re-current training in Germany, I met a tornado named Gwen Alcott. She worked at a New York advertising agency's London office. A sorority sister of Rena Ballantine's in college, Gwen was staying with the Ballantines for a week. Rena called the squadron to set up a date pairing Gwen and me, saying, "Gwen is the smartest woman I know."

"The dumbest woman you know might be a better match," I said. That might have gotten a laugh out of Hacksaw, but not Rena.

Gwen and I met in a *tapas* bar in Las Cuevas section off Plaza Mayor. Gwen was dressed for a board meeting. I was dressed like every other twenty-something male in Madrid in a navy blue sweater and khaki slacks. Gwen ordered octopus in its ink. The black juice stained her pearly white teeth, giving her an Addams Family aspect. After chit-chatting for a while, she told me that she knew all about me. She said she was going to change my life and she leaned forward in her chair to dominate the conversation.

"You have a tragic past. Tragedy is opportunity. Stitch, Stitch, Stitch, do not let this opportunity pass you by." She was not short on enthusiasm. "Develop your brand. I see an inspirational book targeted at the Christian market. I know the perfect ghostwriter. I see you giving motivational speeches on college tours. The name *Daniel Cromwell* will be everywhere." My brain had to work fast to keep up with Gwen. "I see a movie. I know the perfect producer. I know how to do this for you." She held my hands in hers. "We were meant to meet on this night."

I had to talk her down. Since leaving hospital, I had been advised by well-meaning acquaintances to "give back," as though I were the recipient of some sweet deal for which I had to pay recompense. I didn't know how to tell Gwen that I didn't want to be a celebrity for what I had done; I wanted to *hide* from what I had done. Sure, I wanted my hands and face back, but I couldn't have them back, so the next best thing was to forget.

———◦«◦»◦———

I couldn't explain my string of successes on the gunnery range in December. Normally two or three sloppy bomb passes corrupted my bombing averages, but not in December. William Tell I was not, so it was a marvel to see my name at the top of the Top Gun board for the first time. Right on my heels in second place was Gunner Gunnersson. He approached me at the squadron candy machine where I was slaughtering a Snickers.

"Stitch, let me have the Top Gun trophy this month."

He had a better chance of convincing me to give him both of my kidneys. "Why would I do that?"

"My Dad's visiting from the Pentagon, and it would mean a lot to me."

It was an insane request, so I turned him down. Gunner gave me the evil eye and stalked away. Two days later, on January 2, I noticed that Gunner had jumped ahead of me on the December Top Gun board. I audited the bombing range records in the Weapons Shop by comparing them to the scores in my personal logbook. I discovered that my immaculate range sheet scores from a sortie on December 13 were missing from Top Gun calculations. I didn't need Hercule Poirot to figure out that Gunner or an accomplice had destroyed my December 13 scores so Gunner could win the trophy. I fumed about this honor violation until I considered the consequences of blowing the whistle. Exposing Gunner would embarrass his lieutenant general father and might derail Gunner's career.

We had no witnesses when we met in an Officers Club men's room. I said, "I know what you did."

"I seem to recall that you stole a ton of brass from Bardenas. Let's not castrate each other."

His threat worked. I chickened out and said nothing. The wing king awarded the Top Gun trophy to Gunner at a noisy celebration in the Officers Club. Gunner extended his hand to me right in front of his father. "Nice try. It was close." That took a lot of nerve. Coward that I was, I said nothing, not even to Dinger. Revenge was another matter. I didn't bear grudges as a rule, but I made an exception for Gunner Gunnersson.

Chapter 5

Treasure:
a faded Hotel Atlántico receipt for five gin-and-
tonics, two meals, four wines, and two flans

I FELT ELIZABETH'S presence constantly. I caught glimpses of her everywhere. Six years after the accident, I still mistook blonde strangers in crowds for Elizabeth. I caught sight of her one afternoon in the Prado, but it turned out that the slim, curvaceous look-alike was one of a group of college kids from Amsterdam. I was still in love with Elizabeth, although I conceded that my concepts of love were a tangled mess. My father had taught me since I was a whippersnapper that God loved me so much that He sacrificed His own son for me. *Ipso facto*, I was good enough for God's love. I wasn't as convinced that I deserved Elizabeth's love, not before the accident, and certainly not after.

I imagined Elizabeth looking down on me from a parallel spiritual zip code and tallying up my deficiencies. I tried to make up for my faults by taking risks with airplanes, cars, and women. I may have tried harder to earn Elizabeth's admiration in death than I did when she was alive. I read French and Russian literary novels beside my fireplace in the evenings. I listened to classical music by Vivaldi and Rossini, leaving the record jackets in plain view to impress visitors. I memorized the names of compositions so I'd be ready to name-drop if the subject ever arose in conversation. Of course, classical music virtually never came up in conversations among fighter pilots unless I primed the pump. Dinger warned me against getting too big for my britches: "Who are you trying to bullshit, you Shakespearean twat?"

I wanted to be sensational. I flew to Paris for a long weekend with the intent of sweeping some girl off her feet with my renaissance tastes. I met an attractive Austrian girl named Jilli at a café. I betrayed Vivaldi by telling Jilli that Haydn, an Austrian, was my favorite. Jilli didn't care. Her real passion was the Klagenfurt Athletic Sports Club, winners of eleven straight Austrian ice hockey Championships. She professed her love for all Klagenfurt hockey players who, as I understood it, loved her in return, every single one of them. How could I hope to compete with a stable of Austrian hockey studs? In a perverse way, she intimidated me, so it didn't work out.

In time, my literary and musical pretensions faded away. I stopped reading dense biographies and listening to classical music. My new pals were Kurt Vonnegut, Bob Dylan, and James Taylor. All I needed, besides three square meals, was flying and sex. Costello's warning that I'd never find a girlfriend without using a tranquilizer gun was too cynical. I dated several girls, but never with any kind of serious intent. My twisted, semi-adolescent rationale was that sex-as-sport was therapeutic and not disrespectful to Elizabeth's memory. I toyed with a German girl named Gretchen, or maybe she toyed with me. I made a date with an English accountant whose name I couldn't remember. I was pretty sure it started with "V" — Veronica or Valerie or Victoria, one of those. Her sassy challenge snared me: "I should accept a dinner invitation from you before I grow old."

I was a pushover for an English accent. No woman had ever made such a proposal to me in any tongue or dialect, so I invited her to dinner at a fancy-schmancy restaurant in Madrid's Hotel Atlántico. I even wore a suit and a silk tie. Granted, the "V" girl wasn't a natural beauty. The loss of five pounds would have done her no harm and her teeth weren't the straightest on the Iberian Peninsula. Who was I to judge? I was far from a perfect specimen myself. While weaving my way through evening traffic on Madrid's Gran Villa, I fruitlessly frisked my brain for the girl's name. I arrived at the restaurant bar at 7:50 p.m., my pocket full of a wad of pesetas thick enough to choke an alligator but without a name.

I had the bar to myself, which allowed time to rehearse a couple of fascinating stories, starring, naturally, me. I ordered a gin-and-tonic. The bartender chucked a lonely ice cube into a slender glass and then drowned it in gin. I saw a hangover in my future. Dinger Countryman once summed up my hangovers best: "The pain in Spain falls mainly on the brain." Approaching nine o'clock, according to my Rolex, the English girl still hadn't appeared. Perhaps, despite her weight and dental issues, she had received a better offer and hadn't bothered to let me know about it. I accepted rejection by buying gin-and-tonics with the money I would have wasted on the tart's dinner. Finishing my third GT at the stroke of ten, I was feeling savagely handsome and witty — more than witty, hilarious. I did the medically prudent thing by moving to the dining room. I knew that a long overdue meal might preclude alcohol poisoning. Serendipity interrupted my menu analysis: the waiter seated a spectacular-looking woman in the chair on my left. My heart palpitated when I realized that it was Jennifer Gunnersson, wife of my outspoken detractor, Gunner. Everything from then on seemed to move in slow motion so I could keep up.

"Buy me a drink?" Jennifer asked.

"*Ginebra y tonica,*" I told the waiter. (Gin and tonic.) I put real effort into the guttural "*g*" in *ginebra* and I trilled the "*r*" like a machine gun. I was a linguistic marvel. The Spanish language was putty in my hands. Jennifer, with silky blonde hair and classic Nordic features, was a marshmallow in a room full of caramels. I told her the truth about being stood up, but I invented the girl's name. "Verity," I said.

"Such irony," Jennifer said. It wasn't long before Jennifer revealed that she was still fuming over a squabble with Gunner earlier that day. "He's *not* a nice man," she confided.

I knew the rules of marital criticism. She had license to slander Gunner until the cows came home, but the instant I dared to say anything negative about her loutish husband, she'd turn on me. All that was required of me was sympathy: "Mm-mm-mm" and "really?" and "oh, no," that kind of thing.

Messing around with Jennifer was as appropriate as a two-year-old playing with a hand grenade. Maybe I desired Jennifer because of her physical resemblance to Elizabeth. Maybe it was simple lust. Jennifer's ego was overinflated.

She dropped names in lengthy monologues and she had an irritating habit of laughing at her own jokes. She told me about her life and times with Gunner in their hometown of Rochester, Minnesota. Gunner was in the graduating class of 1970 at the University of Minnesota. Jennifer graduated in the same year from Boston College. She showed me a picture of their wedding in Sweden that summer. I had to admit that the Gunnerssons made a striking couple. The king and queen of Sweden were plodders by comparison. For the record, nothing could have interested me less than descriptions of her wedding, but I faked it, calculating that paradise lay a story away if I feigned interest long enough. We finished dinner at eleven, just as the locals were getting started.

I excused myself for a belated visit to the men's room. Every step was a miniature agony because I had been pounding diuretics since eight o'clock. Halfway down a corridor, I was astonished to encounter Rena, Hacksaw Ballantine's wife. She was dressed to the nines and arm-in-arm with a mountain of a man. I was a hypocrite, immediately assuming the worst of Rena while giving Jennifer Gunnersson and me a free pass for the same transgression. I didn't know the rules for greeting a cheating wife. Rena surprised me with a cordial hug and surprised me again by introducing Hacksaw's younger brother Hunter. She put me at ease concerning her faithfulness to Hacksaw: "Hunter's a junior at Texas A&M."

"Howdy," I said.

"Howdy." Hunter's voice was as deep as Hacksaw's during our Cliff's Notes of a real conversation.

I needed the men's room urgently. "Excuse me. I really need to …."

"Go. Go. Go." Rena said. I got only ten paces closer to the lavatory before Rena chased me down. She said, "It's probably better for everyone if we don't talk about seeing each other tonight."

Obviously, she had seen me with Jennifer. I said, "It's not what you think."

"Sure it is. But, my friend, I didn't see you. Hunter didn't see you either. You've had enough trouble in your life, you don't need any more." She kissed me on the cheek and glided away to join Hunter.

Back at the table, I commented on the remote odds of running into Jennifer like this.

"I knew you'd be here," she admitted. "Your date's name isn't Verity, it's Victoria. Sticky Vicki is what they call her at our country club. And she's not an accountant. She works in the pro shop. I overheard her bragging about having a date with an American sky god, and that's a quote." I was flattered and probably showed it. Jennifer said, "I gave her two thousand pesetas to stand you up so I could do a so-called *surprise prank birthday thingy*. She promised not to tell anyone."

"Why did you do that?"

"When your father told you not to do something, what did you do?"

"Whatever he told me not to do."

"Well Gunner's been down on you since the moment you got to T. J. His knickers got in a knot because I chatted with you at the pool party. He told me to stay away, so, voila, here we are." We finished our flans and brandies. She said, "I have a key."

In comparison to any hotel room I had ever seen, Jennifer's Hotel Atlántico seventh-floor masterpiece was enormous. I opened French doors leading from the suite to a balcony that overlooked the Gran Villa and Madrid's constellation of lights. I felt weightless. I imagined that I could spring over the balcony railing and soar above the Puerto del Sol. Jennifer wrapped her arms around me from behind.

"Are you expecting the good captain?" I asked.

"I'm expecting him to be an arrogant tyrant for the next fifty years of my miserable life."

Time flew by. Even with my elastic morals, I knew better than to proceed down this path. I was an officer, but not much of a gentleman. I had felt sorry for myself for so long that respect for Gunner was the last thing on my mind. At the moment, I was wearing nothing but a leather necklace, a memento that Elizabeth had given to me when I first soloed in jets. It consisted of three beads strung on a narrow strip of leather. The reason I was wearing nothing but a leather necklace was that Jennifer had undressed me at the pace of a one-armed nurse with an acute interest in male anatomy. I sprawled on my back while Jennifer introduced me to a gossamer baby blue garment called a "teddy." She crawled toward me on her tummy like a marine on covert maneuvers. No matter what she did, she was stunning. I was not. Displayed on my thighs, hips, chest, and abdomen were rectangular three-inch by four-inch donor site scars left by doctors who had harvested skin to graft onto my hands and face.

Jennifer traced a manicured index fingernail over the edges of a scar near the top of my left thigh.

"Wyoming," she said. She rested her finger on the corner near Yellowstone before sliding to my abdomen. Fingering the next scar, she said, "Kansas." Her sensual Rand McNally play was ecstasy. She scooted closer to me and traced the border of another rectangle closer to my navel. She said, "Colorado," and kissed the area around Pueblo. She worked her way up toward my chest and traced the outline of still another rectangular scar. "New Mexico," she said. She had covered much of the Southwest. She scooted even closer to a donor site on a patch of skin covering the right side of my pelvis. Her tender tracing along the borders of my wounds was magical, and, for a little while, my scars didn't seem to be scars. "Utah," she said, aware that she was near the epicenter of my desires.

"How about Florida," I asked, "and the Twin Cities?"

"Let's leave Florida and the Twins alone right now."

"Must we?" I knew better than to get too frisky. It was early days.

"We must." She snuggled against my chest and pulled the sheet over us.

"You're breaking my heart."

"Oh, Stitch, don't let an impossible thing break your heart." She patted my chest. "Gunner wouldn't approve of this," she giggled. "No, no, no." If Jennifer was on a mission to get even with her husband, I hoped she intended to keep the payback secret. She was a child jeering behind a parent's back. Perhaps she was being juvenile, but dynamite couldn't have blasted me out of that bed. "Gunner despises you, Mister." She pinched my left buttock. "You and I are free spirits. His world is strict and ambitious. His father's a lieutenant general with grand ideas about Gunner's future."

"I heard your father's a general, too."

"No. Gunner made him a general when we got to T. J. My dad's no general. He's a pharmacist. Gunner needed a wife whose father was a general. He shapes the facts to suit his needs." Her right hand frolicked under the sheet, a playful rodent making fantasies come true wherever it tarried.

"You're incredible," I said. Encourage the good and discourage the bad was my motto.

As accustomed as she was to adulation, she kissed me for the compliment, making me glad I hadn't offed myself on the burn ward. Still, I had questions. Was Gunner as nasty as Jennifer claimed? If so, why did she stay married to him? Was I anything but a convenient tool of revenge to her? I admired her restraint, and I was amazed by mine. I was so sexually aroused that I was surprised that nothing broke.

"Jennifer, what are you doing here with me? I've got too many rough edges for you."

"Rough edges are underrated." She was playful: "You know, women just want the twenty minutes before and after the most thrilling three minutes in sports. All you guys want is the three minutes. Tonight you gave me what I wanted without forcing me to give you what you want. That's sweet. Would you like me to move in with you?"

Her insane hypothetical was a cold shot of acid injected into my heart. Was she nuts? Gunner was a former football player, a Golden Friggin' Gopher. He'd rip me to shreds if he found out that his wife had flown the coop to bunk up in my house.

"Bad idea."

"What if I tell Gunner about Wyoming and Kansas ... and Florida?"

So, lunacy was the price of beauty. "Jennifer," my tone mildly rebuked her.

She giggled and resumed jabbering as she would have done with a girlfriend at a slumber party. I was so relieved to get off the idea of her moving in with me that I encouraged her to continue babbling. "Stitch, here's something you don't know: Bo has artificial thingies."

"Who might *Bo* be?" I asked. "And what are *thingies*?"

Bo was Gunner's pet boxer adopted during his year of pilot training at Laredo, Texas. The size of Bo's testicles fell short of Gunner's lofty standards, so Gunner searched for a vet in Laredo who would surgically enhance his pooch. He struck out in Laredo, but it was a different story on the Mexican side of the Rio Grande where fiercely competitive vets were eager to customize Bo at a discount. According to Jennifer, the low bidder inserted implants, enlarging Bo's assets by a sensational 40%.

"Appearances are important to Gunner," she said.

"I guess so." I was gaining insight into Gunner's peculiar mind. I could have steered the conversation in so many directions, but, before I could inquire about Gunner's own surgical history, Jennifer asked me a question.

"Were you the pilot of the plane that crashed?"

"Yeah, I was."

"Are you over it?"

"No." Boundless Gloom sucked joy from the room.

Chapter 6

Treasure:
a hand-written note on violet paper signed by
Gretchen, my former German girlfriend

GRETCHEN COULD HAVE been a contender if she hadn't been so zealous about politics. She was a real looker, but she drove me over the edge nattering about the European Economic Community's decision to add Denmark, Ireland, and the United Kingdom to the EEC fold. Despite this fault, I might have given her more at bats if she had shown me more respect. Every day, the Six-Twelfth trained to shoot down guys named Ivan because Russian fighters outnumbered us in the European Theater 13-1. Gretchen teased me by calling me "toy soldier" even when we were otherwise engaged on her lumpy mattress.

"You will all be dead in the first twenty-four hours if the Russians cross the Rhine." She might have been a brilliant political and military tactician, but she had a lot to learn about foreplay.

A peek at her passport revealed that she was two years

older than she had admitted, so I called our relationship off over the issue of trust. A true romantic might have ingested a jigger of sleeping pills, but radical pharmacological reactions weren't Gretchen's style. The *Fräulein* responded as if I had told her to rotate her tires. Her Teutonic composure took the wind out of my sails. It was *auf wiedersehen* without a whimper except for an odd letter she wrote to me in amateurish English in present tense: "You are a huge disappointer. You break my hart (sic)!! Your (sic) playing at life like nothing matters and you must grow up. Some day you are to miss me very much. I am dating a child. You will see!!"

I didn't waste time lamenting Gretchen's criticism or Sticky Vicki's fickle heart because Shelley Countryman told me about a sensational Belgian girl named Trudie Michiels whom she planned to invite to Dinger's birthday party. A background check revealed that Trudie had studied at the University of Amsterdam before moving to Madrid to work as an au pair for a wealthy Spanish family.

I faced a Benelux Conundrum. I had never met anyone from Belgium, the Netherlands, or Luxembourg. I imagined that the men there were as virile as right whales, proud mammals whose testicles weighed 1,000 pounds each. No less an expert than Dinger had once said, "I have a lot of respect for a mammal who takes reproductive duties seriously enough to pack around a set of half-ton balls." Belgian men likely were logarithmically more intelligent than some mundane guy like me from San Antonio. If they had no other advantage, most of them could speak in two or three tongues: they would never run out of stuff to talk about. I didn't like my chances. So I prepared for the mission by reading a newspaper column advising men to resist talking about themselves and to focus attention on the women they desired. What a novel concept. I swore that I wouldn't brag about myself, even though that probably meant that no one else would brag about me, either.

Finally, at the party, I got to meet Trudie Michaels. My first impression of her was that she was a serene Belgian Candice Bergman. I committed the careless blunder of telling her so. I got by with the faux pas, however, because Trudie wasn't petty that way. She was frank, but amiable. I asked her an endless chain of convoluted questions.

"Is this a job interview?" she asked.

"Is it true that you speak five languages?"

"Not at the same time." Modesty at its best. Near midnight, she started playing song requests on Shelley's upright piano. I was hooked by then. I watched her like a proud uncle, my eyes moist. She had never mentioned "piano" once, yet here she was, tickling the ivories to everyone's delight. If I could play that well, I would have tattooed "piano player" on my forehead.

On a perfect sunny Saturday, Trudie joined me for a 60-mile day trip to Segovia. We shared tapas and wine at a small outdoor table with a view of Segovia's imposing First Century Roman aqueduct. Trudie talked about growing up as an only child without a father. My affection for her grew by the minute until I positively ached with desire for her. Trudie was much more than a Candice Bergen look-alike. She made me want to be more than a buffoon with a short attention span and a long bar tab. I wanted to be good enough to deserve Trudie Michiels.

At the next weekend, we drove 45 miles to Toledo. I

bought a ceramic pitcher as a gift for Trudie before join-ing a German couple at an outdoor table beside the *alcázar*. Their four-year-old son couldn't leave the pitcher alone and he fumbled it onto the ground. The parents were horrified to see it shattered on the stones, but Trudie saved the larg-est, most ornamental shard and told them, "My memory of this perfect day will last much longer than any piece of pot-tery." It was a considerate sentiment, and I was glad that she trusted me enough to say it.

Our two road trips went so well that I pushed my luck by inviting Trudie to take a 70-mile Saturday excursion with me to the ancient walled city of Ávila. We hiked around the 2,500-year-old city for hours. At one point she opined that Americans smelled like scented dryer sheets. I told her that she might change her opinion if she hung around a fighter squadron on a Friday afternoon in July. Once she ended a sentence with, "if you decide I'm the one." She caught herself right away and said, "I didn't mean for it to come out that way." I had already decided that Trudie was "the one," but I didn't have the sauce to say so. I felt so comfortable with her that I let her in on the secret of my speech therapy. We drove back to Madrid with the convertible top down and both of us chanting in unison at maximum volume into the rush of wind, "Tell Tom to tread tentatively on tangled tree twigs."

The squadron deployed to Italy for two weeks, so Trudie and I put our next junket on hold. I reserved two nights in a posh Valencia hotel near the beach. On my return from Italy, while we were lazing around Valencia, Trudie told me stories about her childhood in Belgium. I visualized the characters populating her tales – farmers in suits riding on tractors and tyrannical nuns reigning over young boarding school girls. I felt as though I had actually met Filthy Fiona, the Irish nun renowned for her snotty nose and soft heart. Fiona had showed her fondness for Trudie by smuggling truffles beneath the folds of her habit. Filthy Fiona taught Trudie to be generous for goodness sake without expecting anything in return. I was falling in love with Trudie, and recollections of other girls were fading, except for memories of Elizabeth. That kind of forgetting might take forever.

We returned to Madrid in time for one of Dinger and Shelley Countryman's recurring parties. I separated Shelley from the herd so I could get her advice on whether I was being reckless to fall for Trudie so fast. "Love doesn't have a speedometer," she said. "Don't look for excuses to mess it up."

Whirlwind weekends with Trudie ended when the Six-Twelfth assembled for a routine deployment to the Middle East. Trudie was on hand in the Torrejón passenger terminal to witness the ritual for her first time. Couples smooched in every corner of the terminal. Kids were clingy and tearful to see daddy leaving. I didn't risk kissing Trudie farewell in public. I played it safe and told her that I'd send her a post card. She said, "Don't bother." I didn't know what to make of that.

⸻ ⬦ ⸻

Pancho was a flight of four on a two-vee-two air combat maneuvering mission out of İncirlik, Turkey on the second Tuesday of the squadron's deployment. Hacksaw was Lead, and I was Pancho Four. In the debriefing, I immodestly claimed three kills on Pancho Two, a junior captain named Duke Errol. Afterwards, Hacksaw took me aside to critique me in private. He said, "When you reside at the pinnacle of aviation as a fighter pilot, it is imperative that you be massively cool at all times. You went a little heavy on Duke. Could you be a little more diplomatic?"

I certainly could be when he put it like that. To soften the criticism, Hack proposed a trade, Duke to Gunner's B Flight in exchange for me moving to Hacksaw's D Flight.

"Duke Errol's from Minnesota like Gunner. You might be happier come evaluation time."

I agreed right away, foolishly thinking that a transfer to Hack's flight would solve all my problems. I joined Hacksaw and a visiting Air Force buddy from his Texas A&M days Friday night at a table in the Officers Club. His friend's call sign was Bat Man. Boy, could Bat Man tell a story. He had flown a tour as a Raven in Laos four years earlier and he entertained a cluster of us all night with tales about the secret operators flying forward air control along the Ho Chi Minh Trail. A Texan named Cowboy Platt was the hero of several stories. Apparently, Cowboy was eccentric enough to fly his pet bear cub on combat missions out of Long Tieng, Laos.

On one of Cowboy's missions, an enemy 14.5 millimeter anti-aircraft round tore up one of the legs of his Laotian observer. Cowboy saved the observer's life by flying the plane with his feet, restraining the observer with one arm, and using his other arm to amputate the shattered leg with a Bowie knife. Bat Man's yarns were tough to top. He couldn't buy a drink all night. I was happy to chip in, acknowledging that, by contrast, I was a pretty dull boy. During his Raven tour, the enemy shot Cowboy down eleven times. After his eleventh downing, he carried his Laotian observer across a paddy and tossed him into an Air America HH-34 Choctaw rescue helicopter. Back at Long Tieng, Cowboy celebrated his escape with his fellow Ravens late into the night. He awoke the following morning paralyzed from the shoulders down. His neck was broken and his spine was fractured in seven places. Cowboy was a tough, tough man. I remembered that Bat Man referred to the band of colorful volunteers as "Connie's Lunatics." I wondered who this mysterious Connie might be. I vowed to step up my game toward Cowboy's level.

<hr />

The Six-Twelfth returned to Spain when the deployment ended. I was eager to find out whether Trudie had forgotten me. I also had often daydreamed about playing "Name the Rectangle" naked in bed with Jennifer. The memory brought pleasure, but it left me with an uneasy conscience, too. My foreboding peaked when I reached the top of the stairway that accessed squadron operations and came upon my former flight commander Gunner Gunnersson hovering over the flight-planning table. I shuddered to guess what he would do to me if Jennifer, his gorgeous blabbermouth wife, had confessed details about Wyoming, Florida, *et al.* Gunner worked out with dead weights all the time and he had muscles everywhere, including several in the jaw that I hadn't previously known about. If he had been born thirty years earlier, he would have made a dandy Nazi. An Aryan wonder, he was so physically superior to me that beating me to death wouldn't have qualified as homicide to him because I was such an inferior life form. I was on high alert for any hint of aggression. He looked up from filling out a mission data card in a haze layer of cigar smoke, a stogie wiggling between his lips.

"Stitch." His greeting was perfunctory, neither the salutation of a dear friend nor the forewarning of an incensed husband intent on revenge. It appeared that he wasn't on the verge of thrashing me. I thought, *God bless you, Jennifer Gunnersson, for keeping your exquisite, mesmerizing lips sealed.* I was elated. "Got a minute?" Gunner asked. Not so fast. I wasn't elated anymore. I stopped three feet in front of Gunner as he stretched to his full height. I flexed my knees the way shortstops do so I could dart left or right as required. "You headed for the crapper?" he asked. "This can wait."

I didn't know I had flexed my knees that much. "I'm okay."

Gunner extended a card to me. "I'm collecting for the Combined Federal Campaign." What a relief. The squadron commander had selected Gunner to collect donations for the CFC, the military equivalent of the United Way, because no one in his right mind would turn Gunner down.

"I was hoping you'd ask." I was such a phony. My bank balance was so depleted that I'd have to take out a loan to cover a donation check. Every year I contributed fifty dollars to the CFC. A whiskey at the O Club cost twenty-five cents, so I was donating the equivalent of two hundred highballs. I always hoped that the non-profits spent the money more wisely than I would have. I reached down near my left ankle to the flight suit pocket that contained my checkbook. A well-timed uppercut by Gunner would have decapitated me. I filled a check out on the spot for one hundred dollars. I also post-dated the check so I could scramble for money to cover it on the morrow.

"Thanks, Cromwell. I respect your empathy." He whisked the check out of my empathetic fingers.

"Glad to help." My conscience was absolved.

I continued toward my air combat tactics debriefing, a post-flight ritual where fighter pilots argued about whether they had scored kills during dogfights. Hacksaw Ballantine, my flight leader addressed people by invented names that he tossed into conversations like croutons into a salad bowl. "Grab your Coke and cigar, Myrtle," he said to me, "Let's get this over with." I joined the third pilot and the three back seaters at the conference table, their tape recorders, Cokes, and cigars ready. Hacksaw closed the door and took a seat at the head of the table. "Light 'em if you got 'em, girls," he said.

The flare of phosphorous match heads, the dense smoke of six off-brand cigars, and the snap-fizz of pulling Coke tabs marked the beginning of the debriefing. Captain Tyler "Dinger" Countryman, my buddy from Tampa, was my fellow wingman in the flight. His claim to fame was a three handicap in golf. He had played well enough during college to earn an athletic scholarship at Texas Tech University. The debriefing became spirited. I claimed a high-deflection gun kill on Dinger, and he took exception. "Don't lay your eggs before you count them," he said. He accused me of pressing to within five hundred feet, which was twice as close as the minimum separation allowed for firing the Gatling gun. Before our argument could ripen, an airman knocked on the door to deliver a written message to me. It said, "Jim Conti," "main gate," and "URGENT" underlined. I showed it to Hacksaw.

"Go on, Sassafras," he told me, "bug out of here. Throw another buck into the pool and git."

I called the Torrejón Air Base Main Gate Security Police to speak with Jim Conti. When he came on the line, he sounded unsure of whether I'd recognize his name. "My wife Mary was your father's secretary in Japan," he said. "Our bags were stolen in *Gare du Sud* in Paris yesterday. We barely had enough money for the train to Madrid and we can't pay for the taxi. Can you help us?"

Here was a chance for a philanderer to do a good deed. I cashed a per diem check from a recent temporary duty assignment to Italy at the on-base credit union. I had earmarked the $127 for a poker game that evening, but I was willing to sacrifice my pleasure to pay my father's secretary's husband's driver's cab fare. I drove to the main gate and paid up. I checked Jim and Mary Conti into the Torrejón Visiting Officers Quarters as my guests. Putting their room and charges on my Officers Club account bloated my balance to an all-time high. I wrangled a release from the afternoon flying schedule using a little creativity and a lot of bullshit.

Jim, about 40, was medium height. He projected the image of a poised businessman. While he showered, I took Mary to the Base Exchange to replace her stolen toiletry items. My heart was afire with philanthropy, but, possessing the wallet of a pauper, I almost tapped out my available cash paying for

Mary's spree. Back in the Officers Club where my charge account was king, I played the role of free-spending benefactor. I signed chits left-and-right: whiskeys, appetizers, steaks, deserts, and wines. A hustler was pedaling roses in the dining room, so I bought Mary three blossoms for unspecified symbolic reasons. Not only did I want Mary to feel better, my expectation was that Jim would write a glowing letter to my father, who would write a glowing letter to me, and I would feel better, too. At one point, while Mary was praising my father's virtues, she referred to him as "Lieutenant Colonel Cromwell." As I remembered it, Dad was a major at all times during his assignment at Tachikawa Air Base. It was a small inconsistency in the grand scheme of things.

The next morning, I arranged for a credit union loan. I bought Mary a one-way ticket on an afternoon flight from Madrid to San Francisco. I bought Jim a one-way ticket from Madrid to Tehran in five days' time. Deficit spending was so routine for me that frittering away money that I hadn't yet earned was no bother at all. Jim and I dropped Mary off at Barajas International Airport for her flight and then we returned to the Officers Club Stag Bar to pound some Jackson-the-rocks. "What do you do in Iran?" I asked him. He told me that he did this and that. I didn't learn much about Jim Conti.

———— ((◉)) ————

Jim couldn't get money wired until Monday. He stayed for five nights in my small three-bedroom house east of

Madrid in a pueblo populated by French and American embassy workers, Spaniards, and several American pilots from the three squadrons assigned to Torrejón. Jim perked up when Trudie came out from Madrid to spend the weekend. He followed her around like a puppy. They popped off in my convertible to play tennis at the hotel club. Reportedly, Trudie beat him in straight sets 6-0, 6-0. "This girl's phenomenal," he raved. We passed the afternoons drinking wine and eating olives, cheese, and baguettes in the filtered sun on my patio. Jim was a power listener. He found out a lot about Trudie and me, but we learned almost nothing about him. When Trudie went indoors to shower before dinner, Jim told me, "You're a block-head if you don't marry that girl."

"That's a big step."

"Flying a supersonic jet to the edge of space is a big step, but you do it every day." He was stroking my ego to win his point. It worked. I pondered life married to Trudie Michiels. "As for flying," he said, "if you don't get mired down in convention, you can make a lot of money flying for the right people." If he intended to pique my interest, he succeeded. "The point is, keep in touch. Maybe I can help you out some day." I waited for him to amplify the point, but he didn't. "I love your routine," Jim said. "If I lived this way, I'd be dead inside a year." That could have been either a compliment or a warning.

Jim got his money wire and he repaid me for the tickets I had bought for him. When I dropped him off at Barajas for his flight to Tehran on Wednesday, I got a glimpse of a gold American Express card in his wallet, but I dismissed my momentary suspicion. After Jim was well on his way to Tehran, the phonetic similarity between "Connie" and "Conti" occurred to me. I wondered whether Bat Man's "Connie's Lunatics" were actually "Conti's Lunatics."

On Friday night at an outdoor restaurant in Nuevo Baztán, Trudie inquired about my recent visitor. "He knows how to treat a lady," she said. I agreed, rising above jealousy because I assumed that I had seen the last of the mysterious Jim Conti. Back at my house with a fire in the hearth, Trudie's demeanor was calm. She exuded a pleasant kind of innocence. Her gentle critiques didn't leave a sting. She spoke candidly without leaving a bruise: "You should care more about people who aren't as fortunate as you." I didn't mount a defense. I would have cared more about unfortunates, but it was all I could do to satisfy my own needs. I skipped rebuttal and went on offense, nuzzling the part of her neck just below her left ear. The ear bone was connected to the heart bone, and the next thing I knew, clothing was flying off left and right, I was breathing hard, and Trudie wasn't quite the saint she used to be.

————— ◖◗ —————

Three days later, I was blindsided by orders transferring me from Spain to Luke AFB, Arizona, curtailing my tour of duty by almost a year. I had no idea whether Trudie would come to the States with me. I chose Rena Ballantine, a native of Selma, Alabama as my counselor because she had a way of simplifying issues without making me feel like a bozo for not figuring them out myself. I explained that I didn't want to be disloyal to Elizabeth by proposing to Trudie. She said, "Stitch, don't you give Trudie anything less than everything you've got in that big old heart of yours." I ended up asking Trudie vaguely what she thought of marriage.

"The timing's not right."

I had hoped for more enthusiasm on her part. I had no plan, so I winged it: "I can't imagine a better time. After I'm gone, you'll start dating some Spanish meathead."

"You're being presumptuous."

"I'm being insightful."

"You have a tendency to see things from only your point of view."

"That's the only point that I have a view of."

"You're too selfish for marriage. I'll admit that you can dial up virtue when it suits you, Preacher's Boy." There was a tablespoon of flattery in Trudie's recipe for turning me down. "You insist on your own way all the time. We can discuss marriage when you're ready to commit to a mature relationship. On the other hand, Jim Conti told me that I'd be a blockhead not to marry you."

"Jim Conti is a wise, wise man," I said. Not so long ago, my self-esteem in shambles, I had doubted that any sensible woman would ever want to marry me. Then along romped Jennifer Gunnersson whose extra-marital shenanigans turned me into a super hero.

Trudie said, "You don't know Jim Conti and you don't know me, either."

I didn't consider the Catholic-Protestant mismatch a hurdle too high or the Belgian-American cultural divide a chasm too wide. Nevertheless, Trudie turned me down, so I extricated my pride by inviting her to a squadron going-away party in honor of me and two other pilots returning to the Land of Round Doorknobs and Soft Toilet Paper. The end of my tour in my first combat-ready fighter squadron was a bigger deal than college graduation. I hoped that parting words of praise might boost my image in Trudie's eyes. It was a case study in flawed reasoning. In the 1970s, farewell parties in many civilized countries were sophisticated affairs that reduced honorees to tears of appreciation. But in American fighter squadrons, ribald farewell roasts brought the soon-to-be-departed to tears of a different kind.

Almost everyone seated in the hotel ballroom for the going-away bash was merry or pretending to be merry except Gunner. His trademark frown was a reminder of how insignificant the rest of us were in the shadow of his splendor. His lovely wife Jennifer was all smiles as she charmed a small caucus of bachelors. I could tell from fifty feet away that she had taken a fancy to one of the squadron's sharpest looking first lieutenants whose credentials included being an ace tennis player at Arizona State. I also could tell that he had fallen under Jennifer's spell and would remain there until she was through with him. For entertainment, Hacksaw Ballantine and Dinger Countryman put on a clever Smothers Brothers skit at my expense. They used guitars as props even though neither of them could play a lick.

"Good evening." Dinger almost ate the microphone. "I'm Tommy Smothers, and this is my brother Dickie. Invention is a necessary mother, so Dickie and I learned to play guitar just for this occasion."

They strummed furiously in E major between jokes as

a cue for the audience to applaud. Any hack could finger an E major. They snubbed my towering achievements and roasted me for a litany of missteps, none of which, thankfully, had risen to the level of a court-martial. I would have been glad to leave these memories undisturbed: buzzing a range officer's truck at 50 feet and 500 knots, returning from a low-level mission with tree branches in my bomb racks, a thirty-day grounding for jumping a Phantom formation, and being fouled off the Zaragoza bombing range for accidentally rippling off a string of six bombs. They quoted my squadron commander's infamous admonition: "Cut this shit out, Cromwell. Resolve your psychiatric issues on somebody else's time." I couldn't read the squadron commander's mind, but surely he was overjoyed to see the back of me. I was martyred for the cause of *esprit de corps*. I'm sure that Trudie considered us all a pack of juveniles.

Toward the end of the evening, without remembering how, I ended up in a dim side room off the ballroom with peerless temptress Jennifer Gunnersson. She wrapped her arms around me, and my heart went into spasm. I didn't care how nearby Gunner was in the adjacent room. Trudie wasn't anywhere in sight, either, so, the next thing I knew, I reciprocated by wrapping my arms around Jennifer.

"Don't you dare forget me, Stitch."

Nothing – not a lobotomy, not raging dementia — could erase my memories of Jennifer.

"And don't you forget what I told you," she said.

That was different. I remembered nothing she had told me except "Wyoming" and "Utah." We kissed and even fondled a little. I might never have the chance again. After she left the room, I rubbed my lips with a cocktail napkin to erase telltale traces of lipstick. I returned to the festivities as self-conscious as a teenager and as flushed as a clown. When I sidled up to Trudie, she sniffed the air.

"What cologne are you wearing?"

"Brut." I actually had once owned a bottle of Brut, so I was nibbling at the margins of some kind of truth. I was a Brut man, by fragrance and by nature.

Trudie said, "If your heart tries to keep up with your roving eyes, you're in for a heart attack."

Brut Man needed a distraction fast: "Trudie, you look beautiful, tonight."

Trudie got the last word: "Compliments from promiscuous lips don't mean a thing."

That wasn't the only uneasy moment I suffered while wrapping up my Torrejón legacy. A letter from my father mentioned that his secretary in Japan was named Keoko, not Mary. Then, with only three days and a wakeup remaining before my C-141 flight back to the States, Gunner requested my presence in his B Flight Commander's office. He came around his desk to greet me quietly. "What're you doing with the brass?" He was talking about the bullet casings I had collected at the gunnery range. They couldn't have been worth more than a hundred dollars to a scrap metal dealer. I truly didn't know. I had not included the brass among my household goods bound for Arizona. I wished I had never collected them. "Give them to me and I'll solve your problem. No one needs to know about your indiscretion." He looked me over and said, "I've been tough on you, Cromwell, but I was tough on you to make you a man." His clichéd words belonged in a hackneyed movie script. I promised to deliver the brass to him. I was relieved to rid myself of them and Gunner Gunnersson.

At the last moment, Trudie came around to my way of thinking. It was classic buzzer-beater. Residential telephones were scarce in the urbanization where I lived. Callers contacted me by telephoning a nearby resort hotel to bribe a bellhop named Juan Luis to saddle up his moped and hand-carry a message to my doorstep. He always pestered me for an outrageous tip on top of the bribe. Trudie cut Juan Luis out the equation, hitched a ride with a Spanish girlfriend, and showed up unannounced as three of the most sluggish workers in the relocation industry were loading my packed household goods. Trudie told me that she had changed her mind and would accompany me to the States. Even though she left the question of marriage unaddressed, I realized that she was taking a huge risk. I bought her a one-way ticket that afternoon before she could change her mind.

The next day, an MGB stopped in front of my empty *casa*. I observed its arrival from my kitchen window. A man in a three-piece suit got out of the right side driver's door and walked toward my front entrance. I was dressed like a clown in blue pajama bottoms and a horrible yellowish dressing gown that I had haggled off a gypsy for 200 pesetas. My slippers had holes in the soles. My burnt orange University of Texas Longhorns cap was greasy from changing the points and plugs on my Fiat. To complete the hobo look, I was smoking a Tiparillo, not because I wanted a smoke or even liked smoking, but because I wanted to finish off the pack left behind by a visitor. The man in the suit was a handsome devil whose body language suggested that he had never seen the likes of me before.

"Daniel Cromwell?" he asked in proper English English.

I nodded. Silence was appropriate for the moment because I tended to use big words when speaking to English people, and I didn't always know what the words meant.

"I'm Peter Gant. Trudie must have told you about me." When I shook my head, he said, "We're rather close. Trudie's not going to America. I have other plans." Time was not in this arrogant fellow's favor. Trudie's ticket was for travel the following day. "No, she's not going to America, and that's final." He shook his head irritably: "You Americans really are an insult to the eye."

He probably got the insult partly right. I didn't have time for him, so I shooed him away.

"I don't want to get rough," he said.

I exhaled a cloud of cigar smoke: "No, you don't."

He took one step toward me, then spun around. "Rubbish," he said. "You Yanks are a disgrace."

"Goodbye, Mr. Gant." I stored his name away in my memory vault in case I ever needed a tactical nuke to lob at Trudie in the future.

Chapter 7

Treasure:
Trudie's boarding pass for an Iberia flight
from Madrid to Philadelphia

I DROVE A rental car from McGuire AFB, New Jersey to pick up Trudy at Philadelphia International Airport for the drive to the Port of New York where I took delivery of a new Alfa Romeo purchased with money I didn't have. We set out for Nellis AFB near Las Vegas where I was scheduled to attend F-4 instructor school. Everything in the States felt big and limitless. I introduced America to Trudie as if I had created it. I wanted credit for its purple mountain majesties. I squeezed the last drops of purchasing power out of my credit cards to pay for gas, hotels, and meals. We arrived in Sin City and headed up North Las Vegas Boulevard. A flight of four Phantoms with afterburners blazing streaked overhead in fingertip formation. The sight inspired me to picture a mature version of me. I would be a sipper, not a guzzler, of spirits. No more flying at the edges of sanity. No more late bill payments. I reported for Phantom instructor training at the 414th TFS, which was Fighter Weapons School, the name for the Air Force's Top Gun School. In dire need of F-4 instructors, Tactical Air Command repurposed Top Gun instructors to train my class.

At a time when I should have been concentrating only on academics and flying, the Strip was an awful temptation. I devised a modified Martingale roulette gambling system that I named the Rangoon Iteration. The system was a printing press for money until I lost spins six times in a row and reached the roulette table's one-thousand-dollar betting limit. Playing the Rangoon Iteration required a razor-sharp intellect – mine — but it was so boring to watch that Trudie took to wandering off. I won eight hundred dollars a night. When Trudie complained, I promised her a trinket because bribing girls had always worked well for me. I was $3,000 ahead, but the grapes of Trudie's devotion were withering on the vine.

I was about to quit and cash in when I noticed Trudie chatting with a sun-tanned chick magnet attired in bell-bottoms, a satin shirt open in the front, and a gold medallion nestled in chest hair thicker than a chimp. He wore sunglasses, and his mustache would turn a Turk green with envy. Trudie was laughing more with him than she ever laughed with me. I didn't know why she was laughing, but she kept doing it, so *I* turned green with envy.

I impulsively decided to put the three large on the black rectangle. I had a 47.37% chance of doubling my bet. The little white ball decelerated onto the track, hit a pocket separator, and clattered around. I visualized how thrilled Trudie would be when I strolled over to her and Ringo with a cool

$6,000 in my pincers. The traitorous ball came to rest in the pocket for Red One. The heartless croupier raked my four nights' worth of chips away. I wanted to cough, sneeze, shit, and cry all at the same time, but the Air Force had trained me to remain calm in stressful situations. I was right back where I had started – broke. I rationalized the disaster so that I felt fortunate to break even. I pulled five twenties out of my pocket to buy more chips, which I stacked on Black Twenty-two. I was betting two weeks of lunch and gas money to win $3,500. Just wham, bam, all on a hunch. A bad hunch. The sick, perverted, psycho white ball settled into the pocket for Red Seventeen. I was worse than broke. I was down a hundred. The croupier raked away my chips with a trace of amusement on her face. It would have been satisfying to give her a good whack on the ass with my tennis racket.

Trudie and Ringo were laughing like old friends when I arrived penniless.

"How did it go?" Trudie asked.

Ringo, a nosy bugger, looked eager to find out, too.

"Tell you later."

"You need sleep."

"*Ciao*," Ringo said. As he strutted away, the thighs of his pants rubbed together and replicated the sound of my ego being ripped apart. Trudie and I headed out of the casino.

"All of it?" Trudie asked.

"Yep."

"Never again."

"Nope."

I stopped beneath the casino marquis and grasped both of Trudie's hands. A thousand lights reflected in her placid eyes. I realized how self-centered I had been for four nights working a boring mathematical progression, leaving Trudie to waste her time roaming casino floors.

"Trudie, it won't happen again." I had made a fuzzy promise to abstain from gambling for money but I didn't say a word about gambling with my life.

Chapter 8

Treasure:
a 311th TFTS Sidewinders patch, a golden
rattlesnake made out of machine gun bullets

THE TEMPERATURE WAS 109 degrees when we left Las Vegas. It had cooled off to 108 by the time we arrived at Luke AFB on the west side of Phoenix. Nine fighter squadrons flying F-4s, F-5s, F-104s, and F-15s comprised the 58th Fighter Wing, more air power than the entire air forces of the vast majority of the nations on earth. I couldn't tell whether the firepower or the temperature boggled her mind more.

I approached my new role as an F-4 instructor pilot in the 311th TFTS Sidewinders with the energy of a born-again convert. On one shoulder I wore a Three-Eleventh Sidewinder squadron patch, a golden rattlesnake made out of machine gun bullets. On the other shoulder, I wore a 58th TFTW patch, a Roman in a chariot drawn by two high-stepping reindeer, nicknamed "the queer and the deer." Lieutenant Colonel Marcus "Fig" Cannon was the

Sidewinder's squadron commander. He was socially remote, a brooder, with no time for inconsequential chatter.

"I've heard that you can be high-spirited," he said, keeping me fixed in his peripheral vision. "I expect you to be a role model for the students at all times."

"Yes, sir."

"I can be very unforgiving about these sorts of things."

I gathered that I wasn't his pet pilot. That distinction belonged to Captain Bob "Thor" Olsen, a native of Eau Claire, Wisconsin. Thor had played college football at Boston College. He was so good-looking that he was "pretty," not a desirable characteristic for a fighter pilot. Americans want their fighter pilots to be rugged, maybe chiseled, but not *pretty*. Ladies, however, were crazy about Thor even though their eyelashes couldn't compete with his. I didn't know Viking mating habits well enough to speculate on the remarkable similarity in appearance between Thor and Gunner back at T. J.

From the moment I laid eyes on Thor's wife Sally, I felt certain I had seen her before. She was an expert tennis player and had a killer tan from hours spent on court. Her eyebrows hinted that her tresses weren't naturally blonde. She was tightly strung, as if every event in her life was a second serve that had to land inbounds. She finished people's sentences in a Boston accent to goose the pace of conversations. She made it crystal clear that she hated my guts.

Her husband Thor hid his contempt for me until Turkey Shoot Day, a traditional day of competition among squadrons held on the last Friday of each month. The nine squadrons in the wing competed for preeminence in either air-to-ground gunnery or in air-to-air simulated combat. It was modern-day jousting. Fig selected me and three other instructors to make up the 311th team. I happened to be "on" that day, and I posted excellent scores in every event — rockets, strafe, low angle bombing, and high angle dive bombing. Our 311th team won the competition, and I won Top Gun honors. I hadn't won a Nobel Prize, but it felt like it after three beers at the Officers Club celebration. Thor Olsen replaced Gunner Gunnersson as Critic Emeritus with one word. "Fluke," he shouted over the din. I challenged him to a five-hundred-dollar side bet the next time we flew a range mission, and he accepted: "Anytime."

What we had here was (1) an insult, (2) an answering challenge, and (3) an acceptance. A duel. It was worth noting that betting more than a couple of dollars was taboo in the squadron. Also, I didn't have five hundred dollars. I needed a second opinion so I called Dinger Countryman, who had transferred from Torrejón to an F-5 Aggressor Squadron at Nellis AFB. He was flying Soviet tactics in dogfights every day against Navy, Air Force, and allied fighter pilots to hone their air combat skills.

"Did I do the right thing?"

"Face it, Stitch, you've got your pawns and you've got your bishops."

Dinger had given me useless inputs before, but this one took the cake.

Since leaving home for college at seventeen, I seldom visited, called, or wrote my parents. My rare letters were propaganda pamphlets intended to conceal my monkeyshines and tout my virtues. When I got over the surprise of Trudie consenting to marry me, I wrote an announcement letter to my parents. It was the first they had ever heard of Trudie. That covered the Cromwells; on to the Michiels. I couldn't ask Trudie's father for permission to marry his daughter because he had deserted his family to move to an unknown location in the Middle East years before. I wrote Trudie's mother a short letter of introduction and intent to marry her daughter. By return mail, Mrs. Michiels cordially wrote that she would attend our wedding only if it were held in Bruges. Trudie and I agreed to have a simple ceremony in America. Out of respect for my clergyman father, I asked him to officiate. Trudie was Catholic and I was Protestant, but Dad agreed. My brother was my best man, and one of my sisters was Trudie's bridesmaid. Waste not, want not. I didn't tell Trudie how I got the money together for a down payment on a house in Glendale, a suburb of Phoenix. It involved a ball point pen miracle.

Less than a year later, Trudie gave birth to our daughter Katrina on a summer day when the Phoenix temperature was 116° Fahrenheit. I took Katrina swimming for the first time when she was six days old. Her eyes weren't focusing yet, but she seemed to sense that something was afoot. Against her mother's wishes, I blew into Katrina's face as though she were a candle on a birthday cake. When she instinctively inhaled, I submerged her by holding her against my chest and bending my knees. I released my hold on her when we were both underwater. She wiggled around with her eyes wide open in the manner of a frog. After a few seconds, I brought her back to the surface so Trudie's heart could resume beating. I blotted Katrina with a towel before Trudie took her into her arms.

"I'm really proud of her," I said.

Trudie said, "Proud of her or proud of you?" Trudie wasn't displeased that her baby was a submariner, but she disapproved of my methods. I called Dinger in Las Vegas and told him that my daughter was as natural at swimming as she was at breastfeeding.

Dinger asked, "I wonder where she got that?"

For her first few months, Katrina slept in a white bassinette that we moved nomad-style in our bedroom. Trudie turned up the pressure for me to buy our child a dedicated baby bed. I told her that it was a substantial investment, considering Katrina would use it for such a short time. Discord ensued. I relented and promised to buy Katrina a crib soon.

———————————

Our transition to married life manifest in several ways. On Sundays, I routinely read scores aloud from the *Arizona Republic* even though I knew that Trudie couldn't care less about college football.

"Mizzou beat Ohio State," I said. "Maybe the Tigers have a decent team this year because they beat Southern California two weeks ago."

"Is that cricket?" Trudie knew damn well it wasn't cricket.

"Football," I said. "It's college football."

"How can you take so much pleasure in something you had nothing to do with?"

Was she jealous? An analogy came to mind. "Trudie, you told me that Belgium won six medals in the Olympics up in Montreal this summer. You were proud that they finished twenty-eighth. How could you take so much pleasure in something you had nothing to do with?" I knew and she knew that I had played it well.

"Are you telling me that, for a few minutes on a Sunday morning, you want me to be a buddy who cares whether Mizzou won or lost?"

"Yes."

"Will you promise to answer me if I ask whether you like the red dress or the blue?"

"Yes."

She said, "I think we have a deal."

I had discovered another reason to love being married to Trudie Michiels.

———◆———

Millions of readers loved a newspaper syndicated cartoon possum named Pogo for his frailties and humor. For the same reasons, I was fond of a captain back seater from Gunnison, Colorado whose call sign was Pogo. He asked me to fly him to Key West, Florida over a three-day weekend so he could attend the funeral of a friend who had died in an F-4 crash. I put him off for a day so I could clear it with

Trudie. She wasn't happy about me going cross-country because of the conflict with my scheduled crib-buying expedition. Trudie knew that I was an accomplished procrastinator, so she put her foot down. I countered: "Pogo's best pal died. He has to attend the funeral. No one else can fly him."

That did the trick. She consented because Belgians emphasized first communions and funerals. I promised to buy Katrina's crib on my return to Phoenix. Pogo and I blasted off in our Phantom on Friday morning, stopped for fuel at England AFB near Alexandria, Louisiana, and arrived in the overhead pattern at Naval Air Station Key West on Boca Chica Key Friday afternoon. I beat up the pattern for a few minutes with touch-and-goes followed by tight afterburner-powered closed patterns followed by *real* tight – seventy degrees of bank — curvilinear downwind-to-final turns. I taxied in to the transient ramp with both canopies up. I was sweltering, unaccustomed to the humidity. My Nomex sleeves were rolled up, my Nomex gloves were rolled down, the sun visor on my helmet shaded my eyes, and my oxygen mask hung by one saber clamp. Same for Pogo. The lone appreciative witness to our flashy arrival was a female enlisted crew chief who climbed the ladder to my cockpit to unstrap me.

Pogo had arranged to shack up with Brandy, a Polynesian beauty from his licentious past. Brandy was a television weather reporter and popular with most everyone on the island. She was easily recognizable in her lime-green Jeep. We passed waving men, women, boys, and girls on streets lined by palm trees. Brandy hopped out from behind the wheel to give me a delightful full-bodied *Bali Hai* kiss when she dropped me off at the Navy Lodge.

Pogo buried his friend on Saturday. I didn't cope well with funerals, so I skipped this one to snorkel, devour shrimp, and swill buckets of margaritas all day. To make matters worse, I lost all my cash playing poker with some Navy pilots that night. I was ahead after the first few hands, but my kismet soured as the hour grew late. Pogo was rolling in cash, so I hit him up for a loan the following day.

Pogo and I took off from Naval Air Station Key West before noon on Sunday. I flew a fancy full-afterburner double rat's ass departure for Brandy's benefit before dropping down for a freelance flight just above the waves up the west coast of Florida. Every time we flew over a pleasure boat, I aileron rolled to remind them that we were on watch at the ramparts. Pogo mended the previous night's excesses by puffing in his oxygen mask on 100% oxygen. "Eternal vigilance is the price of freedom," he said.

We stopped for gas and oysters at Eglin AFB in the Florida Panhandle. Rye, another of Pogo's maidens, met us with four bushels of Apalachicola oysters in the trunk of her car. I gave Pogo and Rye privacy so they could whisper sweet nothings while I loaded the oysters into a travel pod suspended under the left wing. The travel pod was the empty hull of a napalm bomb with a door cut in the side for access. When I finished loading the odoriferous bags, I buttoned up the pod and pulled Pogo away from the momentary love of his life to get him strapped into his ejection seat. I had reserved a rendezvous time with a tanker in a refueling track over North Texas and I didn't want to miss it even in the name of romance. I got clearance for a burner climb up to Flight Level 320 to keep the oysters cold. The Oklahoma

Air National Guard tanker was waiting for us, so I got on the boom, got my gas, and headed west toward Luke. Pogo patched me through to the command post on a telephone call so I could ask Trudie to conduct a "tactical recall" of a few students and fellow instructors and their wives to attend an oyster orgy that night. I asked her to get catering to set up some tables and condiments. The line went dead.

Pogo told me that Sherry, another of his girlfriends, was waiting with a trunk-full of ice. Pogo's foresight was impressive, but I was more fascinated by his girlfriends' names — "Brandy, Rye, Sherry."

"Coincidence is so random," Pogo said.

Sherry had uncommonly long legs. No one, including me, could meet her and not be distracted by her legs. She had packed so much ice into the trunk of her Volvo that the front end pointed upwards like a Nike missile ready to blast off. We split up the four bushels of oysters before driving our separate ways. Despite the short notice, Trudie had filled plastic-lined liquor boxes with ice, stocked them with beer and wine, and positioned them on makeshift tables around the pool. She had arranged condiments on my repurposed poker table. I asked her about the catering stuff, and she told me that our checking account was overdrawn and our credit card had been declined. There was no catering.

Gulp. The goblins of my financial negligence were on the march and closing in. Seven days before payday, the well was going dry. I asked Trudie where she got the money for drinks and condiments. She had raided her Sabena Fund. Pillaging the sacred fund saved for Trudie's airline tickets to Belgium was a desperate last-ditch maneuver. I knew I'd hear about this desecration after the party. I would have to replenish the Sabena Fund soon. For the time being, Trudie suppressed her anger and assigned me small tasks. I would have danced a jig on hot coals for peace in the valley. We consumed every single oyster. Even the babysitter overdosed on what she insisted on calling mollusks. Discarded shells scattered around the back yard resembled debris after a mortar attack. By the time of our last guest's departure, I was too shattered to clean up and I went straight to bed,

I woke up to the hum of a thousand Allied bombers flying overhead. Unknown to me, the Arizona Department of Agricultural had airdropped bazillions of sterile flies over Phoenix the previous day so an entire generation of flies would never emerge to ruin Arizona's crops. Flies, sterile or fertile, loved the smell of oyster shells. Word got around in the insect community, and several thousand critters assembled in the back yard. The buzzing was deafening. I wanted to delay facing the frightening swarm so much that I fed our cat Tonka twice. Then I went out to face the music. Insects flew into my eyes, ears, and mouth while I collected oyster shells. Over lunch, Trudie presented a summary of my financial blunders. The facts weren't in dispute. As awful as the tongue-lashing was, the oyster debacle turned out to be providential as it postponed my purchase of a crib for Katrina with money I didn't have.

———— ◉ ————

After a day of flying, while inching my Alfa Romeo from my 110-degree driveway to park it inside my 109-degree garage, I noticed a large cardboard box sitting on the front porch. I wrestled it into the house, and Trudie and I popped the cork of our last bottle of wine and opened the mystifying box together. We'd never laid eyes on a finer baby bed, the creation of Amish craftsmen in Pennsylvania. We assembled the crib a few seconds before we finished the bottle of wine. Trudie found a card among the packing: "Stitch, I'll never forget what you did for us in Madrid. Congratulations on your new baby girl. I'll call you soon." Signed: "Jim Conti."

Our benefactor in Tehran had good intelligence sources and a generous spirit too. Once again, procrastination had paid off. I fired off a thank you note to Jim immediately. Katrina's bassinette days were over. No longer a gypsy, she was the proud new owner of an Amish baby bed set up in a permanent place in her own bedroom. The unseen hand of Jim Conti had saved my bacon. I pondered on these things as I watched my innocent little aqua baby slumber in her Amish crib. I knew better than to depend on an acquaintance to provide for my child. I faced the possibility that my lengthy hospitalization had made me self-indulgent. I didn't know the meaning of the word "budget." Perhaps Trudie had been right about me. Perhaps I was too immature to deserve a wife and child. I abstained from eating out or drinking alcohol to break my profligate spending habits for a solid month. Despite Trudie's skepticism, I did it. I managed to save $178, which I promptly spent on new swimming pool furniture.

Greed, arrogance, and ignorance were underlying causes of my persistent poverty. During two years of hospitalization, modest military paychecks had piled up in my bank account. By the time I entered pilot training in 1972, my bank balance was over $15,000, enough to buy a small house at the time. The United States had withdrawn from the Bretton Woods Treaty the previous year, ending the convertibility of U.S. dollars to gold. As a consequence, the value of the dollar fell and the stock market nosedived.

Released from hospital and starting to care about such things, I attempted to improve on dismal returns in my savings account. I didn't trust investment advisors, so I invested every dollar I had in steel stocks at the height of their valuations on the advice of some egghead at *Kiplinger's*. Diversification was for sissies. Steel stock prices buffeted at their tops on the edge of a stall and then plummeted. Believing that the egghead had it only halfway wrong, I borrowed money to buy more steel shares at lower prices. The stock market declined even more in 1973, weighed down by the Arab oil embargo in October. It was all I could do to service the interest expense on my margin loans. I suffered losses in stoic silence. While dating Trudie I never revealed how near I was to insolvency, afraid that she might stampede. By 1977, my net worth hovering within a rounding error of zero, I still showed little fiscal discipline. I barely made mortgage payments, but I always found cash to waste on extravagances such as oysters and beer. Martinis were more important to me than baby cribs. My disgraceful record of managing money put me in a financial hole, and I was desperate for a way out.

Chapter 9

Treasure:
a walnut plaque awarded to the 311th TFTS Top Instructor

"THIS IS JIM Conti. I got your letter. Very classy."

"The baby bed is a work of art. Thanks very much, Jim."

"Enough small talk. I've got a deal for you. You've flown T-Birds, haven't you?"

The precise answer was "no," but I sensed that the conversation would stagnate unless I said "yes," so I twisted the English language into a knot.

"I don't have a boatload of time in the T-Bird." Modest. Deceptive. Just right.

I knew that the T-Bird, officially called the T-33 Shooting Star, was the two-seat trainer version of the single-seat F-80 Shooting Star jet developed by the Air Force near the end of World War II. F-80s had seen action during the Korean Conflict, including the first shoot-down of a North Korean MiG-15.

"An American company needs a test pilot to fly an attack version of the T-Bird for a foreign client." Jim told me that the test flying would be in Arizona and might last for as long as two years. He wouldn't go into details until I committed, but he did reveal that it was a twelve-plane package. "The contract will pay in the neighborhood of one thousand dollars a flight." My heart seized up. My monthly paycheck as an Air Force captain on flight status in 1977 was only two thousand dollars. Jim Conti was offering me a way to pay off my debts and even take a chunk out of what I owed on my home mortgage. "What's your security clearance?" I told him I had a top secret clearance. "Good. Don't repeat this, but the CIA is refurbishing twelve T-Birds to sell to a South American government for drug interdiction."

I didn't dare hesitate for fear that some other greedy bastard would grab the opportunity. I couldn't see how Trudie could object. "I'm your guy, Jim."

"Outstanding. I'll build a resume for you."

That seemed backwards, but I trusted Jim to know what he was doing. I had a feeling that this gig was going to work out better than the Rangoon Iteration. Five days later, the mail man delivered a piece of fiction that Jim called my resume. I'd never seen so much bullshit in one pile. It seemed that I had an aerospace engineering degree from Georgia Tech and a Master of Science Degree in Flight Test Engineering from Air University. I was a graduate of U.S. Air Force Test Pilot School at Edwards AFB. I had flown hundreds of hours in the T-Bird, T-37, T-38, F-100, F-4, F-104, and F-106. In truth, I had never sat in the cockpit of a T-Bird, a Super Sabre, a Starfighter, or a Delta Dagger. In a word, the resume was outrageous. It eased my ethical indigestion over these blatant lies that the last three claims were true: I had current certificates of altitude chamber physiological training and centrifuge training and I had a current FAA medical. I had strayed from my parents' teachings on morality in the past, but I'd never gone on this kind of fibbing rampage before. I called Jim to protest, but only enough to suggest that I owned a moral compass, not enough to queer the deal.

"I'd have to be forty years old to have these credentials."

"It's an insurance thing," Jim said. "It'll also satisfy this prick at CIA. Don't worry. I'll take care of the packaging. You just deliver on the flying." He called again the next day: "A thousand bucks a flight has been approved. Also, they've agreed to pay you an allowance of five thousand if you can borrow a couple of T-Bird batteries for two months. Three thousand if you can get your own parachute. And I got you a two-thousand-dollar allowance for a flight manual, flight suits, and a helmet. Do you see how this is going to go? Welcome to *Operation Twisted Piccolo*. I want you to meet a Mister Bruno in Scottsdale next Monday night. Sign his paperwork and you'll start in a month."

My hands were trembling when I hung up the phone. I scribbled benefits on a yellow pad – debts paid, cosmic cash flow, piles of money, dreams. I waited until after dinner that night, with Katrina asleep in the Jim Conti Memorial Crib, before I swore Trudie to secrecy and told her the news. I made believe that it was an offer that I hadn't accepted yet. I still couldn't tell her how much we needed the money because she would have gotten too sidetracked on my financial ineptitude to give *Piccolo* a chance. Neither did I tell her about the fabrications and false credentials. Even so, she asked questions.

"How much do you know about Jim Conti? What if he set you up from the start? Isn't it strange that such a cosmopolitan guy would lose his money and credit cards in a train station?"

I remembered my glimpse of an American Express Gold Card in Jim's wallet, but I dismissed Trudie's cynicism because I wanted to hang on to the job that Trudie seemed intent on rejecting. She asked me if I'd be covered by insurance, who would pay me, and how I'd keep the secret from the Air Force. I didn't know any of the answers. I went through the motions of getting Trudie to consent, but what I really wanted was to be a dictator who did whatever he pleased.

"Imagine your daughter with no father," she argued. "No. I won't have it."

Driven by greed and vanity, I wanted to seize this windfall more than I wanted anything. I lusted for the money, hungered for the adventure, yearned for the thrill of the secrecy. I spent three days concocting variations of the truth and outright lies to change Trudie's mind.

"Think of the money." (The money was all I could think about.)

"I'm the most qualified pilot they can find." (Gross exaggeration.)

"The ejection seats are state-of-the-art." (Lie.)

"Jim Conti could lose his job if I don't help him out." (Not credible.)

"*Operation Twisted Piccolo* could be a real feather in my cap." (Not likely.)

"How would you feel in the future if your daughter died of an overdose of drugs supplied by the Colombian cartels?

Piccolo will put them out of business." (A stretch.)

"Just stop." Trudie finally surrendered. "Just do your stupid secret thingy, but if you kill yourself, you'll spend eternity unforgiven."

⸻ ⬩⟨◉⟩⬩ ⸻

I generally refrained from recommending restaurants because experience had taught me that most of them were staffed by short-tempered cooks called chefs, surly bartenders, overly bubbly waitresses, and nose-picking busboys who didn't care whether you survived or died. Still, the reputation of *Triento's* in Scottsdale was first-rate. The Mr. Bruno waiting for me hadn't missed many meal times. He was as sturdy as a tackling dummy. Two martini glasses coated with condensation adorned his place setting. I assumed that one was for me, but I was wrong.

"What will *we* be drinking?" the waiter asked. My pet peeve was waiters who referred to me as "we" as if they would spend happy hour perched on my lap.

"Yeah, what's your poison?" Mr. Bruno asked.

"Martini."

"One or two?"

"Two." When in Rome.

Mr. Bruno had a deep, dark tan, the kind of world-class tan you have to fly thousands of miles to get.

"Jim Conti and I go way back," he said. "We got out of Cambodia on the same plane when Prince Sihanouk got his tit in a ringer." He pulled papers from his briefcase. "How's your wrist?"

"Solid."

"Sign wherever there's a yellow flag." He produced a small flashlight that was brighter than a stage light. I started to read the pages with care, but Mr. Bruno steered me away from the path of due diligence. "Don't bother reading that shit. Just sign beside the yellow flags."

I signed the last page as my two martinis showed up. I didn't know *what* I had signed, but for a thousand bucks a hop, I was inclined to sign anything. "Do I have to date these?"

"No. I've got a meathead in the office who'll do that." Mr. Bruno handed me a check for $10,000 drawn on the account of Everest Aviation. All it said in the *for* line was *life support equipment.* "The company spurns attention," Mr. Bruno said. "Will you keep this to yourself?"

"I have no doubts about that." I was euphoric about holding a check for $10,000.

"Jim will appreciate it. So will I."

The waiter was back, itching to recite a litany of specials to impress us with his memory. "What'll *we* be having tonight?"

I wanted to tell the annoying prick I'd be having ten grand, but, instead, I said, "Surf and turf." I wanted Mr. Bruno to perceive me as a decisive maker of deals, not one to be trifled with.

Mr. Bruno didn't blink: "The company's glad to find a guy with your credentials. You wouldn't believe some of the maniacs we had in Laos." He caught himself. "But, let's not get into that."

We were old pals laughing away by the third drink. He

told me that Bruno wasn't his real name. What a surprise. He said it didn't matter because I wouldn't see him again unless I screwed the pooch. Neither of us got personal, so we yakked about football, poker, women, and golf. I was a relative amateur in all four disciplines, so I left the conversational heavy lifting to Mr. Bruno. He insisted I join him for a Bailey's after the meal. I remembered the time in Spain when Jim Conti had advised me that I could make a lot of money by flaunting convention and flying for the right people. Logically, these had to be the right people because the flying wasn't conventional and I was going to make a lot of money.

"You'll be a good guy to work with," Mr. Bruno said. "You got my stamp of approval. Conti always comes through with a good guy." He handed me my copies of the documents I had speed-signed and gave me one last piece of counsel.

"Don't let no clowns talk you into anything stupid."

<hr>

Angelo Costello. More than five years had passed since I had spoken with the legendary hospital slacker and fixer extraordinaire. He told me what an honor it was to hear from me and told me that he had been promoted to sergeant and then to staff sergeant. "E-Six, Baby," he said. "Cream rises to the top." I thought, *given enough fiber, so does a turd.* I emphasized that I was on a tight budget. I needed a T-33 parachute, a black Nomex flight suit, a T fitting so the oxygen hose from my Air Force oxygen mask would connect to the oxygen system of a T-Bird, and a T-33 flight manual, the "Dash One." Costello insinuated a vast network of affiliated scalawags at Army posts and four Air Force bases — Travis, Tinker, Randolph, and Langley. "My empire stretches from sea to whatever. I'll treat you right, L.T."

"I'm not a lieutenant anymore," I said. "I'm a captain now."

"That's a massive accomplishment," he said. "Congratulations, Captain Cromwell." He and I both knew it was *not* a massive accomplishment because the promotion from first lieutenant to captain was automatic. We entered negotiations. Each item cost a hundred bucks except the parachute, which was a thousand. The total was thirteen hundred dollars, which pleased me more than I let on. I was hoping for a discount for old time's sake, but Costello said discounts were like cancer and he insisted on cash.

I left my home in Glendale a week later at five o'clock Saturday morning to drive 450 miles to the designated corner of the El Paso International Airport parking lot to meet Costello. Today's high was going to be a lot more than 82 degrees. I opened all the windows on my Alfa and kept the motor rotating at a rapid rate. If Jennifer Gunnersson thought I looked like a fool dropping to the deck for a game of Dead Bug, she should have seen me shouting my speech therapy sentences rolling through the desert on Interstate Ten. I let the words fly at the top of my lungs: "The abominable aliens filibustered the association." And then, "Indomitable anemone intimidate murderers subliminally." Three times. "United by agnosticism, residents of the isthmus employed onomatopoeia." There was no one within ten miles to hear my goofy sentences: "Today's high is eighty-two degrees."

On a typical day, I might carry as much as eight dollars

in my jeans, but, on this momentous morning, I could feel the one-hundred-dollar bills bulging in my pocket, a hockey puck of treasure. I had stashed another $500 in cash under the spare tire in case Costello threw me a curve ball. I recognized Costello the moment he stepped out of his shiny red Porsche 911. He was attired in blue jeans, a white tee shirt, cowboy boots, wrap-around sunglasses, and a well-rolled cowboy hat. He immediately started bitching: "Damn. Took eight hours to get here. San Antonio and El Paso were only three inches apart on the map." Costello was no Magellan. "Add two hundred bucks for my time." I could see that coming miles away. Costello offered me the privilege of shaking his hand, saying, "I drove six hundred miles."

"Texas is bigger than most," I observed. Standing there shooting the shit about the dimensions of the Great State of Texas, we were the Bobbsey Twins in our jeans and white tee shirts. "If Brooklyn could see you in your Stetson and your shit-kickers," I said. I dug around in my trunk for an extra two hundred dollars and delivered $1,500 to Costello. From a distance, it would have appeared to be a drug deal. I tipped him a bottle of Maker's Mark in the futile hope of disgracing him for adding the $200 surcharge.

I drove the 450 miles back toward Phoenix in an exuberant mood. I hadn't flown a single hop, but I was already up by over $8,000 after expenses. I stopped at the Scottsdale Airport to pick up two T-33 batteries from a civilian who owned a T-Bird. I gave him a rental check in advance for $400. The next night, seeing as how I was rolling in dough, I took Trudie to Pinnacle Peak for the best steak dinners on the menu. Katrina's baby sitter, a pouty little package of discontent, was delighted with my oversized tip. I acted like a rube who'd hit the jackpot. Almost every night for a month, I studied the T-33 Dash One to learn the aircraft systems and emergency procedures. The secrecy of *Operation Twisted Piccolo* excited me because, from among all the pilots in America, Everest had chosen me.

I was on a roll. My inaugural flight in a Shooting Star was approaching fast. My bank account hadn't been so flush since my days in hospital. The graduating class of 311th TFTS Phantom crews honored me as the Top Instructor. I also won Top Gun honors again at the most recent month's 58th TFTW Turkey Shoot. I was somebody. Thor Olsen appeared in the scheduling office on the following Monday.

"Don't read too much into your instructor trophy," Thor said. "It was a compassion thing. The students feel sorry for you."

His malice surprised me. "What have I ever done to piss you off?"

"Figure it out. You're a lame horse. You're an embarrassment." Ouch. Sticks and stones could break my bones and, it seemed, words could do some damage, too. "I'm glad we chatted," Thor said. "You know where you stand with me."

I couldn't figure out why guys like Gunner and Thor disliked me so much. Perhaps my scars reminded them of what could happen to them if their luck ran out.

Chapter 10

Treasure:
a receipt for a Cessna 150 rental from Glendale Aviation

THE LARGEST GHOST air force in the world was located at a gigantic aircraft storage facility on David-Mon-
than AFB (DM) near Tucson. Nicknamed the Boneyard, it
contained hundreds of mothballed military airplanes. Everest Aviation mechanics started resuscitating twelve Boneyard
T-Birds for me to ferry from DM to Marana. The mechanics
purged and leak-checked fuel bladders, replaced tires, test
ran engines, serviced hydraulic systems, replenished engine
oil, repaired pneumatic leaks, and checked electrical circuits
for continuity while I waited back in Phoenix. Time was not
my friend. I imagined an authentic test pilot showing up to
displace me. I worried about missing my chance to shake the
money tree. An Everest secretary called to announce a weekend meeting in the Everest hangar at Marana.

I drove to Marana, west of Interstate Highway Ten between Phoenix and Tucson. The Director of Operations
Bryan Presley, 50, arrived first dressed in a safari jacket and

cowboy boots. We established that he was not a relative of the King. A weed whacker would have burned through a tank of gas clearing the bumper crop of hair growing in his ears. He constantly jiggled a finger in one ear or the other to relieve tickling, maybe itching. Despite the distraction of his fur-lined ears, Presley and I hit it off from the start. I wished I could say the same for the roly-poly three-hundred-pounder named Mr. Hernandez. I didn't know what the Director of Maintenance had lunched on, but I could tell from three feet away that it involved a ton of garlic. Sitting beside a flame-thrower would have been preferable. He obviously considered pilots prima donnas. He exhaled through his blowhole every time he looked at me.

Ferrying a plane from Point A to Point B was about as simple as aviation got. The direct course from DM to Marana was only 32 miles. All I had to do was select a route of flight, an altitude, an airspeed, and a fuel load. Mr. Hernandez insisted that the planes would take off, fly the short route, and land with landing gear pinned down and flaps left in place at 31.5 degrees. His guiding principle was that an airplane wouldn't break as long as some knuckleheaded pilot didn't touch it. Leaving the wheels down for the entire flight meant they'd be there for landing. Leaving the flaps untouched precluded split flaps, a condition that could cause loss of the aircraft. Flying in a "dirty" configuration would burn more fuel, but I didn't care about that: I could fly for 32 miles upside-down. Mr. Hernandez was itching for a fight, so he was surprised when I agreed with him. The lovefest ended on the subject of fuel load.

Mr. Hernandez wanted me to carry a full load of 683

gallons of fuel. I wanted to carry no more than 200 gallons. Fuel quantities in modern aircraft were measured in pounds, so working with gallons was as cumbersome for me as using a foreign language. My goal was to land with a fuel reserve of fifty gallons, about 340 pounds. I remembered an old axiom: "There's nothing as worthless to a pilot as runway behind him, altitude above him, and fuel he doesn't have." I didn't want to run out of fuel and have to perform a dead-stick emergency landing in the desert. Bending a T-Bird would acquaint me with a lot of important people who would want to skin me alive, notwithstanding my incredible resume. On the other hand, I wanted to carry as little fuel as possible to minimize the size of the bonfire if I crumpled the jet. My fancy resume said that I was practically an astronaut, so my word had to count for something.

"If we stop and piss on each other every time we have to make a decision," Presley said, "this little pow-wow is going to last all day. Give him two hundred gallons." Mr. Hernandez gave in, but he said he'd defuel the first T-Bird after landing at Marana to determine how much fuel I had burned. He proposed a $100 side bet on whether I'd shut down with fewer than fifty gallons of fuel remaining. Presley took the "over" and doubled the bet. As we left the conference room, Presley whispered to me, "I hope you know what you're doing."

━━━◄◦►━━━

Aware that I intended to commute from Glendale Airport to Marana Airport using a rented Cessna, Bryan Presley telephoned me on Friday evening to ask me to bring along an Everest mechanic named Guillermo the following morning. In retrospect, I should have rented a larger, more expensive model than a Cessna 150 to accommodate Guillermo's added weight. The prospect of thousands of dollars cascading into my greedy hands made me feel special, so I was over-ripe for a slapdown for my complacency. The Phoenix weather forecast called for unseasonal rain and seasonal heat, the kind of high temperatures that penalized engine and wing performance. It was an hour after sunrise, and I was already roasting in my black Nomex flight suit out on the Glendale ramp. On the positive side, I looked fabulous. I didn't bother with a weight and balance calculation because, compared to a 58,000-pound Phantom, my 1,000-pound Cessna 150 seemed as light as a feather. It wasn't a state secret that I was taking off in excess of the maximum limit of 1,600 pounds. No doubt, at some time in the past, a test pilot had taken off weighing more than 1,600 pounds, but Cessna 150 certification brainiacs had established 1,600 pounds as the limit to prevent hamburgers of my variety from dinging an airplane.

Guillermo showed up twenty minutes late with a small overnight bag. I could tell at a glance that he was fond of doughnuts and tacos. His loving wife told me to take good care of him as if she were leaving him at a day care center. She might have had a premonition of what was about to transpire because she skedaddled away hastily. I shoved the pair of T-Bird batteries behind Guillermos's seat and snugged the parachute up behind mine, thereby shortcutting weight-and-balance calculations in the most perfunctory of ways. In our hurry to get back on schedule, Guillermo sat on my military sunglasses and bent the frames past the point of salvaging. Was it an omen?

The runway length of the Glendale airport at that time was only 2,400 feet. The elevation of the airport was 1,701 feet above sea level. Takeoff roll in a properly loaded Cessna 150 was about 800 feet on a cool day, but I was a tad over-grossed and the temperature was 92° Fahrenheit. Winds were calm. I was stupid. The density altitude that morning was over 4,000 feet above sea level. That meant that the little Cessna was doomed to perform like a constipated pig. Taxiing toward the runway, I selected 10 degrees of flaps. Positioning the airplane so I could use every inch of runway, I added power, released the brakes, and glanced at the airspeed indicator, which took its sweet time budging off zero. More than a thousand feet down the runway, the airspeed indicator showed 50 mph. I rotated at 55 mph as the remaining runway kept sliding beneath the glare shield. The nose was heavy. The more I pulled back on the yoke, the more persistent the grating blare of the stall warning horn got. A scrunched-up Cessna 150 sliding across Glendale Avenue looked imminent.

"Pull the parachute onto your lap," I shouted. My arrogance and calm under pressure were long gone. I ventured one peek at Guillermo, as the pace of events didn't allow time for a more thorough character study. His eyes were the size of onions due to the rapid approach of Glendale Avenue. "Now," I shouted even louder.

Guillermo spun in his seat and dragged the parachute onto his lap. The stall warning horn went silent and I rotated enough to get off the ground before the perimeter fence disappeared under the nose. By the narrowest of margins, we were airborne, but I couldn't coax the airspeed indicator above 60 mph. Ground effect protected us from plowing a furrow in the cotton field beneath us. A web of high-tension power lines supported by menacing erector set towers loomed in our immediate futures. There was no viable option: I flew underneath the power lines.

"Is that normal?" Guillermo asked.

"It's not normal normally," I said.

Guillermo hugged the parachute until his fingers turned white. We gained a couple of miles per hour flying above a field under irrigation. Then a thermal gave us a tiny boost upwards. I yawed to the right and managed a hundred feet per minute climb at 65 mph. I steered clear of controlled airspace and kept gaining altitude. I flew a detour around the west side of South Mountain and continued climbing, now at a whopping 70 mph. All the while, Guillermo cuddled with the parachute.

"What's the best angle of climb speed in this thing?"

"Depends," I said. Did this guy think he was Chuck Yeager?

I kept climbing as we paralleled Interstate Ten, offset to the west by about half a mile. By the time we limped up to 3,000 feet above the ground, the size of Guillermo's eyes had normalized. The parachute against his body was hot, so he asked me if he could put it back behind my seat. I told him to try it to see what would happen. He hadn't comprehended yet that I didn't know all the answers. He delayed for a while before laying the parachute to rest as gently as he would have handled nitroglycerine.

"What was that all about?" he asked.

"I had to move the center of gravity forward." I didn't want to utter the words *stall* or *warning*.

I didn't know whether Guillermo was seeing past my smoke screen, but I was almost sure he'd never hitchhike with me again. I could see rain clouds on the horizon in the direction of Tucson as clouds and reduced visibilities moved in from the south. I chastened myself for overlooking a proper weight and balance calculation. My ability to fly a Phantom two-and-a-half times the speed of sound didn't excuse me from the most basic of airmanship responsibilities. I remembered an old Dinger saying: "Even virtuosos have to tune their violins." On the other hand, I didn't want to beat myself up over my imperfections, either. I had important stuff to do, like flying a T-Bird for the first time. Regardless of how I flew the T-Bird, it would surely entail more decorum than my morning fandango, which had been about as dignified as a monkey diddling a football. I checked the southeastern sky toward Tucson where the clouds were dark, indeed. I landed the Cessna 150 without drama at Marana.

"That's the best landing I've ever seen," Guillermo gushed. I could tell that he was trying to get on my good side now that we had survived.

"Not as spectacular as the takeoff, was it?"

He smiled like someone at a funeral, knowing that he'd never have to deal with the deceased again. A ground handler guided me to park the Cessna 150 beside a Cessna 206 on the ramp outside the Everest Aviation hangar. A guy about twenty years old introduced himself as Todd, the pilot who would fly me in Everest's Cessna 206 Caravan to DM to pick up the first T-Bird. "We'll be delayed because DM's got rain and reduced visibility right now," he said. "I'm not instrument rated." If they required ratings for mustaches, Todd wouldn't have gotten one of those either. Tiny follicles sprouted over his top lip in dozens of directions. I hoped his flying was better than his grooming.

At the time, Air Traffic Control (ATC) directed Tucson International Airport and DM traffic inside the boundaries of a Terminal Radar Surveillance Area (TRSA). I *was* instrument rated so I told Todd that I could take the Caravan's controls any time we were in the weather, including the Instrument Landing System (ILS) approach to DM. I suggested that we press on to DM so I could return to Marana with the first T-Bird while he waited at DM for the weather to improve to allow him to fly back to Marana under Visual Flight Rules (VFR).

Because of the Astronaut Effect, Todd agreed with anything I proposed. He would have flown by way of Tucumcari naked if I had suggested it. He introduced me to his girlfriend, a greyhound-lean maiden in tight cutoffs. She conversed through her nose in a high-pitched whine. I wanted to warn Todd about listening to that over breakfast for the rest of his life, but I kept in mind that I was a world-class test pilot, not a marriage counsellor. She produced a copy of Alan Cartwright's book *The Incredible Shooting Star* and she asked me to autograph it. My impression of her improved. I was a phony, a joker who couldn't be bothered to do a weight-and-balance, yet there I was autographing a book I hadn't written about a jet I'd never flown.

Chapter 11

Treasure:
a picture of a T-33 flying over downtown Tucson

A PHANTOM WAS a thousand mph faster than a T-Bird and 1,500 mph faster than a Cessna 150, but the Cessna could stuff me in a casket as surely as a Phantom. The embarrassing takeoff fiasco at the Glendale Airport was a wakeup call. I was about to fly a T-Bird for the first time, so it was time for extra diligence. Todd was responsible for getting me to DM. He had installed only three of six seats in the Cessna 206 to make room for cargo. I sat in the front to his right, leaving the single second-row seat for his paparazza girlfriend. Compared to my morning cockup, Todd's takeoff was routine. While we were still clear of clouds, I radioed Tucson TRACON for an IFR (Instrument Flight Rules) clearance to DM. Todd gave me control of the airplane to fly into the clouds at four thousand feet in moderate rain.

Todd gave his girlfriend a tutorial on flying in clouds. We remained in the weather during descent and an ILS approach until we broke out a mile on final, 300 feet above the ground. Todd took control of the airplane through landing and taxi-in to a ramp where Everest mechanics had lined up three scruffy T-Birds, their "U.S. Air Force" lettering, bureau numbers, and insignia oversprayed with black paint. A cord stretched from a power cart to a T-Bird parked at an unsettling tilt, its left main gear strut properly serviced and it right main gear strut as flat as a pancake. The Air Force Supervisor of Flying (SOF) parked his staff car nearby. He was an amiable colonel cradling an FM radio. I maintained anonymity and volunteered as little as possible to prevent the SOF from figuring out that I was a moonlighting active-duty Air Force pilot.

"I loved flying the old T-Bird," he said. "Where'd you get your time?"

"Korea." I had never set foot in Korea, but lying was my new pastime. My aptitude for dissembling grew more robust with use.

"Osan or Kunsan?"

"I can't discuss it."

The SOF seemed miffed. He took refuge from me and a warm mist by retreating to his staff car, which he positioned to get a clear view of the pending spectacle. A middle-aged character in jeans, his flaming red hair tucked into a cowboy hat, approached the Caravan. His eyebrows, as bushy as raspberry brambles, kept his hat from sliding down onto his nose. He stuck out a knuckle-crusher disguised as a calloused, freckled hand. We shook.

"You the test pilot?"

"I go by Stitch."

"I'm your lead mechanic. Name's Red." Of course it was.

Red told me he was from San Angelo, and I told him I was from San Antonio. "Damn, Stitch, maybe this is going to work out. I bet flying this old dog's going to bring back some sweet memories."

"Sure enough."

Todd helped me pile my gear beside a BB gun on a table inside a tent situated fifty feet from the Leaning Jet of Arizona. Todd's girlfriend snapped pictures as though her supply of film was endless. Red retrieved a maintenance logbook to brief me on the airplane's status. "This jet's not going to win a beauty contest," he said. "We're just trying to get her up the road to Marana to zero-time her. New avionics. Overhaul the engine. New fuel bladders. You won't believe how sweet she's going to be. Course she's a pile of shit now." He read each write-up like a doctor enumerating symptoms of a patient. "You've got two hundred gallons internal fuel and empty drop tanks. Trying to keep the blaze as small as you can, I reckon." Red had the earthy wit of a firefighter crossbred with an undertaker. "We ain't got cartridges yet, so the ejection seat's disabled. If anything goes wrong, you'll have to sit on your parachute pack and ride it in."

This might have been a showstopper for some pilots, but I didn't mind flying without an ejection seat. I could kill myself as fast punching out as by emergency landing in the desert. Red seemed grateful that I didn't reject the airplane over the inoperative ejection seat.

"She's going to be a bitch to taxi because the right main gear strut won't hold a pneumatic charge."

I had a bad feeling about the flat strut. The T-Bird, unlike every jet airplane I had ever flown, had no nose-gear steering, so, because I had never taxied or flown a T-33 before, I had no idea of how much differential braking would be required to steer.

"The engine's good," Red said. "We've fired it up twice and we got it up to 99% RPM without an over-temp. There's no navigational gear, but, what the hell, Marana's just up Interstate Ten that-a-ways." He dipped the brim of his cowboy hat toward the west-northwest. I could live with that. "Also, the UHF radios don't work. Don't know what you're going to do about that."

I didn't either, at least not right away. I considered cannibalizing a radio from another T-Bird and bringing the radio back to DM after the first flight, but then I asked Todd if he'd ever flown formation before. He looked alarmed and shook his head. I proposed a multi-step plan:

Step One: Todd would get a VFR clearance out of the TRSA when the weather improved.

Step Two: We would taxi in formation so I wouldn't have to contact Ground, Tower, or Departure.

Step Three: I would take twenty-second spacing on his takeoff.

Step Four: Todd would fly as fast as he could.

Step Five: I would fly as slow as I could.

Step Six: I would join up on his right wing to fly out of the TRSA.

Todd was quick to agree to my plan: "My girl will get some cool shots of you."

This bird had more write-ups than any airplane I'd ever flown. Red resumed reading discrepancies, so many that I wondered whether he was kidding me. "The canopy won't stay closed even though we re-rigged it twice, so we're going to have to wire it shut."

"So I'll be wired inside the cockpit?"

"Yep. The guy who meets you in the chocks at Marana will unwire it so you can get out." Having been trapped inside a burning airplane before made me twitchy about being "wired in," but I didn't want to be a sissy. I remembered Mr. Bruno's advice about clowns sweet-talking me into the Land of Stupid. On the other hand, Todd's girlfriend was taking pictures, so I figured things would work out okay. By the time we got through his list of broken things, the visibility had improved and the drizzle had stopped. Clouds were breaking up. The weather was good enough for Todd to fly legally. I motioned for him to get a clearance for our formation departure.

I'd flown the F-4 for so many years that strapping into a Phantom cockpit was as comfortable as settling into a favorite reading chair. By contrast, strapping into the T-Bird for the first time felt odd. I was sitting low to the ground in the T-Bird compared to a Phantom. The tilt toward the flat right strut felt creepy. All the instruments were old school. The fuel gauge was calibrated in gallons instead of pounds. The airspeed indicator was marked in miles per hour instead of knots. The attitude indicator was from the Revolutionary War. Some of the fuel switches were different from the diagrams in my flight manual. It was not a time for hurrying. I was excited. I was about to fly a plane I'd never touched before, which was bliss for an adrenaline junkie. Red's headset cord jack didn't work, so we couldn't communicate on interphone. He screamed at me to be heard, and I screamed back at him in a sort of pre-industrial-age communication ritual. Red juiced the power cart and cleared me to start. I followed the flight manual procedures, but the engine didn't start. My heart was thumping. Red hustled over with a ladder, climbed up, and looked inside the cockpit. He pointed at a red guarded switch.

"You've got to flip that ignition switch on for an auto-start," he shouted.

I flipped the red guarded switch to on, and a bomb went off. Todd and his girlfriend bolted for cover. The SOF backed his staff car fifty feet further away. I aborted the starting sequence as Red slid down the ladder and jogged toward a nearby fire extinguisher. A second mechanic, who had been watching the show from a safe distance, climbed up the ladder to the cockpit.

"Whoo-whee. You torched a flame a hundred feet long. Never seen that much fire out of an engine before. There was even fire coming out of the intakes. You was a Roman candle."

My heart was racing. Red replaced the mechanic on the ladder. "How hot did she get?" he asked.

"Never topped eight hundred," I told him. "These switches are different from my manual."

"Tell me something, Stitch; you ever flown one of these things?"

The jig was up. Although I didn't want to lie to Red, I didn't want to get fired on my first day at work, either. I decided to break with my recent trend and to tell the truth.

"Never have," I said.

Red howled laughing. "You're even a bigger bull-shitter

than I am. We're both Texas boys, though, so let's keep it between ourselves. We all got to make a living."

The engine started without histrionics the second time around. Todd and his girlfriend were seated side-by-side in the Caravan with the prop spinning at idle. I closed the T-Bird canopy so Red could wire it shut from the outside. The canopy lever resembled a 1960's auto steering wheel suicide knob, which seemed appropriate for this undertaking. The Phantom could blow the base gym off its foundation with jet exhaust at idle power, but the T-Bird needed a lot of power to taxi. The flat strut meant I had to add even more power, so, after Red pulled the wheel chocks and signaled to me, I added power and stepped on the left brake to keep the jet from lumbering in the direction of the flat gear strut. That killed forward motion. I had to start all over again. The nose bobbed up and down and left and right in fits and starts. I resembled Dean Martin trying to taxi after a night on The Strip.

The SOF had seen enough. He evacuated for high ground to give himself plausible deniability for whatever was about to happen. By throttling up to 70% RPM, I was able to taxi in trail behind the Cessna 206 toward the runway. The Caravan rolled onto the runway and came to a stop. I couldn't hear any radio transmissions, so I was operating in ignorance as to what clearances he was being given. I moved into wingman position on his right wing and flashed him a thumbs up. Todd poured the coal to his engine and he accelerated down the runway. I counted to ten seconds before advancing the throttle. What a dog. My pulse topped out before the engine did. Phantom afterburners were a mule kick; the T-Bird's old Allison J33-A-35 engine was a feather nudge. It took forever to accelerate to 70 mph where the rudder started working and to 80 mph where the elevator had some effect. Once airborne, I closed the gap on the Caravan and settled into formation three feet clear of his wingtip. Todd gestured thumbs up for the umpteenth time and led us out of the TRSA while his girlfriend shot up rolls of film.

When we reached twenty miles from Marana, I hand-signaled goodbye to the Caravan and flew on ahead for a straight-in approach to Runway Three Zero. My first T-Bird landing was smooth, especially compared to my first T-Bird engine start. I parked the jet by the Everest Aviation hangar, shut down the engine, and claustrophobically waited in the hot cockpit for a mechanic to unwire the canopy so I could get out of the greenhouse. A fueling truck arrived to defuel the airplane so we could calculate how much fuel the flight had taken. Judging from the cockpit fuel quantity gauge at sixty gallons, Presley had won his $200 bet with Mr. Hernandez. I sat there sweating and grinning like a knucklehead. I had just made a thousand dollars. This gig was way better than the Rangoon Iteration.

The second ferry flight was relatively uneventful. Red and I played our parts as if we had at least scanned the script. The second T-Bird's engine started without pyrotechnics. The canopy locked properly, so I wasn't a hamster wired into a cage. The struts held pneumatic pressure, so taxiing was a breeze. The UHF radio was operable, so I got my own ATC clearances. After returning to Marana, Todd grounded his Caravan because of an oil leak. While a mechanic tinkered with it, Todd and I agreed to substitute my rented Cessna 150 for his Cessna 206 for the third flight to DM that day even though the Cessna 150 rental agreement listed me as the only approved pilot in command. I was gambling that nothing would go wrong in 32 miles. Todd's girlfriend used Todd's car to drive to her apartment to develop film. Our plan didn't derail until I was readying the third T-Bird for its flight out of DM.

A new SOF, a skinny major, showed up to monitor our antics. He had pencil thin mustaches and dark, cavernous eyes. He reminded me of a butt ugly version of David Niven. Because he was carrying an FM radio, commonly called a brick, he was of the opinion that he was somebody special. He drifted over to me and gave my black sanitized flight suit the evil eye. Without asking permission, he extended a bony hand toward my helmet, situated on top of the canopy bow. I could tell that he smelled a rules infraction or a policy transgression and he wanted to peel back the electrical tape to uncover squadron colors on my visor cover. I had to stop him to protect my financial way of life.

"Sir, you can't be within fifty feet of the aircraft," I said.

The major got into my grill. "Mister, this is my aerodrome. I can't allow you to operate until you've shown me some identification and licenses."

I wasn't carrying a wallet or wearing dog tags. I looked more like a hippy than a test pilot in my leather necklace strung with African beads. I had a single dog tag laced into the strings of my boot where the coroner could find it to identify my charred remains, but the major didn't notice my boots because he was too busy bullying me with his stare.

"I'm not allowed to carry identification on these missions," I said, making stuff up on the fly.

"That so?"

"Yes, sir."

Red got into the act. "This is an Agency operation."

"La-de-dah. That doesn't matter to me." The SOF transmitted on the FM radio: "Tango Charlie, tell the tower officer on duty that I'm marking my position with a flare." It was a classic intimidation move. Without any warning, the major fired a flare into the heavens. "Do you have me in sight."

The brick emitted static then, "Roger, Sir. We sure do."

"Tell them that this T-Bird doesn't move until I say so. Got that?"

"Yes, Sir."

I could hear a muted siren in the background. A fire truck was racing from the firehouse to the spot on the major's aerodrome where his flare had landed and ignited a brush fire. The major didn't notice the siren or the blaze. On second thought, he reminded me more of Peter Sellers than David Niven.

"You stay here until I come back," he said to me. "I'll bring two large individuals with M-16s, and we'll see who's got the biggest dick around here." The major stalked to his staff car, cranked it up, and accelerated away to muster his reinforcements.

"That there's a prize-winning asshole," Red said.

I worried that this dipshit would blow my cover. Todd was about my size, so I motioned for him to follow me to the tent. I told him to trade clothes with me. He looked at me as though I were insane. I took off my boots and removed the dog tag from the left boot. I unzipped my flight suit and dropped it to the ground. The world's foremost test pilot was down to a T-shirt and boxer shorts. Todd started stripping without conviction. I asked Red for some BBs out of the BB gun. He cupped six BBs in his hand. Todd was out of his comfort zone as he handed me his jeans, shirt, and canvas boots that smelled like a decaying corpse. He said the odor was from a fungus. I handed him two BBs and told him to swallow them. I demonstrated by swallowing one myself. Todd hesitated: "Are they for the fungus?"

I said, "I want you to feel sick right now. X-rays will show the BBs. Food contamination. You have to go to the emergency room right now." I pointed to a landline telephone on the table in the tent. "Red, call Nine-One-One and get an ambulance for this sick pilot whose name is classified."

Red dialed the rotary phone. Against his better judgment, Todd swallowed the BBs.

"Todd, I've got all your ID cards and licenses. I'm you now," I said, "and I'm flying the Cessna back to Marana before shit-for-brains gets back."

Despite Todd's preference for a more deliberate cadence of life, he eagerly donned my black flight suit and laced up my flying boots. He was the real deal now.

"Red, follow the ambulance in your truck and get Todd to an off-base hospital. Call Jim Conti as soon as you can and get the CIA to lean on this SOF lunatic. Do *not* tell anyone my name."

"I'm on it," Red said.

Dressed in Todd's baseball hat, jeans, shirt, and smelly shoes, I whisked my helmet off the T-Bird canopy bow, pulled my parachute out of the cockpit, and loaded my gear into the Cessna 150. I started the Continental engine and asked for a taxi clearance to depart VFR right away. As I pulled away from the ramp, I could see Todd already lying down on the asphalt with Red hovered over him. I also spotted ambulance emergency flashers approaching the ramp. Tower cleared me, and I did a rolling takeoff, skipping the magnetos checks because I wasn't going to abort the takeoff unless the wings fell off. When I landed at Marana, Bryan Presley called me on Unicom to come to his office. I left my helmet and parachute in the Cessna 150 and strode apprehensively across the hot ramp to the hangar to report to Presley in his office.

"You've got to stop feeding BBs to my nephew."

"I didn't know Todd was your nephew."

"Yeah, he is. I told my sister I'd watch out for him. I don't want him getting stomach cancer."

"I had to throw the x-ray technician a bone," I said.

"Really?" Presley said. "There was no x-ray." He obviously had received an update from Red. "Todd was dehydrated. Red's driving him here as we speak." Presley opened his refrigerator. "You want a beer?" He had never offered me a beer before. I took the offer as a sign that I wasn't getting fired. "I called Conti and he called the Agency. They'll take care of everything. You won't hear from that major again. Look, Stitch, don't get flamboyant on me. Todd's already convinced that you're cooler than school. He wants to join the Air Force. You're poisoning his mind in the prime of his life."

Red and Todd arrived within the hour. Todd and I exchanged clothes. Presley doled out beers to promote bonding among management, maintenance, transportation, and flight operations.

Todd embellished the episode: "When I swallowed the BBs, I imagined I was taking cyanide pills."

"You've got an active dream life," I said.

Red said, "So do you."

———— ((◉)) ————

I ferried twelve T-Birds in less than six weeks without a major emergency or another run-in with the skinny major. My anonymity intact, I parked the last T-Bird on the Marana ramp where four bigwigs waited. Three of them were Everest Aviation kahunas and one was a CIA big shot, at least a bigger shot than we were used to seeing at Marana. When I descended the ladder from the cockpit, the CIA representative shook my hand, and asked if I was getting the support I needed from Everest.

"Everest is first-class. These birds will be perfect when Everest gets through with them."

Brown-nosing didn't cost me a thing. My sycophantic praise pleased the Everest contingent. As they and the man from CIA left the flight line, Presley whispered to me, "Can you spell *bonus check*?" The way he scattered money around was an inspiration to me.

Everest Aviation was the big dog on the Marana Airport. Two T-Birds were in overhaul inside the Everest hangar at any one time. The other ten T-Birds were parked in a row on the ramp. Presley told me to stand down for two months to give Maintenance time to prepare the first two jets for test flights. I remained in Phoenix, flying a full Phantom instructor's schedule on weekdays and enjoying time off with Trudie and Katrina on weekends. On weeknights, I studied T-33 systems and test procedures. Any time I got drowsy and the words started to merge, I'd blow a single blast of a whistle to spike my adrenaline count. My dad gave me the whistle when I was twelve along with an exaggerated tale of its provenance.

"I was fly-fishing up in New Hampshire one time," he said, "wading in a clear crystal stream. The conditions were so perfect that the trout were jumping out of the creek into my creel. (Introductory hyperbole.)

"The creel was as heavy as an anvil and it was about all I could handle as I tried not to slip on the round river rocks. (Peril everywhere.)

"A fall could have drowned me if my waders had filled up with water. (Living on the edge.)

"The biggest, hungriest black bear in all of New England showed up and he had an agenda. (Man against Nature.)

"I was over a mile from the car, so, if the bear would have mauled me, I'm not sure I could have crawled back to the car with my intestines dragging along after me. (Act of supreme courage.)

"I jangled my car keys at him, but that just attracted him closer. (Suspense.)

"I can tell you, some sad images crossed my mind. What if I wasn't there to make sure my son did his pushups each night. (Devastating loss hanging in the balance.)

"And then it came to me, placed in my hand by an angel, this ten-cent Japanese whistle made the racket of a million-dollar foghorn. (Inspired problem-solving.)

"My ears rang for a week, but the terrified bear loped all the way to Maine. (Sacrifice. Reward.)

"Here, it's yours. It might get you out of a jam someday." (A tender moment, a gift from the master.)

I loved my dad's corny stories, but a ten-penny whistle wasn't going to extricate me from my predicament of un-authorized moonlighting. If my squadron commander discovered my extracurricular hijinks, he'd yank me out of *Operation Twisted Piccolo* in a heartbeat. I worried and count-ed my money.

Ever since I was a pup, I was better at losing mon-ey than hanging on to it. I pretended that I didn't care so I seldom discussed money. Now that bucks were fly-ing around the joint like manna from Heaven, however, I turned chatty. For the first time, I confided in Trudie about matters of the purse. She appreciated having a say in the distribution of our checking account surpluses. We discussed investment ideas over tea as we imagined millionaires did. To my dismay, Trudie wanted to give a chunk of dough to her Catholic church. I reckoned that the Vatican was flush enough without me forking over my hard-earned cash. I argued that we should chip away at the mortgage. Trudie could give a wad to her church when the mortgage was paid off. The atmosphere grew frosty. I slipped up and mentioned that I had paid off mar-gin account debt that had plagued me for years. She said, "Margin debt? That's the first I've heard anything about margin debt." I explained what a margin account was and she accused me of gambling. Trudie could speak five languages, but economics wasn't one of them. She was no financial wizard, and she pointed out that I wasn't, either. "For all of your good qualities, Stitch, you're a selfish man." Any dreams about buying a Porsche or an airplane vaporized. We agreed to pay $4,000 in estimated tax payments to the Internal Revenue Service, $5,000 to chip away at mortgage debt, and $1,000 to Trudie's church. That left enough for a case of Corona beers for me, selfish bastard that I was.

Money wasn't the only secret I had kept from Trudie. She didn't know that I hadn't even tried to get Lieutenant Colonel Cannon's permission to fly for Everest. In an ideal world, I would have filled out a Form 3902, cleared it through the Judge Advocate's Office, and then gotten Fig's sign-off. I followed the lead of so many scoundrels before me by grabbing the money now and being prepared to ask forgiveness if my scheme unraveled. I documented cases of moonlighting by military personnel at Luke for use as mitigation. There were bouncers, bartenders, Amway franchisers, ministers, lifeguards, cowboys, and one Playboy bunny. It was vital for me to conceal my moonlighting. I told Trudie that the CIA demanded complete secrecy. I asked Jim Conti for a document that would protect me if Fig ever found out about my scheme. Jim said he would do it, but weeks raced by with the promise unfulfilled.

Costello called late one night to tell me that he was in possession of a load of top-of-the-line barbecue grills and he could let me have one for almost nothing. I told him to take me off his solicitation list.

"Before I go," he said, "how about some handsome cotton golf shirts. Top quality. Hyper cheap."

"What colors?"

"I don't know," Costello said. "I ain't stole them yet."

Chapter 12

Treasure:
an aeronautical chart of a route from
Marana to Cartagena, Colombia

EVEN THOUGH I kept my head down at the Three-Eleventh during the lull in T-Bird flying, unwanted attention found me on one dark and stormy night when I was leading a four-ship designated Blinky Four-One flight on an air-refueling/night ground attack mission. During air-refueling, the student flying Blinky Four-Four got into the most severe pilot-induced oscillation (PIO) I had ever seen. I felt helpless watching the student's gyrations from my position on the left wing of the KC-135 air-refueling tanker. His control inputs were a millisecond too slow, so his plane repeatedly dove away from the tanker then back toward it. On one of the violent pitch-ups, his Phantom struck the tail of the tanker. Blinky Four-Four Bravo – the back seater — had seen enough for one night and he ejected before the front seater could ram the tanker again. The brilliance of ejection seat main gun explosive charges and rocket pack ignition lit up the night.

The student pilot regained control, so I told the instructor in Blinky Four-Three to escort the damaged Phantom back to Luke. The tanker commander, an Air Force reservist, recovered his Stratotanker at Sky Harbor International Airport for repairs and, I assumed, a stiff drink. The back seater survived a frigid three-hour camp-out in the Arizona desert before a helicopter rescued him at dawn. Fig eliminated the front seater from the program. Such mishaps invoked the Rule of Fives: the brass wrote five new regulations and rounded up five lambs to sacrifice. I managed to dodge that bullet, but Thor went behind my back and advised Fig to suspend my flight lead status. Thor's sabotage attempts failed, but my inimical relationship with Thor continued downhill. Most importantly, my clandestine involvement in *Operation Twisted Piccolo* remained a secret.

⬤

Greenbacks started to roll in again when the first batch of T-Birds was ready to be test flown. I flew six test hops on the first day. The contrast of grossing $6,000 in a single day compared to my Air Force salary of $2,000 a month made me giddy. Maintenance had transformed the mothballed T-Birds into works of art. They removed all paint from the exterior, leaving a polished aluminum finish. A clean-wing T-Bird, one without wingtip drop tanks, aileron rolled five times faster than a T-Bird with the drop tanks installed, so it was natural that I liked clean-wings best. I followed up test profiles with aerobatics sessions or by hunting for targets of opportunity.

During this phase of overhaul, the airplanes didn't have any markings, not even registration numbers. Anonymity made me bold. One afternoon, after completing a test flight profile, I stumbled upon a formation OV-10 Broncos at 7,000 feet. I jumped them from the rear with a couple hundred knots of overtake. I flew a big barrel roll around them and then shot off to the north executing a series of tight aileron rolls to give them something to talk about during their debrief. A week later, I attacked a flight of four A-10 Thunderbolts. I paused upside down sixty feet above them to witness their surprise. I saluted them with an Eddie Rickenbacker hi-ho and peeled off to the south to camouflage my actual direction of travel. Absent a court-martial, I'd never know what the Warthog pilots said when they got back to their squadron at DM. I always completed all test flight items before I started horsing around by jumping formations or practicing aerobatics. I memorized the vertical distances required to clear the dirt at the bottom of loops or split Ss so I could have fun without making Trudie a widow.

My standard recovery at Marana was a 500 mph pass a few feet above the runway, chop the throttle to idle, aileron roll, 4-G pitch up to downwind, and, with the throttle remaining in idle, fly a curvilinear final turn to touch down at exactly five hundred feet down the runway. One day an improperly rigged throttle shut down the engine when I chopped it to idle. I improvised a deadstick pattern that worked out fine. On the rare occasions that an acceptance pilot or an engineer was flying in my back seat, I would warn him not to eject while we were upside down at a hundred feet over the runway.

On a blistering hot Saturday, when there were no Cessnas available to rent for my commute from Glendale, I drove my Alfa Romeo to Marana for a single test hop. I completed the test profile with plenty of fuel to spare, so it was show time. I knew better than to buzz cars because terrified drivers often did unpredictable things, but trains stayed on their tracks no matter how frightened the engineer might be. I dropped down just above a set of railroad tracks parallel to Interstate Ten that stretched west-northwest away from Marana. Flying just a few feet above the tracks, I roared along at 460 mph in light turbulence. I put on a pro bono show for a train engineer and diners at a restaurant near Picacho Peak. Red met me in the chocks when I returned to Marana and he commented on the layer of insect corpses coating the canopy. Red was no dummy. He knew I had been hot-dogging down in the weeds and he winked to signal that it would remain our secret. He asked me for a ride to Casa Grande on my way back to Phoenix. I agreed and promised him lunch and beer.

Before I could head for the shower, Bryan Presley and a stranger approached me beside the jet. "This is Colonel Kutain from DM." Bryan peeled off for the safety of his office.

Colonel Kutain was dressed in khaki chinos and a golf shirt. I couldn't see his eyes because he was wearing military sunglasses. He asked me to join him in the shade of the hangar. He told me that our chat wouldn't take long, which made me worry about losing my Everest pork barrel.

"Ever heard of Richard Bong?" the colonel asked.

"He was a World War Two ace. Over 30 kills."

"Correct. He had 40 kills, to be exact. Did you know

that he died in a *Shooting Star* on the same day we bombed Hiroshima?" (I didn't.) "Did you know that he got grounded for flying aerobatics underneath the Golden Gate Bridge and for buzzing Market Street in San Francisco?" (I didn't.) "Do you know what General Kenney wrote in his letter of reprimand?" (I didn't.) "Something like I wouldn't want you in my Air Force if you didn't want to buzz Market Street, but don't do it anymore. You get where I'm going with this?" (I did.) "You've got a sweet deal going here. Don't mess it up by bouncing my formations. Deal?"

I was overjoyed that it was him and not the major with the skinny mustache. He was giving me a face-saving way out so I took it: "Yes, Sir. I won't jump any more military aircraft."

"Just a suggestion," he said, "I wouldn't bounce any civilians, either." He removed his sunglasses so I could see his steel gray eyes and he extended his hand, which I gladly shook.

"Thanks, Colonel Kutain."

"No names. I don't know yours, and you don't know mine." He strode away saying, "Press on."

I stuck my head into Bryan's office: "It won't happen again, Bryan."

The boss never looked up from his desk. "I don't know what you're talking about." He was making so much money on this *Piccolo* thing that I don't think he cared whether I bounced Air Force One.

In less than an hour, Red was sliding into my dark blue Alfa dressed in a clean set of Everest Aviation overalls and smelling of cheap cologne.

"What's your plan for Casa Grande?" I asked.

"Got a squeeze waiting for me. Crazy about my style."

I exited the freeway a few miles down the interstate from Marana and parked at the Picacho Peak restaurant with the best view of my morning air show. In the cool air of the bar, I told Red about my aerobatics demo as an explanation for the bugs on the canopy. I ordered up two Coors for each of us from a lanky waitress with Lauren Bacall pipes. We each ordered a burger dressed with everything available on the premises. I asked Red where he had worked on airplanes in the Air Force.

"All over, including the 366th Gunfighters at Holloman and Da Nang."

"You worked on Phantoms?" I asked.

"Night and day."

"That's my real gig," I said.

"I know."

I didn't know how he had figured it out. "You married?" I asked.

"I try not to get hitched if I can help it. I tried it a couple of times, but it never took." Red fed my ego: "Bet you gave them tourists a hell of a show."

I asked the waitress whether she had seen anything unusual during her shift.

"What do you mean *unusual?*"

"I heard something about a jet."

"Oh, some jackass was raising hell a couple hours ago," she said with a flip of her wrist.

In Biblical terms, I had cast my pearls before swine. Red said, "Some chicks are hard to impress. By the way," he asked, referring to Colonel Kutain, "who was the guy in the khakis?" "There was no guy," I said. Red accepted my version of the facts like a good Gunfighter.

————⟫«⟨❂⟩»⟪————

Mechanics were the unsung heroes of *Operation Twisted Piccolo*. They were so proficient at working on the T-Birds that I wrote up only a few discrepancies after the first test flight in each aircraft. Sometimes I'd come back from flying the fourth test profile on a jet and have no write-ups at all. One malfunction upset me more for the events that followed the incident than the inoperative system itself. I flew Tail Number 2008 back to Marana one afternoon when the nose gear wouldn't extend. I had enough fuel in reserve that I was able to repeat the Dash One emergency procedure three times. The nose gear still wouldn't budge. I asked for a fire truck to lay down a narrow 2,000-foot long strip of foam on the centerline of the runway starting at a point 2,000 feet down the runway. Fire fighters foamed the strip while I secured my loose equipment in the cockpit and flew a circuit overhead. Word had gotten around. I spotted a dozen mechanics in Everest Aviation overalls and some secretaries lined up outside the main hangar to witness whatever it was that I was about to do. I imagined that the mechanics were all praying that I wouldn't put a scratch on "Two Double Nuts Ocho" while the rest of the curiosity-seekers were hoping for an inferno.

I flew a four-mile straight-in approach and touched down within fifty feet of the approach end of the runway. I flew the nose down to the ground just past the start of the foam strip. Once the skin of the fuselage started grinding on the asphalt, I got on the binders to stop the T-Bird before it slid out of the foam strip. The plane came to rest nose-down in a sea of foam. A fire truck sprayed more foam on the main landing gear. The brakes may have been glowing hot, but neither main tire deflated. The crash-seekers were disappointed. I pinned the ejection seat myself and climbed out of the T-Bird to ride in a maintenance truck to the Everest Aviation hangar.

Out on the runway, mechanics rigged a sling under the forward fuselage of 2008 so they could extend the nose gear manually for towing to the ramp. I was relieved because I didn't want a reportable incident to derail my gravy train at Everest Aviation. I intended to keep milking my cash cow by writing as boring an incident report as possible.

A fuel truck pulled away from a six-passenger, two-engine propeller-powered Piper Seneca parked on the Everest Aviation ramp. Two children waited beside the plane with a woman who looked familiar to me. I strained to make out her face as I stepped down from the truck in front of the hangar.

"What have we here?" The man's voice came from behind me.

I turned to face Thor Olsen. He didn't extend his hand to shake, and I didn't extend mine.

Thor aimed a forefinger at me and said, "The man in black." He glanced out at the T-Bird on the runway and then back to me. "Doing a little double-dipping, are you?"

"What are you doing here?" I asked. Thor was the last

person on earth I expected to see at this remote airstrip in the desert. I had to prevent word of my moonlighting from getting back to Fig.

Thor gestured with his thumb toward the Seneca. "I'm headed out with Sally and the kids to Marfa, Texas to watch my brother in a glider competition." He pursed his lips and nodded his head in a deliberate appraisal of me. "How long have you been doing this?"

"Not long," I said.

"Did you get Fig's approval?"

"Not required," I said.

"Yes, it is." Thor was at his most sarcastic. "You've screwed up again." I guided Thor away from eavesdroppers. "I told you, Cromwell, you're an aviation hobbyist, not a professional."

"Look," I said, "it's the weekend. You're flying a Seneca and I'm flying a T-Bird. Neither one has anything to do with the squadron."

"The difference is that I'm not getting paid. I haven't killed anybody, either." The son-of-a-bitch had just invaded a private place. I wanted to plant a fist in his smug face. "I know what you've done," he said. "Sooner or later, you're going down for it." I was too steamed to respond. "It must be awful for you," he said. "One minute you're a hero and the next minute you're a goat." Thor stepped past me on his way to the Seneca. "See you back in the world."

<hr />

Four days later, I bumped into Thor Olsen in the squadron parking lot as I headed home. He was smirking as he approached me. "Let's pow-wow," he said in a half-whisper. He looked around us to make sure no one was within hearing distance. "I need to borrow four thousand dollars."

His thinly-veiled demand reinforced my assumption that he hadn't reported me to Fig. I didn't like it, but I didn't see that I had a choice, so I said, "I can do that."

He pushed further: "Interest free."

"I can do that, too." His request for a favor was degenerating into a demand for blackmail.

"Principal-free, too," he said as he glared at me with pure hatred.

"If you promise me that this is the last I'll hear about Marana, I'll do it."

"Done deal," he said.

He insisted that I bring cash to the parking lot at Ducky's, a popular Glendale pilot bar. The encounter made me feel impotent and resentful. I wanted to choke him. I knew I had to keep the blackmail payment a secret from Trudie. If she found out about it, she'd want to know what I was doing that would subject me to blackmail. The answer was almost everything related to flying the T-Birds.

I arrived at my bank just before closing time. I couldn't have felt any more self-conscious if I had showed up in a loin cloth. I withdrew four thousand dollars in cash from my checking account. The teller counted out eighty fifty-dollar-bills, taking longer than I expected. I fancied that everyone in the bank was looking over my shoulder. The teller banded my stack of fifties.

I didn't know whether blackmail was a crime. There was no law against Thor telling Fig something about me that was true. He might even claim that he was obligated to report me. There was no law against Thor asking for a gift of $4,000, either, but the combination of the two actions felt illegal. I needed advice, but I didn't have time to find a legal advisor. After driving home, I stewed about Thor's shakedown all evening until I headed out for Ducky's.

"Where are you going?" Trudie asked.

"I'm going to hit a bucket of balls at the driving range," I said. "I can't study anymore or I'll puke." I pocketed the car keys on the move, and she returned to reading her book, obviously displeased.

I waited for Thor in the rear lot at Ducky's. By the time he drove into the lot, I had justified the financial setback as a cost of doing business. It took less than a minute for me to locate his car and pass the brown sack containing the money through the open driver's window.

"There," he said. "Wasn't that easy? We're done." He started his engine and drove away as if we had conducted the most common transaction in the world.

I went inside Ducky's, took a booth, ordered up a beer, and fantasized about violent acts of revenge against Thor. Tammy, a girl with impossibly long brunette hair, entered the bar and headed straight for my booth. I bought her a margarita, as I had done in the past. Tammy was in her last year at the Arizona State University College of Law. She was prone to expounding on the law without me asking her to. Now that I wanted to know about blackmail, she said very little. The margarita loosened her tongue.

"It's a statutory thing," she said. "This guy might even have a duty to report you, but, when he offers to refrain from squealing on you in consideration for money, he runs into difficulties."

One of Tammy's classmates lured her from my booth. No sooner had Tammy left than a dodgy character named Chimmy slipped into my booth and focused on me with his one functional eye. He insisted on buying me a beer. I'd seen him prowling around Ducky's before. I wasn't about to ask where he was from. He asked me whether I was a pilot and whether I did any recreational flying. That was the standard format for recruiting pilots to transport drugs. The smugglers weren't interested in hard-core jet pilots who weren't familiar with light airplane flying. Probably half the guys in the squadron had been approached by someone willing to pay for nocturnal aviation services. Everybody knew that, even if your morals were corrupted enough to haul for a cartel, you still didn't want to get involved because, once they got you in their grip, they'd never let go. To my knowledge, none of the fighter pilots at Luke ever fell for the offers of the Chimmys of the world. Military pilots also knew that reporting incidents of this sort to authorities would invite suspicion and susceptibility to government pressure to be a confidential informant. My best course of action was to tell Chimmy that I didn't fly private airplanes.

"I seen you at Glendale Airport," he said.

"I'm mistaken for a lot of guys," I said. "I get Robert Conrad all the time."

"I don't see it," he said. The night was young. He moved on to interview other suckers who might be the right fit for his pitch.

———⸺«⟨❉⟩»⸺———

During the following weeks, my fears about a second blackmail demand appeared to be unfounded. I even flew in Thor's flight of four on an air-to-ground gunnery mission, and, if anything, he was almost amicable to me. It was as if the shakedown had resolved our differences.

My commutes to Marana were routine. The money kept pouring in. Months had passed since my inaugural T-Bird flight in the single-legged, radio-less, winged coffin. I had already flown fifty of an estimated seventy flights. Bryan Presley called me into his office one Saturday in September. He asked me to recommend the method and cost of moving the T-Birds to Colombia. "By land or by sea, Paul Revere?" He told me that he was up against a deadline for avoiding late penalties. I asked for time to review T-33 performance charts and navigational charts covering Arizona, Mexico, and Central America. I contacted Mexico and El Salvador about landing rights, ground support, and jet fuel. I added a hefty profit margin to everything and, two days later, I submitted a figure of $25,000 for each plane. I recommended that I deliver them three at a time, which meant I'd have to subcontract two more ferry pilots. Presley didn't blink before accepting. He told me to contact Mr. Bruno. I contracted a stomach-wrenching case of negotiator's remorse, wishing I had jacked the proposal up to $30,000.

———⸺«⟨❉⟩»⸺———

The nature of my pending $25,000 haul ratcheted up from a windfall to a certainty to a necessity. I mentally squandered the whole shebang before the first penny rolled in. I was so confident that the payday would solve my financial headaches that I became paranoid about loose ends that could queer the deal. I trusted no one. I stayed clear of Thor Olsen for fear that he'd squeeze me for more money. I worried that he might tell Sally and that Sally might blab. I worried that Fig might find out. I worried whether I could find two additional contract pilots. I worried that Everest would find a cheaper way to move the jets to Cartagena.

Trudie joined several other squadron wives for a Saturday girls' night at the greyhound races north of Phoenix. I was the designated baby sitter, and, when Katrina went down for the count, I had five hours to myself. I was poking around in the garage in search of aviation charts when I found a sealed liquor box full of Elizabeth's personal items. I hesitated to open the box out of respect for both Elizabeth and Trudie, but curiosity and nostalgia won out. The first item I unwrapped was a portrait of Elizabeth. My response startled me: my chest ached, and tears flowed down my cheeks. I examined a photo album filled with snapshots of Elizabeth and two small children from the summer she had worked as a governess for a family at Lake Tahoe. I paged through another album of photos of Elizabeth and her family taken in Hawaii. Next, I leafed through Elizabeth's sophomore yearbook from Stephens College. A round-trip carbon copy of a ticket for a TWA flight between St. Louis and Boston marked page 46. A group picture of her sorority dominated the page. The caption listed the girls' names and hometowns – Pacific

Palisades, Scottsdale, The Woodlands, Plano, Highland Park. It was easy to spot Elizabeth's sparkling eyes and blonde hair. Another girl with blonde hair flowing to her shoulders stood to Elizabeth's immediate left. I read the caption: "Elizabeth Van Drake, Rancho Cordova, California" and "Sally Byrne, Brookline, Massachusetts." I was shocked to learn that Sally Byrne Olsen and Elizabeth had been sorority sisters. I took the yearbook into the house to examine the picture under a stronger light. I found a message in the front of the yearbook hand-written from Sally to Elizabeth: "Perfect weekend in Boston! Hold on to Cody for a wild ride! On to B.C. next fall, Sorosister!!! Love, Sally." Elizabeth had never told me about Cody. Jealousy tainted my heart.

⸺ ❖ ⸺

When I called Costello at his home in San Antonio, I noticed that he had lost more of his Brooklyn accent. He had upgraded his personality, too. He was delighted to fill my order for more flight suits, flight manuals, T connectors, and T-33 parachutes. He charged me $3,600 for the whole package plus C.O.D. shipping charges. My next task, in order to realize the richest bonanza of my lifetime, was to find two pilots to wear the gear. I was willing to wheedle, beseech, whatever it took to recruit them. Scoring a year's pay in three days was my irresistible bait. I compiled wingman candidates by cutting-and-pasting emergency recall lists from my fighter squadrons — the 27th, 612th, 414th, and 311th. Then I culled the herd. I eliminated the faint-of-heart, the committed careerists, the humorless, the cautious, and the braggarts. I needed risk-takers who could keep a secret. Not every jock would agree to fly an antique airplane over unfamiliar territory even for $25,000. I eliminated everyone in my current squadron because I was concerned about a leak close to home. Fig might overhear a conversation or Thor, that greedy bastard, might intermeddle if he got wind of *Operation Twisted Piccolo*.

I came up with two all-star candidates. The first was Tyler "Dinger" Countryman, my friend and counselor from the Twenty-Seventh Squadron in Tampa and the Six-Twelfth Squadron in Spain. He lived three hundred miles away in Las Vegas, so logistics would be a snap. He was a known vacation hoarder. I expected him to hem and haw at first because his wife Shelley would come up with a dozen practical reasons to decline. Dinger could sell snow cones to Eskimos, however, so his chances of persuading Shelley were better than even. My second blue-chipper, also a Six-Twelfth alumnus, was Bobby Joe "Hacksaw" Ballantine. He had transferred during the previous year from Torrejón to Hill AFB near Salt Lake City, Utah. He was aggressive and fearless, and I was confident that my proposition would appeal to him. Surely he could get three days off for *Piccolo*. The big question was whether he could coax his wife Rena to agree to it. She was keen to be a general's wife and she wouldn't regard Hacksaw farting around with me in the skies above the Land of Pancho Villa as career-enhancing. On the other hand, Rena was a profound admirer of the American Dollar, so the $25,000 carrot would exert monstrous sway over her. A pressing follow-up question was whether Rena could keep her lips shut about it. I pitched my plan to both pilots and waited.

———— ‹(◉)› ————

Biting a kernel of corn that was harder than industrial-strength steel broke off a cusp of the crown of one of my molars, so I left the formal squadron dinner in search of a bright light and a mirror to inspect the damage. On my way to a men's room in the Officers Club foyer, I passed a window overlooking the swimming pool. I spotted Sally Olsen standing by herself near the deep end of the pool. I exited the hallway by a glass door leading to the pool. Sally was breathtaking in a violet cocktail dress. Her skin was bronze from hours on tennis courts. When she detected me in her periphery, she sighed irritably and stepped toward the dining room.

"Sally," I said. "Just a moment." I reached her side.

"You don't remember, do you?" she challenged me. "We met in Tower Hall. You were a senior at Mizzou and I was a sophomore and Elizabeth's roommate at Stephens College. You were picking her up for the Oklahoma-Mizzou game. I came downstairs to tell you she'd be delayed." A memory stirred. "Do you remember what you said? You said, 'That's annoying.'" She pointed at my chest. "*You* were the one who was *annoying*. Elizabeth and I had spent the previous weekend in Boston with our fiancées – Cody and Bill who were juniors at Boston College. Cody was the perfect match for Elizabeth."

It was the first I had ever heard about a fiancé. Elizabeth had never mentioned having a fiancé or even a beau in Boston or anywhere else. Sally started crying. "Why she married you, I'll never understand. Elizabeth was going to be my roommate at B.C. Then she died because of that horrible crash."

"It was an accident, Sally."

"You were the pilot. You were responsible." Sally crossed her arms and stepped backward. "How can you act so care-free and just forget her?"

"I haven't forgotten Elizabeth. I can't stop *remembering*."

Now I had tears in *my* eyes. I wanted Sally to know that I atoned for Elizabeth's death every day, but Sally's personal grief ran too deeply for her to care about mine.

"Your negligence killed my best friend and part of me."

I extended a hand to console her, but she pulled away and strode toward the O Club. I retreated to the foyer men's room and examined my image in a mirror. My pristine white mess dress jacket decorated sparsely with only three medals couldn't divert attention from the scars on my face. I hated what I had done to my face. I hated what I had done to Elizabeth. Boundless Gloom threatened to swallow me up and I wept. I retired further into a stall with a stout door lock. The involuntary spelunking of my tongue in the Carlsbad Caverns-sized space left by my missing tooth fragment no longer mattered. Nor did it matter that the chip of tooth and the malign corn kernel that caused it were likely creating all manner of mischief in my small intestines. All that con-cerned me was disguising my remorse and holding it at bay. Booze. I needed booze, and I knew where to get it — down the corridor in a ballroom full of jolly colleagues adorned in formal evening attire.

———————

Dinger turned me down. His rejection really surprised me, shocked me, really. I was willing to bet Shelley had nixed it. Deadline pressure made me irritable. I called Dinger that night.

"So Shelley makes your decisions for you now, you wuss."

"It's not Shelley's decision, it's mine."

"What?" I had too much at stake to let Dinger spoil the party. "I need you to help me out for only three days, and you won't do it? It's not like I'm asking you for a handout. I'm offering you twenty-five grand. Are you squeezing me for some of my share? Okay, I'll give you an extra five grand."

"I don't want more money, Stitch. Look, this must be a shady deal or they wouldn't be paying so much. It doesn't pass the smell test."

"They're paying me for my expertise, dammit. There's a deadline, and I need your help."

"I can't help you. I'm out."

"Damn it, Dinger. That's not final. I'm coming to Vegas."

I drove from Phoenix to Las Vegas like a maniac. I spent more time over 100 mph than under. When I got there at two in the morning, the Countryman's house was dark. I knew they seldom locked their doors, so I walked right in and stumbled around until I found the master bedroom. A voice broke the silence and froze my heart.

"One more step and you're a dead man." I had never heard Dinger sound so severe.

Shelley awoke. "Tyler?" I sensed her fear in the darkness.

"Dinger, it's me, Stitch."

A bedside lamp turned on like a strobe light. Dinger was pointing a pistol directly at me. "For the love of God, Stitch. Do you know what time it is?"

"It's time for you to help me out."

"I told you: No."

"I won't take *no* for an answer," I shouted.

Shelley interrupted: "Stitch, you've been hurt by a terrible tragedy in your life, but you don't get everything you want because of that."

"What do you know about ...?"

"Go back to Phoenix," Dinger said. "I gave you my answer."

"To what?" Shelley asked.

"He wants me to fly a plane to Central America."

"When?" she asked.

"Next week."

"Then put down the gun and help him out," she said.

Dinger looked at her in disbelief and lowered the gun.

"He's got the judgment of a fifteen-year-old," Dinger said.

"Well he drove all the way to 'Vegas for a reason, so help him out."

I couldn't believe she took my side. Dinger sputtered for a while as he explained the deal to Shelley. She did the math, gave her blessing, and got up to make coffee. For the record, as she scrambled in her nightgown to pull on a dressing gown, I noticed that she could have, in fact, sunk a thousand ships.

"I should have shot you," Dinger said, "done us both a favor."

Chapter 13

Treasure:
a charcoal rubbing of a Krugerrand

HACKSAW CALLED TO tell me that he wanted in on the Cartagena deal the day before I was to meet Mr. Bruno for dinner. Everest Aviation's bagman no longer intimidated me the way he did at first. He was like a pineapple, an abrasive exterior with a soft inside. I watched him flex his expense account muscles over margaritas at a popular steakhouse in Tempe. He scribbled on bar napkins while he overindulged his appetite for steaks and booze. As usual, he dominated the conversation, telling me about his revolutionary method for paying me for the Cartagena gig.

"So, who are the two geniuses you've hand-picked to fly down to Colombia with you?"

"Bobby Joe Ballantine and Tyler Countryman."

He printed the names on a cocktail napkin. "They sound like hicks in a bluegrass band," he said. "No offense." He explained that we were being paid in advance in gold so we'd have gold for contingencies. He told me to send three flight suits to him so he could sew five thousand bucks worth of Krugerrands into each waistband. He also told me to leave our three parachutes in Bryan Presley's office safe so he could have $20,000 in Baird & Co. ten-ounce gold bars sewn onto each set of risers. "Presley will keep the golden flight suits and parachutes in his wall safe until the day you guys take off for Colombia."

"I expected a check."

"It's better for you this way," Mr. Bruno said. "No taxes, unless you're an idiot. It's better for the company, too. The gold is off balance sheet, left over from Southeast Asia, so it won't count against the T-Bird program. For lots of reasons, we have to do it this way. Don't forget I'm acting as an agent for the Colombian government. Everest Aviation is just a vendor for the Colombian government. You'll be flying Colombian airplanes. When you cross into Mexican airspace, your link to Everest is history."

I didn't pay as much attention to those details as I should have because I was fixated on being paid in gold. I asked, "How will I know the metal is gold if it's sewn into the waistband and parachute risers?"

"So, now you're a gold expert? Are you going to be difficult? Don't worry about it. I'll demonstrate when I return the flight suits to you. I'll need copies of your passports and your FAA certificates. You'll each get an American Express card issued by a Colombian bank to defray unexpected expenses. Once again, it's between you and the Colombian government. It has nothing to do with Everest. It has nothing to do with the CIA. It has nothing to do with the United States government."

We bickered over the gold. He called me a thug. The less I opened my mouth, the smoother things went. Mr. Bruno ordered another round and kept cajoling me and sweetening the pot.

"Each of you will carry five grand in U.S. fifties for per diem, fuel, and bribes. You've got to have bribery money in Central America. You can keep the cash you don't spend as a bonus. Here's some advice: no babes. No, siree, no babes. Babes are on your own nickel. Ha, ha, ha." Mr. Bruno was assuming that I was more of a man of the world than I really was. "I'll give you the bribery money in Tucson when I show you how to access the Krugerrands."

Mr. Bruno's extravagance impressed me. I was accustomed to receiving ten dollars a day in Air Force per diem. Despite Mr. Bruno's lavishness, I affected the demeanor of a stern bargainer, a wheeler and a dealer well-oiled by three margaritas. He asked how far it was from Marana to Cartagena. I was sure he already knew. I told him 4,800 kilometers instead of 2,600 nautical miles so he'd feel that he was getting more for his money. He wasn't fooled. He could do the math.

I left the table first, but I waited in my car in the parking lot to observe Mr. Bruno exit the restaurant and drive away. As soon as he was out of sight, I reentered the restaurant and told a skinny waiter named Chad that I needed to review the tip amount on my credit card slip. Searching by table number, Chad located a check and copy of a credit card imprint.

"Here you are, Mr. Brewer." The imprint revealed that Mr. Bruno's name was Robert Brewer. I tipped Chad ten bucks.

I briefed Dinger and Hacksaw late that night by telephone. They weren't happy about the payment in gold, but I mollified them by telling them about the extra $5,000 in cash. I made it sound as though I had wrung the cash out of Mr. Bruno in an arduous negotiation.

"You're a magician, Cromwell," Hacksaw said.

———⟨◉⟩———

I received two T-33 Dash Ones from Costello on Tuesday, and I mailed one each to Dinger and Hacksaw. They were itching to begin cramming airplane systems and procedures. I carried flight suits and parachutes to Bryan Presley as soon as they arrived so Mr. Bruno could perform his $25,000 alterations. I spent most of my evenings planning the flight segments from Marana to Cartagena. I had an ADF receiver and a single-head Very High Frequency Omni-Directional Range (VOR) receiver to work with, so I picked a route down the western coast of Mexico and Central America navigating by a chain of VOR stations. At 2,660 nautical miles, the Mexican land route was 400 miles longer than the overwater route, but I felt that simplicity and safety were worth extra flying time and higher fuel consumption.

I divided the route into three legs. Leg One was to commence with a sunrise takeoff from Marana, cover 1,125 nautical miles, and end with a nine o'clock landing at Acapulco for servicing. Leg Two was to begin with an eleven o'clock takeoff from Acapulco, cover 645 nautical miles, and end with a one o'clock landing at El Salvador for a twenty-hour layover. Leg Three would begin with a 0930 takeoff from El

Salvador, cover 890 nautical miles, and end with a noon landing at Cartagena. The three legs would cover the total distance of 2,660 nautical miles in about eight hours of flying. Ignoring winds aloft, the first leg of 1,125 nautical miles was equal to the maximum range of the T-Bird with a full fuel load. I could have shortened the first leg by stopping in Manzanillo or Zihuatanejo, but both airports charged more for fuel than Acapulco and neither fixed base operator seemed interested in providing me with a start cart unless I passed him a big wad of cash under the table. Every dollar I saved on fuel or servicing stayed in my pocket. If the winds turned against us, we could divert into one of several viable alternate airfields scattered along the western coast of Mexico. I set up a conference call with Dinger and Hacksaw to rubber stamp my plan. I was naïve to assume it would be that easy.

"Build in more slack on the first leg, Amelia," Hacksaw said. "We've never flown this silver lawn dart before, so cut us some slack." He wanted to fly only as far as Manzanillo, 300 nautical miles closer to Marana than Acapulco. Dinger agreed with Hacksaw, who disapproved of my layover point too: "Isn't El Salvador in a war zone?" The Farabundo Marti National Liberation Front and the government of El Salvador were engaged in a bit of a donnybrook, but the Salvadoran Air Force flew T-Birds, so I had arranged to borrow their T-Bird ground support equipment at *Aeropuerto Internacional Monseñor* Óscar *Arnulfo Romero*. The Salvadoran Air Force Captain I contacted agreed to let me use one of his power carts at no charge. What a deal: three engine starts for three courtesy bottles of Jack Daniels.

"Where do *you* want to spend the night, Hack?"

"I don't want to *spend* the night, Mr. Marriott," Hacksaw said. "I want to fly straight through to Cartagena. And I don't want to flame out on the first leg doing it, thank you very much."

I stuck to my guns during the three-beer argument. I should have been more open to suggestions from my wingmen. They deserved more consideration on their first navigational flight in the T-Bird, but they tired of arguing and gave in, extending me way too much credit.

———◦(◦)◦———

Two weeks before the flights to Cartagena, my trusty wingmen flew to Phoenix to spend the weekend with me. We had my house to ourselves because Trudie had flown with Katrina to Las Vegas to visit Dinger's wife Shelley and her son. I could imagine the two wives together for the first time since Spain, murdering cups of tea and watching their one-year-olds discover that other small people roamed the Earth. The following morning, I flew us down to Marana in a rented Cessna 172. Each of us brought a sanitized helmet, a sanitized olive drab flight suit, an oxygen T fitting, and a flight manual. I intended to demonstrate an external inspection of a T-Bird, spend an hour with cockpit familiarization, and then take Hacksaw and Dinger up for a few touch-and-goes in the Marana traffic pattern so they could get their hands on the airplane. Maintenance had agreed to install cushions in the place of parachutes because Presley had instructed a trustworthy seamstress to sew gold bars into our parachute risers. Neither Hacksaw nor Dinger had ever flown a jet without an ejection seat or without a parachute.

Aircraft painting was complete, and Tail Number 2010 looked magnificent in its Colombian Air Force skin of polished aluminum and its yellow, red, and blue tail flash. Even the main gear wheel wells, a repository of dirt and hydraulic fluid on most planes, were immaculate. Hacksaw, the first guinea pig, climbed into the front seat, and Dinger crouched on a ladder hung on the right side of the cockpit. I settled onto a ladder on the left side. Hacksaw performed the preflight cockpit set-up by accomplishing the checklist items line-by-line. Dinger and I followed along. I occasionally demonstrated my vast knowledge of the T-Bird by answering a question. As often, I revealed my vast ignorance of the T-Bird.

"It takes a real man to admit he doesn't know something," I said, "but I'm still alive after seventy-three hops, so if I don't know something, it must not be too important."

I strapped into the backseat of T-Bird 2010 behind Hacksaw in the front. Hacksaw worked his way through the checklist to bring the T-Bird to life. I could tell that he couldn't believe how much power it took to get the jet rolling. The plane bobbed and weaved on the taxiway until he convinced himself that it took a handful of throttle to taxi. We took off to the southeast and stayed inside the airport traffic area without exceeding 250 mph. Hacksaw flew initial at 1,500 feet above the ground, pitched out, lowered the flaps and gear, and flew a nice visual pattern to a touch-and-go. He flew three more patterns before landing full stop and taxing back to the barn to shut down. He made room for Dinger to replace him and get his three bounces. I entered the flights in their logbooks and signed as an instructor. I wanted to leave a clean paper trail in case we bought the farm and they buried us on the lone prairie. I gave each of them a copy of a signed ground training form of my invention. They each scored 97% on the written exam. Who's perfect? Me, I guess. I gave myself a 100% and asked Dinger to sign it.

"Who would have guessed?" Dinger asked. "You aced the test."

I flew us back to Glendale in the Cessna 172. After showers and fresh clothes, we went to a Mexican restaurant to celebrate mastering the T-Bird. I gave them a five-question T-Bird oral exam that they both passed brilliantly. They insisted on buying margaritas, and I insisted on drinking them.

———— ((◦)) ————

Everything was falling into place until, as I was leaving the squadron for home on Wednesday afternoon, I heard Thor Olsen's voice growling from behind me. He caught up with me and said, "You've got a lot of nerve pushing Sally around."

I assumed he was referring to my tête-à-tête with Sally beside the O Club pool. I scanned the lot to make sure no one else was within hearing. "I didn't push her around."

"I need two thousand more in cash by tomorrow or, I swear to God, I'll tell Fig what you're doing."

"Fig will want to know why you didn't tell him sooner."

"I'll say I just found out. He'll believe me over you. Two grand by tomorrow night."

I tried not to reveal how much his ultimatum infuriated me. I felt powerless to do a thing about it. I weighed siphoning off $2,000 to line Thor's pockets against losing the whole enchilada. I couldn't take the chance.

"Okay, but this is it." I was attempting to save face.

"Be on-time at Ducky's."

Chapter 14

Treasure:
a plastic hospital wristband bearing my name

TRAVELING WESTBOUND ON Camelback across the street from Grand Canyon University, I turned left to drive southbound on 35th Avenue. During the turn, I squinted into the setting sun and spotting a horrifying red blur. A bomb exploded. Slam cut to black. I had entered the intersection in a jolly frame of mind. I exited the intersection in no frame of mind. I was unconscious and lying on an ambulance stretcher.

I woke up with cottonmouth and a pounding headache. I inventoried my fingers and toes by wiggling them. My fingers were mostly present and accounted for. IV tubes dangled from bags suspended from hospital floor stands. A chubby nurse told me I was in intensive care following a car accident. Two beanpoles in blue scrubs rolled me on a gurney to imaging.

"How's my brain?" I asked.

The lead beanpole told me, "You're brain's fine." How

would he know? I figured he was a nurse because a brain surgeon would have used Latin words. I was lying flat on my back and staring straight up at perforated ceiling panels whooshing by. I reckoned that it was late at night. I ended up in a private room with subdued funeral home indirect lighting. I had never sensed the link between hospital rooms and mortuaries so strongly before. Trudie glided into the room. She held selected fingers of my left hand, the one with the intravenous needle taped to the back.

"What do I look like?"

"Better than the Alfa. It's totaled. So's the Corvette that hit you. The police told me that you were doing about fifteen and the Corvette was doing forty when you met head-on.

"Was it red?"

"Used to be. A witness saw you shoot through the windshield and tumble across Camelback."

"My head hurts."

"It *should* hurt." Trudie was more accusing and less consoling than I would have liked. "I could murder you for not wearing your seat belt."

"My shoulder hurts too." I wanted to deflect attention from my negligence. I wanted sympathy.

"You're lucky to be breathing." She wasn't going to let me off the hook. "Your head's enormous."

"Am I going to live?"

"I guess so or they wouldn't have bothered putting ten stitches in your head."

That seemed a low number of stitches for so much commotion. Feeling as terrible as I did, I would have expected thirty or forty. Trudie's bedside manner needed fine-tuning.

She informed me that I had an abrasion on my left shoulder and bruise marks down my chest and stomach from smashing against the Alfa's steering wheel on takeoff. Her fortitude cracked, and she broke down crying, which put me in the mood to sob, too. It was therapeutic to share a good cry with the woman I loved.

The following evening, Lieutenant Colonel "Fig" Cannon visited me. "You look awful," he said. He scooted a bedside chair closer to my bed for intimacy. Trudie perched near me on my bed holding my left index finger, the one uninjured and socially acceptable thing for her to hold onto.

Fig was acting differently from the detached commander I was accustomed to seeing around the squadron. He was fatherly and almost chummy in an impish way. I guessed that he had visited Happy Hour at the O Club on his way to the hospital and he was sharing his buzz to distract me from my funk. He gave me a gift-wrapped box of macaroons that, according to him, possessed curative properties. He offered to sample them along with me and Trudie. He asked me to choose which color we should devour first. It was empowering. I said, "Tan."

"I've canceled your personal leave next week so you won't lose it," he said. That was a jolt. I had requested two week's leave to ferry the T-Birds to Cartagena and to boat on Lake Powell on our return. I didn't trust myself to say the right things, so I remained silent. "The flight surgeon has placed you on medical leave. You'll be DNIF for as long as you need." DNIF was duty not involving flying. "Forget about work and concentrate on getting well." Fig's hospital deportment was exceptional. He surprised me by saying, "I've never told you how much I admire you for overcoming your burns."

I didn't tell him that I wasn't convinced that I *had* overcome my burns. Nor did I tell him that, if ever trapped in a fire again, I had predetermined that I wouldn't beat my way out with my fists like the first time. I simply couldn't go through it again. I would never tell Trudie, either. No one who loved me could understand such a choice. No, I'd never tell Trudie for fear of breaking her heart and I'd never tell Fig for fear that he wouldn't admire me anymore.

Trudie and I chatted sporadically. I had to remember *not* to bring up Thor ripping me off for six thousand bucks. I hoped I hadn't babbled while drifting in the murky zone between Dreamland and consciousness. Trudie touched my fingertips with hers.

"I'm going to leave now. Gina's watching Katrina for me. I'll bring Katrina with me tomorrow."

I couldn't remember who Gina was. I couldn't wait to see Katrina. I apologized for putting Trudie through this unpleasantness. The pain medication worked well, so I lay there admiring Trudie's calves, thin waist, graceful tilt of the head, and strands of blonde hair shimmering in the ceiling lights.

"I'm just glad you're all right, Stitch. Dinger's flying down from Vegas tomorrow morning. He'll cheer you up with his bullshit." Before leaving, she said, "I love you."

———※———

My feelings about hospital visitors were mixed. On one hand, the sight of Dinger, a muscled, sun-tanned specimen, was an inspiration; on the other hand, Dinger's fitness was a reminder that I had a long way to go to return to health. A nurse spotted Dinger in my room and she started hanging around fluttering her eyelashes. She pampered me more in five minutes than she had in the previous several hours. A bulldozer couldn't have pried her out of there. When she left, Dinger opened his Texas Tech Red Raider gym bag and pulled out a sack of tiny Snickers bars.

"See? There's a reason we don't wear our underwear on the outside."

Dinger was making less sense than usual. He mystified me even when I was at full capacity, which I obviously was not. He tossed a Snickers to me which I caught one-handed. My ribs and sternum ached from the exertion. As though feeding a trained walrus, he tossed me a second Snickers at the exact moment the nurse reentered the room.

"I didn't see that," she said. She was a team player. When she was gone, Dinger opened his gym bag to show me a glorious cluster of clattering miniature Cutty Sark bottles.

"The secret to life is knowing which rules to bend, Stitch. I called Hack to tell him about your accident and I told him that the Cartagena trip was off."

"Who said it's off?"

"Trudie told me."

"It's not off. Don't listen to her."

"Your head's the size of a watermelon. You couldn't fit on a helmet if you used a crow bar."

"The swelling will go down."

"Maybe by Christmas."

"There's no way I'm giving up twenty-five thousand bucks. We're flying those jets."

———·«(O)»·———

On my second day home from hospital, while Trudie was still being especially considerate and sensitive to my medical needs, I tackled the task of replacing my pulverized Alfa Romeo. Being a red-blooded American materialist, I had wanted to own a Porsche for years, but I had never squeezed the trigger. What better time would I ever have to tout the Porsche brand to Trudie than the present? I finessed my loved one by presenting her with two brochures that Dinger had picked up for me. I placed the Chevrolet and Porsche brochures side-by-side on the kitchen counter. "Trudie, Sweetie, which model do you prefer?" My flowery word choice and overconfident mood were the results of over-medicating on a newly-approved pain-killer called Percocet.

"I don't know," she said. "Which one do *you* prefer?"

I nudged the Porsche brochure forward. "The Porsche is safer," I said. "German engineering."

"How much do they cost?" Trudie was quick to slash to the core of the matter.

"The Porsche is somewhat more expensive," I said. How true.

"Then it's a no-header."

"No brainer."

"No brainer," she said. "Get the Chevrolet."

That's why a Chevy was parked in our garage.

Fickle winds of Fate threatened to turn against me, jeopardizing the ferry flights to Cartagena. I kept momentum alive by calling Hacksaw and Dinger each evening to keep them invested in the final stage of *Operation Twisted Piccolo.* If the news was good, I told them about it; if bad, I censored it. Speaking of bad news, Thor was promoted on Monday to major "below the zone." That was the term-of-art used to refer to an officer advancing on the fast track. Thor hosted an impromptu party at the Officers Club. If I hadn't been too ill to attend, the sight of Thor strutting around the club in his new golden oak leaves would have been enough to put me back in the hospital. Bad news kept rolling in.

On Tuesday, the Three-Eleventh Operations Officer vacated his position as second-in-command of the squadron to attend Air Command and Staff College at Maxwell AFB, Alabama. In such a case in the normal chain of events, Fig would name another major in the squadron as acting Operations Officer for the ten months. Pogo called me at home that afternoon to tell me that Fig had named Thor to the position of Acting Operations Officer. I assumed it couldn't get any bleaker until Wednesday when I got another call from Pogo to announce another development.

"Fig's taking off for two weeks of leave to fly with his wife to Scotland for an anniversary present."

These were fast-moving times. "Who's going to cover for Fig?"

"Are you lying down?"

As a matter of fact, I was. My entire circulatory system froze stiff when Pogo said, "Thor." The squadron line of succession threatened to block my pathway to riches.

On Thursday, one of Thor's first decrees as Acting Squadron Commander was to notify me by telephone that he wanted me to work on syllabus rewrites at the Training Center until I could return to flying status. This was the equivalent of being told during sexual climax to carry out the trash.

"I can't do it, Sir," I said. "I'm too sick."

"Sure you can. It's light duty. It'll do you good."

What would have done me good was for Thor to buzz off so I could deliver the T-Birds to Colombia and pad my bank account. Bryan Presley had made it clear that Everest couldn't slip the deliveries because of punitive late penalties in the contract. If I admitted to Thor why I had to have the time off, he'd have even more leverage to put the screws to me. Perhaps I could get sicker. I needed a non-terminal disease that would relieve me from all Air Force duty so I could fly a jet to Central America for the CIA. Off hand, I couldn't come up with such a specialized disease, so I did a very stupid thing. I tried to appeal to Thor's sympathy.

"Major Olsen, I've got to do some work for the company down at Marana."

"You've got to be kidding me."

"I've got to have time off. A lot's at stake."

"You are *unbelievable*. Meet me at Ducky's at eight. Your career depends on it."

"I'm recovering in bed."

Thor exhaled dramatically and hung up on me. When I told Trudie that I was going out after dinner without telling her why or where I was going, her internal volcano erupted. She wouldn't even glance in my direction, not that there was much to see. From the neck down, I didn't appear to be as bad as I felt. My khaki shorts and navy blue golf shirt covered all but a few "road raspberries." My head was another story. Bruises and scrapes were signs that something violent this way had passed. I left the stitches in my swollen head exposed in the hopes of stirring Thor's sympathy. My newly-appointed fearless leader was waiting for me in a booth in Ducky's.

"You look awful."

I responded in kind of a pathetic muffled bleat and I winced at the slightest jab of pain to remind him of the sacrifice I had made just to be there. I came clean with a bewildering version of some of the truth.

"Thor, I'm working for the CIA."

"And I'm the Crown Prince of East Bum Fuck," he said.

The fact that I had paid two blackmail demands in the past cast a shadow of suspicion on my claims. I was hoping that my forthright confession might get him to back off. Instead, he demanded even more.

"The best way I can see this working out is for you to gift me four thousand dollars. I'll put you back on DNIF and nothing ever happened."

His appalling abuse of authority stunned me. I felt fearful and royally pissed off: "Give me a break."

"You're trying to dodge responsibility and blame, but you can't."

"I could report you to the I.G.," I said.

"You've got no proof."

The executive summary of the five minutes that ensued was that I agreed to give him $4,000 in cash the next night at the same time and place. It wasn't a negotiation; it was appeasement. I drove home uttering murderous rants directed at Thor Olsen. Trudie had never seen me so upset.

"What's wrong?"

"Nothing."

Trudie didn't care for secrecy and she hated lies. Anything I could tell her was one or the other, so the atmosphere was lethal. I started to pack a small duffel bag.

"You're not going anywhere." she insisted. "You should be in bed." Her instincts for caretaking were as strong as her will.

"I'm going and that's final."

She went silent and marched out of the bedroom.

How could I cut off the advice of the woman I loved? Greed had come between us. I opened the top drawer of my chest, a repository for cuff links, medals, spare wings, and silk fighter squadron scarves — gold for the 27th, blue-and-white checkered for the 612th, and powder blue for the 311th. I passed them over and selected my chamois dogfight scarf. I stuffed it in my small duffel bag and carried the bag to the garage to lock it in the Chevy trunk. After stowing the duffel bag, I turned off the garage lights and sat inside the Chevy in the dark trying to see myself as Trudie did. On the outside, I was scraped and bruised all over as if I had been dragged through a cactus patch. I felt even worse on the inside. My head throbbed in time with my heart and my shoulder ached to a beat all its own. I had taken a huge risk by taking Thor into my confidence. I decided to double-cross him. I wasn't going to pay him another dime. By the time he showed up at Ducky's the following night, I'd be in Tucson. Thor would flip out of his mind with rage. If he attempted to take me down, I'd try to drag him along with me. I realized that my rebellion might well end in career suicide.

I returned to a darkened house for a truncated night's sleep. Trudie had gone to bed and turned off lights to signal her unhappiness. I navigated to bed by a nightlight in Katrina's bedroom and the aqua blue glow of the swimming pool light that filtered through the master bedroom curtains. I was in too foul a mood to bother to turn it off. I never slept well when Trudie was cross with me, and this abbreviated night was no exception. I held several truths to be self-evident: I was avaricious, selfish, and irresponsible. My character flaws had caused me to lose Elizabeth, and now Trudie was slipping away. I was a discredit to the Air Force Officer Corps. I dabbled in shady deals. I paid blackmail. Mulling over the $25,000 payoff was my only antidote for depression. It was miraculous that I slept at all.

I left Trudie in bed wrapped in slumber at an hour before dawn. The blue glow of the swimming pool light diffused by the bedroom curtains illuminated her delicate features. Lips that had criticized me the night before were parted so her breaths and dreams could mingle and pass. I looked in on Katrina as she lay in the arms of serenity in the Jim Conti Memorial Crib. I loved Trudie and Katrina enough to bring tears to my eyes, but not enough to call off my pursuit of treasure. Before leaving the house for the airport, I left a note to Trudie on Katrina's changing table. I knew she'd find it there because little Katrina could generate more scat than a buffalo herd at all hours of the day and night. The note told Trudie to be ready to celebrate my triumphant return with friends on a houseboat on Lake Powell as if that would make up for all the misery I had brought her. "I'm doing this for you and Katrina," the note said, even though I knew all too well that I was doing it for me. It occurred to me for the first time that I might never see my wife or my daughter again.

Chapter 15

Treasure:
a picture of T-Bird 2010 painted in Colombian Air Force colors

I ARRIVED IN Tucson hours ahead of Dinger and Hacksaw. I got an early check-in and rubbed Arnica pomade onto my battered body parts, sucked Gatorade, and rested during the day. A double dose of anti-inflammatory tablets had reduced the swelling in my head. Gauze and surgical tape covered the stitches in my scalp, so I no longer gave the impression of a zombie on walkabout. My chest still looked like a goat carcass that had been flogged with a rubber hose, but the pain that accompanied every breath had subsided. My left shoulder range of motion improved. I didn't mention the car accident to Everest Aviation's Director of Operations Bryan Presley because I worried that he might invoke my contract's cancellation clause and cut me off from my bonanza. He might resort to some radical alternative, perhaps trucking the planes all the way to Central America. In the afternoon, Dinger showed up at my hotel door wearing a Hawaiian shirt that would have made a blind man cringe.

"I'm here to add elegance to an otherwise drab affair," he said. He raided my mini-bar and fixed himself a vodka and tonic. "You look a skosh better," he said. "Have you squeezed on your helmet yet?"

My head was still too swollen to try a Cinderella-esque helmet fitting. Dinger helped me sort Jeppesen high altitude charts, sectional charts, and approach plates for each cockpit in stacks on the hotel room desk before pausing to answer a knock at the door. He opened it to Hacksaw, who recoiled and replaced his sunglasses at the sight of Dinger's shirt.

"Tune up the ukuleles, Don Ho."

"Jealousy is the ultimate form of compliment," Dinger said.

Hacksaw latched on to two miniature Old Foresters from my mini-bar. He emptied two packets of sugar from the coffee tray into a glass. With the flair of a magician, he produced three lemons. "From the hotel courtyard," he explained. He lopped off an end from each lemon with his survival knife, squeezed the lemons, and added ingredients into a glass half-full of ice cubes. He sealed the glass with a shower cap, and shook the glass. "Whiskey sour, girls." He scrutinized my face. "You're a sorry sight."

Dinger took the ice bucket for a stroll to the nearest ice machine. He returned in the company of Mr. Bruno, who was wearing an insurance salesman's black suit and carrying a fiberglass suitcase. I couldn't tell which startled him most, Dinger's shirt or the condition of my head: "What's *that?*"

"I had a fender bender."

"More like a head banger." Mr. Bruno twisted the tops off three Beefeater miniatures and tilted his glass toward the ice bucket: "Hit me." Dinger plopped ice cubes into the glass until Mr. Bruno said, "Whoa." I introduced my posse to Mr. Bruno. He asked Dinger, "You from Hawaii, Hawkeye?" Dinger seemed to know it was a rhetorical question. Mr. Bruno opened his suitcase and pulled out a black flight suit with "Ballantine" scribbled on a white tag attached to a zipper. He offered it to Hacksaw. "Check it out and tell me whether you can find the Krugerrands."

Hacksaw couldn't feel any coins. "But there is something in the waistband."

"Correct. Thirty-one Krugerrands, to be exact. Worth five thousand bucks."

"How about the gold bars?" Hacksaw asked.

"You've got twelve ten-ounce bars sewn into your parachute risers. Presley's got them in his vault at Marana. They're worth twenty grand on the spot market. This method of payment gives you contingency money while you're down range and, this way, it's all tax free." Mr. Bruno was not big on giving unto Caesar. "By the way, it's legal for you to own Krugerrands now, but to avoid conflict with CF 4790 bringing them into the United States, here's what you do: deposit your left-over Krugerrands and gold bars in a Colombian bank. You can liquidate them over time and avoid taxes. There's no paper trail."

"It's okay with me," Dinger said.

"Who made you Secretary of the Treasury?" Hacksaw asked.

None of us had the juice to ask what a CF 4790 was or to object to cheating on taxes. Mr. Bruno produced a sample coin sewn into Nomex fabric to show us how to extract it.

He slit the woven pouch and a plastic sheath inside the fabric with an Exacto knife. A Krugerrand fell out onto the desktop. We passed it around, as curious as three yahoos who had never left the home place. We were seduced by Mr. Bruno's cloak-and-dagger panache. The Krugerrand added credibility. Mr. Bruno moved things toward a conclusion: "I'd love to stay and chat, but I have to go." He replaced Hacksaw's modified flight suit into his suitcase and locked the clasps. "This is going back into the safe until you show up to fly in the morning." He drained his Beefeaters and donned his sunglasses.

When Mr. Bruno was gone, Hacksaw said, "That's a real live gangster for you."

"How would you know?" Dinger asked.

"I can spot a gangster from a hundred yards." He took a peep at Dinger's shirt. "Pimps too."

We were as excited to be involved in *Operation Twisted Piccolo* as kids on a sleepover. We were elated to be flying off the grid. It was a real kick to work with the Agency on foreign shores. Forty years hence, we could embellish the story to impress our grandchildren if they turned out to be gullible enough to listen to us.

———※◉※———

Before dawn on the first morning of our Colombian escapade, a limousine company van picked up Dinger, Hacksaw, and me for the ride from our Tucson hotel to Marana. Each of us carried a small duffel bag like a brat bound for summer camp. The van deposited us in front of Bryan Presley's office at the Everest hangar. Mr. Bruno had informed Presley of my skull condition because the first thing Presley said was, "I heard they botched your brain transplant." Everybody had a head gag.

I hadn't tried to fit on my helmet for fear of tearing stitches. I had rented a Dave Clark headset and boom mic in case my head wasn't down to size by game time. I was prepared to duct tape my oxygen mask onto my face for flying above 10,000 feet if I had to. Presley opened his wall safe and distributed our gold-laden flight suits. He passed out our deluxe parachutes, eight pounds heavier than normal because of the attached gold bars. Hacksaw wiggled into his parachute harness and said, "Girls, I've never been worth as much as I am right now." He pointed at the leather thong hanging around my neck. "I hope that thing has good mojo." I assured him that it did. When we were suited up, we lugged our kneeboards, charts, helmet bags, and duffel bags out onto the dark ramp.

"I feel naked without a G-suit," Dinger said.

The T-Bird's G limit was 7.33 Gs, but we were flying to Cartagena straight and level, so we didn't need anti-G protection. I reached T-Bird Number 2010 nicknamed "The Dime." On the nose in large block font, detailers had painted "2010," which, I told Dinger, happened to be my vision at the time.

He called my observation a brain fart. He said passengers would take a train if they knew half of what pilots thought about before flight.

Because we were taking off with full drop tanks, I verified that 330 pounds of ballast had been added to each nose armament compartment to compensate for two machine guns and full magazines of ammunition removed for the aircraft deliveries. I sat in the rear seat of 2010 long enough to ensure that all switches were in the correct position for solo flight. I secured my duffel bag on the rear ejection seat before moving up to the forward seat. I told Red that we were tight on gas, so we wouldn't have time to yak and scratch after engine start. I also told him that if one of us ground aborted or crapped out in the air, we'd all come back.

He nodded and handed me my shoulder straps so I could connect them to my lap belt. He armed my ejection seat and stowed my ejection seat safety pins. I put on my thinnest helmet liner with care to avoid pulling out the stitches in my scalp, possibly springing a leak and bleeding to death on my way to Acapulco. My helmet was custom-made for a tight fit, so I pulled it on gently, the way I would have pulled on a jock strap filled with razor blades. Red plugged a long interphone cord into the aircraft and checked in with me. When he cranked up the power cart, the whine pierced the darkness and echoed off exterior hangar walls. We started the jets simultaneously on schedule. I checked the flight in on VHF radio tuned to Unicom frequency.

"Polo Flight, check."

Dinger: "Two."

Hacksaw: "Three."

I radioed in the blind: "Marana Unicom, Polo Flight taxi three of the world's finest departing Runway One-Two."

As I taxied past Red, he snapped to attention and popped me as smart a salute as anyone could get on any base in any air force in the world. I returned his salute and taxied in front of Hacksaw's nose. Dinger fell in line behind me, followed by Hacksaw. Our spacing was perfect. Several Everest mechanics had gathered in front of the hangar to watch our pre-dawn departure. Their hard work over a year-and-a-half span had reconditioned abandoned Korean-era ghost planes into these gleaming T-Birds. I would have liked to reward the mechanics' hard work with a three-ship fly-by after takeoff, but fuel was too scarce. We lined up on Runway One-Two in echelon left formation, a tight fit on a width of only a hundred feet. We lowered our canopies on my signal. I radioed a reminder to set fuel tank selector switches and transmitted a blind departure call on Unicom before switching the flight to Tucson Departure Control.

I signaled for my wingmen to hold their brakes and run up their engines. The ambient temperature was 70° Fahrenheit and the elevation of Marana was 2,010 feet above sea level. Even at such an agreeable pressure altitude, the old T-Bird engines were slow to accelerate. I released brakes and steered toward the center of the runway for my takeoff roll. I counted on Dinger and Hacksaw to do the same in ten second intervals. Once airborne I throttled back to 96% for the straight-ahead rejoin to give my wingmen a chance to close into fingertip formation. Dinger came aboard first. Then Hacksaw. I wiggled my rudder to move the boys to route formation, two plane-widths on either side of me.

I navigated toward Nogales and requested an IFR clearance to Acapulco. Tucson Departure handed us off to Albuquerque Center. We were climbing through Flight Level 230 on our way to Flight Level 390 when Albuquerque Center handed us off to Mexican Air Route Traffic Control.

The sun popped over the eastern horizon, and we crossed into the Mexican Upper Identification Region. After checking in with Mexican ATC, I sent the flight over to VHF frequency 123.45 so we could chat about fuel switches and other weighty matters. Our fuel was on schedule. Oil pressures were normal. The motors were purring. I noted a variance among our indicated oxygen pressures. I had 360 psi (pounds per square inch); Dinger, 380, and Hacksaw, 300. I asked Hack whether he had rotated his pressure dial from "normal" to "safety" climbing through Flight Level 300 on the way to FL 390.

"Sure did, Lindberg." Hacksaw was in high spirits.

I returned the flight to ATC frequency, and we settled in for flying straight and level to save fuel by minimizing bank angles and power changes. We rarely did that in Phantoms, flying entire sorties twisting and turning at the edge of violence. We leveled off one minute ahead of plan and twenty gallons ahead on fuel. I was the master of my universe as I led the formation over waypoints Hermosillo and then Ciudad Obregon. An hour into the flight, however, halfway from Obregon to Culiacan, things deteriorated. I could tell that we would be late and behind fuel schedule at the next waypoint. The forecast beneficial winds aloft weren't there. I gave a hand signal for an oxygen check. I had 300 psi; Dinger, 310, and Hacksaw, 190. I calculated oxygen rates of use and fuel burn. A descent from FL 390 to FL 200 would double our fuel consumption. With a normally operating oxygen system, Hacksaw's oxygen pressure of 190 psi would last for an hour and 48 minutes, but he was using oxygen at a rate much higher than normal. I faced up to the conclusion that, by having to fly at a lower altitude, we weren't going to reach Acapulco.

We overflew Mazatlán five minutes late and 24 gallons down on fuel. I prepared for a diversion into Zihuatanejo (Z Town), 111 nautical miles north of Acapulco. Menacing thunderstorm cells obscured the horizon ahead. An oxygen check revealed that I had 240 psi; Dinger, 250, and Hacksaw, 140. At a time when all my attention should have been on the problem at hand, extraneous considerations distracted me. Everest Aviation had paid me through my last test flight, and my ties to Everest terminated when I crossed into Mexican airspace. I couldn't prove that the hulls were insured. I hadn't actually seen the gold allegedly sewn into my uniform and parachute. I had never had any real communication with the CIA, so the Agency had no motive to hang it out for me. My liaison contact with the Colombian Air Force was a captain whose name I couldn't remember. The Salvadoran letter of introduction was an ornate, but generic-looking document with no signature. I certainly couldn't claim that I was acting for the United States Air Force. If things got gnarly, none of these entities would have any motive to get involved with saving my bacon. I felt stupid and alone.

Because of Hacksaw's oxygen depletion, I took us down to Flight Level 240 approaching the thunderstorms. Our T-Birds weren't equipped with radar, so I knew I'd have to maneuver in clear air to avoid storm cells. Hacksaw's oxygen was down to 100 psi. I put the Zihuatanejo approach charts away and started studying the charts and airport layout at Manzanillo, some 200 miles closer to us than Z Town. By the time we crossed overhead Puerto Vallarta, it was apparent that we needed to descend even lower for Hacksaw's sake. If his oxygen system pressure fell to zero at 24,000 feet, he'd turn blue, succumb to hypoxia, and spiral into the ocean four-and-a-half miles below us. I got a clearance down to 14,000 feet. Next, we had to deviate fifteen miles west for thunderstorms. My blood pressure was rising.

"Boss," Dinger radioed, "Recommend diversion to Manzanillo." In dozens of Phantom sorties we had flown together in Europe, I'd never heard him challenge a flight leader. I zippered, clicking the transmit button twice so my tone of voice wouldn't reveal my irritation. We overflew Manzanillo eight minutes late and 35 gallons over burn.

"Hey, Doolittle," Hacksaw radioed, "I'm out of oxygen."

Dinger's nerves were frayed: "Lead, we need to divert to Manzanillo."

I zippered again. I felt flushed with embarrassment. In a sense, I had been caught showing off. My head was thumping. I descended to twelve thousand feet. The situation was getting untidy at a rapid rate. Making matters worse, I had to zig-zag continuously between thunderstorms. I considered turning back to Manzanillo, but pride intervened, and I decided that we could make Z Town on fumes. I wouldn't have been surprised if Dinger and Hacksaw had mutinied, declared lost wingman, and turned back toward Manzanillo, but they hung on to my wing as if they were glued there. I weaved around and between storm cells. We passed over a small private airfield, so I grabbed a sectional chart to identify it. I fiddly-farted around so long that we were halfway to Z Town by the time I knew without a doubt that Dinger was right: I should have diverted into Manzanillo. I felt physically ill. My gut was churning. I located a private airport named Atl Ixtaca depicted on the chart short of Z Town.

Atl Ixtaca. I was on the verge of committing to a small private runway that I knew nothing about. I didn't know the condition of its surface. I didn't know if there were obstacles on the runway. I didn't know if the taxiway could support a T-Bird. I doubted whether Atl Ixtaca had jet fuel or a starting cart. Indecision had boxed me in. I wasn't positive that we had enough gas to reach this tiny airport whose name I couldn't pronounce 120 miles short of Zihuatanejo. I cancelled IFR with ATC and throttled back to flight idle. I turned my transponder to standby out of embarrassment. I didn't want to be seen on radar by anyone, not Mexican ATC, not even God. The possibility of three T-Birds flaming out over the Pacific coastal plain of Mexico made me sick to my stomach. I maneuvered to keep the formation clear of clouds and to keep a safe distance from the rising terrain inland. I pondered the problems of landing deadstick on a highway if we flamed out. I even considered abandoning the jets by punching out. If I had worked at it all day, I couldn't have fouled up any worse. I sent the flight over to a discreet frequency for the remainder of the flight and braced for the dismal fuel remaining numbers I was about to hear.

"Polo, fuel check ... one's got seventy gallons."

"Two, fifty-five gallons."

"Three, forty-five gallons."

"Guys, we can't make it to Z Town. We're going to land on Runway One-Niner at Atl Ixtaca Airport. It's on the nose for sixty miles. It's four thousand, nine hundred feet long and ninety-eight feet wide. Elevation thirty-nine feet. We'll land as singles in the order, Three, Two, One." I got silence for an answer. Neither of my wingmen acknowledged my brief. I could sense that they were boiling mad at me. They probably were mentally rehearsing ejection procures to be ready for the moment their engines went silent for lack of fuel. We descended below the 4,000-foot bottoms of the broken cloud layer. I estimated visibility in the haze layer at less than ten miles. I strained to identify a runway ahead of us, briefly fearing that we may have overflown it already. Mountains soared 10,000 feet into the clouds to our left. The Pacific Ocean stretched to infinity to our right. Overconfidence collapsed into humiliation.

"Hack, say fuel," I radioed.

"Fifteen gallons." His voice was terse.

Fifteen gallons was a lot of fuel in a Toyota, but nothing but fumes in a T-Bird. My right hand was trembling on the stick. Did Atl Ixtaca even exist? I spotted a reflection of sunlight off a pane of glass about seven miles ahead. By squinting, I could make out two buildings east of a small runway.

"Hack, call the airport in sight at your right one o'clock, four miles."

No hesitation: "Tally."

I radioed, "Polo Three's cleared off right to land."

Hacksaw banked away as though he were balancing his last fifteen gallons of fuel in a pitcher on a tray with one hand. I reminded Hacksaw that the runway was a narrow. Atl Ixtaca wasn't long enough to leave any runway unused.

"Hack, confirm three down and locked." Suddenly I was as coddling as Captain Kangaroo.

"Ayfirm, *Commandante*."

"Target speed's one-twenty-five indicated with full flaps." Or Mister Rogers.

"Roger."

"Use moderate braking and roll out to the end. There's no parallel taxiway."

"Roger." I could tell by Hacksaw's tone that he didn't want any more aviation tips.

I cleared Dinger off to set up for his right turn to final. Hacksaw landed hard, which was better than flaring high in search of a crowd-pleaser. I told Dinger to confirm three down and locked. His confirmation was grudging. Hacksaw radioed to Dinger, "Step on the binders, Alice. I'm stuck down here at the end with nowhere to go." Dinger came to a halt at the departure end of the runway near the left edge, a few feet behind Hacksaw, leaving me the right side of the runway to skid past and off the end if I couldn't stop my jet. It was a wise move, considering how my day was going.

I touched down on the first brick, got the jet stopped, and doubled back six hundred feet from the departure end of the runway. I waited for Dinger and Hacksaw to join in trail formation to taxi toward the ramp. It was nothing short of a petro-miracle that Hack's antique Allison engine didn't flame out. I tapped my helmet and nodded, and three canopies rose to the open position in unison. Fighter Pilot Axiom 77: "better to die than look bad." Fighter Pilot Corollary 77: "when you screw things up beyond all recognition, at least look good." We raised our flaps in unison on my command. We were out of fuel and at the wrong airport, but, by God, we were looking magnificent. We taxied in with perfect spacing and parked facing west in front of a hangar that needed paint worse than I needed a drink. What a pity that no one was present in this forsaken place to marvel at our precision.

"Hack, say fuel."

"Zero."

"Shut 'em down. Safe your seats," I said. I sounded bossy, but I was feeling the opposite. I had suffered this desolate disillusionment before: crashing in the Sierra Nevada, being overwhelmed by the loss of Elizabeth, and hurtling toward disaster on takeoff at Glendale. Now with this amateurish diversion into Atl Ixtaca, I was tortured by the awful certainty that, in every important way, I had failed.

All three engines spun down, and I could hear the strident calls of birds. There, was that a monkey in the jungle? Monkey or not, the warning shriek lingered in the oppressive heat and humidity. The thick air smelled of salt and rotting kelp from the ocean, not three miles away. Heat waves rose all around and nothing stirred, not even a rumor of a breeze.

I set the parking brake, removed my helmet, and propped it on the canopy rail. Small tracks of blood had seeped into my cotton helmet liner. I safety-pinned my ejection seat and unstrapped so I could climb down over the left intake and aft to the left wing. The aluminum surfaces were as hot as a griddle in the merciless sun. Sweat poured from my forehead and my stitches pounded to the beat of my heart as I bent toward the heat-soaked ramp beneath the wings to pin the main landing gear. Standing back upright, I balanced on quivering legs. I wiped perspiration from my face with my chamois scarf and waited for my wingmen to join me. My brain caromed between two impossibilities: I wanted time either to freeze in place or to race to a miraculous resolution.

I experienced a flashback to the time I demolished the exhaust system of my dad's 1958 DeSoto on an unexpected speed bump. One of the bravest acts of my sixteen years on Earth was reporting to my dad to confess the damage done to his once pristine DeSoto. He asked me how fast I was going when I hit the speed bump. At that stage in my development, I often fibbed when truth was required and spoke the truth when nothing but a good lie would do. "Less than a hundred," I said. It took all summer to pay him for the damage.

To scale, the depression I felt over the DeSoto wasn't even a molecule in the vast universe of humiliation I felt at being stranded on a steaming hot ramp in Atl Ixtaca, Mexico. I might never get over it. I might never be able to cover it up. I felt gutted, disgraced. My legs and hands trembled. My chest ached from the bruising at Camelback and 35th and from an awful sense of failure. I had turned a routine task into a colossal disaster. Shock descended on me slowly, the way preoperative anesthesia sneaks up on a patient. Breathing came hard, and sweat was trickling down my back. Dinger stopped directly in front of me. His face was so contorted that I could scarcely recognize him. He threw his kneeboard onto the asphalt ramp. "You dumb son of a bitch," he shouted.

His outburst hurt worse than Nurse McCloddy's bullying, Gunner Gunnersson's scorn, Thor Olsen's contempt, or Sally Olsen's bitterness. Dinger yelled, "I should have gone lost wingman at Mazanillo."

Hacksaw chimed in: "I've seen better."

Dinger bellowed, "I told you to divert, but you wouldn't listen."

Hacksaw tried to deflect Dinger's rage: "The Colombians must be having second thoughts about the three imbeciles flying their airplanes."

Dinger seemed about to throw a punch, so I took a step backwards. The three of us stood there for an awkward few seconds. To a distant observer, we would have appeared to be three typical fighter jocks taking a typical break during a typical cross-country flight, stretching stiff legs and looking for a place to cash a check, but, up close, we were falling apart. I eased away from the confrontation and slinked on unsteady legs toward a cheesy office tucked under the roof of a beat-up hangar. Dinger and Hacksaw tagged along, Dinger still fuming.

The office door was unlocked. The inside of the disheveled office was as hot as a furnace. If there was an electrical grid in that tumbled-down domain, the office wasn't connected to it. A trapped bird was causing a tremendous flap trying to figure out how to escape its prison. Dust coated everything – chairs, tables, and an empty bookcase. Dinger was still too angry to speak.

Hacksaw said, "So, Carmen Sandiego, this is Atl Ixtaca?"

The hopelessness of our dilemma was sinking in. The solitary telephone in the room was missing a receiver and its three-foot tail of a cord dangled toward the floor. In all of Mexico, no room needed air-conditioning worse or was less likely to get it than this one. Hacksaw was the first of us to hear the sound of vehicle engines in the distance: "Unless I'm mistaken, here comes the cavalry."

Desperate for deliverance, my momentary relief faded as I squinted down the taxiway. I couldn't name it, but something didn't pass muster. "Boys, stow your Rolexes." I stuffed my treasured watch inside the neck of my right sock and rolled it into my boot. Dinger and Hacksaw did the same. I stood beside them, looking tough but feeling untough and wondering what was about to happen to us.

Chapter 16

Treasure:
a corroded bottle opener imprinted with a Pacifico logo

TWO PICKUP TRUCKS rushed toward us, their mirages shimmering above the blistering ramp. As they drew closer, I could make out men crowded into the back, their rifle barrels jutting upwards.

"That's a mangy-ass cavalry, General Custer," Hacksaw said.

A pack of hayseeds wearing baseball caps and straw hats descended on us. The first truck skidded to a halt, and four bozos leaped out to jab at us, using their carbine barrels in the place of cattle prods. They forced us to lie on the asphalt, which was hotter than any frying pan in the State of Guerrero. I squirmed on the scorching tarmac while a rough character, whose body odor was indistinguishable from a porta potty, searched my flight suit pockets. He stole my cash, credit card, passport, and letter of introduction to the Salvadoran Air Force. A second load of nitwits arrived, brandishing their weapons and compounding the chaos of the scene. A jowly jackoff with a shabby cowboy hat and scrub brush whiskers motioned for us to get on our feet. He chewed on an unlit pipe as he poked at the gash on my head.

"*¿Pilotos?*" (Pilots?)

Dinger chose that moment to use one of the ten words in his Spanish vocabulary.

"*Sí.*"

"Does anyone speak English?" I asked, reeking of sincerity. I labored to be the opposite of a gringo smart-ass. "Anyone?"

The chunky, stubble-faced whack-job slapped me. "*Silencio,*" he growled.

It was all I could do to keep from shoving his pipe up his adenoids. We eyed one another malevolently. I spotted one of e*l jefe's* (the boss's) minions moving a pickup truck to the front of Hacksaw's T-Bird and tying a heavy rope around the nose gear. He attached the rope to his trailer hitch with the intent of towing the jet, but, when he forced the transmission into first gear and played out the clutch, the plane didn't budge. I was still stinging from the first masculine face slap I had ever experienced in my life, but I had to speak up to prevent the nose strut from being ripped off the jet.

"*Los frenos,*" I shouted. (The brakes.) "*Peligro.*" (Danger.)

El jefe gestured to stop tugging on the plane. Then he ordered me to fix things. "*No vas a ningun sitio.*" (Don't try to get away.)

The dumb shit was worried that I was going to make a break for it. He didn't know that Hacksaw's jet didn't have enough fuel remaining to start a lawnmower. I hustled toward the T-Bird and lowered myself into the cockpit the same way the Lone Ranger would have mounted Silver. I released the parking brake and motioned to the driver of the pickup. For an ignorant novice, the truck driver did a decent job of towing. I had to step on the brakes once when he slowed down and the jet continued rolling toward him. We averted disaster and got the T-Bird into the hangar. Six men hand-pushed the jet backwards to make room for the other T-Birds, and I set the parking brake again. The truck driver untied his maze of knots and signaled for me to hop into the back of his truck so he could drive me back out onto the ramp to repeat the process. It was hot work.

With the planes towed out of sight, *el jefe* ordered his worker bees to close the hangar doors. As far as the outside world's satellite cameras and reconnaissance planes were concerned, we no longer existed. *El jefe* and his rag-tag gang herded us into the sweltering office inside the hangar. He had a little English after all. His arms were windmill blades when he spoke.

"Your country pay us for these lifes." He pointed his pudgy forefinger in our faces.

I appealed to his reason. *"Tenemos no importancia."* (We are not important.)

"Not truth. *Pilotos* is many moneys. *Y los aviones, mucho dinero tambien."* (And the airplanes, a lot of money too.)

I tried to make him comprehend that the government of Colombian was our *jefe*. We were just contract drivers, nothing more. Hacksaw, seemingly unconcerned that our asses were in a bind, seemed amused by my clumsy efforts. I stepped out of the office into the hangar and pointed at the Colombian insignia on the nearest T-Bird fuselage: *"Muy fuerte.*" (Very strong.) "*Muy importante.*" (Very important.) When I pointed to myself, I shrunk my shoulders inward and crouched over. "*Pequeño.*" (A little one.) I said. "*No soy importa.*" (I'm not important.)

"*Una gamba pequeña,*" (A little shrimp) one wit mocked me, "*pobrecito.*" (Poor thing.) The guerillas, bandits, gangsters, whatever they were, laughed. Viewed from almost any perspective by my mono-linguistic wingmen, my performance was pathetic. The conclave ended, and our captors moved us to the convective oven upstairs. A pockmarked gunman dropped our parachutes onto the floor and pressed his palms together to one side of his head, the international sign for *pillow.*

Opening every window that would budge didn't get rid of the hot air. Dinger's animosity toward me was losing steam, replaced by hostility for our captors. He hid our Rolexes in a desk drawer, which he referred to as our *vault.* I hung a length of telephone wire to make a clothesline. We stripped off our sour-smelling Nomex flight suits, folded them at the waistlines, and draped them on the wire. A locker room with the laundry staff on strike couldn't have stunk worse. We hung up our soaked tee shirts too.

"What the hell is that?" Hacksaw pointed to a puncture scar just below Dinger's right rib cage.

"Skiing accident," Dinger said. "A broken bough impaled me. I was a marshmallow."

"Sonny Bono." Hacksaw glanced at my skin-grafted torso: "Stitch, you're a checkerboard."

I pointed to my groin: "I've got a lot more."

"Keep your boxers on, Frankenstein, I've seen enough.

We should hide you-know-what somewhere before Che Guevara finds it." He stretched out on a table temporarily, too tired to move.

Dinger collapsed on another tabletop. I did the same before my knees buckled. Maybe I deserved to die of dehydration in a warming oven, but Dinger and Hacksaw were blameless in this debacle. A wafer-thin para-military guard unbolted our door at sunset to give us a single bowl of coarse-textured rice contaminated with what appeared to be twigs. A second bowl contained black beans congealed in wallpaper paste the color of feces. He placed a plastic bowl of water onto the floor as though he were watering mongrels. We huddled on chairs around a table and took turns using dog tags like tortilla chips to scoop globs of rice and beans into our mouths. Hacksaw made napkins by crumpling sheets of abandoned printing paper. We didn't chance drinking the water. After our repast, we sat on our parachutes on the floor because the air was theoretically cooler at the lowest level of the room. Light was fading fast. The door opened and a skinny hand rolled an object into the room. I panicked and flattened myself against the floor. The object came to rest against my temple. I had no experience with explosives, but I knew that a hand grenade detonation in such close proximity would blow my head clean off.

The fearsome object was a bottle. I heard a second bottle roll in and then a third. A metallic object clattered into the room. The guard's skinny arm stretched into the room and left a candle in a holder on the floor. Hacksaw located the bottle opener and popped the top off the beer bottle nearest him. Froth everywhere. I could barely make out the yellow label in the candlelight. *Pacifico.*

"My kingdom for an ice-cold Lone Star." Hacksaw placed the candle on the table and he perched on a chair. Dinger and I opened our warm beers and joined him. Hacksaw was studying the corroded bottle opener by candlelight: "I'm going to slit the guard's throat with this so we can make our escape."

"No, you're not," Dinger objected. "There's nowhere to escape to." Depressed by our gloomy prospects, Dinger said, "If these dimwits show our passports to the Americans to get a ransom payment, the Air Force will find out and our careers will be shot to hell."

"It won't matter because these dildos are going to put a bullet in your head," Hacksaw said.

Trudie had once told me that my habit of making light of things was a defense mechanism. Well, at present, I wasn't making light of anything. Stuck in a hellhole that smelled of urine and sweat, I could only dream of the way it could have been, three of us sipping cool beverages in a Cartagena hotel with $75,000 in gold stashed in the room vault. I had brought all of this misery down on us by complicating a simple game of checkers into a complex chess match. "Face it," Dinger said, "we're here. There's no use bitching about how we got here." It wasn't an apology, but it was as close to an apology as I was likely to get.

An hour after the last drop of *Pacifico* was gone, the Lord of the Thugs reappeared with henchmen bearing gothic lanterns. My heart almost stopped when he went straight to the flight suits on the improvised clothesline. He unzipped every pocket and groped around the insides with the delicacy of a bear in a beehive. What could I say if he found the hidden gold? The alpha bandit found nothing but Hacksaw's comb. His lantern holders had been boozing, and their foul breaths mingled with the musty ammonia smell of our honey bucket to create a fetid asparagus odor. A young tough guy brought us two more candles and a box of matches.

When the intruders had departed, I lit a new candle and convened a meeting to discuss our bargaining chips: Rolexes, $15,000 in Krugerrands, and $60,000 in gold bars. Dinger suggested that we use broken shards of window glass to cut the Krugerrands out of our flight suits so we could hide the gold somewhere in the room. The motion carried.

Hacksaw said, "Give Pancho Villa a couple of grand to let us go."

Dinger disagreed. "He'll take all the gold and then shoot us anyway."

I sided with Dinger. We agreed to hide the gold in the room while we still had access to our flight suits and para-chutes. Dinger used the bottle opener to remove screws holding a grill near the floor on the back wall. We formed a unique sewing circle cutting gold bars out of parachute har-nesses with glass fragments by candlelight in our skivvies. We deposited our gold bars into the black hole in the wall as if mailing parcels into a concrete mailbox. Dinger was nimble at cutting Krugerrands out of his flight suit. He was so good at it that he cut the coins out of our two flight suits as well. We wrapped our Krugerrands in yellowed printer paper rolls before depositing them into the slot. The last items to disap-pear into the void were our three Rolexes. Dinger replaced the grill to seal up our $100,000 of treasure.

With the candle extinguished, I lay on the floor of our

dark, stifling hotbox with my head resting on my parachute. I speculated about negotiations for our release. No doubt, the bandits would test the deep pockets of the U. S. government. The second worst thing that could happen was that the Americans would refuse to pay ransom for us and this band of misfits would kill us. The *worst* that could happen was that they would torture us before killing us. There was an old saying that fear of torture was worse than torture itself, which was bullshit, if you asked me.

Hacksaw asked, "These pudknockers won't kill us, will they, Cromwell?"

We whispered. We dozed. Sometimes we dozed in the middle of a whisper. We pissed in the honey bucket until we ran out of piss. The night dragged on. I plagiarized the Bible by numbering the days of this unexpected junket as the days of creation were numbered. This was Day One. I reflected on Trudie and Katrina, things I should have done, things I should have said. I puzzled over the paradox of living so many years of my life broke, but now, with my personal wealth at its zenith, I was on the verge of dying. I wasn't ready to check out. I had reasons to live, many of which were hidden in a stucco wall in a dilapidated hangar in Mexico. Major Thor Olsen's $4,000 grudge against me was surely festering. If I could get out of this mess to return to duty by Day Ten, my career might still be salvaged. The Colombians, Everest Aviation, and the CIA had probably established our last position report with Mexican ATC. Bryan Presley might have notified our wives that we were missing. Would our wives cancel our houseboat reservation at Lake Powell? Would they call the Air Force?

Deep into the night, Dinger assumed I was asleep and he whispered, "You awake, Hack?

"Yeah."

"What a dick dance. I can't believe Cromwell crapped his brain so bad."

Hack was marginally kinder: "A mind's a terrible thing to waste."

The whispering stopped. Sounds of nocturnal creatures owned the night until the shots rang out.

⸻ ⦿ ⸻

Bang. Bang. Two distinct reports, so near that they might have been in the downstairs room.

"We're up shit creek now," Hacksaw said.

I kept quiet so the shooter wouldn't get an idea that I was a target. I positioned my parachute between my body and the door and did my best to get inconspicuous.

"They're shouting something in Spanish," Dinger stage whispered.

"They're Mexicans," Hacksaw whispered back, "that's what they do." A short clip of automatic fire rattled not far from our second-floor holding cell. "Shit, Mandrake, machine guns."

"Quiet," Dinger hissed. Bullets shattered glass and careened off concrete.

I remained motionless, speechless, breathless, any kind of "-less" that would keep us from being added to the body count. Somebody found somebody, because, for a few seconds, intermittent gunfire became more robust. Semi-automatic rounds cooked off and automatic fire, too.

"Sweet, sweet Jesus," Dinger whined.

I could barely make out Hacksaw maneuvering to barricade himself behind his parachute and a table tipped onto its side. "Been nice knowing you boys," he said, making no pretense of whispering. It was as if he wanted gun-slinging maniacs to find us and to end our suffering. Shattering glass and screeching metal below us preceded a tremor that shook the whole building. A single gun fired three quick shots. I heard a spent casing skitter across a concrete floor. I would have traded every last Krugerrand I owned to have my Sig Sauer in one hand with a bag of ten ammunition clips in the other. A car horn wailed. Men shouted at one another. The horn went silent.

"I can't believe you got me into this, Stitch," Hacksaw lamented from behind his wooden barricade.

"Me, neither," Dinger said. He had fashioned a rudimentary fort out of his parachute and a chair.

"Check the window," I said.

"Check the window yourself, Zorro," Hacksaw said. "I'm staying right where I am."

I creeped to a grimy window and raised my head enough to scan the ramp. On the windowsill among broken glass lay a mangled bullet, still hot from recent impact. I could see that one of the bandit pickup trucks had rammed into our building. Another truck sat idling twenty feet further away on the tarmac. Men were tossing dead bodies into the back of it. I counted three corpses.

"They're piling bodies onto a truck," I said.

"Sweet, sweet Jesus," Dinger moaned.

"Use that chair to smack whoever opens the door," Hacksaw said.

"It's bad policy to use a chair on a guy with a machine gun," I said. Our unity was rupturing.

Dinger continued his metaphysical inquiries: "Why me?"

I retreated to a corner and pulled my parachute in front of me like a baseball catcher's chest protector. The idea was to slow down a bullet enough that it would merely maim instead of kill me. More shots rang out from further away. I discovered that I was the kind of person who lost his voice when terrified. Hacksaw was the kind of person who found his. He kept asking what was going on. A knock at our door was almost polite. The voice that came after it was sonorous, confidence-inspiring.

"¡Policia Federal!" Knock, knock, knock.

"We are unarmed," Hacksaw shouted.

Dinger rose to the occasion: "No tenemos armas." ("We don't have weapons.")

Hacksaw called out again, "We mean you no harm."

"No tenemos armas." Dinger had attained his linguistic stride and his words were more forceful this time, his accent less touristy. He spoke at half speed as if he were addressing a retarded person.

"¿Norte Americanos?" asked the resonant voice from the other side of the door.

"Sí," Dinger shouted, "Norte Americanos."

"We come in peace," Hacksaw yelled.

"Shut up," Dinger hissed.

"You gringos got any guns?" The man with the golden voice spoke good English. American style. Better than most.

"No guns. No knives. No nothing," Dinger replied.

"We're coming in," the voice announced. I heard the sound of a bolt sliding. The door opened to reveal two men in black assault gear brandishing flashlights and pistols. I could make out black helmets and *POLICIA FEDERAL* stamped on black bullet-proof vests.

"Thank God," Dinger said.

More flashlight beams from the hallway pierced the darkness. I leaned forward from behind my parachute barricade on unsteady knees. Dinger leaped up with the energy of a kid greeting Santa Claus. Hacksaw clambered to his feet, too. "Man, we're glad to see you guys."

"You can relax," the leader said. "You're safe, now. My name is Carlos." Carlos was a sturdy six-footer, no stranger to the weight room, and accustomed to being the big dog.

"Who were those guys?" Hacksaw asked, referring to the deceased.

"Common crooks. They were planning to collect a ransom for you."

"You shot them all?" Dinger asked.

"The world's a better place," Carlos said.

More men in civilian clothes squeezed into the room. At first I assumed they were undercover cops, but, the more glimpses I got of them, I realized they were too rag-tag to be cops. It was confusing. I was over-stimulated. A second uniformed gunman's pat-down was a groping. He remarked on nothing. I supposed that, stripped down to our underwear, we didn't have much to remark on. Carlos produced a notepad. As if on command, his pawns aimed their flashlights at the tabletop for illumination.

"We already rescued your passports from the bandits," Carlos said. He didn't mention the money or credit cards. "Write down your current home addresses and telephone numbers so we can notify your families that you're safe. Tomorrow we'll take you to a telephone, but this'll do for now."

"I appreciate it, Carlos," Hacksaw said. He was the first to write his address on the pad as flashlight beams jerked across the table surface.

"Salt Lake City," Carlos said. "Nice town."

"You've been there?" Hacksaw had transformed himself from a state of paralytic fear to engaged conversationalist.

"I've been everywhere," Carlos said.

Dinger wrote down his home address in Las Vegas next, and Carlos said, "Sin City." For the benefit of his cohorts, he repeated in Spanish, "*Ciudad del Pecado.*" They laughed.

I was next. I scribbled my Glendale address and my home phone number.

"I know Phoenix well," Carlos said. His chummy comments calmed us down. "Now, you need food and sleep. My men will bring you water, beer, food, and cots. For your safety we'll keep you sequestered here." *Sequestered*? This guy knew the English language better than I did.

Carlos was scoring points at a rapid rate because *beer* and *food* were magical words to fighter pilots. A flunkey entered the room and left a lantern on the table. Carlos told us to sit. He babbled in Spanish to his subordinates. Blowing away bandits had tired them, and they plunked down on chairs strewn around the room with their rifles resting against their thighs, the barrels pointed more often than not toward the ceiling. Carlos sat backwards on a chair at the table and slumped the way an American might do it.

"Did you find our credit cards or money?" Hacksaw asked.

"No," Carlos said. "Now tell me how you got here."

I explained our fiasco to Carlos in a way that omitted details about our full-time employment and flying experience. The last thing I wanted was for Carlos to contact the Air Force or State Department or any American government agency to report on our status. I wanted to get back in the jets, fly them to Cartagena, and get home. Ideally, our wives would never know that anything had gone amiss.

In my opinion, the Mexican food that a gofer brought in for us was excellent. The beer was boiler plate *Tecate*, maybe a little warm, but wet. A teenaged kid whisked away our chamber pot. Two of Carlos's henchmen escorted us one-at-a-time to the jungle behind the hangar to do what Carlos called "our business." The teenager upgraded our dinky piss pot to a manly five-gallon paint bucket. In a bizarre twist, Carlos handed each of us a cuddly stuffed animal to use as a pillow. Mine was a tiger. *Bully for Old Mizzou*. Dinger's was a camel and Hacksaw's was a mustang. My tiger smelled fresh from a good scrub in a tub followed by air-drying in the sun. Carlos's underlings vacated the room. I stretched out on my lumpy cot, head on my tiger, and listened to the snoring of the guard on the other side of the locked door. The melody to "Silent Night" kept playing in my head. Later, but before dawn, Hacksaw whispered to me, "Stitch, it's not your fault we got a shit sandwich for headwinds and my oxygen leaked."

I appreciated what Hacksaw was trying to do.

"Yep, all's forgiven," Dinger yawned. "We're in good hands now." He nodded off again.

Chapter 17

Treasure:
a label cut from clothing:
"Hecho en Guatemala"

I AWOKE LATE in the morning of Day Two, the day after the OK Corral shootout. I was hot, dirty, and thirsty. Hacksaw, Dinger, and I took out our frustrations by lobbing insults at one another. We squabbled about our deadlines for returning to the real world before the Air Force could discover our questionable conduct. I was stuck somewhere between Fig's permissive leave policy and Thor's refusal to cut me any slack at all. Hacksaw had taken leave for ten days. Dinger always wrangled more days off than any officer I ever knew. He negotiated personal days off as rewards for doing undesirable tasks, so his official leave balance kept accruing month after month.

Carlos arrived in a humorless mood. "Drop your drawers for the girl. Shower time." The *Mestiza* girl, pretty but expressionless, removed our flight suits from the clothesline and held out a basket to collect our undies. She was sixteen at most and not constrained by rules of etiquette. She drifted among us, sneaking peeks at Dinger's loins. I suspected that she had seen a lot for her tender years, but, judging from the way she was gaping at Dinger's nether regions, she'd never seen a blond high *or* low and certainly not an oddity so blond, high *and* low, as Dinger.

"Hold the starch." Hacksaw tossed his underwear into the basket the way he'd shoot a free throw.

Naked, we trooped downstairs at the point of a battered carbine wielded by one of Carlos's raggedy henchmen. Dinger opined that federal police wouldn't herd us around at gunpoint. Out on the sunlit ramp, a young flunky handed Dinger a community bar of soap as big as a block of cheese. We waited for a hose while gunmen gathered to gawp at us.

"In a world without dignity," Hacksaw said, delivering his impression of a movie trailer in a deep, bass growl.

At last, a pint-sized worker bee shuffled toward us dragging a filthy hose with water flowing from its corroded end. We lathered up in the sunshine. Hacksaw snatched the hose out of the man's grasp and sprayed us and him, too. Our uncouth audience thought the adolescent stunt was hilarious. They might never have seen a human ass as white as Dinger's. I hadn't. I heard the word "*gringo*" more than I liked, but I was in no position to be thin-skinned about it. I noticed Carlos eyeing my scars and the black-and-blue bruise marks on my torso. I didn't volunteer information about the car accident, and he didn't ask. We three gringos shared the same small stolen *La Casa Que Canta* towel to dry off. One of our captors or protectors, depending on assumptions, tossed a store-bought tee shirt and briefs to each of us. The labels said, *"Hecho en Guatemala."* (Made in Guatemala.)

Hacksaw donned his briefs: "You got to be hung like a mule to fill these monsters out."

Carlos translated for his posse, and they hee-hawed again. "Pilots are supposed to have the *cojones* of elephants," he quipped, showing his playful side.

Being on public display didn't improve my disposition, but gritty soap and running water made up for it. Carlos inspected my seeping head wound and sent a boy to fetch ointment. We still hadn't shaved, but it felt wonderful to wear clean cotton underclothing. One of Carlos's grunts brought us *bocadillos* and bottled water. The ramp was hot on our bare feet so we converted the tailgate of a shaded Toyota pickup truck to our lunch table. I noticed a portable compressor and a fuel truck with a "JET A1" sign on the side parked outside the hangar. A minion carried a portable fan upstairs to our dormitory. Another Einstein fiddled with the wiring to our building and hand-started a portable generator.

Carlos advised us to rest. "We'll discuss our next phase tonight." I asked him if we could refuel and get on our way. "You'll have to stay in the safety of your room for now. It's complicated." The subject wasn't up for debate. I swallowed my *bocadillo* and my protest. Hacksaw glared at Carlos, but even the Aggie knew that it was no time for argument. We stifled our commentary until we returned to the privacy of our room. We assessed our situation and spoke in low voices masked by the hum of the fan.

"Carlos is no cop," Hacksaw said. "We're hostages, and our lives aren't worth a nickel." A compressor cranked up outside. I observed two men wearing facemask filters and toting paint sprayers enter the hangar. Hacksaw said, "Carlos is nothing but a dude in a cop shirt who happens to speak American."

At about four in the afternoon, two brusque guards intruded without knocking. The fat one aimed his rifle in my direction while a pockmarked sidekick dropped a box filled with tacos onto the table. He lugged in a cardboard box lined with a plastic bag and filled with ice. The necks of twelve *Tecate* beer bottles stuck up out of the ice like Polaris missiles. Carlos was playing "good cop" again. He knew how to win the hearts and minds of his charges, hostages, prisoners, or whatever we were.

"Now we're getting somewhere, Groucho," Hacksaw said as he murdered the first taco and opened a frosty *Tecate*. "Fresh skivvies, a taco, and a cold beer – can't beat that with a stick," Hacksaw belched and revised his opinion of our captor: "Ol' Carlos is all right."

I nurtured a faint hope that Carlos might shake down the Colombian Air Force for money to free us to fly to Cartagena by the next day. On the other hand, I didn't want him to mess with the American State Department because they wouldn't give him a dime anyway and everybody and his brother would get in on the act to our detriment. I was counting on Jim Conti to certify that the CIA had prohibited us from informing our commanders of our patriotic service to the country. In other words, we weren't scalawags moonlighting for cash under the table, we were heroes serving the American people. I was most worried about Trudie. Belgians were a resilient breed, but discovering that your husband was a prisoner in a country notorious for violence and murder would distress even a Belgian. I hoped that Trudie would delay cancelling our Lake Powell reservations in case we got a break on getting out of Mexico.

Near sunset, Carlos's crew set up tables end-to-end on the ramp below our dormitory windows. A guard escorted us downstairs. Barefoot and dressed in cotton tee shirts and undershorts, we three gringos sat together facing sunset. The remaining chairs were occupied by Carlos's motley band. Their firearm safety procedures were non-existent. Most of them carried a sidearm and an automatic rifle hanging from a shoulder strap. The barrels pointed at the ground, at the sky, and in our faces. An ugly character seated next to Hacksaw hunched over his food and inclined the barrel of his gun toward Hack's head.

"Do you frigging mind, shit-for-brains?" Hacksaw protested. He nudged the barrel of the gun away from his head. The gunman couldn't translate what Hacksaw had said, but he knew it wasn't a compliment. In a blur, the unsightly man produced a machete and held it a whisker from Hacksaw's throat. The sight of the man's decaying teeth combined with the ruthlessness of his scowl put Hacksaw in a sweat.

Carlos's voice broke the silence that followed the flash of steel: "Tell him you're sorry."

"How?" Hacksaw asked.

"Say, '*lo siento*,'" (I'm sorry) Carlos told him.

Hacksaw did better than that. He said, "*Lo siento, Amigo.*" (I'm sorry, friend.)"

The swordsman broke into laughter. He withdrew the machete and sheathed it. Then he grasped his firestick and thrust it into the air in a kind of spontaneous celebration.

Hacksaw smiled and, being the new crowd favorite, pointed alternately at the revolting celebrant and himself. *"Amigos."*

The incident underlined the vast chasm that separated our world from Carlos's. Our condescending view of these rough-hewn simpletons wouldn't get us very far in Carlos's domain, a place full of hooligans who would exploit any advantage in the most extreme and violent way. We gringos had no standing among them. Because of my stupidity and greed, my friends and I might never get back to our privileged lives. I scanned the ramp hoping for a diversion. I noticed that the compressor outside the hangar had fallen silent and sat idly beside the kind of cart used to start T-Birds.

"You found a power cart already?" I asked Carlos. "How'd you do that?"

Carlos leaned toward me and said, "I told a guy named Eduardo to bring me one or I'd slaughter every male member of his family and feed their livers to dogs." Dinger exhaled an odd kind of laugh-cough, an amalgam of belch, fart, moan, and whine. If Carlos was a police officer, he was a rare breed of lawman, indeed. Whatever he was, he was sending us a stern message. "Tomorrow night we're moving the airplanes to a forward operating base to be in position for a big drug bust," he said.

"Who's doing the busting?" I asked.

"Mexico. And the U.S. It'll be huge. It'll set the cartel back years." He slammed a fist into an open hand and his crew of naughty boys murmured on cue.

"Who's moving the planes for you?" Dinger asked.

"You are, of course. It's all worked out with the Colombian Air Force."

His story wasn't supported by even the faintest trace of plausibility, but I didn't have the guts to confront him. Hacksaw, of course, did. The Aggie hadn't capitulated yet. "I don't have any intention of putting me or my plane in harm's way." Brave words from a man wearing only underwear.

"Of course not," Carlos assured him. "Hell, no. Move the planes seven hundred miles to a secret facility, then we'll get you guys back home." He slapped me on the back. "Back home to *mami*."

"I should speak with the Colombian Air Force," I said.

"Not possible," Carlos said. "We're on a communications blackout until after the operation. No leaks. That's why we had to secure you in your dormitory."

The whole set-up seemed wobbly. What role could Colombian T-Birds play in such an operation with their machine guns removed?

"Do these guys know about the bust?" I asked, gesturing with my head to avoid pointing at the potentially trigger-happy killers sharing our banquet table.

"They've got no clue," Carlos said. "It's not their job to know. They're local irregulars."

"Undercover?" I asked.

"No. Sort of mercenaries."

"Are you prior military?" I asked.

"Can't say." Carlos remained a man of mystery.

"Where's this secret base?" Dinger asked.

"Well, they call it a secret base because it's secret. I can't tell you until you flight plan. I *can* tell you that the climate's decent and you'll have air-conditioning. It's better than this dump."

"Wouldn't it be simpler if we just caught a commercial flight home?" Dinger asked. "Let the Colombians come get their planes."

Carlos ignored Dinger. "It isn't optional."

"If we move the planes, do you guarantee that we can go home?" I asked.

"Absolutely."

I decided to keep my powder dry and cooperate with Carlos at least until I found out the destination the next day. It was time to decide whether we were going to incur Carlos's wrath by resisting or to nurture his good will. I was betting on the good-will angle, and my companions followed my lead. I gorged on black beans and the ribs of either a goat or a cocker spaniel. We swilled beer until the heat didn't matter. I dreamed up escape scenarios in overdrive. In one scenario, the three of us would fake collaboration until we could take off for the secret base and divert to Marana. We'd get back to our families and return to our squadrons in time to prevent the Air Force from learning of our injudicious activities. Who'd even believe such a story? We'd forget the money and we'd stay north of the border for the rest of our lives, older and wiser. Back in our upstairs dormitory room, woozy from beer, stuffed with meat, and away from the gun-toting posse, we hashed it over. We agreed to put a plan together the following day and make our break for freedom the next evening. The prospect cheered us up even though we faced another steaming hot night on the cots-from-hell.

Chapter 18

Treasure:
a diagram of El Hoyo auxiliary airport

IN THE MORNING of Day Three, Carlos arrived with lackeys carrying food, bottles of water, antique aviation sectional charts, and flight manuals and Jeppesen charts from the T-Birds. During the night, Hacksaw had barfed the remains of his beans and ribs into our five-gallon-chamber pot three times by my count. Vomit and urine didn't mix well. The warmer the room got, the worse the stench. An errand boy emptied the pot and brought Hacksaw pills wrapped in aluminum foil. Hack was trending worse and he lay motionless on his cot as though he had forfeited his will to live. Under Carlos's direction, Dinger and I shoved two tables together and started flight planning. Carlos circled Atl Ixtaca with a red pen and then drew another circle up in Northern Mexico in the middle of nowhere south of El Paso/Juárez.

"Where's the destination airport?" I asked.

"Airport?" Carlos sneered.

I examined the chart again. His red circle was located in

the middle of a vast basin surrounded by escarpments and mountain ranges in elevations of over 10,000 feet. The center of the circle bisected a straight stretch of Highway 45 connecting Chihuahua and Juárez.

"You want us to land on a two-lane highway at night?" Dinger was incredulous. "Not me."

"It's called El Hoyo." Carlos ignored Dinger's short-lived revolt. "There's a full moon tonight. Plan to fly low-level to avoid all populations and radars."

I estimated the straight-line route to be about 800 nautical miles. Even with full internal fuel tanks and full wingtip drop tanks, a T-Bird couldn't fly that far at low altitude because the old bird was a real gas hog down low. "We'd have to refuel to make it at low altitude," I said.

Carlos was prepared: "There's an airport about halfway to El Hoyo, southeast of Durango, called Hidalgo de la Frontera. It's not on these old charts." He dropped an airport diagram of Hidalgo Airport onto the table. The field elevation was 6,208 feet above sea level. The runway was 75 feet wide and 6,000 feet long. It was oriented northeast to southwest on magnetic headings of 060º and 240º. The runway had two perpendicular taxiways at the ends and a narrow parallel taxiway. "You can't use Durango or any other airport where you might be seen, so it's either Hidalgo or a highway. We'll coordinate a refueling truck for you when you've finalized your plans."

"Carlos, this isn't right," was my last feeble attempt to beg off the dangerous flights.

"You're going to fly those three airplanes to El Hoyo tonight, period. I'll be back in two hours for you to tell me how you're going to do it." Carlos strode out of the room.

Dinger and I brainstormed about flying a low-level route until clearing the first mountain range, after which we could climb to altitude and make it back to Marana with tail winds. Dinger warned that Carlos might assign chaperones to ride in our back seats. As a measure of how desperate we were, I offered the preposterous idea of punching out, thumbing a ride to Z Town, and surrendering to police.

Hacksaw was lying on his side facing away from us. His voice was just a whimper: "No way."

"A nighttime ejection over the cactus capital of the world?" Dinger said. "That's ridiculous."

"No ejecting." Hacksaw groaned more adamantly. He retched and groped for the chamber pot to make another deposit. The door burst open and Carlos entered in the company of two armed bodyguards. He plopped an old tape recorder onto the table and punched the play button.

"You bugged the room?" Dinger said.

"Of course, num-nutz." Carlos's temper was showing. "I've tried to be straight with you clowns." He pointed at Dinger. "Come with me."

Dinger put his foot down and refused to move until Carlos gestured for a guard to aim at Dinger's chest. Dinger exited the room first, followed by the first guard, Carlos, and the second guard, who crouched as if for a bayonet charge even though he didn't have a bayonet.

"What've I done, Hack? These guys aren't cops."

Hacksaw didn't answer. He was heaving worse than a worn-out sump pump.

From the floor below us, at a volume that dwarfed the

whir of our fan, a loud slap – leather on flesh – was followed by a soul-rendering human shriek.

I leaped to the door and pounded on it: "Carlos!" The image of Dinger being flogged horrified me. The whip cracked again, followed by a cry more despairing than the first. I pounded on the door again.

"We'll fly the planes, dammit," I screamed.

After a pause, the door cracked open. "Step back," Carlos warned.

Dinger entered unscathed. Carlos ripped duct tape off Dinger's mouth, cut his plastic wrist restraints with a knife, and shoved him further into the room.

"I'm just trying to make a point with you," Carlos said. "Think about consequences. You'll each have a guy with a machine gun in your back seat. Now, stop wasting my time and plan the flights."

My pulse was still elevated as I spread the charts out on the table. Dinger, seemingly unfazed, researched performance data in a flight manual. We knew we couldn't refuse to cooperate without risking our lives and we knew the room was bugged so we put a plan together by pointing more than talking. We knew how to plan low-level missions quickly. Not so long ago, back at the Six-Twelfth Squadron in Spain, we had frequently planned for a selective release of a nuclear weapon on a target announced at the last moment. It was called SELREL, and we had gotten good at deciding how to ingress to a heavily-defended target, nuke it, and get the hell out and maybe even survive the experience one per cent of the time. This was different: The T-Bird was slow and its range was short, we weren't carrying nukes, and there weren't any enemy missiles or anti-aircraft artillery sites along the way to blow us away. The mission was simple enough. We finished flight planning the two legs in forty minutes.

———⟐———

In the afternoon, a hodgepodge of lesser goons brought tamales and water bottles to our little piece of Hades-on-Earth. Hacksaw refused to eat a bite. He forced himself to drink water even though he puked it back up seconds later. One Samaritan gave Hacksaw more pills and gestured for him to swallow two. Hacksaw swallowed three and lay back down. Dinger and I made a list of questions for Carlos. He showed up in a wife-beater undershirt worn beneath a Guayabera shirt and a gold medallion nestled in a tangle of chest hair thicker than a gorilla on Rogaine.

"Nice Guayabera," Dinger said. In two words, he communicated that the earlier staged whipping was forgotten and that we accepted the reality that Carlos was in control.

"It's called a Yucatan shirt down here," Carlos said. "How's our patient?"

"He can't fly tonight," I said.

Carlos ignored me: "Just brief me on the flight to El Hoyo."

"We can make it non-stop at high altitude. If we fly low, we'll have to refuel."

"You can't fly high. Too many leaks. The cartel has informants all over the place. The more people who know about positioning the airplanes at El Hoyo – controllers, anybody – the less chance we have of keeping the operation secret."

Carlos had all the answers, but I still had my doubts about his so-called sting operation.

"We'll need decent weather to fly low-level through the mountains," I said. "And the winds will have to be benign for landing on the highway at El Hoyo."

"I know, I know," Carlos interrupted me. "You Air Force pansies make such a big deal out of everything." Carlos knew more about us than he was letting on. "You're worse than lawyers. The moon's going to be full and the winds at El Hoyo were almost calm last night."

I elevated the hostage/kidnapper bond a notch by asking questions. Would Hidalgo have runway lighting? *No.* Would we have a start cart at Hidalgo? *No.* What was the width of Highway 45 where we had to land at El Hoyo? *Thirty feet.* Was the turnoff to El Hoyo stressed for a fifteen-thousand-pound airplane? *Yes.* Carlos knew the answers as though he had deliberated over the flights himself. I told him we'd need lighting to mark the touchdown and turnoff points at El Hoyo. When I asked for a follow-me truck to lead the way in the dark from the highway to the parking area, he ridiculed me.

"You're not Air Force One and you're not landing at Andrews Air Force Base, for crying out loud. You'll get a guy with a flashlight on a motorcycle." Carlos further informed us that our ejection seats would be disabled, our parachutes replaced by cushions, our transponders removed, and all oxygen bottles capped. That meant we couldn't fly above ten thousand feet for any length of time, we couldn't signal to ATC, and we couldn't punch out.

Without a start cart at Hidalgo, we'd have to refuel with

our engines running. Carlos promised to provide at least 1,500 gallons of jet fuel for each T-Bird. He promised us that the fuel truck would be grounded so static electricity wouldn't blow us to smithereens. He guaranteed that the fueler would know where all seven fueling ports were on the airplane and would gas us up without dropping a wrench down an intake. "Okay," Carlos said, "that's enough. Be ready to launch at one o'clock this morning. Sleep all you can." He pointed at Hacksaw. "You, keep popping pills and drink water till you puke."

"He's already puking," Dinger said.

"You know what I mean," Carlos scowled. "I'll bring you weather tonight with your food." He was as pompous as Curtiss LeMay before the bombing of Dresden. "The three guys who'll fly in your back seats are downstairs. Tell them what they need to know." He left the room.

"That cocksucker's a pilot," Dinger said. "He said *wilco* and *piece-of-cake*."

I agreed, but I held up a forefinger and pointed around the room as a reminder of bugs. Dinger was impatient: "What do we do with Hack?"

"Give him another couple of pills in an hour." I sounded more heartless than intended.

"Piss off," Hack moaned, personifying the wrath of a ram and the force of a lamb.

———— ((◦)) ————

A guard brandishing his rifle like a pitchfork escorted me downstairs and into the steaming hot hangar. I was surprised to discover that Carlos had painted all three T-Birds the color of hearses. It wasn't a professional job, but you didn't have to be Rembrandt to spray black paint on everything. His painters had even covered tail numbers and insignia so no distinguishing marks of any kind remained. Waiting for me were three little *Mestizo* dudes whom Carlos had assigned to ride in our back seats. I could tell by their body language that they weren't volunteers. My job was to acquaint the reluctant "tail gunners" with the T-Bird's rear cockpit, the claustrophobic-inducing little box where they would be trapped for almost five hours on the way to El Hoyo. They couldn't have been more solemn if I had been fitting them for a casket. They followed me as I climbed onto the right wing of the nearest jet. We huddled around the rear cockpit as I helped the least timid of the three men slide into the rear seat. I gestured for him to leave his machine gun with one of his pals so he wouldn't aerate the cockpit with bullet holes. I proceeded to mutilate their native tongue.

"*Esse,*" I said, "*es un avion.*" (This is an airplane.) They were with me so far. I pointed to the rear cockpit control stick. The Three Amigos eyed it in awe as though I was about to teach them to fly.

"*No temerlo,*" (Don't fear it) I said. They looked puzzled. Wrong verb. I pointed at the stick again and said, "*No tomarlo,*" (Don't drink it). Another dud. I couldn't remember the verb for "touch." My brain raced. The three little men couldn't hide their smiles. Once upon a time, I had learned that "*tocar*" was the Spanish infinitive for "touch," but, now, when I needed it, the word eluded me. I pointed at the stick again with my right hand and slapped it with my left hand.

"*No hace falta joder con eso*," I said. (You don't need to screw with that.) That got my audience laughing. Shazam, I was a stand-up comedian. I worked my way around the cockpit repeating the phrase. Each time, they broke into peals of laughter. "*No temes todo*," I said. (Don't fear everything.) "*No jodes con nada*," (Don't screw with nothing).

In a short time, I proved that I shouldn't attempt to speak Spanish and that they shouldn't touch the switches. I didn't dare ask them if they had any questions. Their eyes teared from laughing at me. One little guy gave me a wooden crucifix attached to a chain. I thanked him and draped it around my neck. The gesture pleased him more than I expected. He crossed himself and smiled. The armed guard escorted me back to my sweltering dorm where Dinger asked me about the machine gunners whom he called the Flying Wallendas. "Never have so few known so little about aviation," I said. I reclined in my cot fingering the crucifix and perspiring. I contemplated all the ways I had disappointed Elizabeth, Trudie and Katrina, and Dinger and Hacksaw. I didn't deserve the peace-of-mind required for slumber, but I fell asleep anyway.

I awoke after 6 p.m. of Day Three. Heat and dehydration dulled my brain and made me indolent. My mind shuffled vignettes of my mother and father. My father had once told me that he set out to make me the perfect child. He must have abandoned the project because he never mentioned it again. When I was three years old, he taught me the Greek alphabet, which gave me a leg up in high school trigonometry. Not only did he make me do pushups, he told me to memorize verses from the bible. I favored the shorter, punchier passages: John 11:35 – "Jesus wept," and an abridged Exodus 3:14 – "I am who I am."

"It's all about discipline," Dad told me.

I didn't know whether he was referring to the Scriptures or to pushups. At the moment, in Atl Ixtaca, the heat was too oppressive for either. Underwear Girl delivered our evening meal of beans, rice, and lukewarm bottled water. Hacksaw wanted nothing to do with a legume of any description. Dinger and I ate his untouched food and coerced him to swallow gulps of water. I had seen Carlos's stormy reaction to bad news, so I dreaded telling him that Hacksaw was too sick to fly. Carlos was overdue, so Dinger and I conspired about popping up to thirteen thousand feet or so, broadcasting in the blind on the radio, and flying erratically to attract a Mexican Air Force intercept. We were headed into some of Mexico's most remote mountains where we wouldn't be able to attract notice even if we set ourselves on fire and flew a Blue Angels airshow. Furthermore, the machine gunners in our back seats might get trigger-happy if we climbed or deviated from the plan. In the end, we figured that we had no choice but to fly to Hidalgo and on to El Hoyo. Carlos finally showed up looking harried a little after sunset.

"Tough day?" Dinger asked.

"Shut up." Carlos was in a touchy mood. He handed me weather reports and glared at Hacksaw. I scanned the long ribbon of current weather and forecasts for every significant reporting station in central and northern Mexico. I normally hoped for *fair* weather before a flight. On this night, however,

I wanted the weather to be too foul for even ducks to fly. I got what I wanted. Weather over the mountains along our route of flight looked gnarly. Convective activity had produced a legion of cumulonimbus cells with tops over thirty-five thousand feet. Cloud-to-cloud and cloud-to-ground lightning was forecast. I argued for a weather abort so we wouldn't have to get to the question of Hacksaw's illness. Carlos grandstanded for a few seconds and rifled through the weather reports before relenting.

"You expect me to argue with you," he said, "but I won't, even though it's a gamble to wait. The planes have to be in El Hoyo for modifications no later than tomorrow night." He gathered the weather sheets off the table. "We'll slip the flight for twenty-four hours, but then we won't have any cushion. Tomorrow night, you seagulls are going to fly. I don't care if it's snowing."

Rain deluged Atl Ixtaca that night. The temperature cooled off by ten Fahrenheit degrees, but it was still as humid as a fish bowl. My backbreaking cot reminded me of prisoner-of-war training at Air Force combat survival school where sleep deprivation and hunger had made the two-week course seem twice as long. As miserable as that experience had been, it helped me tolerate being a captive now in Mexico. Nothing helped Hacksaw who appeared to teeter on the edge of death.

Chapter 19

Treasure:
a metal E-6B analog aviation circular slide rule

ON THE MORNING of Day Four, a girl, who apparently hadn't eaten a decent meal in a decade, brought us food. Maybe she had a thyroid condition. We called her Slim. She stacked tortillas on three plates and ladled a top coat of beans and eggs, sort of industrial-grade *huevos rancheros*. Hacksaw peeked at the eggs before spewing green goo into the honey bucket. Her mission was to bring food in and take out our underwear for laundering. She didn't appear to be overly interested in the nakedness of three men, two of them munching and one moaning. When she left with our undies, a guard popped his head through the doorway and announced that it was time for *el baño* (the bath). Hacksaw reiterated his promise to die that morning and refused to budge from his cot. Dinger and I went downstairs exposed once again to the ridicule of our captors. One chubby fellow I hadn't seen before showed a troubling degree of interest.

"If I get a chance to coldcock one of these pig-pokers,

I'll do it," Dinger grumbled. "I'm sweating half the time and freezing my nuts off the other half. Look at Cantinflas over there yucking it up."

We dried off with a soiled hand towel before being ushered back upstairs in the nude. We stayed that way until Slim returned with our laundered undies. When I wasn't dozing, I reviewed aviation charts. The embryo of an escape plan was taking form in my mind, but it was too far from ripening for me to confide in either of my comrades. Hacksaw's condition was in such decline that he probably would have turned down a first-class ticket on the Concorde directly to the Mayo Clinic.

Carlos waited until nightfall before telling his legions to pull the black T-Birds out of the hangar onto the darkened ramp. A fueler driving a modern fuel truck replenished the fuel tanks. He knew what he was doing. I chose "Kiko" as our flight call sign in honor of Dinger's corgi. A Las Vegas rescue puppy became the inspiration for three gringos to wander around Mexican airspace in three antique jets. The weather forecast was better than on the previous night. Hacksaw's fever had broken, but he was still poorly. He arose from his sickbed long enough to pull on his flight suit and boots before collapsing back onto his cot. He had the reek of a field hand returned from cutting sugar cane all day. I knew a confrontation with Carlos was brewing and I'd have to be the one to face up to him. I abhorred confrontation. The feelings of impotence that I felt during an argument were too similar to the helplessness I had felt lying in a hospital bed. I would detour a long way to wiggle out of a dispute, but there was no avoiding this one. Carlos showed up at ten o'clock in a vile mood, abrupt and short-tempered. My knees were shaking with trepidation.

"We're a no-go, Carlos. Hacksaw's still sick as a dog."

Carlos snapped at me, "I decide whether you fly or not." His eyes were flashing carbon. His voice was flinty. "Tonight's not optional. All three of you have to fly."

"Hack can't do it, Carlos."

"You don't get it, do you? Those planes have to be at El Hoyo before sunrise. Period."

"We're not going." My voice seemed to come from outside my body. Carlos got right into my grill.

"If you have any hope of ever going back to the States, all three of you will get into those airplanes and fly them to El Hoyo." He pointed at Hacksaw: "Once you're there, you'll get well and you can sleep all you want." Carlos pulled two colored pictures out of his chest pocket and thrust them toward me. The first picture, showing the leader of the bandits at Atl Ixtaca, made me queasy. The man's body lay in the back of a pickup truck covered with blood. His severed head with his pipe propped in his mouth was arranged on the truck bed to face the camera. Carlos forced the second photo closer to my face. The picture showed three bodies stacked on a truck bed with their decapitated heads arranged in a grotesque row. I thought I'd pass out if I viewed the repulsive pictures any longer. I pushed his hand away.

"Do you get it, gringo?" he taunted me.

"That's sick, Carlos." I was so upset that even my lips were quivering.

Hacksaw's resurrection was brief and unconvincing. He sprang up and sat astraddle his cot. Any enthusiasm had to be artificial because it appeared that the angel of death had been gnawing on his face all day. His voice was much too cheerful to be sincere: "I can do it, Stitch."

Carlos shoved his forefinger into my chest: "That's a player for you." He patted his new teacher's pet on the back. "Don't mess with me," he snarled before pacing out of the room.

"No sweat. I can hack it," Hacksaw said before flopping onto his back again.

I was the sorry joker who had gotten us into this mess so I had nothing to say. Dinger gathered his gear and headed for the door. Hacksaw struggled to his feet and trooped out after Dinger. I went last. A rotund guard lugging a shotgun guided us downstairs to the back of the hangar to water the jungle. Hacksaw had downed buckets of water throughout the day, so he took a long piss on a palmetto. For an encore, he dry-heaved the lining of his stomach right on top of it. I was squeamish about expelled body fluids of any description, so I vacated Hacksaw's toxic waste site on the double.

My tail gunner was waiting at the aircraft. His machine gun and construction hardhat made him appear smaller than real life. He was pleased that I was wearing his crucifix. He repeated his name three times as if seeking to form a meaningful relationship with me. I didn't care what his name was. For all I knew, this could be the last flight of my life. I turned lights off in the rear cockpit to eliminate distracting reflections on the canopy. I coerced my petite passenger to occupy the rear seat. He wasn't pretending to be happy about buckling into a tiny cockpit for the first airplane ride of his life. He couldn't have been any more frightened if I'd dumped a box of tarantulas on his head. He had stuffed paper napkins into his ear canals for hearing protection. He looked ridiculous with a lime green hardhat on his noggin and napkins protruding from his ears. I made sure that he positioned his barf bag beneath his crotch so he could grab it quickly. His face was a portrait of terror. I patted him on the left thigh to encourage him, but he wasn't expecting it, and he recoiled as though I had shoved a red hot poker up his ass.

"*Buena suerte,*" I shouted. (Good luck.)

Even though his face brightened when I dry-kissed his crucifix, he seemed ready to bolt from the plane and dash for the jungle if he could figure out how to unstrap himself. I didn't comprehend what Carlos gained from stuffing his gunmen into our back seats without parachutes. How would they know whether we'd done something Carlos didn't want? How would they benefit by shooting us for some unauthorized maneuver? Wouldn't they die in a crash a tenth of a second after us? My opinion didn't matter. Once Carlos decided on a plan, he stuck with it. I stopped by Hacksaw's airplane. On a scale of zero to ten, zero being dead and ten being dandy, I scored him a marginal *two*. "You okay, Hack?"

"Piece of cake." His earnest eyes seemed to have receded into their sockets. "You're a good friend, Cromwell. Don't kill me tonight."

I wanted to ask his forgiveness, but I turned away. Unspoken regrets took a toll. Hacksaw didn't need any more distractions. He had fewer than four hours of flying time in the T-Bird, and I was asking him to fly sick at night in an unfamiliar jet carrying an overly weaponized dwarf to land on a ribbon of asphalt in the dark. I could guess at how disorienting it must have been for him. Twenty-five thousand dollars seemed a paltry reward for what I was asking him to do.

Carlos stayed out of our way. Painting the T-Birds black removed almost all pretenses that he was on the side of justice in the fight against drug cartels. The charade that we were part of a massive drug bust was flimsy, and Carlos's masquerade as a cop was half-hearted. As time for engine start approached, he perched on a lawn chair in the bed of a pickup truck from which he could watch every move we made.

We used a single power cart to start all three jets. I lined up in a tight echelon formation on the narrow runway. My heart was thumping when I advanced the throttle full forward and released brakes for takeoff roll at 0012 local time, Day Five. Kiko Two and Three were to follow me at twenty-second intervals. After takeoff, I raised the gear and flaps and circled the airport at two thousand feet above the ground in a thirty-degree left-hand bank to allow join-ups by Dinger on my left wing and Hacksaw on my right. I aimed the formation north toward the mountains and descending to low-level altitude with speed set at 345 mph. Our goal was to fly comm-out, using as few radio calls as possible.

On my signal, Hacksaw dropped back 2,000 feet behind Dinger. Then Dinger dropped off my wing to take 2,000 feet of spacing on me. I turned off my exterior lights and rotating beacons and dimmed cockpit lighting as much as I dared. The moon was a silvery white ball overhead. As my eyes adapted to a world without artificial light, I could see the mountains ahead in moonlight. I tried to imagine my diminutive back seater's thoughts as we streaked two hundred feet above the ground along valleys at the bases of 10,000-foot mountain peaks. I imagined his bewilderment as I rolled upside-down to cross saddlebacks in ridgelines. At the apex of each crossing, all he would have been able to see was a world of rocks a hundred feet from his face. He probably wished he had kept the crucifix for himself. I could imagine him praying to saints he hadn't troubled in a long time.

I approximated a course parallel to the straight-line magnetic course toward Hidalgo without benefit of any navigational aids. Heading, time, speed, and distance were my tools as I kept my eyes out of the cockpit to keep from smashing into mountainous terrain. I suspected that the contents of my back seater's stomach were in his barf bag by the time we entered a long canyon running upward between two ranges of mountains so craggy and remote that I was sure that no one had ever planted a foot there.

I was used to flying Phantoms at a hundred feet off the deck at twice my current speed, so the hour and sixteen-minute flight to Hidalgo through Mexico's most desolate topography seemed to be slow motion. In one isolated valley, I spotted a tiny stone cabin with a light in a single window. What would the hermit make of three earth-shaking reverberations of unknown origin hurtling by his hut in the darkness? Would he report unidentified flying objects? Did he even have a telephone? Untouched by modernity, would he be as mystified as his forebears would have been a thousand years earlier?

As we flew north, the mountain peaks stretched higher into the night sky. The scorched sand reflected moonlight, and I had no trouble avoiding obstacles. I sneaked peeks at my fuel gauge. I planned to land at Hidalgo with 180 gallons of fuel remaining. The seventy-sixth minute had almost elapsed when I spotted the lights of Durango glowing behind a mountain on the horizon straight ahead and a little to my right. I had strayed off-course to the west, so I corrected back to a northeasterly heading to try to find Hidalgo de la Frontera. I slowed to 180 mph. During an easy left-hand turn overhead the expanse of desert where the landing strip should be, I turned on my navigation lights and rotating beacons. My wingmen, co-altitude at my seven o'clock position, did the same. I was relieved that I hadn't scraped either one of them off on a mesa. Halfway through my first circle, I made out the Hidalgo runway. A line of four pickup trucks marked the southwestern end of the runway with their headlights. Twelve smudge pots marked the touchdown zone at the approach end. I set up for a left teardrop entry to position for a left hand turn-to-final for the approach. Dinger took thirty seconds spacing on me and Hacksaw took thirty seconds on him. I crabbed to adjust for a slight right crosswind and descended at eight hundred feet a minute, aiming to touch down between the smudge pots set on either side of the runway.

"Wind two-five-zero, ten knots," I radioed.

Two sets of zippers. They knew that my wind report was a SWAG, a scientific wild-ass guess. Even with the benefit of moon glow and the illumination of my landing light, I could see only a tiny area of asphalt ahead of my plane as I pulled the throttle to idle and flared for the touchdown at 120 miles an hour. There were no centerline markings. It wasn't my smoothest landing ever, but I didn't chip any teeth. I strayed to the right edge of the runway and had to increase left braking to steer back toward the middle. As I slowed to taxi speed at the departure end of the runway, I turned right and followed a bicyclist holding a flashlight onto the parallel taxiway. I turned off my taxi light, so the moon was my only source of exterior light. Off to my right, I could see Dinger rolling out and Hacksaw touching down.

It was obvious that Bike Boy had marshalled aircraft before. He left his bike near a fueling truck and used lighted wands to direct a forty-five-degree right turn and brake to a stop. Another ground handler appeared from out of the darkness with a set of wheel chocks. He put them in place on either side of my nose wheel. The two ground crewmen jogged off to Dinger's jet and directed him to stop two hundred feet behind me also on a forty-five-degree angle. By the time they had positioned Hacksaw another two hundred feet back, a fuel truck had parked at my four o'clock position.

Two fuelers attached truck-connected cables to iron grounding loops fixed in the taxiway. They each stretched a hose toward my jet. My canopy remained closed. I couldn't see into the back seat, but I imagined that my miniature chaperone was wondering when his nightmare would end. When my seven tanks were full, a guy in tan overalls stood off to my left and gestured with two raised fingers in a horizontal circle to indicate that all seven fuel service caps were secure. He gave me a confident thumbs-up signal. This guy knew his way around campus. I returned his thumbs-up, and the refueling truck moved toward Dinger's plane. A ground handler pulled my chocks and the lead handler used his wands to indicate chocks out and clearance to taxi out. As I passed by him, he saluted me. Where had Carlos found these characters? If they weren't military, they had to be trained airline personnel.

It was time to execute the single-ship leg of the mission. Leaving Dinger and Hacksaw behind on the taxiway to take on their fuel, I taxied into position on the runway between rows of smudge pots. I took time to arrange my chart on the kneeboard strapped to my right thigh and to orient myself with the magnetic course toward El Hoyo. Off to my right, I could make out Dinger's plane as fuelers wrestled fueling hoses into his wingtip drop tank fueling ports. Hacksaw waited his turn.

I figured that there were ten souls in the middle of the huge expanse of desert southeast of Durango – three pilots, three machine-gunners, two ground handlers, and two fuelers. Eight witnesses would survive to tell the tale if I screwed up and created a fireball on takeoff. That was the most negative pre-takeoff notion I'd ever entertained. I maintained radio silence by flashing my landing light once to signal "*adios,*" a primordial communication suitable for an unsophisticated airplane in a primitive place.

——— ((O)) ———

I pushed the throttle forward and released brakes. By squinting to estimate the unmarked centerline of the runway, I managed to keep the jet on the narrow runway surface until airborne. I turned left in a thirty-degree banked turn, climbing no higher than three hundred feet over the terrain. I raised the gear and flaps, turned off my navigation lights and beacons, accelerated to 345 mph (300 knots), and established the desired magnetic heading parallel to the straight-line magnetic course to El Hoyo. Carlos had warned me to avoid the city of Chihuahua and to stay low to remain undetected by the radars of United States ATC in the sectors across the border and both El Paso and Juárez approach controls. More important than remaining unseen by radar was avoiding lethal contact with the desert floor. The most difficult task of all lay ahead — landing the T-Bird on a thirty-foot-wide highway in the dark.

El Hoyo was a geographical point on my chart at a lat/long of N 30:01.6 W 106:23.1. The El Hoyo Waypoint was a position on Highway 45 halfway between the cities of Chihuahua and Juárez. What made that section of Highway 45 distinct from other portions of the road was that power lines and a railroad bed that paralleled Highway 45 were at their most divergent points from the highway. Measuring from the center of the El Hoyo mining complex, the power lines were a mile west and the railroad was two miles east. Portable lights would mark the touchdown zone and the turn-off to the mining complex. It was time to land on a ribbon in the dark.

A skinny 30-foot-wide ersatz runway was a set-up for a hard landing because pilots tended to flare late when landing on runways narrower than the conventional 150 feet. A late flare would slam the aircraft onto the runway, compromising directional control and possibly driving the struts into the wings. The T-Bird wingspan exceeded the width of Highway 45 by nine feet so it was vital to keep the airplane in the center of the highway. There wasn't another 100-watt light bulb within fifty miles of the mining complex, so the lights of El Hoyo were easy to identify. I called Papi, Carlos's El Hoyo radio operator, on VHF frequency 123.45. "Papi, Kiko One. Say winds."

The thickest Spanish accent I'd ever heard responded, *"No prahlem. Wince un-aay-zhero a' twelf."*

"Roger," I said, "One-eight-zero at twelve knots."

"Rhayer, Rhayer, no prahlem."

The portable light carts came up brightly at the touch-down zone followed by those at the turn-off point to the mining complex. Winds were down the snot locker, so I didn't crab much at all. When I chopped the throttle to idle, I glided in ground effect before the main wheels slammed onto the road surface. When the effectiveness of the rudder dissipated, I applied wheel brakes gently. The airplane jerked to the right and the right main tire left the road surface onto the edge of the shoulder. Despite the sound-dampening qualities of my helmet, the noise was terrible. I imagined that it sounded like the end of the world to the little man with paper napkins stuffed in his ears in my back seat. My sphincter was so torqued down that I probably wouldn't shit for a month. I wrestled the beast back onto the highway and slowed down before I reached the exit to the mining complex. A guy on a motorcycle was waiting off to my right with a flashlight that was brighter than some strobe lights I'd seen. I was too grateful to be on the ground to resent the follow-me motorcyclist for destroying my night vision with his flashlight. My landing had been crappy even with calm winds and a hundred T-Bird landings under my belt. I had real concerns about the chances for a successful landing by either Dinger or Hacksaw.

I raised the canopy. The desert air was sweet and cool. I followed the motorcycle uphill to the hangar where a ground handler chocked my main wheels and motioned with a lighted wand to shut down my engine. I cut the engine and performed the shutdown checklist. I pulled my helmet off my aching head and removed my soaking wet cotton helmet liner. I unstrapped, climbed out of the cockpit, and slid back on the intake to help Machine Gun Garcia unbuckle his straps. He was beaming brighter than an astronaut just returned from space. My flashlight revealed that the crotch of his pants was wet. It wasn't perspiration. His bloated barf bag was lying on the cockpit floor, tied off with a length of parachute cord.

He shouted, "*Maestro. Maestro,*" as he forgot his machine gun and embraced my shoulders. Perhaps no man in history had ever been so glad to return to earth. I broke up his celebration-of-life ceremony by pointing at his barf bag so he would remember to throw it in the trash. He imitated my slide off the wing onto the ground. His legs were unsteady after almost five hours in one position. He trotted off toward the mining complex in search of a crapper and a shower, maybe a chapel. I performed a flashlight inspection of the right main tire and found no damage. I asked to see Papi, a cheerful older man sitting at a picnic table beside a bulky VHF radio connected to an industrial grade extension cord. A crude six-foot "T" antenna was fastened to a clothesline with old-fashioned wooden clothespins on the "T" end and alligator clipped to the antenna pigtail at the radio on the other end. We shook hands.

"¿*Con permisso, Papi?*" (Do you mind, Papi?) I asked.

"*No prahlem, Señor.*"

Papi eagerly passed off radio duties to me by sliding side-ways on the picnic table bench and handing me the headset and the mic. An antiquated lantern illuminated the radio knobs and switches. No one was shoving a rifle in my face. Carlos wasn't there barking orders. It was almost as good as freedom, although in a place where I didn't want to be. I donned Papi's headset and double-clicked the mic button.

"Kiko Two, you up?" I transmitted on the radio. I waited. Silence.

Papi scrutinized me as though I had issued a command of vital significance. My right hand was still trembling four-teen minutes after planting my T-Bird on a skinny-ass high-way posing as a runway. I trimmed the wick of the lantern to improve my night vision. Out of the airplane, my existence no longer depended on laser-sharp eyesight, so, of course, my night vision was spectacular. I could see the silhouettes of men a quarter mile away at the portable lights on Highway 45. "Kiko Two, you up?" I transmitted again. No answer. Papi wasn't accustomed to such portentous events and he was ner-vous. As the minutes creeped by toward Dinger's scheduled arrival time, Papi farted around with a coffee spoon trying to tighten the loose screws holding the faceplate on the radio. I pulled my E-6B analog circular slide rule out of a flight suit leg pocket and showed it to the old man.

"*Whiz wheel,*" I said.

He gestured that he was impressed. "*Wiss will,*" he said.

He was even more mesmerized when I pulled the metal

slide out of its track and showed him how to use it as a screwdriver. He began tightening screws, and, after each one was secure, he looked at me for approval as though he had tightened the critical screw on an Apollo rocket booster. Time passed slowly with Papi screwing screws and me replaying my screw-ups. Dinger's arrival time came and went. Papi had finished tightening screws and he was trying to make sense of the E-6B's tiny numbers by holding the computer up to the lantern. If Kiko Two didn't show up soon, I might never know why. I checked Papi's watch. Dinger was overdue by seven minutes.

The radio speaker crackled: "Kiko Lead, this is Two. How copy?"

I transmitted, "Kiko Two, you're five by." That was pilot lingo for "loud and clear."

"Three minutes out, northbound over the tracks. No joy."

I used Papi's walkie-talkie to tell the men operating the portable lights to turn them on. In response, I heard the generator motors starting down on the highway. The improvised runway lights turned on.

"Tally the lights," Dinger radioed. "Winds?"

"One-eight-zero at ten," I said. "There's a lip from the road down to the shoulder."

"Don't figure I'll use the shoulder," said Dinger, cocky for a guy making his fifth T-Bird landing on the equivalent of a balance beam with his eyes closed.

"Christmas tree," I radioed.

Dinger's navigation lights and rotating beacons lit up, and I spotted him low over the railroad tracks about three miles south. Watching Dinger fly the approach so soon after flying it myself was a curious experience. I could imagine what he was seeing in the cockpit and what he was thinking. He turned left onto final and lined up with the highway southbound, from my left to my right. He contacted the road surface between the touchdown zone mobile light trailers. Smooth. As I watched his landing from the side, I realized that he was braking harder than I had done. As far as I could tell, he kept his T-Bird on the highway surface throughout the landing roll. The executive summary was that Dinger had done a better job than me. The motorcycle follow-me vehicle led Dinger to the same place I had parked.

I left the picnic table and strode over to the T-Bird as the engine wound down. I climbed onto the left wing, and Dinger raised his canopy. His oxygen mask was hanging by one clip, and I could see a big smile on his face. His tail gunner's face was the same color as the Jolly Green Giant, however he was anything but jolly. As I got closer to the canopy rail, I could smell vomit. I focused my flashlight beam on the little back seater. It was obvious that he had been too slow grabbing his barf bag. What a mess. I helped him out of the plane and pointed toward a water hose beside the hangar: *"Agua."*

That was music to his ears. He climbed out of the plane and raced for the hose. He even left his machine gun and yellow hardhat in the cockpit. I crawled to the forward cockpit to help Dinger unstrap as a ground handler leaned a conventional ladder against the left canopy rail.

"I be doing fine, Bro'. That's how it goes down in the big leagues," Dinger said.

"Aren't you a master of ebonics."

"I like to season my speech with a little cultural diversity, yes." He slid his helmet into his helmet bag and passed it to me. "I couldn't see shit." I took his helmet with me when I crawled back to the wing and slid off it onto the ramp. Dinger used the aluminum ladder. He pointed toward his back seater being hosed down by a ground handler. "Pancho isn't cut out for this line of work," Dinger said. "He puked five minutes after takeoff, and I've been smelling that shit ever since." Dinger pointed at his boots. "Look at my legs." His knees were tuning forks. "The low-level was fun, but you can keep the landing part."

Ground handlers arrived to chain the nose gear and to prepare the T-Bird for towing into the hangar.

"Where *is* everybody?" Dinger asked.

"This is it. Nobody's packing heat here except for the Wallendas."

We stayed close to the radio in preparation for Hacksaw's arrival.

Dinger asked, "They got any beer around here?" He didn't wait for me to answer. He motioned to the handler driving the tow truck. "*Hey, Jefe,*" (Chief,) "*Cervezas.*" (Beers.)

It was always Happy Hour in Dinger Land. Two minutes later, Dinger and I were sucking down chilled Coronas. Our friend Hacksaw was long overdue. He could have been burning to death at that very moment while we chugged beers at a picnic table in the middle of the Chihuahuan Desert.

"Hack's going to have his hands full," Dinger said.

"Okay, girls, Kiko Three's up. Give me lights and say winds." Hacksaw's voice sounded awful.

"Out of the south at ten knots," I radioed. Next, I told Papi to instruct his crews positioned on the highway to turn on their portable lights. Trouble. The generator for the left touchdown zone portable light array wouldn't start. I told Papi to move a functioning runway end light to replace the inoperative approach end light. This shuffle was quickly taking on the features of a protracted goat-rope. I told Hacksaw to extend his downwind to give us time to replace the left touchdown zone light. The pickup truck towing the portable light array was still half a mile from where it needed to be when Hacksaw turned from base to final. The lights couldn't be in position for Hacksaw's landing in time, so I told Papi to tell the driver to get his truck and the portable light trailer off the highway.

"Hack you have only one approach-end light marker on the right side of the highway. You copy?"

"Ayfirm."

The driver pulled off onto the east shoulder of the provisional landing strip. I gestured to Papi to get the whole rig completely off the highway to prevent Hacksaw's left wing-tip from colliding with the pickup truck or trailer. Papi yelled into the walkie-talkie. The driver shouted back at him and executed a panicky three-hundred-sixty-degree turn.

"Hack, be ready to reject the landing," I said.

"Don't send me around, Stitch. I'm barely hanging on to this thing."

Hacksaw's wings dipped spastically as he tried to figure out the relationship between the lone threshold light and

Highway 45. I shouted for Papi to get the pickup off the highway. Papi screamed into his walkie-talkie. The driver of the pickup froze on the eastern edge of the highway, his headlights aimed south, away from Hacksaw's approaching T-Bird. Hacksaw landed hard.

"Hack, go around," I shouted on the radio. The truck driver did a donut on the highway. The T-Bird engine accelerated and the wheels slammed onto the highway a second time. Papi cringed as the plane closed on the pickup truck. The plane and the truck seemed to merge, and I waited for an explosion. The T-Bird leaped into the air, missing the pickup truck by a precious few feet. The roar of the jet made a believer out of the truck driver. He drove straight down the steep embankment from the highway shoulder into a ravine in a cloud of dust. I was surprised that neither the truck nor its trailer rolled over on the bank. The T-Bird turned left and climbed back toward downwind.

Hacksaw's voice was a parched whisper: "I'm leaving the gear down because I hit hard."

"Did you impact the road or the shoulder?" I asked.

"Fuck if I know."

"The truck's clear," I radioed. "You're clear to land."

"Roger."

I told Papi to telephone a doctor. Literally translated, I told Papi that Hacksaw was "insane." Papi knew what I meant. He limped to the office to place his call, leaving his walkie-talkie with Dinger, for all the good that was going to do. I was concerned that Hacksaw might have blown a tire during his touch-and-go. This dick dance was my fault. My arrogance and poor judgment had led to this moment.

Hacksaw's life was in the balance with everything stacked against him. I felt sick to my stomach.

I radioed, "Line up the single lights and fly that thing, Hack." My nerves were jangling. Dinger drained his beer and grabbed mine. Hacksaw was on glide path again at about a mile out, thirty seconds to go until his destiny. His wings were more stable this time. He slammed onto Highway 45 again, and his T-Bird bounced into the air at least five feet. He fought the T-Bird back down onto the asphalt surface. The plane's right main gear dropped onto the right shoulder. He overcorrected, so the left main went off onto the left shoulder. He got on the binders hard and skidded to a stop in the center of the highway. I could see dust clouds billowing on both sides of Highway 45.

Hacksaw radioed, "Not bad for an Aggie."

I told him to hold his position so I could go down to inspect his tires. I motioned for Dinger to take over the radio. I grabbed a flashlight and saddled up behind Papi on his motorbike, and Papi drove me down the access road onto the highway and to the T-Bird. I hopped off the bike and stooped under the T-Bird. In the beam of my flashlight, I could see cuts in both tires, but the pressure was holding. I gestured for Hacksaw to taxi in trail with the follow-me motorcycle. Outside the hangar, handlers chocked the plane. Hacksaw raised his canopy, shut down his engine, and removed his helmet. I hopped onto the left wing and slid forward on the intake toward the cockpit. I'd smelled more aromatic septic tanks. The back seater's face was blanched by terror. Hacksaw looked as bad as anyone can look and still be alive. He was dripping wet and flushed bright red. Dinger used the aluminum ladder to join me in helping Hacksaw down to the ground. He was so weak that he was wobbling to remain upright on the asphalt.

"I've got a doctor coming, Hack," I said.

Hacksaw's flight suit reeked of stale perspiration from two days of fever sweats, and his bowels hadn't functioned up to snuff, either.

"Sorry, Stitch. I'm a mess," he groaned.

"There's a hose by the hangar over there. Papi," I shouted. "*¿Tiene jamon?*" (Got any ham?)

Papi teetered toward us. "*¿Como, Señor?*" (What, Sir?)

Dinger interjected: "*Jabón.*" (Soap.) "*Jamon* is ham. Soap is *jabón.*"

Papi got a whiff of Hacksaw and knew right away that I wasn't in the market for pork.

Chapter 20

Treasure:

a yellow shuttlecock

OUR ROOMS SMELLED like hyena cages in a zoo, but uninterrupted sleep in dry high desert air did wonders for Dinger and me. Not for Hacksaw. A week's rest in the Savoy wouldn't have tamed his wicked mood. As compensation for his suffering, I offered to bring him breakfast in bed at noon of Day Five of our captivity, but he declined gruffly. He shared guidelines on where I could shove breakfast. I told him that Dinger and I had decided not to antagonize our captors. Hack said, "Just get us back to the States before these boneheads kill me."

Carlos had told us we'd stand down for a day while the T-Birds were being modified and while Carlos and his brain trust made the 800-mile journey to El Hoyo by truck. A young English-speaking doctor from Juárez examined Hacksaw and reckoned that food poisoning had brought the Aggie to his knees. I pleaded with him to take Hacksaw with him back to Juárez, adding that Dinger and I would accompany him to assist in any way possible. The doctor knew the lay of the land and he knew about Carlos. He wasn't about to risk spiriting the three of us back toward the border, but, as a parting favor, he removed the stitches from my head.

The dry El Hoyo air felt like a spa compared to Atl Ixtaca. Dinger and I scrubbed all our flight suits and hung them on the clothesline that doubled as an antenna frame. Some twenty El Hoyo grunts were indifferent to us lounging around in our Guatemalan underwear while our laundry dried. Even the armed men were as amicable as the Flying Wallendas, who were making themselves scarce in case Carlos arrived with the idea of flying them again. Papi instructed me on the rules of internment as I loafed at the picnic table in the shade of the hangar. He pointed eastward toward Highway 45.

"You no pass *carretera* (highway)."

"Okay."

"You pass *carretera*, it make many guns."

Dinger joined us and passed me a beer. "What's the old codger yapping about?"

"He said they'll shoot us if we cross the highway."

"Many guns," Papi said for emphasis.

This triggered more Dinger Spanish: "*Sí*. Many guns in El Hoyo. And an astronomically huge number of whack-jobs, too."

Papi, blissfully ignorant, nodded agreement. He pointed to the desert west of us. It looked uninhabited as far as the eye could see, maybe all the way to Baja California. "You no pass *carretera*, okay."

"He says it's okay to roam around in the desert out that

way," Dinger said, offering Papi a beer, which the old man refused.

"*Mucho trabajo,*" he said. (A lot of work.)

Dinger opened the beer for himself. "Work my ass."

Later that morning, I found Dinger bench testing six three-foot sections of oxygen lines he had removed from the three airplanes. They had been contaminated when Carlos capped all the oxygen bottles, so Dinger wasn't worried about purging the lines after his unapproved tinkering. The lines connecting oxygen bottles to cockpit oxygen regulators were identical except for the one from Hacksaw's system. Unlike the other five samples of tubing, Hacksaw's line included a suspicious segment four inches long.

"I mounted each section to an air accumulator bottle. The other five sections held a compressed air charge of four hundred psi for fifteen minutes," Dinger said. He held up Hacksaw's oxygen line: "But Hack's lost pressure at a linear rate. I submerged Hack's segment in my proprietary home-made solution to locate the leak, then put it under a micro-scope and discovered a calibrated orifice."

"So somebody wanted Hack's oxygen system to leak?"

"They sure did," Dinger said. "Someone didn't want Hack to get to Alcapulco."

———————

That afternoon a likeable new worker bee dropped by the picnic table that Dinger and I had appropriated as our officers club. The new guy was the only black man in the camp. Papi called him by a long name that had no chance of catching on with us gringos. His face was an uncanny replica of Richard Pryor's. He had never heard of Richard Pryor or *Silver Streak* or *Blazing Saddles*. I called him "R. P." from then on, and every time I did, he rewarded me with a big Richard Pryor smile. "Sweet," he said as he moved dust around with a broom and pretended to do other odd jobs in the shade beside the picnic table. R. P. pointed to the three African Millefiori-painted clay trading beads dangling from my neck on a leather thong. "Sweet."

"Morocco," I said. I didn't know whether that meant anything to him, because his world clearly was well contained inside the borders of Mexico. I removed one of three ornate tubular beads from the leather strip and gave it to R. P., and he thanked me as though I had given him the keys to a Ferrari. He threaded the single bead onto a piece of copper wire to make a necklace.

"Hermanos," he said. (Brothers.)

Dinger said, "Dude's got a man crush on you." R. P. hustled off toward the hangar. "He's looking for a gift to reciprocate for the gizmo you gave him." R. P. returned with a yellow shuttlecock in hand. I had no idea of where the rest of the badminton set was. I admired his gift and made appreciative noises. "For the man who has everything," Dinger said. "Now you've got two cocks." I told Dinger to get his own boyfriend.

R. P. and Papi drifted away to tend to mystery chores. Dinger and I stayed in the shade, frat boys drinking beer in our underwear, unable to do anything about our predicament.

Dinger said. "That gold we left at Atl Ixtaca, "you figure we'll go back and get it someday if these dildos ever let us out of here?"

"Oh, yeah."

———⚬———

Emerging from our dormitory, entering stage left into bright afternoon sunshine, Hacksaw appeared as naked as a possum and amazingly carefree for one in a state of undress. Formerly an endangered specimen, our Aggie was clean-shaven, and his short hair was still wet from an indoor shower. Being the only nude person in the compound, he caught the attention of El Hoyo ranch hands. One of Hacksaw's admirers was a little man resting in the hangar shade with a beat up guitar on his lap.

Hacksaw called out to him: "Hey, Guitar Man, you going to play that ax or is it just decoration?"

Guitar Man's interpretation was that Hacksaw was asking permission to play the guitar, so he jumped to his feet and extended his instrument to Hacksaw who waved him off and pointed to me.

"Go ahead, Stitch, show him how y'all do it down in Old San Antonio."

Guitar Man handed the guitar over to me. I twanged the strings, tuning a couple of strays with the confidence of a sound engineer. I strummed and launched into "*Where Have All the Flowers Gone?*" in C major. In only a couple of bars, I realized that this was the best I'd ever sounded. The acoustics outside of a make-do hangar in the middle of the Chihuahua desert were as magic as any studio in Austin or Nashville. I concluded my performance with a simple downward pass on the strings.

"That's some fine picking, Hoss," Hacksaw said.

Guitar Man offered me a wrinkled candy bar wrapper and Papi's ballpoint pen. The pen worked only intermittently on the backside of the candy wrapper, so the second autograph of my lifetime could have passed for Arabic. My new fan left us to bring a second guitar from his sleeping quarters. His face contorted emotionally as he sang a somber selection in A minor. He played slowly so I could keep up and fill in with a little riff here and there. He wailed melodramatically as laborers from the hangar gathered around to sing along. It may have been an overstatement to say that we were bonding.

At the conclusion of the sing-along, Hacksaw, still nude, said, "That'll bring a tear to the eye of a mighty tough man, Elvis." He laid his hand on Guitar Man's shoulder and said, "Pablo, music makes me thirsty. How about rustling me up a cold *Tecate*?"

"*Tecate*" was the key word. Guitar Man dashed off to the nearest refrigerator.

"These guys aren't your personal valets," I said. I was sensitive to the cultural implications of bossing our captors around.

"It's good for him," Hacksaw said. "Makes him feel part of something bigger than himself."

I abandoned my defense of egalitarianism and performed *Blowing in the Wind* in D major. Dinger sang along in a key in the vicinity of D major. Guitar Man came back with Hacksaw's beer.

"Nice job, Guitar Man." Hacksaw then explained to me, "I find that expressions of gratitude are never wasted."

I continued entertaining the workers at El Hoyo, amiable, generally homely characters with the attention spans of children. I wrapped up my set with another crowd-pleaser that sounded the same as the first two. A bushy-haired, bearded intruder appeared carrying a newfangled boom box that was blaring mariachi music.

Hacksaw said, "Hey, we got a hootenanny going on, Dingleberry. You want to tone that shit down?"

The radio enthusiast mistook Hacksaw's words for encouragement, so he moved even closer and favored us with a couple of solo dance steps. He uttered something in a deep, gravelly bass, and, when he did, we three gringos looked at one another in amazement. Except for the language, his voice was an exact duplicate of a syndicated disc jockey on Armed Forces Radio. We said his name almost in unison.

"Wolfman Jack."

"Hey, Dickbreath," Hacksaw said, "you ever heard of Wolfman Jack?"

"¿Como, senor?" (What?)

"Wolfman Jack. On the radio."

I gestured for Wolfman to sit at the picnic table beside me. He nodded when I pointed to the boom box radio, so I tuned the frequency to 1570 on the AM dial. I had listened to super-powered Mexican clear channel radio station 1570 as far away as Tampa, Sacramento, and Columbia, Missouri.

"This is Wolfman Jack coming at you from Del Rio, Texas on X.E.R.F. ... two-hundred, fifty thousand watts of power ... so get naked and lay your hands on your radio and squeeze them knobs."

"Wolfman Jack," I said, pointing at the boom box as the

disc jockey began to howl .

The face of our radio hobbyist was lit up. He was listening to himself. "Wolfmang Yack," he said.

Dinger said, "*Sí.*"

Wolfman latched onto Hacksaw, who weaned him off mariachi music and onto rock-and-roll broadcast by the border blaster station in Villa Acuña, across the Rio Grande from Del Rio. "Surfin' Safari" by the Beach Boys became Wolfman's new standard. The audience drifted off before I could do my not-to-be-missed rendition of "Proud Mary" in E major, and we had our privacy back.

Hacksaw said, "We need an escape plan."

Dinger said, "Maybe we can get to the highway and hitch-hike to Juárez. It's only a hundred miles or so down the road."

Hacksaw was skeptical: "You might show up in Juárez minus a liver, Hondo. Body parts are big business around here. You blink and the next thing you know, you're a lung short."

Dinger said, "Maybe we could steal a truck and drive to the border. A guy in Ybor City taught me how to hotwire an ignition."

"We'd never make it," I said. "Highway 45's the only way to Juárez. They'd call ahead, cut us off."

"How about those railroad tracks off to the east?" Hacksaw asked.

"They'll shoot us if we cross the road," Dinger said.

"We've got to do it together," I said. "Carlos will decapitate anybody who's left behind."

Hacksaw shouted out to Wolfman: "We need three more *Tecates* here."

"¿*Tres?*"

Dinger said, "*Sí.*"

———⊙———

Through the window in my room, I watched Carlos arrive with seven sidekicks in a three-truck convoy late that evening. He immediately went to the hangar to inspect Hacksaw's damaged T-Bird. Next he observed workers constructing wooden cradles in a pair of pickup truck beds positioned beneath each of T-Bird 2010's wingtip drop tanks. Almost an hour later, Carlos sauntered into my room with a beer in hand and told me to go with him to the hangar in the morning to test-jettison a set of wing tip drop tanks. I could read the tea leaves, so I wasn't astonished when he told me that I'd have to fly another sortie. I complained, but he told me to shut-up and do what I was told if I valued the lives of my two friends. He wasn't pretending to be a cop any longer. He laid three laser-printed black-and-white pictures on the bed beside me.

"Here's a snap from Arizona."

The picture of Trudie pushing Katrina in a stroller in front of our house in Glendale gave me the shivers. I felt foolish for volunteering my home address in Glendale the first night in Atl Ixtaca.

"When was this taken?" I asked. The answer would help me know whether Trudie had stayed in Glendale or driven as planned to Page, Arizona to meet the girls on Day Four.

Instead of answering me, Carlos showed me a picture of Hacksaw's wife Rena and said, "Here's a snap of Salt Lake

City. And Las Vegas." The last printout showed Dinger's wife Shelley and child in front of an Albertson's grocery store. "Do what I say and we don't touch them."

Objecting or arguing would have done no good. I pleaded for the safety of our wives and I asked him not to show the pictures to Hacksaw or Dinger. The arrogant prick didn't give me any assurances.

———— ((O)) ————

Carlos guarded details of my pending flight as if they were national secrets. As I strolled through the rear of the hangar on Morning Six, I noticed a line of six fabricated wooden drop tank cradles. Two others were mounted on the beds of two pickup trucks parked under the wingtip drop tanks of T-Bird 2010. Carlos was supervising the evacuation of fuel vapor from the left drop tank. When that was complete, the mechanics filled the tank with nitrogen.

"We've already stabilized the right drop tank," Carlos told me. "Put power on the airplane and drop the tanks when I tell you to."

I climbed into the cockpit from which I had a straight-line view of Carlos messing with a stopwatch as though he were conducting a time/motion study.

"Jettison ... now." He started the stopwatch.

I pressed the emergency bomb salvo switch on the front lower instrument panel near my left knee. The bomb shackles holding the drop tanks snapped open, and the drop tanks fell about six inches onto their respective wooden cradles. It was less impactful than dropping barbells on a mat. On Carlos's hand signal, drivers in both pickups creeped away from the airplane and parked off to his right. I removed power from the airplane, climbed out of the cockpit, and sidled up to Carlos. Workers had begun cutting a five-foot-long access plug out of the top of the first tank. One worker oiled the cut line, and the other operated a low-speed saw.

"You're not needed anymore," Carlos dismissed me.

I returned to our dormitory and brushed my teeth with baking soda at the miniature sink in my room with a cast-off toothbrush that no one in the States would let within a brush handle's length of his mouth. I replaced the tooth-brush on a wooden shelf where bacteria thrived. I had be-come orally slipshod. I peered through my bedroom window to watch welders heliarc ribs, face plates, and fasteners in-side the opening in the first drop tank. Hacksaw and Dinger paid me a visit and gestured for me to follow them to a spot overlooking the compound. Guatemalan underwear was the uniform of the day.

"Carlos is making me fly another mission."

Hacksaw predicted more flights based on the num-ber of wooden cradles in the hangar, and I didn't doubt his conclusion.

"Don't move a wheel for that son-of-a-bitch," Dinger said.

"I have to, Dinger. If I don't, he'll mess with you two." I didn't mention the jeopardy our wives were in. "We're stuck and there's nothing we can do about it."

The sunset on our sixth day in Mexico was a bold pallet of red and gold. According to our tattered original plan, we three, along with our wives and children, should have been enjoying vacations together on a sixty-foot houseboat on Lake Powell. Instead of celebrating our new wealth, however, we remained prisoners of a drug trafficker on the Mexican frontier while our wives presumably worried about whether we were alive. Tom Sawyer could have concocted a better cover story than the yarn we had left for our wives: "We're fishing in New Mexico, parts unknown." Our cover stories varied depending on the party asking for our whereabouts. Everest Aviation, the CIA, and the Colombian Air Force knew our real itinerary. When I hadn't called from El Salvador to check in with the Colombian liaison officer by the end of Day One, I presumed that the Colombians would have started looking for their three airplanes. I also assumed that Everest had informed our wives that we were missing. I hoped that Trudie and the girls had gone to Lake Powell without contacting the Air Force. Hacksaw was on leave until Day Ten, so, if we could resolve things by then, the Air Force might never know about our unapproved boondoggle.

Hacksaw asked me at what point we'd go from missing to assumed dead? How would I know? I imagined the mindset of each party involved. Our wives might have canceled Lake Powell reservations, stayed home, and might be burning up telephones lines between Phoenix, Salt Lake, and Las Vegas. They might have requested a police search in New Mexico to legitimize our fishing story, although that alibi was stinking up the joint now that we were overdue. The police might pressure our wives for the truth, making our wives as mad at us as everyone else. Mexican authorities might be looking for three smoking holes based on our IFR flight plan. Thor Olsen, angered by my failure to make the $4,000 blackmail payment, might interfere at any time. Bryan Presley was probably reading insurance policy fine print and floating a fresh resume. Mr. Bruno would be grumbling, "I told you so." I could only hope that Jim Conti would come through with a CIA cover letter to protect us from the wrath of the Air Force.

Carlos got me alone in an office and told me where, when, and why I was scheduled to fly the next night so I could start planning the flight. At one point, while Carlos and I stood side-by-side looking out of an office window, I spotted a flatbed truck hauling away the eight drop tank cradles. I knew their destination now: Texas.

———•«◉»•———

During a morning meander through the hangar on Day Seven, I noticed that modified drop tanks had been reinstalled on my jet. Drop tanks had been removed from the other two T-Birds without my help, so I figured that Carlos had added a T-33 maintenance guru to his private air force staff at El Hoyo. Cutters and welders were installing access doors in the remaining drop tanks. It was obvious that his latest promise to release us was as bogus as previous ones.

Hacksaw and I were loitering beside the picnic table when a pitiable creature brought us lunch. Every square inch of his exposed skin was covered with thick keloid scars. His face wasn't human. His fingers and thumbs were so malformed by connecting webs of scar tissue that he could hold only a single bottle of beer at a time as he packed *Dos Equis* bottles into a cardboard box containing ice. His hair, eyebrows, nose, and ears had been burned away. His eyes darted around beneath a mass of scars resembling molten wax. I felt special compassion for him because, if I had been trapped in my burning airplane in the Sierras for a few seconds longer, I might have passed for his twin brother.

He got a glimpse of my scarred hands when I reached for a beer. He cupped my hands in his and studied the smooth grafts. He examined my face in wonder. We were two aliens planted in separate places on Earth among millions of normal human beings and, against staggering odds, we had found one another. He made a moaning sound, threw his arms around me, and squeezed me as if to keep from slipping away. I self-consciously halfway hugged him in return. His exterior was reptilian, but I sensed that his heart was filled with the divine. I was moved to tears because I understood the suffering he had endured. I couldn't imagine his infinite loneliness. I barely could fathom my own. Carlos appeared on the scene and stopped in his tracks to absorb the sight. Wax Man released me, as if suddenly embarrassed. He backed away, his right arm trailing after him to sustain the connection.

Hacksaw said, "Stitch is playing nice with his losers." He may have intended it as a throwaway smart-aleck comment, but it stung me. I expected better from Hacksaw.

After lunch, a small dump truck full of sawdust rolled into the compound. The driver parked the truck on the downwind perimeter of the complex. Worker bees removed a heavy tarpaulin cover and began blowing sawdust off the truck with gas-powered leaf blowers. The fine particles mushroomed in clouds that billowed away from the compound on the wind. The removal of mounds of wood particles in broad daylight exposed scores of compacted cocaine packed in plastic bags. The bags had been reinforced by duct tape. Dinger, Hacksaw, and I watched the process from my room. Dinger challenged us to figure out the street value of two T-33 wingtip drop tanks filled with compressed cocaine, assuming street value of a kilo of cocaine in New York City at $25,000. By my reckoning, a T-33 could carry a load of coke worth $40 million, a sum so high that I checked my computations for decimal errors.

Hacksaw announced, "Thirty-six million."

Dinger took the cake: "Forty-two million. Did you forget to put three hundred pounds of coke in the place of machine guns?"

It was no longer a mystery how Carlos could afford his small army of mercenaries, mechanics, pickup trucks, fuel trucks, and a start cart. The cost of ground support equipment was chump change compared to his millions in revenue. The chances of Carlos being a cop, a clean cop anyway, were nil.

Dinger said, "We've got to escape even if we buy the farm trying."

———— ⚙ ————

Approaching midnight of our seventh day in captivity, I pre-flighted my ebony T-Bird, formerly Number 2010. I slapped my gloved hand against each wingtip drop tank; cocaine made a different sound than jet fuel, a trivial fact that I hoped never to note again. Dinger and Hacksaw weren't on the hook to fly, so they were helping themselves to bottles of *Dos Equis*. They persuaded Papi to drink a beer, too, and the two mischief-makers slouched around the picnic table watching the old man wire up his homemade antenna to the clothesline. R. P. met me at the bottom of the boarding ladder and handed me an official patch of his favorite football club, *Club Deportivo Guadalajara S.A. de C.V.* I duct-taped the patch to my blacked-out helmet visor housing, which pleased R. P. no end. Dinger and Hacksaw razzed me. "It's true love, Cromwell," Hacksaw called out.

I told R. P. thanks for the third time so he'd stop pestering me. Midnight had come and gone, so it was technically the start of Day Eight when I strapped into the cockpit and pulled my helmet over my skullcap. R. P. and Wolfman drove off in pickup trucks to tow portable light trailers toward Highway 45. Dinger and Hacksaw were still chirping at my expense. I supposed that Stockholm Syndrome was at work at El Hoyo because there I was hauling $40 million of cocaine for a drug lord while my friends horsed around as though we were charter members of the cartel. I was too occupied flying the sortie to consider how bizarre my situation was at the time. I strapped in and started the engine. I could tell I was over maximum gross weight because, after an easy taxi downhill on the service road to Highway 45, I had to cob the power to get up onto the highway. My maximum internal fuel load wasn't quite enough to fly low-level round-trip between El Hoyo and Texas. The drop tanks carried 3,600 pounds of cocaine, and Carlos's boys had even strapped down sixteen kilos of cocaine in the aft seat. The back seat alone was worth about $400,000. I refused to dwell on ethical questions such as how many people would die of overdoses as a consequence of the crap I was carrying. I was doing what I had to do to protect my family and get home alive. I lowered my canopy and waited for the clock to show 0123 local, my scheduled takeoff time. I strained to see into the void ahead of me. I turned off the dimmest taxi light in aviation, and my forward visibility actually improved. R. P. and Wolfman turned on the portable lights. They hadn't aligned the lenses downward enough to prevent my night vision from being cauterized by a zillion lumens of light.

Hacksaw's voice transmitted on short count frequency: "Big Dog, you're cleared to roll."

Papi's radio call was of more use: *"Wince two-sayce-zero at ten. No prahlem."*

I turned on the taxi light, pushed up the throttle, and released the brakes. I couldn't see beyond forty feet ahead in the dim taxi light beam. I squinted to make out the white-hashed centerline markings disappearing under my nose. As I accelerated past one hundred mph, a blur and two iridescent eyes lurched at me out of the pitch-black night. I yanked back on the stick to rotate the nose upwards, and, as improbable as it seemed, the nose gear missed the animal. If the T-Bird had weighed just five hundred pounds more, I would have transformed Wiley Coyote into an oil slick on Highway 45. After takeoff, I leveled off about 300 hundred feet above the desert, raised the gear and flaps, and steered on a magnetic heading of zero-seven-one degrees in the direction of Texas. As my night vision improved, I descended to a hundred feet above the terrain. I turned off my exterior lights and rotating beacons and flew at 345 mph. The internal wing fuel tanks were feeding as designed. All I had to do to avoid radar detection was fly low without smacking into the ground for 110 nautical miles. I planned to cross the Rio Grande a little northwest of Candelaria, Texas, and land on U.S. Highway 90 near Ryan, Texas, population zero. I crossed the first ridgeline at a hundred feet above the ground and about 7,000 feet above sea level, rolling inverted over the top so I could pull down to the desert floor after clearing the saddleback.

The section of two-lane highway I planned to land on was directly beneath the middle of the Valentine Military Operating Area (MOA). I hoped that the Air Force, Army, Navy, Border Patrol, Drug Enforcement Administration (DEA), Bureau of Alcohol, Tobacco, Firearms and Explosives (ATF), Texas Public Safety, Presidio County Sheriff, and Texas Rangers all over West Texas were sound asleep. I crossed the border nineteen minutes after takeoff. I faded my heading a little to the right towards the town lights of Marfa. A couple of minutes later, I started to slow down so I could lower flaps and gear. I transmitted on short count: "Lights."

Sure enough, off to my left eleven o'clock, four portable light arrays illuminated. I set up for a left base-to-final turn at a speed of 160 mph. The two-lane highway and the paved shoulders on each side gave me a primitive sixty-foot-wide runway. I lined up to land northwesterly on a heading of three-two-zero. I stabilized on final at 125 mph with a sink rate of 600 feet a minute. I touched down abeam the first set of lights and rolled out toward the other set about three thousand feet down the highway. I stopped just past the second set of lights and turned off my landing light. I set the parking brake, raised the flaps to takeoff setting, and raised the canopy. I had 80 gallons of fuel remaining. A ground handler in front of the aircraft nose gave me the chocks-in signal. Two pickup trucks drove from an unpaved access road onto the highway in front of me. Each was carrying a drop tank cradle, which I recognized as those slapped together in the hangar at El Hoyo. One truck backed under the left wingtip drop tank. The truck under the right wing was too high for the cradle to fit under the drop tank, so four men dressed in black hopped into the back of the truck to lower it to clear the drop tank. When the cradles were aligned beneath their respective drop tanks, the handler signaled for me to push the emergency bomb salvo switch. The plane jerked up when the bomb shackles released the 3,600 pounds of cocaine. Each pickup truck was instantly 1,800 pounds heavier, so both drop tanks easily cleared the wingtips.

The cocaine-laden tip tanks disappeared behind me and two fuel trucks approached the aircraft from my ten and two o'clock positions. The fuelers from each truck drove rebar rods into the desert to ground the trucks and the aircraft electrically. They extended their hoses to reach the two fuel filler caps on each wing. By manipulating a hand-held mirror, I could observe a black-clad figure offloading kilo packages of cocaine from the seat behind me. He passed them to an assistant on the right wing. The assistant passed them on to another handler on the ground in front of the right wing.

Before the internal tanks were full, I spotted red and white flashers on fast-approaching vehicles closing on us from the northwest about three miles up U. S. Highway 90. I panicked and gave the emergency abort signal to a fueler who quickly shut down refueling, secured gas caps, and stowed hoses. Meanwhile, the lead ground handler had seen my abort gesture and he signaled that I was cleared to close the canopy. The fuel trucks pulled away onto a dusty parallel service road. I confirmed the brakes were set while he removed chocks and verified my path was clear of obstacles. I was about thirty gallons short of a my planned fuel load, but I had enough to barely get back to El Hoyo if I didn't fart around with any wasteful detours.

I was itching to shove the power up to get out of there before trouble arrived. I fully intended to hug the dirt tighter than maple syrup on a pancake all the way to El Hoyo. I was thirty-five nautical miles from the border, so, at five miles a minute, I could cross over into Mexico in seven minutes. The flashing lights were getting closer. The handler gave me an unceremonious salute and hopped into a pickup truck that accelerated away on a sandy road leading into the desert.

Leaving my exterior lights and rotating beacons extinguished, I poured the coal to the T-Bird engine and turned on the taxi light so I could keep the beast on the paved surface. The gross weight was below 11,000 pounds without wingtip drop tanks, so the jet accelerated well and jumped into the air. The T-Bird without wingtip drop tanks was agile and a delight to fly. The oncoming flashing lights were closing from a mile away. I banked left to a heading of two-five-zero degrees and raised gear and flaps. I never got higher than a hundred feet off the ground all the way to the railroad tracks east of El Hoyo. Wide runways had become an unnecessary luxury so, despite a five-knot crosswind, my landing on Highway 45 was uneventful. It was a good thing because I didn't have enough fuel left to dick around with a second approach.

Dinger and Hacksaw had been well-oiled even before my takeoff, so they were orbital by the time I taxied in. Dinger shot a victory arch over my plane with a pressure washer. Hacksaw set off strings of firecrackers tied to Papi's clothesline antenna Cinco de Mayo style. I climbed out of the jet and bumped into Carlos, who was elated. I told him about the emergency flashers on U.S. 90 coming toward the Ryan drop.

"They were ours," he said. "We put roadblocks up on Ninety at both ends."

R. P., Wolfman, and Carlos's other henchmen were in a festive frame of mind for three o'clock in the morning. Discarded beer bottles and cans surrounded the picnic table. Wolfman turned up his ghetto-blaster volume tuned in to the real Wolfman Jack. In the interest of playing nice, I opened a cold bottle of *Dos Equis* and shot darts with R. P. and two other rascals in matching red *Club Deportivo Guadalajara* tee shirts. In my wildest dreams, I had never foreseen celebrating with a crew of simple-minded drug smugglers. Unbelievable. The Mexicans were as irresponsible as children, not that we gringos were much better. The Mexicans had twisted senses of humor, too. One of them fired a dart into the back of a colleague's head and laughed until he cried. After a slow start, I drank until five a.m., forgiving myself for fraternizing with the enemy because, although I hadn't disclosed my plan to Dinger and Hacksaw, I knew how we were going to escape to America.

Chapter 21

Treasure:
a Jeppesen diagram of the municipal
airport near Deming, New Mexico

WHEN I AWOKE hungover late in the morning of Day Eight, one look out my window answered the question of whether I'd have to fly for the cartel again. What to my wondering eyes did appear but a long-bed pickup carrying the wingtip drop tanks I had jettisoned the previous night. I watched Carlos's worker bees offload the empty, dented aluminum drop tanks and their wooden cradles from the truck. I noticed that the modified drop tanks from Dinger's jet had already been suspended on the bomb shackles of Aircraft 2010. No doubt, I was going to fly again that night. The identical dump truck from the day before rumbled up from Highway 45 and parked on the downwind side of the compound. R. P., Wolfman, and other leaf-blowers cut loose and blew the layer of sawdust away on the wind, revealing another colossal cargo of cocaine in kilo bags. In a matter of minutes, the dump truck backed up to the hangar, and R. P.,

Wolfman, and their mates started packing the bags into the newly installed drop tanks on Aircraft 2010. After the dump truck left the mining complex, I moseyed out to the hangar where Carlos was supervising dent removal from the first night's drop tanks.

"What's that God-awful smell?" I asked him.

"Our guys in Texas sprayed the tanks with air freshener and pepper spray to neutralize the drug dogs at the border. We're also adding fender strips to the cradles so the drop tanks don't get beat up."

"I guess I'm flying tonight."

"Yep. Same place, but I want you to ingress on the south side of Candelaria."

"Your light crews torched my night vision last night," I said. "Can you put Dinger and Hacksaw on the portable light crew so they can prevent that?" I didn't have much faith that he'd agree to do it.

Carlos jutted out his chin and gazed at me for a couple of seconds. "Sure," he said. I hid my delight. If my plan worked, my next midnight flight really was going to be my last.

———— ◉ ————

A hot, dry southwesterly breeze whispered over the Chihuahuan Desert. Perspiration evaporated fast in this parched land. We gringos made an absurd spectacle strolling in our Guatemalan underwear and black flying boots in the middle of a moonscape. Black Nomex flight suits were solar panels in the sun. Plagiarizing Lawrence of Arabia's fashion sense, I wore a frayed towel on my head as a *keffiyeh*. Security was lax because the idea of us going anywhere dressed as three Fruit-of-the-Loom mannequins was absurd. Our captors let us roam anywhere in the domain west of Highway 45. We loitered 200 meters upslope from the open door of the hangar with a view of Carlos strutting around in his aviator glasses.

"Dickhead," Hacksaw murmured. He turned his sarcasm on me, "No offense, Lawrence. I forgot you and Carlos were bosom buddies." Hacksaw's grumbling was proof positive that he had recovered from his bout of food poisoning. "You going out again tonight?"

"Ayfirm. And I'm not coming back." That got their attention.

"Do you know what they'll do to me and Dinger when you don't come back?"

"You guys are going with me." I explained my escape plan starting with the part about them operating the portable lights down on Highway 45 beside R. P. and Wolfman. We planned our escape not with charts and compass but by wandering around the desert in our whitey-tighties.

Carlos sat beside me at lunch in the primitive chow hall. He was still upbeat about how well the operation had gone the previous night. I guessed that he had gained favor in the eyes of his bosses. "I got the idea from the Berlin Airlift," he said. Carlos: smuggler and historian. It was best to appear resigned to serving at Carlos's pleasure for the duration. The safety of my family depended on it. I also had to pretend that I believed Carlos would release me when he was through with me. That meant I had to grovel and ask questions about how long I had to fly loads of cocaine into Texas. A guy planning an escape wouldn't ask such a question, would he? Carlos answered my question, "Until I say so."

I asked him whether he ever thought about the people who died using cocaine.

"No. And neither should you. Users are losers. Americans are soft and stupid. All they care about is leisure, entertainment, feeling good. They're addicted to sugar and coke and fun. They wring their hands about the opioid epidemic. It's an IQ test, and the stupid ones die. I'm just satisfying demand. It's making me rich." He pointed toward the laborers seated around the room. "I could hire five thousand of these guys at a hundred bucks a month."

I didn't know what to make of Carlos. Although I hadn't seen him perform a single violent act, I surely wouldn't nominate him for citizen of the year. I recalled how detached he was showing me photos of headless people. He unexpectedly mentioned that he was raising his kids Catholic. I hadn't imagined him married or religious. I asked him whether he was a U.S. citizen. "You're not my biographer," he said, "and we're not fraternity brothers. The less you know about me, the better off you are."

During the afternoon, between napping and rehearsing my escape plan, I daydreamed about Trudie and Katrina. If I could get back to the States by the morning of the tenth day, I'd move Trudie to a safe place away from Carlos's reach. I'd face up to Thor Olsen at the squadron. I'd cling to the straight and narrow as if this nightmare had never happened. Everest might fire me. I might not even get paid for this debacle. I didn't care anymore. I'd be satisfied to get back to America and Trudie safe and sound.

My extensive military education trained me to delegate distasteful duties such as meeting Carlos's Chihuahua mail run courier to get printouts of weather forecasts. I deputized R. P. for this task while I enjoyed a morning beer with my pals at the picnic table.

"Stitch, here comes your attaché with the launch codes," Hacksaw said.

R. P. was all business as he scurried up the slope toward us. Hacksaw and Dinger were slouched in their favorite folding chairs in the shade of the hangar. I was reclined on the picnic tabletop in my underwear. R. P. handed me a Manila folder, his eyes bugging out the way Richard Pryor's eyes used to bug out when he didn't know what was going to happen next.

"R. P., *Tecate.*" Dinger tossed his empty can to my eager assistant who trotted off to the main office refrigerator. "I'll teach these fungos to recycle before we're done here," Dinger said.

It would have been easy to dismiss the El Hoyo worker bees as shiftless halfwits, but they were a cut above the thugs back in Atl Ixtaca. I was genuinely fond of the El Hoyo gang. They just happened to be running vast quantities of cocaine because it paid better than other jobs they could find. Mix the variables of life a bit, and I could have been R. P. Although R. P. had laudable qualities, he was becoming as pesky as a mosquito flitting around me all day. He made a big deal out of giving me a water-spotted photograph of himself in his beloved red *Club Deportivo Guadalajara* tee shirt. Just to pull my chain, Hacksaw taped R. P.'s picture to the instrument panel of T-Bird number 2010 the way they did in corny World War II movies. The gesture transported R. P. into ecstasy. He displayed his African Millefiori-painted clay bead on the outside of his shirt as a reminder of our intimate connection. I sat upright on the bench facing west to read the weather reports in R. P.'s folder. R. P. returned with Dinger's beer, then perched over my shoulder and read along with me, trying to astound everyone with his intellect by reading "Laredo" and "Presidio" aloud. He pretended to comprehend the page with the flying schedule on it. Reports from a spy on the ground near Ryan gave Carlos the confidence to send me on the same profile I had used on the previous night. He had set the takeoff time for my second flight at 1:40 a.m. local Chihuahua Time. Ryan was in a time zone an hour later than El Hoyo, so the schedule had me landing at El Hoyo before my takeoff from Texas. R. P. observed the exotic contradiction and fussed about it in Spanish. R. P. had no grasp of the concept of time zones, so Dinger was delighted to make trouble. Hacksaw ordered a beer from him, somethings R. P. *did* understand.

"*Dos,*" he said. "Your hero needs one, too."

"*Dos,*" R. P. parroted before scampering away.

Hack told me, "Boy, do you suffer fools?"

I bagged a siesta in the afternoon and another after dinner, so I was stone sober when the other two Americanos and I suited up in black in preparation for our nocturnal trickeration. Before leaving my bedroom at midnight, I left two gifts in the drawer of my bedside table. I scribbled "R. P."

on a torn-off piece of aeronautical chart that I had used to wrap around the two remaining African Millefiori-painted clay trading beads. I wrote "Papi" on another piece of chart paper and folded it around the wooden crucifix. I was re-gifting before re-gifting became fashionable. As I headed to the ramp for my mission, I encountered Wax Man in the hallway. His eyes, always wet from eye drops he used for relief, bored into mine from behind his mask of keloid scars. We paused for only a moment face to face. Wax Man was a monument to his lost wife and five children taken by the fire that had disfigured him. He thumped his malformed right hand against his heart and then pointed at me. I wondered whether he somehow knew that we were crossing paths for the last time.

"*Quiero seguirte y trabajar para ti.*" (I want to follow you and work for you.)

"*Lo siento, pero no es possible,*" I apologized.

I had no gift for him; what could I give a man who had nothing? I moved away before he could see tears in *my* eyes. I felt ashamed for any time I had pitied myself. I had suffered nothing compared to Wax Man. I worried that he might not be the only person at El Hoyo to intuit my escape plan.

———◦《◯》◦———

I cranked the engine on T-Bird 2010 at 1:25 a.m. near the beginning of Day Nine. The tailpipe temperature gauge peaked near 900 degrees Centigrade, higher than I had ever seen it before, including the eye-opening DM Blow Torch Incident. I normally would have shut the engine down, but not on this flight. I was going to fly that T-Bird to Gringo Land even if it left a meteor tail of molten metal across the night sky and burned half the fuselage off getting there. I was jumpy taxiing down the slope toward the junction of the mine service road and Highway 45. A lot of moving parts had to sync up for my plan to work. For example, Dinger and Hacksaw had to knock R. P. and Wolfman unconscious down at the portable light trailers.

Dinger had never coldcocked anyone before by his own admission. Hacksaw hadn't either, but he had opinions on everything: "Estimate how hard you have to hit him to knock him out and double it." Off to the right, ten feet below my cockpit perch, Dinger and Hacksaw were directing R. P. and Wolfman to aim the portable bank of lights away from my field of view and toward the mining complex. R. P. grinned at me and pointed with pride to the football logo on his tee shirt. He waved at me the way a kid insists on his mother's attention. I felt foolish doing it, but I waved back.

I lined up for takeoff with my nose wheel on the centerline of Highway 45 pointing into the light wind out of the south from Chihuahua and pushed on the toe brakes hard. I completed the before takeoff checklist and waited nervously, unable to actually see the drama unfolding on the ground beneath the airplane. Violence was in the air. So was doubt: what if Dinger and Hacksaw failed to overpower R. P. or Wolfman? That would screw up the works royally. I couldn't fly to America without my two pals. Only by straining forward and twisting to my right, could I catch sight of the mining complex, which the portable lights were illuminating as bright as a manger scene. Blinding Carlos,

Papi, and the rest of the El Hoyo Militia was an important part of the plan. I felt the plane shudder when Dinger and Hacksaw each clambered onto a wing and rushed toward the rear seat. I couldn't see behind me, so I had to assume that they were tossing bags of cocaine out of the rear seat and onto the ground behind the flaps as planned. I peered into the darkness ahead of me down Highway 45. My right hand trembled on the stick grip. The airframe stopped wobbling, so I figured Hacksaw had settled on a cushion of cocaine in the rear seat with Dinger plopped on his lap. It had taken an argument and a coin toss to settle on that cozy arrangement. They planned to skip strapping in to expedite our departure by flying *au naturel* — no seat belts, no helmets, no parachute, no cushions, no microphones, no earphones, no nothing except, in Dinger's words, their "balls, dicks, and a one-way ticket to America."

The canopy motor whined as the canopy jerked downward on the jackscrew a couple of inches. That was my signal from Dinger that their bodies were clear of the canopy rail and I could lower the canopy all the way down without amputating their arms. I locked the canopy closed and then advanced the throttle to takeoff power. I turned on the taxi light and was about to release the brakes when a figure hopped into the middle of Highway 45 in front of me. His arms and ankles were bound by a rope Joan of Arc style. Whoever had smacked him had hit him hard enough to make him bleed, but not hard enough to keep him in Dreamland. The taxi light revealed R. P.'s bulging eyes, his confusion, and his betrayal. He bounced around in the glare of the taxi light as if he were in a potato sack race without a potato sack.

Blood splatters clung to the left side of his face. An African Millefiori-painted clay bead flailed around his head. I half expected Gene Wilder to jog across Highway 45. R. P. assumed a protestor flop onto the ground a few feet in front of my nose wheel. I shoved the throttle another inch toward the firewall and released the left brake. The T-Bird lurched to the right and rolled forward. A few feet later, I reversed the braking and brought the nose back onto the highway centerline. Running over R. P. would have made the plane bump upward the same as a car crushing an armadillo. It would have slowed acceleration. That didn't happen. I hadn't flattened R. P. into a pancake, but I may have torched his eyebrows as the jet roared over his body. I wondered how a few bucks a month could motivate R. P. to lay down in the path of a jet. I didn't take him for an Oxford Man, but surely he was smarter than that. Loyalty came cheap in Mexico. I squinted to see the centerline in the darkness. I pulled the stick back at rotate speed, and the T-Bird lifted into the air.

In a left hand turn toward the north, I raised the gear and flaps and climbed to four hundred feet above the ground, accelerating toward 400 mph indicated. The engine was running hot. My hands were still trembling. I tried to see what was going on in the light-drenched compound. Somewhere below in the darkness out of my sight, R. P. was probably recovering from being tumbled by jet exhaust across Highway 45. I spotted Papi beside the radio antenna, but I couldn't identify any of the other figures staring up into the night sky. I reached down to turn off my position lights and rotating beacons and realized that I had never turned them on. I was carrying 3,600 pounds of cocaine in my drop tanks and 400 pounds of pilots crammed two-high into the back seat with my lights blacked out because there was no other traffic to hit in this remote part of Mexican airspace.

I heard Papi's voice on the radio, *"Steech, thahs no* the direction to *Tejas."*

No shit, Sherlock. I wasn't heading for Texas. I was bound for New Mexico. I said, *"Adios, Papi."*

When my eyes had accommodated to the darkness, I descended to a couple hundred feet over the desert. I flew a course of 325 degrees. The distance from El Hoyo to Deming was 148 nautical miles. I flew over a lake called Laguna Santa Maria, a looking glass in the moonlight. I resisted the temptation to descend to fifty feet for fear of terrifying my *incommunicado* back seaters. Skimming just above the mirror surface of the water, I thought of Wolfman, Wax Man, and R. P. — three unpretentious souls trapped in a mind-numbing existence. I remembered Weird Carlos, too. I wasn't going to miss the ominous kingpin of the El Hoyo Mafia and Drug Transportation Company. I laughed in my oxygen mask to think of his predictable tantrum over losing $40 million of white powder.

Approaching the U.S. border, I tuned in the Columbus VORTAC Channel 111.2 and flew five miles east of the station. Then I steered directly for the Deming VORTAC Channel 108.6, 27 miles away. Past the Florida Mountains, I set up for a left base to land on Deming's Runway 26, which was 4,314 feet above sea level. I tuned the VHF radio to frequency 122.8 and clicked the mic button seven times to turn on the runway and approach lights. The Deming Airport lit up as bright as the Vegas Strip. The engine overheat warning light down by my right knee illuminated and glowed amber. The tailpipe temperature gauge had climbed through the 720-degree Centigrade maximum limit. A mile on short final, the red fire warning light started blinking. With twenty seconds remaining until touchdown, all I could think about was getting the jet on the ground before the wings burned off.

———◦(◦)◦———

A T-Bird could warn a pilot of a fire, but provided no way to extinguish it. No light burned brighter than a fire light in the cockpit of a pilot who couldn't do anything about it. Dinger and Hacksaw could see the warning lights, too, and all they could do was pray that I'd get it right this time. I landed and taxied double-time to the fixed base operator's ramp with the warning lights still glowing. The tailpipe temperature gauge had stabilized over 900 degrees Centigrade. I spotted a portable fire extinguisher and taxied toward it, raising the canopy as I parked the jet into the wind beside the fire bottle. I flipped the fuel switches off, the main fuel shut-off valve switch on, and retarded the throttle full aft. The engine wound down. I set the parking brake and released my harness and lap belt. I evacuated the front seat in record time, brushing past Dinger, who had already leaped out of the rear seat so Hacksaw could egress after him. I shouted, "Fire bottle."

The pre-dawn ramp was silent except for the popping of overheated engine parts. I sprinted for the nearest fire bottle.

Dinger pushed a second extinguisher bottle toward the left side intake. I discharged foam into the right engine intake. I moved aft under the wing toward the tail pipe and squeezed the trigger again. The exhaust stack popped and sizzled as foam hit the superheated metal. Hacksaw pulled a third portable fire bottle to the smoldering T-Bird. When I was satisfied that the jet and its $40 million cargo wouldn't go up in flames, I stopped spraying and joined Dinger and Hacksaw upwind of the T-Bird. "We're in America," Hacksaw shouted. He man-hugged me as if I'd scored a touchdown. We were free. I could stop obsessively counting days in captivity at nine, just as I had stopped counting my days in hospital at 777. We walked carefully in the darkness to the Turner FBO building. I peered into the shadowy interior through locked glass doors. Hacksaw put a boot through the glass for entry as though we owned the joint. I turned on the overhead fluorescent lights. From my left flight suit chest pocket, I pulled three pictures — Shelley. Rena. Trudie. I pressed them flat on the customer counter.

"I didn't want you to see these until we could get the girls to safety." Now they understood Carlos's leverage over me. We commandeered phones in separate cubicles and punched discrete phone lines to call our wives. We outdid one another trying to sound calm while warning that our wives' lives were in danger. Trudie answered my call on the second ring.

"Stitch? Daniel?"

"Are you alone?"

"Of course I'm alone. I was worried that you might have gone down."

"I couldn't call. I was kidnapped."

"Where are you?"

"Back in the States. Listen, wake Katrina and get out of there right now. Get a taxi to Luke and check into the BOQ. Stay there until I join you."

Trudie told me there was no need because two DEA agents were guarding the house.

"Are you sure they're DEA agents?"

"Sure I'm sure. They gave me a number for you to call."

"Don't let Katrina out of your sight. I'll call right back."

The number Trudie gave me connected me to the Duty Officer at the El Paso office of the DEA. He assured me that Trudie had been under protective watch for eight days. I wondered how the DEA had known to protect Trudie from the start. The DO told me to sit tight at the Deming airport for a couple of hours until DEA agents arrived from Las Cruces to impound the aircraft. As soon as I hung up, I relayed the information to Dinger and Hacksaw. I called Trudie again to tell her that she didn't have to leave the house after all.

She said, "Major Olsen's been trying to reach you. Where were you?" I told her. "You had no business messing around in Mexico in the first place."

"We're okay now. I'll be coming home as soon as the Feds question us."

I telephoned Jim Conti and told him about being detained in Mexico and escaping to Deming. He wanted an accounting of the three airplanes. I had an eerie feeling that he knew about El Hoyo and only the Deming piece was news. I told him that my Air Force boss would sauté my liver when he found out about my moonlighting, and I reminded him that I needed a CIA letter for protection. Jim faxed exactly what I was looking for twenty minutes later. It was addressed to Major Robert Olsen, and it said that I was "vital to the success of *Operation Twisted Piccolo*" and "confidentiality was essential in the national interest." I called Jim back to confirm receipt. He told me that representatives from Colombia and the CIA would fly in on a chartered executive jet from Tucson to Deming. He must have heard me breathing hard. "Calm down, Stitch. You've got me behind you. I'm your sponsor. It's going to work out."

When I told my buddies that we needed to get our story straight, Hack said, "The truth might work."

I liked the truth angle, with minor tweaking.

Three DEA agents from Las Cruces showed up and things started hopping when I told them that the wingtip drop tanks contained $40 million in cocaine. An FBO mechanic arrived for his shift, and the agents ordered him to tow the T-Bird into an empty hangar. They brought in reinforcements to guard the plane. Having recovered from the shock of seeing his glass door shattered, the FBO manager gave me a razor and some soap. I shaved and showered in the FBO transient facility. No one expressed sympathy when we described our ordeal except one female agent who inquired whether the Mexicans were responsible for the gash on my head. I told her that I'd done that myself in a car accident. It appeared to me that the DEA agents were positioning to soak up as much credit as possible for the big bust. I was happy to give them all the glory as long as my name stayed out of it.

A business jet landed and taxied to the FBO ramp. Three figures emerged from the jet and strode into the building. Mr.

Bruno announced that he was representing the Colombian Ministry of National Defense. He introduced a lawyer and a CIA employee whom I'd met once in Bryan Presley's office. The DEA on-scene commander convened an all-inclusive meeting. Always the diplomat, Mr. Bruno praised the on-scene commander for hiding the T-Bird quickly. Not a single reporter had showed up. The on-scene DEA commander gave us business cards with appointment times jotted on them. My appointment was at the Federal Building in Phoenix two days later. In a private meeting excluding DEA agents, the CIA rep watched as Mr. Bruno gave Dinger, Hacksaw, and me $8,000 each in cashier's checks drawn on a Colombian bank. I wasn't sure who the lawyer worked for. He guided us as we signed receipts, termination agreements, and CIA non-disclosure agreements.

"You can't reveal any of this for forty years," Mr. Bruno said. The lawyer and the CIA representative both nodded gravely. I didn't care whether I had to wait for a hundred years to spill my guts. The lawyer questioned me in the presence of Dinger and Hacksaw. It was embarrassing to stretch the truth in front of them, but hearing my version of events meant they could harmonize their stories. I blamed our diversion from Acapulco on everyone and everything but myself. Polo Three's oxygen regulator malfunctioned. Winds aloft were worse than reported. Our fuel gauges were inaccurate. On and on I went, trying to obscure the fact that I had screwed up. The way I told it, Dinger, Hacksaw, and I were heroes. While the subject of money was fresh on everyone's mind, Hacksaw asked Mr. Bruno if we could recover any of our stolen gold. The lawyer of unknown allegiance said that we might have had a claim if only we had delivered the aircraft to Cartagena. It was the most artful "no" I had ever heard.

Out in the foyer, workers had almost finished repairing the broken glass door. DEA agents milled about, excited about the huge drug bust for which they could take credit. Mr. Bruno, speaking for the Colombian government, seemed unconcerned about the locations of the three T-Birds. He told me that Everest hadn't been penalized for late delivery because the Colombians had accepted delivery the moment we flew into Mexican airspace. All parties present seemed so satisfied with the outcome that Dinger, Hacksaw, and I more or less sneaked out the back door.

We flew on Mr. Bruno's jet back to Tucson where a flunky met us and took us by van to the commercial airline terminal to buy our tickets home. We had no civilian clothes to change into. My pals had no carry-on luggage; all I had was my helmet. I ended up boarding the airplane dressed in black Nomex and I sat in the back away from everyone. I couldn't help comparing the luxury and serenity of the DC-9 cabin to the rustic surroundings at Atl Ixtaca and El Hoyo. I wasn't worried about my reunion with Trudie. She might bitch and moan on the telephone, but I was sure that, when I embraced her and laid a fifty-pound Hoover of a kiss on her, she'd melt as sure as a stick of butter on a Phoenix pavement.

Trudie, in fact, did *not* melt like a stick of butter on a Phoenix pavement. She was, however, as blistering hot as a

Phoenix pavement. I couldn't get anywhere near her. Katrina was my sole ray of sunshine. From the minute Katrina set eyes on me, she gave me a big smile and held her arms up toward me. I gathered her up and carried her to the kitchen. Trudie was banging pans around and refusing to acknowledge my presence. I took a tentative step forward, and her hand shot out. "No!"

"The Mexicans treated me better than this."

"I'm so mad at you. I will not tolerate you being slaughtered by a bunch of hooligans."

"No harm done, Trudie. I'm back." I pointed at my head: "I got my stitches out while I was down south." I tried to buy her forgiveness: "There are nine more T-Birds to deliver, and, if I fly them all, that'll be more than two hundred thousand bucks." I didn't mention that Mr. Bruno had severed my umbilical cord to Everest because I still hoped to edge my way back onto the gravy train by appealing to the good graces of Jim Conti and Bryan Presley. "We could easily pay off the mortgage."

"Would you stop?" She was looking at me now with tear-filled eyes. "I don't care about the house. I don't care about your damn money." Trudie threw her arms around me and begin sobbing. "You *idioot*," she cried, "I don't want your money, I just want *you*."

⸻◈⸻

Two days later at the Federal Building in downtown Phoenix, I met my assigned DEA interviewer. She had the beady eyes and face of a weasel and she had perfected a weasel's twitch, too. Her irises and pupils merged into one blob. I wanted her to believe every word I said and send me home. I wasn't under oath and I wasn't wired up to a polygraph machine. If I read the rocks on her ring finger right, she was married to some long-suffering soul who had given her a galaxy of tiny diamonds. She twiddled the ring with her thumb. I suspected that she was trying to hypnotize me. She narrowed her eyes at the end of each question as if squeezing off a secret fart.

"You believed that your wife would be killed if you didn't fly the drugs in?" Squint. Squint.

"Yes. I also believed that they'd kill my two friends."

"That's Tyler Countryman and Bobby Joe Ballantine?"

"Correct."

"For the record, your wife was not in danger. The DEA provided pictures of your wives to our mole only to persuade you to cooperate with the sting."

That didn't seem legal to me, but I would be pleased to overlook it if she'd let me go. "I'm glad to hear that. Thank you." I wondered who the mole was. Carlos had given me the pictures, but he seemed too high up the food chain to be a mole.

The Weasel asked, "Do you know who beheaded the bandits at Atl Ixtaca?"

"No. The bandits had already lost their heads when I got a tally ho." I wasn't trying to be an aviation wiseass, I was just nervous.

"Plain English, please. Earlier you told me that you saw them before they were decapitated."

"Yes, Ma'am. I meant I saw them in the afternoon when

they captured us. Then, after the firefight, there they were, headless." I was one malapropism away from bursting out in a hee-haw.

"You told me that Mexican bandits stole your passport, cash, and gold bullion." As if performing a magic trick, she laid a passport on the table. "Recognize this?"

I opened it, and, *alakazam*, it was my passport. "Wow."

The Weasel apparently expected me to be more astonished. I tweaked up my energy. "Amazing. That's it, all right." What truly would have amazed me was pouring my pile of gold onto the table.

"We've found no trace of the gold." She looked at me full in the face for an extended time. I refused to blink. We were two kids playing the stare game. Behind her through a glass door, I spotted a familiar person down the hallway no more than twenty feet away. It was Carlos. He wasn't in handcuffs and his hair was a lot shorter than it had been down in Mexico.

"That's him. That's the leader of the drug smugglers."

"Calm down," the Weasel said as though she were dealing with an excitable grade schooler. "He's ours. He's DEA. He's not undercover any more since the raid." She left her chair, opened the door, and called out to Carlos, "Got a minute, Raul?"

I expected Raul, a.k.a. Carlos, to greet me effusively now that he could drop the bad guy act and salute me as a colleague on the side of justice. Instead, he shook my extended hand unenthusiastically. No smile. No personality. No congratulations.

"Was I right about you being a pilot?" I asked.

He ignored my question and said, "We planned for you to divert into Manzanillo. That's where I was waiting with my guys. You threw us a major curve ball by diverting into Atl Ixtaca."

"How did you know we'd divert?"

"We messed with your wingman's oxygen regulator to force you to land short of Acapulco. We drove as fast as we could from Manzanillo to Atl Ixtaca. We almost got there too late."

"Does that mean the DEA planned our kidnapping?"

"It was a win for everyone. The DEA got its biggest drug bust in history. The Colombian defense ministry leased the three T-Birds to the Trujillo Cartel and almost covered the purchase price of the T-Birds. Plus it set up the cartel for the bust. The DEA was happy to take credit for the drug bust and let the CIA assume the risk. I got a promotion, so I'm happy. Everybody's happy."

"I'm not happy," I said. "I was kidnapped *and* I lost my contract for future deliveries."

"The cartel was planning six smuggling flights before turning the airplanes back over to the Colombian Air Force. You got off easy."

"It didn't feel easy. We only got a fraction of the pay we agreed to."

Raul already knew the details: "Eight thousand's pretty good for loafing for a week drinking beer."

"We didn't know whether we'd live. We were prisoners for eight days."

"I know what you were," Raul said. "I was there. Don't overestimate your importance in all of this."

"Did Jim Conti know about this?"

"He's the guy who came up with the idea." Carlos, a.k.a. Raul, wasn't so stingy with words now that he was on the right side of the law. "We wanted you to keep flying drugs into Texas so we could keep impounding the cocaine and make more arrests. Of course, you had to go and escape. I'm on my way out. Remember, if you ever run into me around town, you don't know me. You don't even see me."

"For forty years," I said.

"At least." Carlos, also known as Raul, didn't hide his disdain for the Weasel and me. He didn't shake my hand in parting. He just left. Soon after that, the Weasel gave me the bum's rush out of her office. I had not impressed her, and she sure as hell hadn't impressed me.

Chapter 22

Treasure:
a golf ball from the Old Course at St. Andrews, Scotland

DEA INTEREST IN Dinger, Hacksaw, and me came to an abrupt and welcome end. Seizures of drugs and arrests of smugglers had exceeded all government expectations. Reading between the lines, I deduced that Everest Aviation and the Colombian Air Force were richly rewarded for co-operating with the DEA. No one from the Columbian Air Force called me out for scattering their T-Birds all over Old and New Mexico. I kept waiting to be chastised, but I heard nothing from Everest, the CIA, or the Air Force. Each day that passed without a call or letter raised my hopes that I was going to elude punishment for one of the biggest foul-ups of my life. Jim Conti telephoned me from Taipei over the weekend. Because I believed that he was the mastermind of the whole convoluted mess, I didn't waste time with face-saving half-truths. He didn't pull any punches, either.

"You'll be glad to know that all your records at Everest have been purged," he said. "Your astronaut resume doesn't exist, not here or at the CIA or at the insurance company. It never happened. Now, forget you ever flew for Everest."

I didn't antagonize Jim by accusing him of risking our lives. I didn't want to be a sissy, and a quarter of a million dollars was still on the table. I pressed Jim to let me deliver the nine remaining T-Birds.

"Don't make a mess of it by trying to get back on the bus," he said. "It's time for you to put some distance between yourself and the company. Something else may come up, and I'll give you a call."

———— ((◦)) ————

That same evening, Hacksaw dropped a nuke on me. He called from Salt Lake to tell me that he had resigned his Air Force commission. He had been hired by Western Airlines in the space of ten days. Sly fox. He never said a word in Mexico, but now he admitted that he had applied to Western, Hughes Airwest, and Braniff a month before our Mexican horror show. He maintained secrecy to prevent embarrassment should all three airlines reject him. I got over my initial stupefaction and congratulated him sincerely. I was ignorant of the airline world and airplanes that flew on-schedule and straight-and-level. Not Hacksaw; he spent an hour advising me how to land an airline pilot job.

Deregulation of the airlines in the United States had spurred immense growth by 1978. Routes that had been protected monopolies were opened up in a kind of airline free-for-all. An airline pilot hiring spree had turned into a feeding frenzy that gobbled up high-caliber pilots left and right. Hack's Western Airlines domicile was Salt Lake City, so he didn't even have to move his residence. He painted such a tempting picture that I flirted with the idea of hanging up my G-suit to fly a Boeing 727 for a living. A question I evaded asking was, "Why would any airline hire a pilot who had been involved in an accident?" I avoided asking the question because I couldn't live with the answer.

⸺⬦⸺

I was the leader of the four Phantom crews comprising Biscuit 21 Flight in an attack on a simulated MiG Airfield on Gila Bend's East Tactical Range. Sweating in 120-degree temperatures, we waited beside our planes for the arrival of the "bread truck, a clone of a UPS package car, a utility van that transported us between the flight line and the squadron life support section. Chugging pints of ice water and draping iced towels around our necks was blessed relief on the ride to the squadron. We turned in our helmets, harnesses, and G-suits to life support specialists and carried our kneeboards and interphone tape recorders toward the debriefing room to try to make sense of the last 1.2 hours of pandemonium.

"Biscuit Two-One, debrief in Bravo Three in five minutes," I called down the hallway.

Thor, the Three-Eleventh Squadron Operations Officer cut me off before I could reach the men's latrine. "You've got problems," he whispered. "I ordered you to submit a Form 3902 to the JAG and the boss to shed a little sunshine on your rogue moonlighting."

I didn't like where this was going, so I depressed the

"record" button surreptitiously on my interphone tape recorder.

"There's more. You've busted Bingo at least eight times in the last three months. And you disobeyed my order to do rewrites at the training center. *And* I'm accusing you of being absent without leave. No matter what it is, you get it wrong, Cromwell. It'll all come out at your court-martial."

"What?" The mention of *court-martial* threw me into a spin.

"On the other hand, paying me the four big ones you owe me will make all this go away."

I was angry enough to smack him, but an operations clerk intervened. Thor, nervous about eavesdroppers and witnesses, sidestepped the clerk by escaping through a seldom-used doorway, tossing over his shoulder, "Take care of that right away."

The clerk informed me that Lieutenant Colonel Marcus "Fig" Cannon had returned from his vacation in Scotland and was requesting the pleasure of my company. On my way to his office, I discovered that I had punched the "pause" button on my tape recorder instead of the "record" button, so I had collected no evidence to prove Thor's blackmail. I reported to Fig in a military manner.

"Sit down, Cromwell."

I couldn't read Fig. His summons could have been for a Medal of Honor ceremony or an execution. He tossed a Titleist golf ball across the desk at me. With the reflexes of a jaguar, I caught it and read the logo imprinted on it: "The Old Course at St. Andrews."

"I birdied the eighth," he said.

"Wow." In my world, a birdie on any hole was a major triumph.

"I stuck it twelve feet from the pin off the tee."

"Sweet, Boss. Wish I could have seen it."

"I told the caddy to beat me to death with my own driver if I missed the putt."

"You'll never forget it, Boss." I didn't know where the conversation was headed, so I killed time by fiddling with the ball as if it were a religious relic. "Bonnie Scotland."

"I hear you've been doing some traveling, too." I delayed answering because I didn't know how much Fig knew. "I'm guessing you're familiar with a guy named Bruno?"

"Mister Bruno? Yes, sir."

"Weird character. Most spooks are. He showed me a letter from a James Conti. Bruno wouldn't let me keep the letter. Said you've been doing some secret stuff."

"I see."

"I presume my security clearance allows me to hear about your stuff."

"Need to know, Sir." I was playing this to the hilt to prevent anything negative from washing up on the beach. "I can't say anything about it for forty years." It felt absurd to say it, but it was, after all, my story, and I was sticking with it.

"Forty years? Long time. Wonder what I'll be doing in forty years. Fertilizing daisies, I imagine. I don't care much for secrets or surprises. You might have kept me informed in a roundabout way."

"Federal statutes," I said. As usual, I was in the deep end, way over my head.

"Well, none of my business, I guess. Don't care much for

your sneaking around behind my back."

The fishing expedition was over, and so was my part in the conversation. No more warm-and-fuzzy chitchat about golf. Fig told me that my future in the Tactical Air Command wasn't brilliant. He said that I was too rough around the edges to advance very far. Not that he wouldn't fly into battle with me tomorrow, no sir. But it took a different kind of fighter pilot to build a rock-solid career as an Air Force officer in peace time. An officer competing for a star would have to fill all the right squares, attend the right professional schools, have a strong sponsor, and look the part. I had lost too much time in hospitals, he said. I was too aloof for my own good. A tad too cocky. He said that he wouldn't deny that I was first-rate in dogfights and at Happy Hour at the O Club. "It's come to my attention that you've busted bingo several times of late. Are you trying to pad your flying time for the airlines."

"Hmm." I was a fool. I would have been an even bigger fool to feign surprise or to deny it.

"You shut down with three-hundred pounds of fuel remaining on Monday. That's seventeen hundred pounds below the minimum. That's stupid. It's a bad example for the students." His eyes bored a hole in mine. "You never called 'Bingo' a single time. Care to comment?"

"No excuse, Sir." I was trapped. Thor had probably called up a report on average time per sortie and followed the data to catch me out to poison Fig's opinion of me.

"You could have been something, Cromwell. You could have traveled around the world preaching flight safety to fighter squadrons everywhere. Zippers up. Sleeves down.

Gloves secure. You could have exploited your scars. But no, you've beamed around in full afterburner doing whatever you please. You're all speed and no direction." He yawned as if this session was wearing him out. "Consider getting out, Cromwell. It's going to be the Dark Ages for the Air Force when Jimmy Carter checks in to the Oval. Since you tend to march to a different drummer, putting in your papers may be your best move."

I didn't need a gong to announce the end of our intimate chat. I thanked Fig for his advice and saluted him smartly even though my ego had just taken a thumping. After leaving Fig's office, I over-reacted sensationally. Within thirteen hours, I had handed in my resignation paperwork. As huge a mistake as that may have been, it was trifling compared to my biggest mistake of all – failing to include Trudie in the decision-making.

<hr />

"I can't believe you quit without discussing it with me." Trudie's Belgian accent was more pronounced when she was angry. "We've got to talk." She was more infuriated than I had ever seen her. She lectured me on the idiocy of resigning without successor employment in the bag. I was aware that my rash decision was all temper and no I.Q. but I wouldn't admit it.

"You and your secrets," she said.

"Does the name Peter Gant mean anything to you?" There, I'd chucked in my concussion grenade.

"You've waited all this time for that?" she said stridently.

"Besides, I'll get on at Western."

"Stitch, you're not Hacksaw Ballantine." I wondered whether she intended for her words to hurt as much as they did. "We need time away from one another." We had been married long enough that I could decipher Trudie's syntax. What she meant was, "I can't bear the sight of you." She said she was taking Katrina to Bruges for a while as a statement of fact, not a request for my approval. Flying to Belgium without consulting with *me* was retribution for my resigning without consulting with *her*. On her way out of the kitchen, she looked in my direction for the first time and said, "If I'd known how much you love money and how little you regard my opinion, I'd never have come to America." She stomped in quick time toward our bedroom. I expected the slam of the door next, but first she shouted, "You're so passive-aggressive. For once, show a little emotion." BAM. The banging door made wall studs creak.

Boundless Gloom was in ascent. I shouted, "Fine. Godammit. Fly off to Mommy." We had argued before, but it had never felt as toxic as this.

———»《0》«———

When I got home from jogging five miles the next day, Trudie and Katrina weren't there. I assumed that Trudie had taken Katrina in her pram to a nearby park. I was reluctant to believe that Trudie had gone through with her threat over what I considered a temporary kerfuffle. When I discovered Katrina's pram in our bedroom with a note taped to it, I caught on to the fact that my wife had left me. The note read, "How could you?" I took the note to mean, "How could you have resigned from the Air Force without my input?" I was indignant because it was *my* career, not Trudie's. Should I have faked consulting with her to make her feel better? I had asked for Trudie's opinion about replacing the Alfa, and ended up with a Chevy for my trouble. I felt that Trudie was being unreasonable, and my pride wasn't going to let her get away with it. I found another note taped to the cat's feeding bowl.

"Don't forget to feed Tonka. You'll forget for five days and then triple the serving, and Tonka will think you're the world's greatest humanitarian since Eleonore Roosevelt while it's me who's fed her every day without fail for two years. What's the use?"

I detected a lot of subtext in Trudie's note. It was revealing that her note to me was three words long and Tonka the cat rated 48 words. My initial tantrum cooled and loneliness began to creep in. I missed Trudie in a hundred small ways: her aroma, her voice, her touch. I missed drinking wine and necking with her by the swimming pool. I would have paid a hundred bucks to hear her laugh.

In Spain I had a gardener named Manolo. Five days a week, he'd walk his burro up the steep hill from Campo de Fuente to my house when dew was still on the grass. A weed needn't fret about longevity with Manolo on the job. He slept mostly. I bought Manolo an inexpensive gas lawn mower. It may have been the first engine he had ever owned. A Rolls Royce wouldn't have made him any happier. On many a warm evening, Manolo in his blue coveralls and I in my olive drab flight suit sat shoulder-to-shoulder on my porch steps drinking bottles of cheap *tinto*. I slayed his native tongue, and he shouted through rotten teeth hoping to make me understand his guttural gibberish. The more we'd drink, the more we'd laugh. I knew I'd miss Manolo big time when his time came, which it did. Until then, he adored me. Or, at least, he loved the way I made him feel. That's the way my love for Trudie worked. Maybe I didn't know her intimately enough to love her in the classical sense, but I was head-over-heels enchanted by the way she made me feel. Maybe that's how love always worked.

The same Trudie could be a stinker, punishing me for getting kidnapped and daring to leave the Air Force without her blessing. At the moment, she was a pouting, ill-tempered brat. I wanted to ring her neck for leaving me in limbo, trapped between bi-polar matrimonial extremes of love and hate.

My Technicolor life faded to sepia without Trudie. I was unaccustomed to having so much free time. I obsessively washed windows and vacuumed floors. I jogged every day religiously and napped beside the swimming pool when I liked. I baked frozen meals at 350 degrees Fahrenheit. I watched far too much basketball on television. I checked the curbside mailbox three times a day. I still hadn't received a response from Western pilot recruitment, that pack of pernicious peasants. But, not so fast. Was it possible that the wonderful folks at Western pilot recruitment might not have received my application because low-life scoundrels at the United States Postal Service had lost it? To be safe, I applied to Delta and American, waited, then applied to Eastern and Pan Am. Maybe some rascal at the post office was destroying all my applications. I feared a conspiracy. Thor Olsen called to threaten me for what he called "reneging on my debt." I reminded him that I was out of the Air Force, so I didn't care what he said or did anymore. He warned me that he and Sally had important airline contacts: "You'll never get hired. I'll blackball every background check that hits my desk."

I didn't know it at the time, but airlines seldom contacted an applicant's military commanders. I gave Thor too much credit. I imagined that his blackball threat was a mortal wound. I took it out on Trudie by resolving not to write to her until she first wrote to me. Nothing arrived from Belgium. I applied to Frontier and National. I listed the house for sale. The only realtor showing interest was battier than her scatter-brained so-called buyer, a nut-job who couldn't have qualified to buy the garage. I was a hermit. I applied to Northwest and Texas International.

Two months dragged by without a single response. I applied to Continental, TWA, and Ozark. I didn't know which rejection irritated me more, the airlines' or Trudie's. I was burning through saved up Everest Aviation checks. The sixteen-year-old bundle of trouble next door popped her head over the fence every other day asking whether she could come over and hang out. I had met her musclebound truck driver father the previous summer. He was from California, a state known for psychotic killers. Jail Bait appeared at the gate one afternoon in a pink bikini and two bottles of Olympia beer. I had a frank one-way discussion with her about staying away and she cried her eyes out before stomping out of the yard shouting, "Loser. Pervert. Fag." So, now I had females mad at me on both sides of the Atlantic.

I applied to Alaska, North Central, and Southern Airlines. I fantasized about the gold hidden at Atl Ixtaca. Still no word from Trudie. I applied to Northwest Orient and Pacific Southwest Airlines. I filled out reams of pages for the airlines, but my injured pride wouldn't let me send even a word to Trudy. I was curled up in my king-sized bed when the phone rang.

"I need to speak to the world's sexiest fighter pilot," said a sensuous feminine voice.

"This is he."

"It's Jennifer." For the next few minutes, all I had to do was listen. I discovered that, after leaving Spain, Jennifer and Gunner had spent two years at Langley AFB, Virginia. Now Gunner was assigned to Luke to transition from F-4 Phantoms to F-15 Eagles in the 555th TFS, the famed "Triple Nickel" Squadron. The Gunnerssons were staying with Jennifer's Boston College girlfriend Sally Olsen and her husband Thor while looking for an apartment. Jennifer joked that she needed a geography lesson bad.

I said, "I'm married now."

"I heard. How irrelevant."

I visualized Thor and Gunner residing under the same roof. In *Monopoly* terms, I'd rather land on Boardwalk with a red hotel on it than be in the same house with those two. Jennifer proposed that we meet at a hotel bar in Litchfield Park that evening. Judas betrayed Christ with a kiss. I betrayed Trudie by agreeing to meet Jennifer. I rationalized my skullduggery by resolving to do nothing but listen to what Jennifer had to say. Of course, it was illogical that I would be more resolute in person than on the telephone. Jennifer had hinted that things were rocky between her and Gunner. Maybe I could help. I didn't deceive Jennifer for a second, but I deceived myself long enough to drive to the hotel. Jennifer and I sat side-by-side in a booth, and I ordered whiskey sours. Jennifer was at the top of her game. Tanned. Fit. Seductive. Teasing and flirting were as natural to her as breathing.

"How is living with the Olsens?" I asked.

"At first it was like we were apartment mates in Boston again right after Sally transferred from Stephens. Thor went by 'Bob' back them. He started hanging around the apartment to be near Sally, who was moping around after Bill dumped her."

"So you and the Olsens are one big happy clan?"

"God, no. Everyone's tiptoeing on eggshells. Gunner's such a cretin. He's pissed that Thor made major before him. He got tipsy and told Thor that Minnesota would've beat Boston College by five touchdowns and that Thor couldn't have made the practice squad at a Big Ten school. What a thing to say to your host."

"So Gunner's on Sally's shit list?"

"Along with you. Did you know that Sally and your wife Elizabeth were best friends at Stephens?"

I recalled the photo of Elizabeth and Sally that I had found in Elizabeth's Stephens yearbook.

"Elizabeth was supposed to transfer from Stephens to B.C. with Sally until you messed the plan up by marrying Elizabeth. When Elizabeth broke her engagement to Cody, his best friend Bill broke it off with Sally. Bill had a crush on Elizabeth and was just going through the motions with Sally."

"It's a soap opera."

"Sally hates your guts because you're the reason Bill dumped her, but she's rewritten the narrative. She blames you for Elizabeth's death. Nothing will change her mind now, so just stay away from her."

"So Thor's pissed at me because of Sally?"

"You can't expect him to feel any other way. Thor played football with Cody and Bill. After Bill was out of the picture with Sally, Thor replaced him. Thor was Sally's second choice."

Jennifer made short work of her whiskey sour. I ordered another round.

"Sally's a psych major and she's got a whole theory about you. She says that everything you do is designed to get you off the hook. She says that you invent close calls so you'll feel heroic for saving the day. Thor gave us an example; he said that you've been landing with empty fuel tanks."

I had indeed, as pointed out by Fig, landed low on fuel a few times, but I couldn't see any reason for Thor to know that unless he was trying to build a case against me.

"She says that another example is that thing you were doing down at Tucson …."

"Marana."

"Okay, Marana. She believes it was part of your subconscious need to make amends for the accident. I'm just telling you Sally's take," Jennifer said. "I don't see it that way."

"Maybe I should apologize to Sally," I said.

"You can't fix it with an apology. Sally's too invested in being a victim to change her mind now. It's been three years since the Atlántico. I heard that you married a Dutch girl."

"Belgian," I said.

"Belgium's a quaint little backwater, isn't it? Rustic?"

I didn't appreciate her inference. My snit with Trudie was no green light for Jennifer to pile on. I found a vestige of a backbone.

"Minnesota's no world center of culture."

"Easy, Tiger. Don't be so touchy." I could tell that she felt in control of me, that she assumed she could say anything, and I wouldn't leave, the same as every other man she had manipulated in her life.

"I shouldn't have come." I slipped out of the booth, which was a bold move for me.

"Sit down," she ordered. "I mean it, Stitch. You won't get a second chance."

From a purely carnal point of view, my timing was off. A world class sex-hound, unfettered by conscience, would have waited until after the coupling to be indignant. I tossed a twenty onto the table to prove I wasn't trying to wiggle out of paying for the drinks.

Jennifer had to have the last word: "Sally warned me about what a flake you are." She flicked the back of her hand at me. "Go. It's your loss."

My father, who had never shared a booth with sexy Jennifer Gunnersson, used to say, "You are what you do when no one's looking." Well, no one watched me stride out of the hotel. On the drive home, I contemplated the sacrifice I had just made. Rare was the man who could reject Jennifer Gunnersson. Damn if I hadn't done the right thing for a change. Of course, there was no reward for being virtuous. I couldn't expect a merit badge for spurning hedonism's call, for winning a duel with temptation. Tragically, Trudie would never know of my virtue because she was off doing God-knows-what in Belgium.

<hr />

I told Dinger about Trudie leaving me when he telephoned me one afternoon. He put on his counsellor's hat: "You really should have asked for Trudie's opinion before you resigned."

"Separating from the Air Force was my decision, not hers."

"Hey, Old School, paternalism is a thing of the past. You should have discussed it with her."

"She's not writing me and I'm not writing her."

"You're kidding. Get on the phone and fix this. I bet there's more to this than your resignation."

I spurned his advice, so he changed the subject to the enrichment scheme he had called about.

"Cromwell, do you remember the you-know-what that we left behind in you-know-where?"

"Of course. I fall asleep dreaming about the you-know-what."

"Well, I went to high school in Tampa with this guy Pratley who lives on a boat docked at Cabrillo Island Marina." Pause. "He'll take us down the coast in his boat to recover the you-know-what. It'll take two weeks."

"Do you have two weeks of leave saved up?"

"More. Plenty."

I was in serious need of you-know-what, so I agreed to

meet Dinger in San Diego in three days. Hacksaw couldn't join us because he was still in his probationary year at Western Airlines and in training to transition and upgrade from Boeing 727 Flight Engineer to Boeing 737 First Officer. He promised to send a check to cover his share of expenses. The expedition team was down to two explorers and a sea captain. I packed a duffel bag and set off for San Diego to meet up with Dinger at Pratley's marina. I knew nothing about boats, but I did know that almost $100,000 in gold and Rolex watches was waiting to be recovered at an abandoned airport in Atl Ixtaca, Mexico.

Chapter 23

Treasure:
a worn leather granny cord for a pair of sunglasses

AS THE SUN rose over Glendale in my rear view mirror, I aimed my Chevy at San Diego on a journey of six hours through the Sonoran Desert on Interstate Eight. I parked in the Cabrillo Island Marina visitors' parking lot next to Dinger's Corvette, a dark metallic blue rocket ship with Nevada plates. The engine was still crackling, so I reckoned that Dinger had arrived only a few minutes ahead of me. I was curious to meet the captain of the good ship *Suffice*. My expectation ran along the lines of Charlton Heston. I found *Suffice* easily, but Charlton Heston was elusive. Barney Fife with a Brillo pad coiffure greeted me. I assumed he was the ship's mate.

"Toss me your bag and come aboard," he called, a trifle melodically.

He caught my duffel bag like a girl with his arms extended and his head turned aside as though a miss might rip his face off. I soon learned that *Suffice* didn't have a mate. Barney

Fife's twin was the captain, Dinger's pal from Tampa, Pratley. Dinger popped up from below decks. Brilliant white zinc oxide cream coated the tops of his ears, the tip of his nose, and his bottom lip. Pratley stowed my duffel bag, I whispered to Dinger, "You didn't tell me Pratley was ...."

"I'm not sure he is," Dinger mouthed.

"I'm sure enough for both of us."

——◅((◐))▻——

We departed the marina for Atl Ixtaca under mild conditions: clear skies, six knots of wind, and swells of no more than two feet. Pratley, possibly North America's most chipper skipper, assumed the helm. Pratley prattled non-stop about anything. Two miles off the coast, as if we had crossed over into another jurisdiction, Pratley's pants hit the deck, revealing an all-over tan that was a dermatologist's nightmare. He was as brown as a leather handbag in places where run-of-the-mill Caucasians were paler than Bo Peep's sheep. Pratley said that he made a concession to textiles only from noon until three o'clock when he donned a tee shirt for protection from intense ultraviolet radiation. His tee shirt on the first day of the voyage was screen-printed with an inspirational message, "... and the horse you rode in on." He also wore a pink baseball hat that read, "Zottonaut." He scattered expensive sunglasses around the 36-foot vessel with a granny cord attached to each pair. Pratley's shortcomings – Art Garfunkel hair and a left testicle that hung alarmingly low – didn't detract from his fetish for top quality sunglasses.

"The Mighty Pacific," Dinger sighed as he gazed at the

sea, "a large body of water with salt in it."

Captain Pratley shook his head. He called Dinger by his real name: "That's a smidgen simplistic, Tyler." They quibbled all day. Whatever Dinger said, Pratley debated with him. Pratley maintained a course parallel to the Mexican coast thirteen miles from land. Two hours before sunset, he engaged the tiller pilot and trimmed the engines for a reduced speed of six knots so we could sit down for our first meal at sea. After dinner, Dinger paid Pratley a $3,000 advance to cover his estimated fuel expense for the round-trip between San Diego and Atl Ixtaca. Dinger had promised Pratley $200 a day payable at the end of the trip. Pratley pressed Dinger to lift the shroud of secrecy surrounding our mission. Dinger explained that we had stashed a "shit load" of gold down in Mexico and we were going back to get it.

"How much gold?" Pratley asked, possibly reconsidering his $200-a-day fee.

"A bunch."

My earliest impression was that this two-week cruise might feel like eternity, but my fears were unfounded, and the days passed pleasantly. I didn't spot a single cloud in six days. Pratley didn't drink much booze because of his responsibilities as skipper, so Dinger and I took up the slack.

"Stitch, you put away a hell of a lot of hooch for a guy with no job," Pratley said. He wasn't being judgmental. He was making a blunt observation. I couldn't argue with him.

Dinger and I had similar tastes in ocean attire: baggy surfer shorts and straw cowboy hats. We slathered on gallons of newfangled sunscreen. By night we took turns monitoring the tiller pilot in four-hour watches. By day we napped, played guitar, snacked, and drank. I wasn't angry at Trudie anymore. I credited the sea, the wind, the sun, and the passage of time for repairing my injured pride and erasing my memories of petty insults.

Pratley and I rarely agreed on anything. I figured out that he was a contrarian. He disputed whatever Dinger or I said, although without rancor. Our opinions differed even in small matters: the weather, navigation, and politics. When I complained about the heat, Pratley went out of his way to disagree. Of course, every day was cool for a chap who roamed around as naked as a jaybird. Despite our different points of view, Pratley and I coexisted without friction . He was amusing in his own way. I could imagine Pratley and Dinger, opposite ends of so many spectra, arguing their way through high school. During idle hours on deck, I turned introspective. I had expected to be rolling in money by now. I had assumed that my loving, adoring wife would be at my side. As for this impromptu gold expedition, I never foresaw myself afloat on the bounding main under the command of an eccentric homosexual exhibitionist. I contemplated what my father had once told me about his prayer for me on the night of my birth.

"Heavenly Father, please don't let him be dull."

In light of my current enterprise, I was a classic example of an answered prayer.

⸺◦⟨◉⟩◦⸺

At the end of our seventh day at sea, Pratley dropped anchor at around midnight in a desolate cove less than three miles west of the Atl Ixtaca runway. Dinger and I were tanned, unshaved, salty, and eager to get underway. *Suffice* was becalmed. It was too hot to sleep below, so we stretched out on inflatable mattresses, I on the foredeck and Dinger and Pratley on the afterdeck.

Compared to the great amphibious assaults at Omaha Beach and Iwo Jima, our landing at dawn was uneventful. Dinger and I motored three hundred meters to shore in an inflatable dinghy powered by a five horsepower, two-stroke museum piece. We hid the dinghy in bushes among the dunes. We shouldered our backpacks and hiked inland on a dusty road that paralleled the beach until it turned ninety degrees left toward the airport. We crossed a narrow bridge over a river a half mile from the beach. The melody of *It's A Long Way To Tipperary* played on a loop in my mind until my imaginary disc jockey changed the featured repeating refrain to the theme song of *The Bridge On The River Kwai*.

Two miles of easy hiking later, we arrived at the derelict main entrance to the Atl Ixtaca airport. Since our previous visit, every structure on the aerodrome had been demolished into piles of cinder blocks, concrete, twisted iron, and stucco. We paced down the middle of the tortured asphalt runway on which we had landed our T-Birds less than a year earlier. We reached the ramp in front of the former two-story office that had served as our dormitory. The eastern wall of our former prison was a pile of rubble six feet high. Dinger and I dropped our backpacks and put on scuba gloves.

We wanted to get our mitts on the gold and beat feet out of Mexico by sunset at the latest. It wasn't complicated or probable. We were so overheated after an hour that we had to stop for a water break. Our progress was paltry compared to what a backhoe or excavator could have done. So far, we had removed fewer than twenty cubic yards of debris in a three-foot wide path into the ruins. The rough texture of cinder blocks abraded my diving gloves. The thumbs were the first to go. My back was aching. As my attitude wilted to new lows, Dinger uncovered a section of the foundation.

"We're getting close, now, Stitch."

Not really. By noon, we had cleared a path along the edge of the foundation without finding the metal grate or the gold interred behind it. We ate jerky for lunch. I was so dehydrated that my urine was mustard. My gloves were in tatters. My wrists hurt. I didn't know how much longer I could last. Dinger was made of stouter stuff and he exhorted me to press on. I rehydrated and reminded myself that I was Daniel Cromwell, one of a long line of Texas-taming non-quitters. Nothing could stop my relentless pursuit of a goal. I renewed the pace. We worked in shifts. I rested in shade while Dinger toiled. When he tired, I replaced him, working until exhaustion shut me down. At one point, I spied a pair of eyes watching us from behind the jungle foliage. I didn't know whether they were human or animal. I didn't care. I pulled our knapsacks near us and loosened the flap securing my pistol. The eyes vanished when I focused on them. When I told Dinger that we were being watched, he told me that I was hallucinating.

We drank our remaining two bottles of water. At last, Dinger uncovered a metal grill: "Behold. The Holy Grate." Shortly after that, he shouted, "Eureka." He handed bars to me one at a time. Many had been gouged by the collapse of the building. Further down in the pile of debris, he found several Krugerrands that had fallen loose from their paper sleeves. By six o'clock, we had ferreted out three Rolexes, 35 Baird & Co. ten-ounce gold bars, and 89 Krugerrands. We were a couple of thousand bucks short. Dinger resumed tossing chunks of concrete and filtering dust through his fingers. He found the last gold bar and two more Krugerrands stuck together. It was six thirty, and we were both exhausted.

"Two coins to go," I said.

"Three hundred dollars? Fuck it. We're done."

We added fourteen pounds of gold to each of our backpacks. I labored to shuffle one foot in front of the other on our return from Atl Ixtaca airfield on the overgrown path toward the beach.

"Company," Dinger said.

A wild-eyed man in a straw hat, worn-out black sneakers, and a dirty tee shirt stepped out from the jungle twenty yards in front of us. He glared at us wickedly and hid his right hand behind his back. Dinger's "*Hola*" (Hello) and my "*Hace mucho calor*" (It's hot) got no response. I reached into my right pocket to cradle my nine-millimeter pistol. Dinger did the same. "*Con permisso,*" I said. (With your permission.) I took a step forward to pass. We weren't going to get permission or anything else but grief from this steely-eyed chancer. He produced a machete in his right hand and pointed it at Dinger.

"*Dinero,*" he said. (Money.)

Dinger pulled out his pistol and aimed it at the interloper's heart. "I'm not in the mood, Pablo."

Our robber was one surprised highwayman. Dinger fired

a round into the ground near the man's sneakers. The effect of the loud explosion was electric. I felt an injection of adrenaline, and I wasn't even the one getting shot at. The man yelped, sliced the air with his machete, and showed us his heels.

"I've always found that a heater gives you piece of mind," Dinger said.

I stepped ahead of my sidekick and fired off a round in the direction of the fleet one. I had never shot at a live human before, or a dead one. I couldn't determine where the bullet impacted, but it was close enough for the would-be robber to ratchet up his pace even faster. Dinger inserted a replacement round into his clip. I was too weary to bother. My heart resumed normal sinus rhythm, but I still had concerns.

"What if his friends down the road are armed with machetes, too?"

"Nah. That's the last we'll see of that peckerwood."

We continued the trudge toward Pratley's dinghy. I was near the end of my physical endurance, but Dinger chatted away as we shuffled down the sandy path. We found the concealed dinghy, but the outboard motor was gone. Dinger scanned the cove from left to right looking for *Suffice*. "Pratley wouldn't go down with the ship. If it sank, he'd be dog paddling out there." I wanted a pizza and a beer so badly that I could have cried. Dinger searched in his backpack for his walkie-talkie. He found it and transmitted to Pratley on Channel Seven. No reply.

"Move further down the beach," I suggested. I soon wished I had kept my mouth shut.

Dinger crossed the sandy beach a hundred feet to the

water's edge. He was ankle deep in water when a wave hit him knee high. The walkie-talkie fell into the foam. I knew who was going to take the blame.

I said a very childish thing: "*You* dropped it, not *me*."

The next two minutes were best forgotten. Dinger dredged up some of my character deficiencies and ancient blunders. We argued about where to hide to wait for Pratley to ride to the rescue. Dinger wanted to stay away from the inflatable dinghy so stray bullets wouldn't puncture it. At the peak of the battle of insults and grievances, Dinger started laughing hysterically, and so did I. In fact, there was nothing funny about our tight spot. We settled into the scrub bushes between the ocean's edge and an inland lagoon. A swarm of insects began feasting on us. We couldn't catch a break.

Dinger croaked, "I'll kill Pratley with my bare hands."

———— ⋙《❂》⋘ ————

"Don't move." I kept my lips rigid when I uttered the words. I focused on the rattle of an insistent castanet, squinting into the blinding rays of the setting sun at a tangle of brush four feet from where I lay. The coiled snake in the shadows flicked its tongue in syncopation with its rattles. Dinger was my best chance out of this pickle, so I remained motionless and repeated, "Don't move."

Dinger was monkeying around with the baptized walkie-talkie. Against my advice, he leaped to his feet. "Don't move," he shouted.

I believed I had already covered that. He awkwardly removed his pistol from his right pocket. In normal times,

Dinger was coordinated and athletic, but he seemed agonizingly slow at present. Not soon enough for my liking, he aimed his pistol and fired five times. The spent cartridges ejected onto my head. The snake disappeared and so did my hearing. I scampered to my feet to locate snake remnants scattered among the bushes. Dinger had scored at least two hits, but the reptile's head was still writhing.

In my fatigued state, everything annoyed me. I scanned up and down the beach to see if the shots had aroused interest. I spied a man running away on the beach road. I recognized his stride. He was wearing black sneakers, and a machete was flailing in his right hand. The would-be robber had followed us from the airport. Dinger fired a shot at him for effect. The man skipped into overdrive.

"There goes the element of surprise," I said.

"You're welcome for saving your life. We didn't have an element of surprise, for crying out loud. Whoever stole our outboard motor knows we're here."

Unfamiliar with rattlesnake culture, I wondered whether rattlers traveled in packs. The bushes could have been teeming with them for all I knew. I flopped onto the sandy beach closer to the surf. The sky was darkening in the east. After broiling in the sun all day, I shivered in the ocean breeze.

"I've got the shakes."

Dinger summed it up: "You've got the heart of a lion and the nerves of a Chihuahua."

Insects, hunger, thirst, reptiles, Dinger's irritating comments, and Pratley's desertion had tattered the banner of our friendship. Motion in the distance attracted my notice. I stood up on aching legs and peered toward the south. Two vehicles raced past long shadows of palm trees leaving clouds of dust in their wake. The scene was reminiscent of the two pickup trucks roaring across the Atl Ixtaca runway in days of yore. I grabbed my backpack and bounded to the dinghy. Dinger helped me drag it toward the ocean. The froth of the surf was a relief to my blistered hands and insect-eaten body. Out past the first line of breaking waves, I tossed my backpack into the inflatable, leaped, and rolled my body into the dinghy. Dinger did the leap-and-roll thing, too, and we collided on top of our backpacks in the middle. We tore the telescoping paddles from their Velcro clips and paddled furiously away from the beach. We were eighty meters off shore when the two pickup trucks halted and the occupants piled out onto the beach. Every meter mattered, so we were paddling at a lung-bursting rate. I heard the crack of the first shot over the pounding of the waves.

"You hit?" I rasped.

"No. You?"

"I'm not sure."

"You'd know."

We were 100 meters from the riflemen and straining to extend the distance. I could imagine the sight picture for these marksmen as they fired at silhouettes dancing mirage-like in the dazzling sunset. Several more reports rang out. Our dinghy maintained its pressure. Our range was 200 meters and increasing.

"They'll wait us out," Dinger said, taking the long view. He told me to slow my paddling. I was flat out of gas anyway. I could barely make out the movements of the sharpshooters beside the two trucks. To the west, the surface of the ocean reflected the crimson sky. The remainder of the sea was as dark as the night sky that embraced the mountains to the east. Bleak images that seldom crossed my mind in the light of day became dominant in the gathering darkness. Black water, darkening sky, hunger, thirst, and numbing fatigue were a bother, but sharks terrified me. Bullets and snakebites were mere aggravations compared to a shark attack. I imagined rows of razor-sharp teeth shredding my limbs. We stopped paddling. Dinger leaned against the starboard gunwale and moaned, "We're in deep kimchi, Cromwell."

Boundless Gloom didn't have time to move in, however, because, at the top of a swell, I spotted a dim green light to the south. I couldn't hear the sound of a motor, but my heart and my brain willed the green light to be the starboard position light of *Suffice*. The shoreline firing squad scored a fluke hit on our dinghy, and a loud hissing accompanied the deflation of the main bladder. Seawater splashed into our increasingly flaccid vessel. Dinger aimed his flashlight at the powerboat and blinked the extraction signal – three flashes, Morse Code dashes for the letter "O." Dinger flashed again. Seawater swamping our boat was ankle deep. At last, three yellow confirmation flashes shone from what I assumed was *Suffice's* flying bridge.

"That's him," Dinger said.

I heard the purr of *Suffice's* engines approaching. Pratley turned on a spotlight aimed aft at his vessel's boarding ladder. We paddled hard to maneuver into the beam of light. With my last British thermal unit of energy, I boarded *Suffice*. Pratley slapped me on the back. He was over-dressed in a shortie wetsuit bottom.

"Where the fuck were you?" Dinger shouted.

Pratley replied that he had gone shopping for fresh food at a harbor down the coast.

"Shopping for grass more likely."

Pratley helped us pull the floppy dinghy aboard *Suffice*. He took the offensive: "Where's my motor?"

"Long story," Dinger said. "We'll buy you a new one."

We secured our backpacks and the battle-weary dinghy on the afterdeck. Pratley jettisoned his diving shorties, and they plopped onto the deck. Most people put their pants on to go to work; Pratley took his off. He steered due west toward international waters. Dinger and I each de-capped a bottle of ice-cold Coors. The luxury. The euphoria. I set out to overdose on beer and gorge on canned beans while soaking my lacerated hands in sea water, but what I actually did was swill two beers in rapid succession, leave the beans unopened, and collapse on a berth in the cuddy cabin off the aft cockpit. All through the night, as Pratley steered northwesterly, I slept uninterrupted, my hands crusted in blood and Mexican silica. I awoke when the sun rose. My breath would have stripped barnacles off a hull. My eyelids were coated with brine. My hands were matted in a purple crust. My body was a mess, but my mind was alert. My future was brilliant. Someday soon I'd land a job, get my financial affairs in order, and banish Boundless Gloom for good.

Suffice made sixteen knots toward the tip of Baja California, paralleling the shore at a distance of thirteen miles. Two hours past sunrise, we paused for a swim, washing away the crud and the blood. The sun and salt alleviated the discomfort of my insect bites. Four hours later, after lunch,

Pratley set a comfortable cruise speed at eleven knots and engaged the tiller pilot. Below in the main cabin, Dinger spread all of the gold we had salvaged from the ruins in a display that incited Pratley to make margaritas. Dinger reimbursed Pratley for his dinghy motor in Krugerrands. He also paid him for fourteen days at his daily rate with Krugerrands. I proposed a five-Krugerrand tip for Captain Pratley. The motion carried three to nil. Pratley didn't technically have a vote, but the point was moot.

Our generosity inflamed Pratley's emotions. "I didn't know what you were up to, but I never doubted you guys." He played with Krugerrands like miniature poker chips. "Gold, gold," he crooned.

During the seven-day voyage back to San Diego, we ate canned tuna until it came out of our ears. We saved the empty cans in a plastic bag for recycling. Even though we rinsed the empty cans in salt water, San Diego probably smelled us coming. Pratley commanded *Suffice* in the nude to within two miles of Cabrillo Island, at which time he put on tennis shorts and a tee shirt that said, "Feed the Greed." When we tied up at the dock, the absence of rocking and swaying and rising and falling with swells was disorienting. After supper, we played three-handed poker using Las Vegas Sands house chips. I asked whether they were authentic.

"Everything on this boat is authentic," Pratley said.

Dinger and Pratley fell asleep at the poker table in a scene from Jonestown. I fell asleep on a couch, which pretty much wrapped up our last night on *Suffice*. The following morning Dinger and I shed our Robinson Crusoe facades by shaving and showering in fresh water at the marina. I had never been so tan in my life. Pratley got emotional when we left *Suffice* to drive home.

"I've always admired you, Tyler. I love you, man." He hugged Dinger with so much affection that Dinger squirmed. The hug exceeded the fighter pilot two-second embrace limit.

"Me too," Dinger said.

We parted in the parking lot. Dinger set off for Las Vegas with two portions of gold – his and Hacksaw's. I drove toward Phoenix with mine. Aiming for an uneventful ride home, I drove for 350 miles on Interstate Eight back to Glendale without breaking the speed limit a single time.

Chapter 24

Treasure:
a 311th Squadron challenge coin

DUCKY'S COULDN'T HAVE been more like a funeral home if it had exchanged its liquor license for a mortuary license. I ordered a pint of Guinness from an Irish bartender who had overstayed his visa. As usual, he rambled on, as if for the first time, about how Guinness in Arizona was nowhere nearly as good as it was in County Wexford. "You look bored," he said. "Did I tell you that before?"

"A few times."

"I've been diagnosed with prosopagnosia," he said, neither in pride nor in shame.

"We're in a lot of trouble, then," I said, "I'm not wearing a condom."

He snorted in the Irish way. "*Prosopagnosia* means I have face blindness."

"That's a disadvantage for a bartender," I said.

"I'm good at recognizing voices. You have a disc jockey voice, same as a hundred other people."

A barfly named Daryl sat down on a stool beside me. "He's right." Daryl was as irritating as a rash. He had been a star pitcher for Mesa Community College for two seasons, got cheated out of making the bigs, pumped gas for his flying licenses, flew a crop duster, and knew all there was to know about everything, including all the national championships Mesa had won in baseball, track, and volleyball. If reincarnated, Daryl would come back as an encyclopedia with M on the cover. He said, "I've been dusting down at Gila Bend. You know anything about flying?" I shrugged. "A crop duster pilot can fly anything. You wouldn't believe what I can do with an airplane. I'm trying to get on at Delta, but what do those grit-gobblers know? They want jet time. Hell, ten minutes of dusting is worth ten hours of sitting on your ass in a seven-twenty-seven. I could do that shit in my sleep." He figured out fast that I wasn't the solution to his empty beer mug problem. "Don't even get me started on fighter pilots. Worthless prima donnas get everything handed to them." He spotted a new face across the bar and he left me alone. I shuddered to think that I was in the same pool of broken-spirited aspiring airline pilots as Daryl.

A clean-cut kid sat on a stool beside me and slapped a 311th Fighter Squadron challenge coin onto the bar. By tradition, I needed to meet the challenge by producing my own squadron coin. If I did that, the challenger would buy me a drink. If I didn't meet the challenge because my challenge coin was at home in the coin plate on top of my chest of drawers, I had to buy him a drink. It was, so I did. His name was Tanner, and he was a first lieutenant student nose gunner in the new class at the 311th.

"I haven't met you," Tanner said, "but your picture's still on the Top Gun wall."

"What's shaking at the Three-Eleventh?"

Tanner lowered his voice and delivered shocking news: "Major Olsen was in the pit of Kranky One-Four with one of my classmates this afternoon. They went down on the East Tac Range."

———— ◈ ————

Thor's portrait was on display in the front of the congregation. The Air Force taught us how to honor our dead with dignity. Fighter pilots died often enough to keep us in practice. Caterwauling, common in some cultures, was unheard of among mourning American warriors. Stoic silence was broken by fighters flying overhead in missing man formation or by rifle volleys or by the hoof clatter of horse-drawn funeral caissons. I made a silent confession: assuming that I wasn't in reality a better pilot than Thor, I was only a twitch of a muscle or a momentary lapse away from being a corpse in my own coffin.

Overwhelmed by the loss of her husband, Sally seemed fragile sitting in the first row of pews in the overflowing chapel. I guessed that the most recent of fighter widows no longer cared that she was the singles champion of the Officers Wives Tennis Club. Her perfect tan couldn't disguise the misery that dulled her eyes and displaced her beauty. Three men in civilian suits sat shoulder-to-massive-shoulder beside her. They were at least six-and-a-half feet tall and probably weighed over 260 pounds each. I watched them from several rows back. Seated beside me, a Four-Twenty-Sixth Squadron pilot in dress blues made it his business to put a name on each face for me. "The three guys with Sally are Manny, Cody, and Bill," he whispered. "They played football with Thor at Boston College." An F-104 instructor in dress blues shook hands solemnly and sat beside the colossus called Manny.

"That's Scottie, Sixty-Ninth Squadron," my informant said. "Cornerback on the same team."

"How do you know these guys?" I asked.

"I played at West Point. We beat B.C. thirty-eight-to-seven at home that year. Sally invited me over last night to meet them. She was engaged to the guy on the right before Thor came along."

I was glad to be far removed from the Boston College Eagles lineup. Jealousy, that most vile of emotions, made me imagine Elizabeth naked in Cody's arms. My chest ached like the time the twins died in Edinburgh. Scottie tilted his head toward Cody and pointed in my direction. Cody pivoted and caught me staring at him. I looked away. While a chaplain praised Thor's virtues and accomplishments, I planned an egress route that wouldn't cross paths with Cody.

After the service, I drove to the Officers Club to attend Thor's memorial reception. When I spotted the three Goliaths passing through the main entrance doors, I considered skipping the reception, but I ended up joining the crowd in the reception room. Gunner and Jennifer Gunnersson stood beside Sally Olsen in the receiving line. On Sally's other side, an older blonde woman – I guessed it was Thor's mother – was wedged between Sally and a grief-stricken older man I reckoned to be Thor's father.

I delayed by wandering among easels displaying enlarged photographs commemorating Major Bob "Thor" Olsen's life. One photo showed Thor in a maroon and gold Boston College football uniform posing beside Sally and Jennifer. I ran across Lieutenant Colonel Fig Cannon among the floral arrangements and gallery of photos. Despite his dismal critique of my career potential, I viewed him through a softer lens since his compassionate macaroon hospital visitation. He pensively examined a memorial portrait in which the artist had captured every flawless feature of Thor's striking face. The death of Fig's protégé must have hit him especially hard. In a senior officer's entire career, he typically chose no more than three young officers to sponsor. Fig had selected Thor to mentor, develop, and fast-track into a star worthy of filling Fig's role. Now, Thor was dead while lesser talents like me lived on.

"Thor had so much promise," Fig lamented aloud. "He was an exceptional officer."

I wasn't about to let six thousand blackmail dollars and my grudge ruin Fig's earnest tribute.

"Yes, he was," I said.

Jennifer didn't budge from her place beside Sally, so I joined the line of mourners behind three exchange pilots in dress uniforms: an RAF squadron leader, a German hauptmann, and a U.S. Navy lieutenant. Just ahead of them in line were the three giants. Bill, Sally's fiancé eight years earlier, wrapped his huge arms around her. She lost composure and nestled her head against his chest. Cody, Elizabeth's former fiancé, also took Sally into his embrace. I couldn't guess whether Sally or Cody hated me more because of my whirlwind marriage to Elizabeth. I also couldn't guess why Elizabeth had never told me about Cody. There were plenty of girls I hadn't told Elizabeth about, but I never had been engaged to any of them. The three giants embraced Jennifer in turn under the somber scrutiny of Gunner.

While the Brit, the kraut, and the squid expressed their condolences ahead of me, I rummaged in my mind for a succinct, sincere way to express my respects. I still hadn't found the right words when I ended up facing Mr. Olsen. "So sorry," I mumbled as I clasped his trembling hand. He didn't answer. "Sorry," I said to Mrs. Olsen. She looked pitiful. She couldn't know whether I was Thor's best friend or worst nemesis. Sally, puffy and disoriented, proffered her hand in ritual, not in friendship. "Sally, I'm very sorry." Neither long nor complicated. Not very satisfying, either.

Sally glared into my eyes before speaking: "I believe you know Captain and Mrs. Gunnersson." Then Sally leaned forward so our heads were close to touching. "It should have been you," she whispered maliciously. She had stored up a lot of hate to say such a thing.

I moved on to shake hands with Gunner who didn't seem surprised to see me. I muttered "sorry" as if I had snuffed out Thor's life myself. My mind was too overloaded to do any better. I *was* sorry, especially for messing around with Gunner's wife. I moved on to Jennifer. If any woman in the world could measure up to Jennifer in a black dress, I would have liked to see her. "Sorry," I said.

She lightly pressed her extraordinarily luscious lips together. "Thank you, Stitch."

I was careful to leave my hand in her's no longer than I would have a stranger's. It was a relief to decouple. I needed to retreat to Ducky's. I hurried away from the sepulchral assembly to the parking lot to locate my Chevy parked beneath a bottlebrush tree. I almost jumped out of my skin when a rumbling voice behind me called my name.

"Cromwell, you said 'sorry.' About what?" I turned to face Gunner. I was sorry for an assortment of reasons besides Thor's death. As for Thor, I could bear a grudge against someone and still regret his demise. I was also sorry that Gunner had me trapped in his intimidating presence in a piping hot parking lot in Arizona. "Jennifer talked on the phone about scars all over your body. How would she know?"

Oh, boy. My misdeeds were flocking home to roost. "You'd have to ask her," I said.

"I did." He closed the distance between us. "She said that she noticed your scars at T. J. at a pool party, but I remember that party. You wore a shirt all evening."

"I can't help you," I said. The afternoon sun was making me sweat, so I sidestepped into the shade. I wanted to tell Gunner what a fool he was for super-sizing his dog's balls and for promoting his civilian father-in-law to general and for cheating me out of the top-gun trophy, but I also valued my health, so I patronized the muscle-bound knucklehead: "You don't have to do this, Gunner."

"Do what?"

"Push your weight around. You're a big, strong guy. You're an excellent pilot. You don't have to put the rest of us down." I uttered any foolishness that came to mind to make him disappear.

"I don't know what there is about getting roasted in a burning airplane that makes your opinion worth diddly squat. Stop dodging my question. How does Jennifer know about your scars?"

It would have been too familiar of me to use the name *Jennifer*. "I don't know. Honor your wife the way she honors you." I was using words on loan from a marriage counseling manual to get out of a jam. *Heavenly Father*, I prayed, *don't let this big son of a bitch pummel me.*

Gunner smirked at me. "You didn't deserve to come back to flying after your accident."

"I'm just trying to get over it the best I can." If there was ever a time that I wanted to appeal to a person's sympathies, it was at that moment.

"You're too stupid to be ashamed. The Air Force is better off without you. Now, slink off to your hole and rot." He seemed to gain control of the demon that brought him into the parking lot after me, although not without scowling and growling one last insult: "If I ever catch you around Jennifer ...."

To my great relief, he hurried away. I vowed to stay far away from Jennifer Gunnersson so I'd never be within the Golden Gopher's radius of lethality ever again. I started to open the Chevy door, but another monster blocked my path. It was Cody. His muscles strained at the cloth of his dark suit. He intimidated me without laying a hand on me.

"I never knew I could hate anybody so much." Cody's voice was steroid-raspy. He jabbed an index finger toward my chest. "Elizabeth was the one perfect woman I've ever met. I have no idea what she saw in you. I'm standing here looking at your worthless ass wondering how you can live with yourself. Fuck you!" He was too livid to say more. When he turned away in disgust, I slid into the Chevy and inserted the ignition key with an unsteady hand. Sensing that I had barely escaped getting the shit beat out of me, I drove straight to Ducky's.

In a remote part of Ducky's parking lot, I molted out my suit and pulled on a wrinkled pair of khaki shorts, a golf shirt, and topsiders. Inside Ducky's cool haven, Daryl-the-cropduster was informing the world about how he got screwed by Delta. I dodged him by sitting in the booth where Thor had shaken me down. The Irish bartender overcame prosopagnosia and took my order for a margarita. "You look like you'll need its twin before long," he said. Bartenders from County Wexford were alive-alive-o. Given enough margaritas, I hoped to cope with the loss of Elizabeth, the absence of Trudie, and, curiously, the death of Thor.

Chapter 25

Treasure:
a picture of a MiG-19 in sky blue camouflage

I WAS AS an indentured servant to disappointment. I checked my telephone answering machine recorder almost as often as I opened my mailbox door. Blank tapes and empty mailboxes were fingernails picking at failure's scab. I must have wounded Trudie deeply for her to cut me off this way. Still, my pride prevented me from calling her. We each had invested too much ego in this spat to back down now, eight months after my ill-advised and ill-timed resignation. Two stubborn people had strayed too far in opposite directions to double back. I doubted whether either one of us had enough patience or forgiveness left to repair the rift.

I distracted myself with minor tasks. Change doorbell battery – check. Pay overdue bills — check. As I audited old telephone invoices, one telephone number among the list of incoming calls stood out from the rest. I examined the squadron recall roster and discovered that the call had come from Thor Olsen's residence. The call had been placed on the same day I had resigned my commission. I mulled over the sequence of events that day to guess why the conversation between Trudie and the Olsen household would have lasted eleven minutes.

I was so useless in my present state that I couldn't even sell the house. A whacky high school teacher who, no doubt, had attended a get-rich-flipping-real-estate seminar, tossed me low balls, which I rejected. Before it was over, he could have offered full price and I would have rejected his offer to deny him the slightest satisfaction. Aviation was getting along without me, too. I hadn't received a single invitation for an airline interview. Dinger telephoned to tell me that he had rented a safety deposit box to store the "you-know-what" belonging to him and Hacksaw. We didn't talk for long because my attempts at good cheer were unconvincing. Hacksaw called only once, perhaps because he was concerned that he might be perceived as gloating about his good fortune at Western. He gave me a prospective lead gleaned from a former squadron buddy of his at Hill AFB. According to this native of Beaumont, Texas, LSU track star, pilot for Delta Airlines, and current pilot in the Louisiana Air National Guard, I qualified for an instructor pilot opening in the Louisiana squadron. This first-rate fighter squadron was known colloquially in the fighter community as the Coonass Militia. Coonass was slang for Cajun which was slang for Arcadian. The squadron was transitioning from F-100s to F-4s and needed current Phantom instructors. I was close to being current, so I pitched my qualifications shamelessly by telephone to get an interview. I flew to New Orleans on two days' notice.

After two hours of interviews, a driver delivered me in a staff car to the hotel where I was staying in Belle Chase, right across the river from New Orleans. One of the Coonass Militia flight commanders was coming to take me to dinner at seven. I waited for him at a table in the hotel lounge and got a head start on the drinks so I'd be at my peak of sociability and wit to make a solid impression. Halfway through my first drink, a stocky guy sat down uninvited and flipped a business card at me. I read the name on the card aloud: "Barry Seal."

"Oops," he said as he replaced the original business card with another. "Wrong card. Barry's one of my top performers." The replacement card read "Ellis MacKenzie."

"Nice to meet you, Ellis," I said.

His handshake was a carpenter's clamp. He had the charismatic personality of a TV game show host.

He asked, "Am I correct in guessing that you're an airplane driver?"

"You nailed it."

He told lots of amusing stories, including one about his second cousin who shot off his right testicle practicing fast draw with a new revolver. "Next, he lost his left nut to cancer. Wrote a book about it – *And Then There Were None.*" Cancerous testicles weren't fodder for humor in polite circles, but Ellis dropped punch lines at the right pace to keep me entertained. Soon we were chatting about more than missing body parts. He told me about a golden opportunity to make big bucks flying nights. "I mean, big, big bucks. I like your style, Stitch. Give me a call. It could be the smartest decision of your life." He looked at his watch and faked surprise.

"Whoa. Look at the time. You're so fascinating I lost track."

I hadn't spoken twenty words, so I doubted that "fascinating" was the descriptor that fit me best. Ellis and I shook hands again as he rose to leave. I noticed a tall man in a flight suit in a side doorway beckoning to me as Ellis left the bar by a back door. I settled the tab and went to the pilot standing in the shadowy side doorway.

"Let's go somewhere else," he said before he had even introduced himself. I followed him. When we were alone in the parking lot, my flight commander host said, "You don't want to mess with that guy."

I showed him the business card: "You mean Ellis MacKenzie? He's funny as hell."

"I'm not saying he isn't funny, but he isn't Ellis MacKenzie." He snatched the card from my fingers, tore it up, and tossed the scraps into a trashcan. "That's Barry Seal, out of Baton Rouge, and he's into all kinds of stuff you don't want to be into. He's the biggest drug smuggler in America. How old are you?"

"Thirty-two."

"They told me at the Coonass that you were a smart guy."

"I'm from Texas." I had set it up for him.

"That would explain it." He spiked it.

The next afternoon I was back in Glendale checking my mailbox. The Coonass called to let me know they had chosen another applicant. I was as low as I could get. Maybe Thor Olsen had blackballed me from the grave. Maybe the Coonass Flight Commander was suspicious of my association with Barry Seal. Thanks, Thor. Thanks, Barry. I was too depressed to stay sober, so I poured a Jack Daniels. The last person I expected to hear from was Jim Conti, but, *abracadabra*, as if to teach a divine lesson on why suicide was usually a premature decision, Jim called. He lifted my sagging self-esteem and launched my hopes into the stratosphere.

"How would you like to nail down three hundred large a year?"

DEFCON *UNO*. Making $300,000 a year was incomprehensible to me. Three hundred billion would have sounded the same to me. "Sure." What an understatement.

"That's all I can tell you, and don't let anyone ever know that I said even that much. As of yesterday, they don't have any other viable candidates, no matter what they represent to you."

"Who is *they*?"

"I can't say. I'm not in the official loop, but I found out about it and it's too good to pass up."

"Where are you, Jim?"

"You know better than to ask that."

I scribbled "$300,000" on a legal pad. Jim gave me a restaurant address in Scottsdale where I was to meet a contact for dinner two nights hence. Jim said that the gentleman in question wouldn't be a stranger, which led me to believe that Jim liked secrets for their own sake. Meeting a gentleman who wouldn't be a stranger narrowed down the possibilities because my list of known gentlemen wasn't a lengthy one. I was so excited that I forgot to ask Jim about himself. He didn't forget me, though.

"How's that good-looking gal, Trudie?"

I answered him jauntily and falsely. "She's terrific. I'll tell her that you called."

I *would* tell her, too, just as soon as I met with the surreptitious contact in Scottsdale to figure out what it would take to bag the $300,000. I intended to use this spectacular news to resolve our communications impasse. I couldn't wait to hear Trudie's little gasp at the moment that love for her miserable excuse for a husband reignited in her heart.

I was desperate enough for a job to duck-walk to Scottsdale if necessary. My brain was working overtime. My senses were percolating. It irritated me no end that it took an hour of my precious time to drive from Glendale across Phoenix to Scottsdale. I wasn't just poking around, either. The Altoid-scented parking valet seemed annoyed about having to park a lowly Chevrolet. I made a mental note to tip him commensurately. Scottsdale's haughtiest maître d', a sliver of a man enveloped by an invisible cloud of lavender and mothballs, escorted me to a corner table. My mystery host, dressed in khaki chinos and sandals and presiding over two martini sentinels, extended his arms godfather style when he caught sight of me approaching. I slid into the boomerang-shaped booth beside him.

"That's no gentleman," I said, "that's Mister Bruno."

"We meet again. Whenever adventure surfaces, you're not far away."

A waiter fluttered to our table, and I pointed to Mr. Bruno's martinis and then at myself. Hand gestures were expedient because Mr. Bruno was blabbing, and I didn't want to impede him getting to the part about the $300,000. He pulled a check from his safari shirt and waggled it at me.

"Five big ones," he said. "Do you agree to keep the substance and details of this meeting secret?"

"There's not much I wouldn't do for five hundred dollars." My wilted attempt at humor was wrongheaded. A sophisticated negotiator with the potential to earn $300,000 would never have said that.

Mr. Bruno pushed a confidentiality agreement in front of me. I signed beside the yellow sticky thing. Next he pushed the check toward me. The signature wasn't Bruno's or Brewer's.

A third voice butted in: "Got a check for me, too?"

I recognized that voice. It belonged to the Big Kahuna back in Mexico, Carlos or Raul, depending on whether he was wearing his drug runner hat or his DEA hat.

"You've met Raul?"

"Yes. Yes, I have. He used to torture one of my best friends."

Raul laughed. I was getting the hang of fraternizing with spooks. We shook hands.

"Ha. You should have seen your face when you thought I was whipping up on your boy Dingo."

"Dinger."

"Yeah, *Dinger*. Old Dinger was pretty sure his ding dong was in a wringer."

Raul slapped me on the back: "You three boys were good sports. I tried to take it easy on you, but of course I had to be tough enough to convince the riffraff."

All was forgiven. In my simple mind, the $300,000 was going to fix all broken things, erase all nightmares, and restore my life to happiness.

"I liked the way you got the job done," Raul said. "That's why I know you're the man for this gig."

Oh, boy. I was so eager to get my hands on the dough that I was double-chugging my martinis. I had to slow that pony down so I wouldn't end up on my knees crawling out of the joint.

"Raul's with Everest now," Mr. Bruno said. I imagined that Raul had directed a tidy sum toward Everest to juice his switch the same way brokers brought their client lists along with them to new firms. "Raul, you're the brains behind this new venture, so why don't you tell Stitch about it."

Raul was nothing if not a salesman. "This job will let you manage an air force of MiG-19s and blow things up and maybe shoot stuff down."

I tried not to act too keen. Visions of running my own air force previewed on the big screen of my mind in full color. I'd make myself a lieutenant colonel squadron commander. Screw that, I'd be a three-star general the same as Gunner's dad or maybe a chief of staff.

"We're close to delivering seven MiG-19s in pristine condition. You'll have ten English-speaking pilots, and you'll be in charge of tactics for interdicting illegal drugs."

"Targets?"

"Jungle labs, trucks, donkeys, distribution sites. You might even get to shoot down some planes."

I was close to frothing at the mouth. This was the chance of a lifetime, a last exploit before I settled down. I longed for Trudie to be sitting at the table beside these schemers who were selecting her husband, from among all the pilots in the world, to head up the whole shebang.

"Where's this taking place?"

"In an undisclosed third-world country where they brush their teeth with sticks and eat fish with the heads still attached," Raul said. "You'll have free housing, a maid, an expense account, and a salary of two-hundred-and-forty-thousand bucks a year. Not too shabby."

I stifled a grin. It was time to wheel and deal. I figured Mr. Bruno was the bank and Raul was the fishing guide who baited the hooks.

"You'll have all the bullets, rockets, bombs, and missiles you need. You'll be flying under color of the military of a friendly nation."

"Could my wife accompany me?"

"Only if you're trying to get rid of her," Raul laughed. Mr. Bruno scowled at him, and he straightened up. "No, no wife. Security will be an issue, but you'll have plenty of personal protection."

I conjured up teenage daydreams of ceiling fans, mosquito nets, and beady-eyed little chaps with Uzis who existed for no other reason than to keep me safe. I put on my best poker face.

"You can't say where it is?"

"No. I'll give you a hint: you won't be spending your free time bobsledding."

"I'll have to check with my wife on this."

Mr. Bruno stepped in, "Of course. You've got seventy-two hours to give us a final answer. If you don't agree by the deadline, we'll tear up the paperwork and none of this ever happened."

It was time for me to get down to the nut-cutting. The prospect of $20,000 a month had pushed me to within a nanometer of laughing aloud with joy, but greed pushed me to want more.

"I couldn't do it for less than twenty-eight grand a month." I teetered between the hope that Mr. Bruno would agree to my madcap request and fear that he would send my avaricious ass packing.

"Wow." This was light work for Mr. Bruno. "We might have to squeeze your king-sized bed down to a queen, but we can swing three hundred and thirty-six per annum." He scribbled in the margin of the conditional contract and initialed it with a *B*. "Yeah, let's do it."

I rediscovered what happiness felt like. Trudie would be staggered when I told her that I was going to haul in ten times an Air Force major's salary. She'd forget every mistake I'd ever made and would make into perpetuity. Who needed the airlines? This salary was almost three times a current airline captain's pay. I could fly Trudie in for the weekend and order my troops to pass in review to the music of a martial band. Trudie could fill a cabinet with Val Saint-Lambert crystal. Katrina could attend Yale. We could sail around the world. I could donate to charity to see Trudie's name etched on a bronze plaque. She could put stained-glass windows in the Vatican, I didn't care.

"It's a two-year contract," Mr. Bruno said, "extendable."

"You could set yourself up for life in two years, my friend," Raul said.

I inventoried equatorial countries that might be in the market for hiring ex-patriot pilots to fly Russian-made fighters against drug traffickers: Ecuador, Colombia, Congo, Uganda, Kenya, maybe Indonesia. "I'll give you a final answer inside of three days," I said.

"Excellent." Mr. Bruno showed me where he had initialed the conditional contract. Raul looked on without showing the slightest trace of envy.

"You have to be forceful with the missus," Mr. Bruno said. "Wives don't always see the big picture." He raised his hands as if to deliver a benediction. "If you don't take this opportunity by midnight Monday, you won't be my go-to guy anymore. I won't contact you again."

I was a lotto winner – undeserving, but oh so happy. Being the chief of staff of an air force — any air force — exceeded the boundaries of my imagination. I chattered all through dinner, but deep inside my brain, where fantasy danced with delirium, I practiced my pitch for Trudie. My choices were starkly contrasting: I could remain poor and unemployed or I could pull down $336,000 a year flying an exotic airplane for the equivalent of two consecutive remote tours. I had to tread carefully to get Trudie's consent. This time, even though I had already signed the contract, I would present it to Trudie as though the deal was an offer, which I would accept only with her blessing. How could Trudie possibly *not* give her blessing? She was headstrong, but she wasn't nuts. I trembled with anticipation. I intended to steer my bride as I desired with the skill and powers of logic I had gleaned over a lifetime.

When I returned home to Glendale after midnight, my emotions were higher than a weather balloon. I tried to call Trudie at her normal wakeup time in Bruges, although, really, there was no bad time to call with such wonderful news. No one answered the telephone. Perhaps the line was down. I placed another call the following afternoon Bruges time. I couldn't get through the second day, either. I telephoned a bar near my mother-in-law's house and asked an English-speaking barman if someone could knock on her door to see if all was well.

"We are not experts with the messages," the barman said.

I offered to give him my credit card number to pay for his trouble.

"It would cost three thousand francs," the barman said, making up the pricing as he went along. That was almost $100, a trifling amount for a high roller knocking down over three hundred large a year. I agreed to pay the profiteer his three thousand francs.

If he left a message, it didn't get through. At least Trudie didn't call me. A $97.44 debit showed up on my credit card account the next day, however, so the barman, regardless of his talents for messaging, was a highly skilled hustler. I couldn't even guess where Trudie was, but I felt certain that she wasn't at her mother's house. At two o'clock in the afternoon of the third day, I gave up and stretched out on our king-sized bed. All the windows in the house were open. The temperature was 74 degrees Fahrenheit. A breeze stirred. My watch read "2200," Belgian Time. I conked out for three solid hours of vivid Technicolor dreams.

When I drifted into the realm of consciousness, I didn't

wake up in the conventional sense, but prolonged a dream in which I was seven years old. My mother beside me was so real that I could have reached out and touched her. I adored her radiant face, soft brown eyes, and angelic smile as she admired the blue silk ribbon bestowed on me that day. I didn't know whether she was enchanted more by the blue silky sheen of the ribbon or the gold letters screen printed on it that read, "Citizenship." Yes, that morning, in front of 24 other delinquents, I had received an award celebrating the supreme quality of my citizenship. My first grade teacher had conferred on me probably the most momentous honor of my fledgling existence.

"This is a very worthy thing," my mother said. She looked at me and smiled affectionately. My heart was on the edge of exploding with pleasure. I was worthy. I sensed no pain, no fear, for I was worthy. I lingered in the moment as time passed slower than a glacier made out of honey. How glorious was this lofty achievement, my mother's smile, and her soft voice, "This is a very worthy thing."

I was in a stupor, and every muscle in my body was flaccid. I visualized a sleek MiG-19 poised on a pristine strip of concrete that bisected a field of verdant grass. The MiG's fuselage was buffed to a high gloss. Formed line abreast behind the MiG, a rank of ten strapping men in navy blue flight suits marched toward me, their commander. Their infinite respect for me was apparent in their piercing eyes and firm jaws. I was demanding of them, but they loved me for it. I loved them in return. My dream cut to a chunk of sky where I was soaring noiselessly in my MiG-19 over sunlit cumulous clouds. I rolled inverted and when I glanced left,

I saw three MiGs in perfect echelon formation on my left wing, and, looking right, three more on the right. My six wingmen stayed glued in double echelon formation as we scaled towering cumulous, then, rolling onto our backs in a lazy half-G top of a loop, straight down as the onset of G forces multiplied and pulled like an insistent friend. At the bottom, we rushed as one over a river of crystal water, our gleaming jets clearing the sparkling surface by a meter. Blinding speed. Perfect precision. My unfaltering wingmen never flinched, never quivered. They entrusted their lives into my worthy hands. When I awoke abruptly, I realized that it was past midnight in Bruges. The press of the deadline led me to imagine the worst. Perhaps Katrina, Trudie, and her mother lay slaughtered on a floor in the house. I should have considered that before. I went nuclear and, after an hour of telephonic dead ends, I reached an inspector in the *Gemeentepolitie*. He gave me the American celebrity treatment, but, after some fiddly-farting around, he informed me that no one was present at the Michiels residence and that there was no sign of anything amiss. I was out of time. I had to call Mr. Bruno before midnight Arizona Time.

Commanding a squadron of MiG-19s would be the pinnacle of my aviation career. The salary was fantastic. Surely Trudie would appreciate the chance for family financial security. She could keep living with Katrina in Bruges until my covert tour was over. Separation, making our hearts grow fonder, was a small price to pay for this opportunity of a lifetime. I would be insane to pass it up.

"Mister Bruno, I'm calling to accept the offer. When do I start?"

"Excellent. Listen, don't tell anyone. Raul will mail you some English text flight manuals to study. Next month you'll attend a familiarization course in Egypt by yourself. You'll get ten hours of flying with an English-speaking MiG-19 instructor. Then you'll fly to Pakistan for three months of ground school and basic MiG-19 training with Pakistani instructors. You'll be joined by five other pilots we've already hired. There's a South African, an Aussie, a Welsh guy, and two former Rhodesian Air Force pilots. Hotels and travel will be provided for you, and you'll receive per diem of eighty dollars a day until you finish training in Karachi; then your salary starts."

The morning after I accepted the mercenary job, my realtor called to announce that The Ardent Trust, an investment group, had submitted a cash offer for my house at my full asking price. The inability to sell my house had squeezed me financially for months, so the unexpected offer from a cash buyer was a green light to accepting the mercenary job overseas. Getting Trudie's consent was the last remaining obstacle. I visualized the steps I would take. I'd get immunized against the worst diseases the world had to offer, making me as invulnerable as a cockroach. I'd study the MiG-19 eight hours a day. I'd get Trudie's post facto blessing as soon as I could. I'd keep the secret from everyone, even Dinger. I had just finished my dinner of burritos and beer when Dinger called from Las Vegas.

"Stitch, we've got to get up to Salt Lake tomorrow. Hack's sick, real sick."

Chapter 26

Treasure:
a round-trip ticket stub for an American
Airlines flight from Phoenix to Austin

I CAUGHT THE first available flight from Phoenix to Salt Lake City and tracked Rena down in a University of Utah Medical Center neurology ward waiting room. She said that she hadn't slept for more than two hours at a stretch since Hacksaw's emergency admission. She said, "Bobby Joe's got a brain tumor, a grade four glioblastoma, an astrocytoma that's growing fast." The only two words I understood were "brain tumor." She rested her head on my chest as though she didn't have the energy to support it on her own. "Hunter flew in from Austin last night. He just left for the first time to get some sleep."

"How did they find Hack's tumor?"

"He threw up and collapsed during a simulator ride. They got him to a hospital immediately, but it was too late to operate. It was too late for anything." She folded her body into a stuffed chair. "Can you wake me in twenty minutes?"

I left her with her crumpled dreams and I entered the ward. I found Hacksaw's hospital room and stepped in quietly.

"Is that you, Dinger?"

"Hey, Hack. Dinger's flying in from Vegas later. This is Stitch."

"Hey, Stitch. My headlights aren't twenty-twenty anymore." Hacksaw struggled to open his eyelids then gave up. "Good old Dinger. He's my executor. Maybe it's Hunter." He wasn't even pretending that he was going to survive this ordeal.

"Either one's a good choice," I said.

Time seemed scarce, as though the angel who runs the clock had reluctantly consented to give Hacksaw a few seconds more so we could get things said. Hacksaw asked, "How did you do this shit for seven thousand days?" He meant seven hundred. "When we met for the first time at Torrejón, you told me how long you were in the hospital. I thought, fuck me in the brain." His laugh was more a truncated cough than a normal Hacksaw hoot. "Well, here I am, and sure as shit, my brain's been fucked."

I clasped his limp right hand in both of mine and held on so he'd feel anchored.

"I've always admired the way you handled your troubles, Stitch. You didn't know we were watching you, did you? Man, Dudley, we did a pile of doo-doo down in Old Chihuahua, didn't we?"

"We sure did, Hack."

"Yep." He licked his dry lips. "Me and the Stitcheroo made a little history." He smiled and squeezed my hand the best he could. "We couldn't have screwed up that first leg out of Marana any worse than we did." He laughed until he coughed again. "I was a tiger in those days. Screw the tiger, I was a lion. King of the goddamn jungle."

"Yeah, you were."

"When I strapped on the Phantom, I was the most powerful son-of-a-gun in the world."

I knew what he meant, so I squeezed his hand to reassure him that he was making sense.

"Remember Wax Man and R. P. back in … that place? Called them Stitch's Losers? Hell, I didn't mean anything by it. I was just mouthing off. Hell, I even had a groupie, what was his name?"

"Wolfman."

"Old Wolfman. I had Wolfman and you had Wax Man."

I said, "The difference between me and Wax Man was about sixty seconds of burn time."

"As long as you know that I didn't mean anything by it."

I wanted to hug this magnificent broken-down fighter pilot legend, but tubes and wires were in the way, so I just held on to his hand and kept watch on him through tears.

"I understand Wax Man now," he said. "I wonder who's luckier, him living or me dying?"

I wanted to respond, but I wasn't sure that words would come out.

"I never told you this, but I almost rammed into Dinger going from Atl Ixtaca to … that first place."

"Hidalgo," I said.

"Yeah, Hidalgo. I lost track of Dinger in the moonlight."

"Hard to see a black plane at night."

"I bet Dinger never told you that he almost smashed into you a little after that."

"Really?"

"Yeah, I'd closed up to eight hundred feet on Dinger and neither one of us had a tally on you until you popped up right in front of Dinger for a ridge crossing." He laughed again. "Damn close to bending some metal. They never would have found the debris. Nothing but scraps of aluminum scattered among rocks." His closed eyelids fluttered in spasm from seeing so many images streaming past. "I was a sick-ass puppy that night, *Commandante*. I had no business driving a golf cart much less a T-Bird. Landing on that highway was the same as landing on the edge of a razor blade. Weren't we something? Immortal." He coughed. "Why don't you give me a Bible verse."

Hack caught me off guard. My memorized verses were notable for their brevity, not their import. One of the longer short ones came to mind, Colossians 2:5: "For though I am absent from you in body, I am present with you in spirit."

"You nailed it," Hacksaw said. "When I clear out of here, I'll be an angel watching you all the time … a non-stop check ride." He paused and adjusted his feet under the sheet. "Wish I'd got back home to Austin one last time, but …."

A seizure hit him without warning. His hand was a vice grip for a few seconds and then it fell limp. The room felt different when he passed away. It reminded me of the night on the burn ward when Tom Speer canceled the rental on his ventilator. The Time Angel had said, "Time's up." I knew that in the instant of Hack's passing away, the world was *not* a better place. But Heaven was.

———=»(())«=———

Dinger arrived in Salt Lake City too late to visit Hacksaw before he died, so he caught a passenger flight from Las Vegas to Austin on the morning of Hack's memorial service. I picked him up at the Austin Bergstrom airport and took him to brunch before we went to church. Six other fighter pilots, some from Torrejón and some from Hill AFB sat together, a row of eight friends in dress blues and me in my charcoal grey suit. Several of Hacksaw's Texas A&M classmates occupied the row ahead of us. They wore Army dress greens and referred to Hacksaw as Bobby Joe. Hacksaw and Rena had no children, so Rena sat in the front row, dignified and alone, a proxy for every brave woman who had ever mourned the loss of her husband.

We filed out of church between a cordon formed by Hunter Ballantine and other members of the Texas A&M Corps of Cadets dressed in senior boots. Cadets lowered an American flag to half-mast as a bugler played taps. F-100 Super Sabres from the Texas Air National Guard flew in missing man formation overhead. I was glad for my dark aviator glasses because I couldn't stop tears from flowing. I didn't know how Rena remained composed. That evening, the former Six-Twelfth aviators in attendance met for a spur-of-the-moment Torrejón reunion dinner. After the meal, when the smoking lamp was lit, Dinger and I excused ourselves to share a moment together on an outdoor balcony. Dinger asked me whether I had spent my Krugerrands, and I told him that I was keeping the bars and the Krugerrands in a bank vault.

"Do you need the coins?" he asked.

"No." I didn't tell my best friend that I was on the threshold of earning over $300,000 a year.

"I don't need mine, either," he said. "Better a ton of health than an ounce of gold. Krugerrands are overrated." Dinger's view of gold wasn't a majority opinion among the pilots I had ever known, but I took his point. "I'm going to give all of Hack's gold and my Krugers to Rena."

For most of my adult life, I had supposed that money was my life's treasure. In the shadow of Hacksaw's death, however, money seemed more like an amphetamine for my ego than a vital element of my life. I was on the verge of being flush with money for the first time ever, but I felt certain that money wasn't the treasure I sought. Money seemed merely ornamental without Trudie by my side. I told Dinger that I'd give Rena my Krugerrands, too.

———«(❂)»———

When Trudie answered my telephone call in Bruges, I wasn't prepared to speak right away because so many of my calls to her had gone unanswered. Trudie was breathless, as though she had sprinted to answer the aged telephone in her mother's hallway. I could hear visitors' voices and a baby's wail echoing off linoleum floors.

"Katrina, go to Bomma," Trudie said.

"How are you?" I asked.

"Katrina, go on to Bomma," Trudie repeated. I could visualize Katrina toddling off to the kitchen.

"Hack died." I led off with that because I figured it would distract her from being angry with me.

"Hack? Oh, God. How's Rena?"

"She's doing well."

"I'm so sorry."

The conversation lagged, natural enough when the subject was the death of a friend.

"Trudie, I've made a big move without consulting with you. I hope you don't mind."

She sighed theatrically as if to say, "Here he goes again."

I didn't dare tell her that Dinger and I had pulled off a raid in Mexico to retrieve our gold. That was an episode best left unaddressed if I wanted to keep her on the line.

"Dinger and I saved up some Everest pay and we gave it to Rena to help with burial expenses."

"That's very decent," Trudie said. "That's good."

"I'm glad you feel that way. It felt right."

"You'll never regret helping a friend." After a pause she asked, "Has the house sold yet?"

I told her about the closing scheduled for three days hence. I asked, "Why haven't you called me?"

"It was your place to call me. You owe me an explanation."

"For God's sake, Trudie, it wasn't that big of a deal. I'm sorry I didn't give you a heads-up about leaving the Air Force. My feelings were hurt. It was a snap decision. There are worse sins."

"I know."

"What does that mean?"

"I know about Jennifer Gunnersson."

A punch to the gut. "What about her?"

"I spotted you two together at your going-away party. I was too stupid to call you out then."

"Trudie."

"Major Olsen told me about you and her, so don't deny it."

"What did he tell you? And *when* did he tell you?"

"That you had sept with Jennifer. He called me the day you resigned from the Air Force."

I pieced together the sequence of events. I remembered Thor's threat in the hallway on the same afternoon as my St. Andrews conversation with Lieutenant Colonel Cannon. I had submitted my separation paperwork the following day. I recalled the invoice record of the eleven-minute phone call to Trudie from Thor that day: Thor had gotten his revenge by accusing me of sleeping with Jennifer. No wonder Trudie had refused to contact me.

"Trudie, I promise you, I did *not* sleep with Jennifer."

"Well, Jim Conti called and told me the same thing."

I was astonished. How would Jim know anything about Jennifer? How would he even know Trudie's number? He must have owned a Rolodex as big as a Ferris wheel. Could my sponsor, my godfather have stabbed me in the back, willing to sabotage my marriage to free me up for the mercenary gig? Step one: I had to get Trudie to agree to patch up our marriage. Step two: I had to get her blessing on the new CIA project because raking in money hand-over-fist wouldn't satisfy me without the assurance that Trudie was committed to me. Convincing Trudie to end the separation was a slow slog. Each explanation exposed new obstacles. When I told her why Thor had sought revenge, I had to admit that he had blackmailed me for thousands of dollars and I had to explain why I had let him get away with it. I didn't mention that Thor had been pulverized on the East Tac Range; I didn't want her to sympathize with him or give him any credibility. I couldn't sacrifice Jim Conti because he was my ticket to mercenary riches. I admitted that I had been in a hotel room with Jennifer but I swore that we hadn't had sex. Anyway, I argued, it had happened before marrying Trudie. Having limped over that hurdle, I tried to explain my impulsive resignation. I told Trudie about Fig's unflattering opinions of me and his advice for me to get out of the service.

"Have you got a job, yet?"

Here was my opening. I had to handle it delicately. "I've got a terrific offer which I hope you'll approve of. If you do, I'll accept it." So far, so good. Lying required a total commitment to the false scenario. "I've been offered a salary of over three hundred thousand dollars a year."

"What? The President doesn't make that much."

I tried to sound modest but deserving: "I'm uniquely qualified for the job."

"You mean it's not flying for the airlines?"

"Not exactly." I had to tiptoe deftly. "It's a job setting up a flying operation overseas." No mention of bullets or rockets and no mention of Jim Conti because I wasn't sure he was in Trudie's good graces after spilling his guts about me and Jennifer.

"Where overseas?"

"I don't know yet because it's classified."

"It can't be a serious offer if you don't know where it is."

"I'll have to be remote for two years." Silence. "Time'll fly by. You and Katrina can live in Bruges with your mom . It'll be wonderful."

"Wonderful? Wonderful? If we're going to get back together, we're going to do it right."

The conversation swerved wildly off-track from my planned trajectory. "There's no other way for me to make this kind of money, Trudie. It's only for two years. Seven hundred, thirty days. Then we'll live anywhere you want to live. It'll be fabulous."

"If you want to be a bachelor, be a bachelor. I won't hold you back."

I should have told her that I would reject the offer, but I couldn't come up with the words. Being a MiG-19 squadron commander was an opportunity too rare. The promise of financial reward was too alluring. The hope of proving myself worthy was too irresistible. I made a split-second decision, hoping that I could repair our marriage after the money was in the bank.

"Trudie, I have to do this. Please understand." I had admitted that I wasn't really seeking her advice or consent. I was asking for her stamp of approval to a done deal. The telephone line went dead, which made me angry enough to affirm my decision. I'd travel to Egypt and Pakistan and make my fortune. I'd live out my fantasy in whatever God-forsaken country Everest was sending me to and make a bundle doing it. Then I'd come back when Trudie had cooled down and put the pieces of our marriage back together again. Doing it my way meant I could have it all. I wasn't going to let Trudie's emotions block my aspirations. Heads up, Cairo and Islamabad. Stitch inbound.

I questioned my decision every time I reflected on Katrina and Trudie. I wasn't sleeping well. I remained wakeful when I should have been sleeping and vice versa. I ignored confidentiality and set my pride aside to call my father. I told him I needed advice, but I was really boasting about my jumbo salary. I wanted to impress him and for him to tell me he was proud of me. It was hard to admit to my pastor father that Trudie and I were separated. He withheld judgment while I explained it all.

Dad finally said, "In a parable, Jesus said that life's worries and riches can choke us."

I could smell a sermon coming.

"Jesus also said, 'For where your treasure is, there your heart will be also.'"

Yep. I'd heard it before. It was pulpit time.

"You've got a *treasure problem*," Dad said. "You have to decide whether to give your heart to a pile of money or to Trudie."

"I want both."

"That's not an option. It's time for you to know your heart."

I didn't get what I wanted from Dad, so I called Dinger and gave him a synopsis.

"Here's what you do, Cromwell. Call Trudie and tell her that you want her back beside you in the States. You're not going to quit on this marriage. You're no quitter. You can't live without Trudie. Or Katrina. Plug her in there, too. Tell her that you'll turn down the job offer, but don't resign at Everest until she gives her word that she'll come back."

"Three hundred thousand dollars," I wailed.

"Forget about that. If she'll come back, you resign."

"What if she won't come back?"

"Then fly MiG-19s and blow up some shit and kill drug smugglers."

Dinger the engineer was a black belt at breaking things down into simple binary decisions. This mercenary job was a chance for me to get ahead. Trudie might come around when the checks started rolling in. On the other hand, if she wouldn't come around, I knew I'd never find anyone to compare to her. It vexed me mightily, but I followed the counsel of my father and Dinger, even though resuscitating our marriage would force me to give up a dream job and remain unemployed. My heart won out over avarice. Love defeated greed. My hand was shaking as I grasped the telephone receiver.

"Trudie, this is Stitch."

"I know who it is." Was she still boiling or just pouting? This was going to require humility. I had experienced more than my share of humiliation, but I wasn't proficient in the practice of humility.

"Trudie, I love you and I want you here with me, no matter what."

"You've worn me out, Stitch. I can't live with you diving through windshields and getting kidnapped. I didn't marry Evel Knievel, I married Daniel Cromwell. Don't take this job."

"Promise me that you'll forgive me and come home and

I'll turn it down." There. I'd said it.

"I'll forgive you, dammit, because I love you, but you've got to pull back on your throttle or whatever you call that thingamabob. You've got to be here for us."

"I will be."

"Stop trying to prove that you're good enough. Elizabeth forgave you long ago. Forgive yourself." I was getting more advice than I'd bargained for. "Don't deny the living trying to honor the dead. Get it through your head that you're all I want. I married you, Stitch, not your wallet. I don't want your money or even a fancy house. I just want you."

In an expression of hope more than a promise, I told her that she wouldn't regret coming home. She called back in an hour with her flight schedule from Brussels to Phoenix. She was flying on Sabena from Brussels to Chicago and then United from Chicago to Phoenix. The last thing she said before hanging up the phone was, "There'll be three of us."

Of course — Trudie, Katrina, and me – three of us. Or she might have meant that I'd be meeting three travelers at the airport – Katrina, Trudie, and Trudie's mother. I loved my mother-in-law, but, for now, I preferred to love her at a distance. I couldn't call back to clarify for fear that Trudie might cancel her reservation as fast as she'd made it.

Chapter 27

Treasures:
two keepsake wisps of blonde baby hair bound by pink ribbons

I DREADED CALLING Mr. Bruno to renege on the mercenary agreement. Admitting that my signature on a contract was meaningless was a degrading confession. Breaking my word to Everest Aviation in order to fulfill my promise to Trudie had seemed a minor bother while I was on the telephone with her, but placing the mandatory call to Mr. Bruno gave me the shakes. On one hand, he would consider me a chump for turning my back on so much money. On another, I despised the kind of controversy my breach of contract was sure to spawn. I'd rather crawl a mile on broken glass than face up to conflict. I didn't have the courage to tell Mr. Bruno the plain truth, so I relied on a time-tested lie.

"I have to withdraw my name because of a grave family illness," I told him. "Totally unexpected. A real tragedy. Involving my mother." I cast my healthy mother, currently residing with my father on a ranch in Oregon, into the role of casualty in this heart-rending, but fictional catastrophe.

Mr. Bruno wasn't bamboozled by my amateur fabrications for a second. He impugned my maturity, character, and manhood. He said that my "bi-polar double-dealing" would devastate Raul. This seemed a stretch because Raul, a.k.a. Carlos, impressed me as man more likely to be the *devastator* than the *devastatee* in any deal. Mr. Bruno colorfully told me that if I leaked *any* part of the deal to *anyone*, he would violate my liver until my dick fell off. To top it all off, he accused me of betraying Jim Conti. "How dare you do this to your champion? It's a disgrace. Disgusting." Mr. Bruno hung up on me.

I consoled myself by looting the refrigerator to binge on Oreos and milk as if globs of fat and calcium oxalate would result in anything besides kidney stones. I browsed through the contents of a cardboard shoebox sitting on my desk. Nostalgia distracted me from my wretchedness as I rummaged through pictures of Trudie, Katrina, and me. Was Destiny whispering that I had made the right choice? Or was Greed telling me I was a sap?

The next time my telephone rang, it was my realtor calling to announce that The Ardent Trust had backed out of buying my house. It seemed more than coincidental that the sale had fallen through so soon after I had turned down the mercenary job. I asked the realtor who the signatory agent was.

"The trustee," she said.

"I mean who signed the purchase and sales agreement for Ardent?"

"Robert Brewer."

It was evident to me that Everest had offered to buy my house as an inducement for me to take the mercenary job.

Now that I had turned down the job, Bruno was backing out of the house purchase to put me in a financial bind again. I didn't appreciate being manipulated and I was still simmering when Jim Conti called, asking me to hear him out.

I butted in first: "Why did you tell Trudie that I had slept with Jennifer Gunnersson?"

"It didn't go down that way. She asked me about it. I couldn't lie."

"How could you possibly know whether I'd slept with Jennifer?"

"I know everything about you, Stitch. I'm your sponsor. Trudie was standing in the way of your success. She needed to know the truth."

"You just wanted her out of the way."

"I knew she'd come back to you when you were rolling in cash. They always do."

"You don't know Trudie."

"You wanted me to lie to her?"

"Why were you calling her anyway? She didn't call you."

"We needed to nail this down and Trudie was in the way. I just wanted to break the logjam."

"By the way, I didn't sleep with Jennifer."

He changed the subject back to the mercenary job: "I heard Bruno lost his cool. Listen, we can unbreak this thing. This is no less than your country calling. I'll be totally transparent about this. The other candidates can't hold a candle to you."

This was killing me. I knew what I had promised Trudie, but my resolve faltered because Jim held all the financial cards.

"Your country needs you. Are you worried about the risk? I'll give you more body guards. You can use a pseudonym. I'll get you a huge life insurance policy. You'll be a king – free house, free food, free booze, and I've punched your annual salary up to three hundred, sixty thousand a year. Hell, we'll buy your house in Glendale for more than you're asking." Every time I tried to object, Jim spoke on top of me. "No taxes. We're going to eliminate taxes for you so you can bank it all. Do you know what seven-hundred, twenty thousand is compounded at eight per cent a year for ten years?"

Of course I didn't.

"One-point-six million." He had built up to a crescendo. "In the name of Jehoshaphat, almost two million dollars. You can build the flying schedules. You can fly as little or as much as you want. Design your own uniforms. Make yourself any rank you like. What an opportunity." I was trying to stay on his good side even though he had played me.

"Jim, I don't know."

"Hell, we'll even pay bonuses for the druggies you kill. Same way you got bounties for coyotes when you were a kid back in Texas."

I realized that Jim knew a lot more about me than he had ever let on.

"I've never put a package together this good for anyone. You can't turn America down."

"Jim, I promised Trudie."

"I know, I know. Look, I can't take 'no' for an answer right now, so get back to me."

—————»《①》«—————

Sure, I had made a promise to Trudie, but the mercenary job was so damned attractive. One way or the other, I couldn't stay in the house. Either I was going to have to turn the keys over to the bank or I was going to sell the house, become a mercenary, and move overseas. While packing, I brainstormed for a way to get Trudie to change her mind. I crammed book cartons with volumes of Vonnegut, Updike, Cheever, Churchill, and Michener. I stuffed liquor boxes with eight track tape cartridges by Bob Dylan, James Taylor, Jim Croce, and Crosby, Stills, Nash, and Young. I wrapped Val Saint-Lambert crystal in profuse layers of wrinkled paper to protect pieces from being shattered by anything short of an apocalyptic earthquake. The cartons I piled up in the garage displaced the Chevrolet. The driveway became a parking space, the garage a warehouse. I scooped up artifacts splayed out on the garage workbench and dropped them into a corrugated box marked "Treasure." I placed Elizabeth's death certificate and the CIA non-disclosure agreement on top of the pile of squadron patches and other mementos.

Airlines were hiring at a frenetic rate. My failure to receive a single airline job interview was a depressing blow to my ego. I was paranoid enough to believe that, if Mr. Bruno could control the sale of my house, he could ruin my employment chances, too. I faced up to my limitations candidly. I was too unimaginative to invent anything. I lacked the energy to be a visionary. My attention span was a candle stub burned down before I could give birth to an innovative idea. I found proof of these blunt truths in a drawer containing unfinished songs and a first draft of a dopey collection of anecdotes that I called a novel. My mediocrity made me melancholy. As a distraction from my unpleasant self-assessment, I indulged in a daydream about my reunion with Trudie that I modified into a dozen versions.

In one adaptation, passengers cleared by Immigration and Customs were arriving at an imposing reception hall bordered by colossal marble columns. Illuminated by a spotlight, Trudie glided down a wide alabaster staircase through masses of fellow travelers who parted to allow her to run to me. Even though she carried Katrina in her arms, the child was lighter than a cherub and, by some unexplained feat of levitation, she remained clear of being crushed as my body form-fitted against Trudie's in an ethereal embrace that, in every repetition, ended in intercourse. The carnal climax was problematic because it disregarded the sensibilities of the hundreds of passengers milling about in my glittering dreamscape. I returned to reality when the telephone rang. I had to leave for the airport in twenty minutes, but I answered anyway. It was Jim Conti.

"Stitch, I know you're short of time, but, look, I'll throw in round-trip tickets and two months of paid leave during your overseas tour so you can stay in touch with Trudie."

I hadn't fully comprehended Jim's power to juice the deal. I wondered whether this latest offer might change Trudie's mind.

"Jim, what's your title?"

"Never mind that. Listen, give your country two full years of your life. Jim had turned the issue into a loyalty test. "I promise, when you finish and come home, you can have a fly-ing job at the airline of your choice. I'll guarantee it in writing."

If Jim had the power to turn on the spigot, he logically had the power to turn it off, too. Jim's intermeddling was a conceivable sinister reason that not one of fifteen airlines had called me for an interview. Perhaps Jim, not Thor, had killed my chance for the Coonass job. I realized that to address my suspicions with Jim could only make my position with him worse because he still held the keys to my treasure chest.

"Jim, I've got to get to Sky Harbor to meet Trudie."

"Okay, okay. United Seven-Nineteen's on time out of O'Hare. I'll leave you to do the right thing. For God's sake and the good of your country, get Trudie on board."

Click. Jim Conti was the Wizard of Oz. He had known about Katrina's birth. He knew private stuff about me. He knew airline schedules. He always knew everything. I had a lot to ponder on the drive to Sky Harbor. The actual re-union with Trudie bore no resemblance to my daydreams. To begin with, Trudie had cleared Immigration and Customs in Chicago, so her Phoenix arrival didn't involve a majestic arrivals hall. Trudie's Boeing 727 didn't even block in beside a mobile passenger bridge. It came to a stop on a ramp in front of an open-air gate. From inside the air-conditioned terminal, I watched a flight attendant lower air stairs to al-low passengers to spill out of the forward passenger doorway. I couldn't see Trudie descending the stairs because a man blocked my view of the ramp. It was Jim Conti.

"Come here for a second," he said. He steered me to a wall-mounted telephone recess. "Have you come around on this?"

"I have to stick with my promise to Trudie."

"Turn Trudie around. Be a man. You're the perfect guy at the perfect time. It's almost too late. This deal is too good to pass up. If you miss out on this, you and Trudie will regret it until your dying day." I started to move toward the sliding door leading to the outdoor arrival gate for Flight Seven-Nineteen. Jim's hand pressed on my sternum and pinned me to the wall. "I called your father."

"You called my father?"

"To get him to reason with you." Jim continued pressing me against the wall. I couldn't imagine how Jim had gotten my father's Oregon telephone number. I had never even told Jim the location of my father's ranch. "He's so excited for you. He wants you to seize this opportunity."

That didn't square with my conversation with Dad. Jim's intrusion into my family affairs especially annoyed me. "You treat me like a child, Jim." I shoved his hand away from my chest and squirmed free to make my way toward the sliding door. Jim's pleading voice called after me.

"I've treated you like a prince," he said. "Turn Trudie around, Stitch."

I reached the pressure mat that opened the sliding door. Through the glass door, I could see a cluster of passengers gathered at the outdoor baggage carousel. Jim roughly pulled me by my right shoulder away from the sliding door.

"Stitch, it works both ways." His demeanor was severe; congeniality was dead. "If you don't answer your nation's call, I promise you that you won't ever get an airline job, not even at the crappiest outfit in the country." He blocked my passage through the sliding doors. His face looked nasty. "You might find some shitty job in Africa, but you'll never fly in the States."

I broke free of his body block. He remained behind me inside the terminal, but he called after me.

"Bring Trudie around. Give me a sign. I know you're a patriot. Don't let your country down."

The throng around the outdoor baggage carousel was starting to thin out. Although Trudie's back was turned to me as she waited for her bag, I recognized her narrow waist, her sexy derriere, the tilt of her head. A diaper bag hung from her right shoulder. Katrina was sucking a thumb and using her free hand to hold on for dear life to Trudie's left pants leg. Trudie didn't see me approach, nor did she see me kneel down in front of Katrina. My little girl leaned against my chest. I whisked her off the ground and held her snugly. Despite her long journey, Katrina's diaper pressing on my forearm was as dry as the Mojave. I kissed her velvet face and inhaled her scent — brown sugar and apple and a residue of cinnamon. A shaft of sunlight illuminated her blonde curls. She stopped sucking her thumb long enough to kiss my left cheek. She didn't care about my burn scars. She didn't begrudge me for trashing my career. No. Some vague memory told her that it was good to be held by me, and, for that, she gave me a kiss.

I extended my right arm to clasp Trudie from behind. I drew her close, burying my face in her hair to smell the fragrance of lemon grass, sea air, and heather from far away. I pressed against her and we swayed slightly off-balance. Katrina squirmed out of my grasp to latch onto her mother. When Trudie turned around, I was astonished to see a baby nestled in a sling tight against Trudie's breasts.

"This is Julia." Trudie's voice was proud, with a trace of defiance. She released Julia from the sling and handed her to me, freeing up her arms to hold Katrina.

A heart attack couldn't have shocked me more. I cradled Julia's small body and filled my lungs with her angelic fragrance, as sweet as honeysuckle.

Trudie's concealment of her pregnancy and Julia's birth struck me as vindictive, but I didn't resent her for it because I sensed how gravely she must have been wounded to lock me out this way. She must have considered the thread connecting our hearts terminally severed to deprive me of this joy.

Pride had blinded me. Now I understood that, while I assumed that Trudie was sulking about my unilateral resignation from the military, she was mostly reacting to Thor's spiteful slander about Jennifer and me. With an aching heart, Trudie had intended for her note to mean, "How could you cheat on me?"

Life didn't owe me compensation for my tragic losses. Elizabeth's death didn't entitle me to an express lane to happiness as a make-up. No one was beholden to guarantee me employment or financial security. No friend was obligated to mend my brokenness. In a rare moment of clarity, I recognized the great hurts in my life as detours. Two years in a hospital bed, false imprisonment in Mexico, and thwarted dreams of prosperity were diversions that kept me from recognizing my treasure. Embracing Trudie, Katrina, and Julia suspended me in a state of tranquility and shielded me from Boundless Gloom.

I spotted the haggard figure of Jim Conti still imploring

me from behind the pane of glass. He had tempted me by laying a fortune at my feet. He was demanding an answer. I shook my head, and his shoulders slumped. Teetering at the rim of Boundless Gloom, I closed my eyes and clung to Trudie. When I looked back at the terminal door, Jim Conti was gone. My heart had turned away from his promise of riches to grasp my ultimate prize, more valuable than gold and more enduring than fame.

Trudie's face simultaneously signaled triumph and unconditional surrender. She was so beautiful. Holding my beloved family in my arms, pressing to my heart my most cherished treasures was my ultimate fulfillment. She asked me why I was smiling like a nincompoop.

I told her, "I think I finally got it right."

CPSIA information can be obtained
at www.ICGtesting.com
Printed in the USA
BVHW041339301121
622871BV00012B/438